What do you live for when there is no escape?

LOST TO A DREAM

COURTNEY ROSALEEN

Hardcover ISBN: 979-8-9903568-2-5

Cover design by: Miblart

Map design by: Courtney Rosaleen

Edited by: Jasmine McKie

For Hannah, this book is your fault.
Thank you.

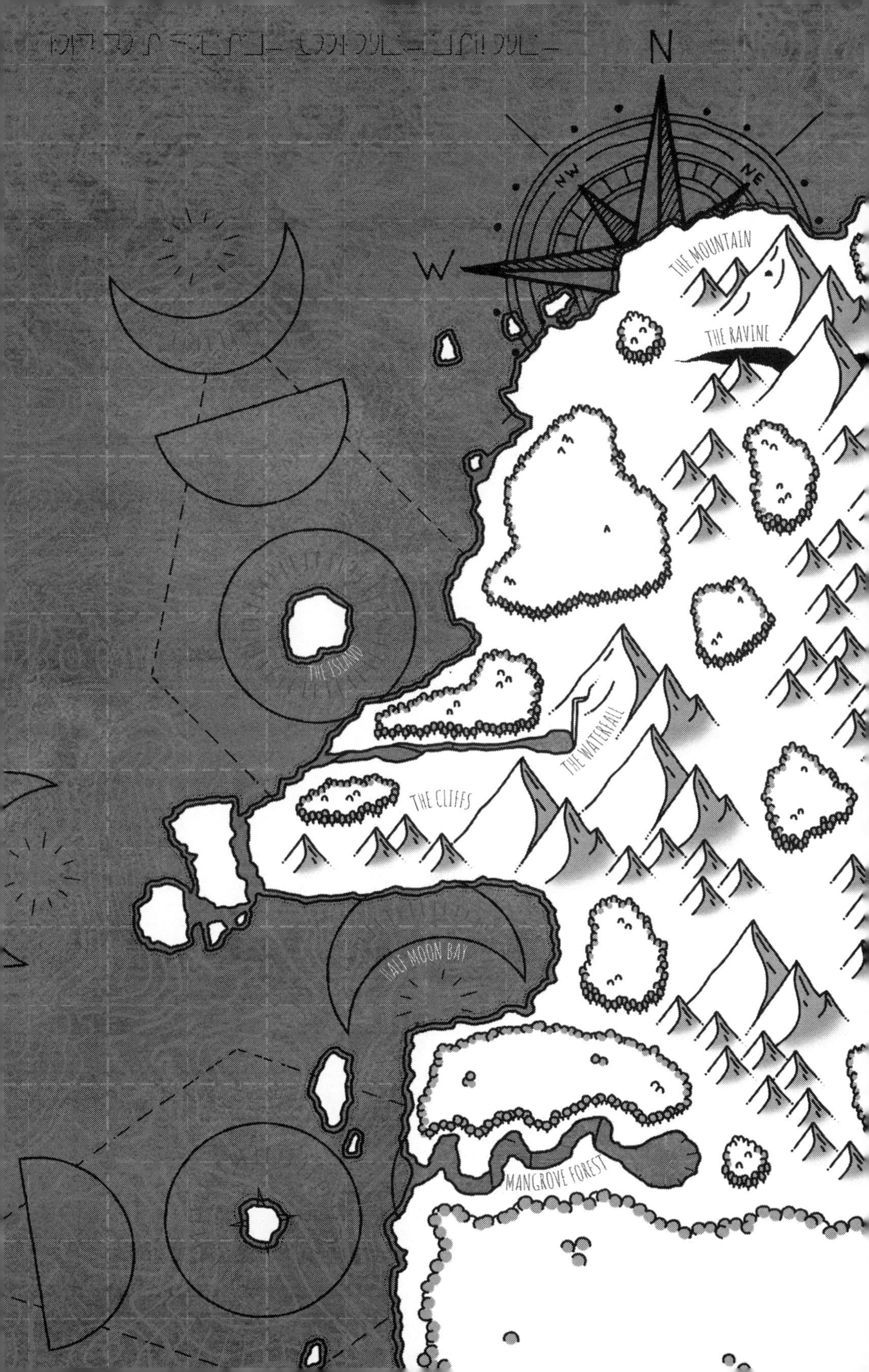
N
NW
NE
W
THE MOUNTAIN
THE RAVINE
THE ISLAND
THE WATERFALL
THE CLIFFS
HALF MOON BAY
MANGROVE FOREST

Lost to a Dream

The Lost Series

Book One

Courtney Rosaleen

"...Yet in these thoughts myself almost despising,
Haply I think on thee—and then my state,
Like to the lark at break of day arising
From sullen earth sings hymns at heaven's gate;
For thy sweet love remembered such wealth brings,
That then I scorn to change my state with kings."

-William Shakespeare

Prologue

Alex

I can't breathe.

I'm suspended in a sea of stars, my body floating among them, but I can't see them, can't feel them. I can't feel anything.

I'm lost.

I'm sure I'm lost.

The world I know is gone, and I'm... *somewhere else.*

"A*gh*, my head. What happened?" I mumble to myself as I gradually regain consciousness. Head spinning, I sit up slowly and blink back the fog from my vision. As I look around, feelings of confusion and fear wash over me.

I'm on an island.

In the middle of the ocean.

Alone.

What the hell? I wonder as a strong breeze blows a curtain of wild red curls into my face. Brushing them back, I try desperately to make sense of what is happening. I search my scattered brain for the last thing I remember until the throbbing in my head urges me to stop.

And that's when the panic sets in.

I can't remember anything past this morning. A wary feeling creeps over my skin and I'm suddenly desperate to get out of here. As I attempt to pick myself up off the sand, I realize that I'm exhausted. My small frame feels a whole lot heavier than usual, but after a few tries, I manage to get to my feet. I stand and take a deep breath, letting the thick salty air fill my lungs. The ocean breeze that rolls over my skin and the hot sand beneath my boots feel real, but they can't be. I have to be dreaming.

That's it... I'm dreaming.

I step forward slowly, surprised to find that I can control where I'm going. Usually in dreams, I don't have a choice in the matter. In fact, more often than not, I end up going in the opposite direction.

But I'm not going in the opposite direction.

I am going precisely where I intend to go, causing that uneasy feeling to claw its way back to the surface. With every second that passes, my head begins to clear a little more and although I am relentlessly tired, I start to feel more aware. More alive. And more... *awake.*

Another wave of panic hits me as I begin to realize, *maybe this isn't a dream.*

The sun is bright, beating down on me from directly overhead. Shading my eyes, I look up. *Must be about noon?*

My feet sink into the sand with every step, making my already sluggish strides even more difficult. Turning in a circle, I look around the small island and see, well, nothing. No trees, no shrubs, just sand surrounded by an endless view of calm ocean waters.

I look to the horizon and after a moment of searching, squinting through the brightness of day, I finally make out the hazy outline of a tree-covered shoreline. A large mountain of cliffs loom far off behind the forest, barely visible through the distant smog. As I stare out over the crystalline water that spreads between us, I suddenly hope that a journey to shore won't become necessary. I have always been a strong swimmer, but it's hard to judge the distance when it comes to water. Sure, it might look close from here, but you never know if there is a hidden current working against you until it is too late and it could easily cause you to wear out before you reach the other side. Besides, if you're lost, then you're supposed to stay where you are, making it easier for someone to find you, right?

God, I hope so.

After some staggering around on weary legs, I find myself beside the sea. There isn't much of a beach, leaving the calm water to gently lap at the edges of the crumbling shore. I sit on my knees, looking down, and ponder the girl staring back at me. Bright green eyes, red wavy hair, a million freckles and even more plans for the future. I'm not sixteen yet, but being trapped in a small town my whole life has made me realize something.

That I want out.

Want *more*.

Running a finger over my reflection, I watch as it dissolves into a distorted image of the girl that was once there. The water is warm and smooth and the physical sensation of it confounds me. It is the moment that my brain accepts the fact that this *isn't* a dream.

This is real.

So, where am I? I wonder. This has to be some kind of joke.

That's it, a joke, I tell myself. Someone must have dropped me off and I hit my head, which would explain why I can't remember anything. Everyone back home is probably laughing their asses off right now. But that's teenagers for you, always taking a good joke too far.

Lucky me. So glad I could amuse them today, I think sarcastically.

As I consider all the theories on how I ended up on a goddamn island, I realize that none of them answer the *where*. I stand and put my hands on my hips, frustrated. This certainly isn't the lake back home and, although I have been to the ocean countless times before, nothing about the woods or the cliffs in the distance are even remotely familiar.

Circling back to the *joke* theory, I suddenly find solace in the fact that if this is indeed someone's idea of a prank, then at least I know they will be back for me before dark. If it is around noon, then sunset couldn't be any more than nine hours away this time of year, so I will just have to wait.

"What the fuck am I supposed to do for a few hours?" I say out loud, because apparently, I have already deemed it acceptable to talk to myself out here. As much as I love to be in the great outdoors and read books about adventures in the wilderness, I have no intention of staying out here without any supplies. Backpacking is one thing, but being stuck on a mysterious island with no food, water or shelter, and no idea how in the hell you ended up there, is something else entirely.

I look down at my hand, still wet from the interruption to my reflection and I'm about to dry it off on my green T-shirt when something makes me pause. I hold both of my hands palms-up in front of me and stare at them curiously, watching as shadows slowly creep across my skin. Looking up, I search for the cloud that is inevitably moving to blot out the sun, but there's nothing. The sky is completely clear.

And yet, it's getting dark.

Shit. How long has it been? Five minutes? Ten?

"Get a hold of yourself," I lecture, because it isn't possible to lose nine hours of daylight in only a few minutes.

Oh, come on guys. Where are you? I think, frustrated, because they should have been back by now.

More than exhausted, I sit down in the sand and hug my knees close, watching with trepidation as the last sliver of light ducks below the horizon. I fall backward onto the sand with a *huff* just as the twilight sky turns into an ocean of twinkling lights. I stare up curiously, because I have never seen so many stars. I heard once that the further you went away from the city, the brighter they would be. But I don't live in the city. I live in a tiny town in the middle of nowhere, so I have seen stars before, *lots* of stars. But never like this. They aren't just brighter, they're everywhere, covering every inch of the velvety sky.

It's breathtaking.

The air suddenly becomes cooler and the chilling breeze rolls off the ocean, prickling my skin. Strangely, I find it to be a welcome comfort after the heat and frustration of my situation.

And then, I hear it for the first time.

A gurgling moan pierces through the silence and my thoughts. Wincing, I cover my ears. I have never heard anything so loud.

Or so *terrifying*.

The drowning noise slowly rolls into more of an animalistic growl. The increasing volume causes the hairs on my skin to stand on end and a shiver runs up my spine. Through the din, I can barely make out the sound of dripping water, telling me that whatever is causing the horrifying noise is coming up out of the ocean.

My heart skips a beat and my body seizes with terror. Holding my breath, I lift my head slowly and look toward the shoreline, my eyes growing wide.

I scramble to my feet and a blood curdling scream echoes from somewhere nearby.

It takes a moment before I realize that the scream is coming from *me*.

Steve

Chapter 1

I slam shut the driver's door of my nineteen ninety-four hunter green Jeep Cherokee, sling my backpack over one shoulder and take a deep, exasperated breath. Standing in the school parking lot, I run a hand through my short messy brown hair and, for a moment, consider getting right back behind the wheel and leaving.

Because here I am again. Staring at another new school, in another new town and wearing *another* new designer T-shirt. One that my parents had insisted on for my first day. I am getting really tired of them fussing over my making a good impression. This morning, they both left late for work to make sure I was ready and out the door in time, like I'm a child, and acting as though my first day is some exciting event, one I should be elated for.

But I'm not.

In fact, I am the opposite.

At the age of sixteen, I have attended eight different schools in the past six years. By now, I am more than fed up with the constant change.

I'm fucking angry about it.

All I want is to have friends, *real* friends. Not the kind who make promises to *stay in touch* and then never do. But I can't blame them. Whenever I switch schools, it isn't like I will be just down the street. Hell, I won't even be in the same state. I will be hundreds of miles away and not by choice. The people I do blame for this, however, are my parents. In my mind I know the practicality of their decision to accept a higher paying position when it was offered to them. I also know that their job requires them to be on site for whatever company startup project they are currently working on.

But I still don't like it.

Sure, my parents are financially better off than most, but whenever they tell me that they are doing it *all for me*, that they want me to *have a future* and all sorts of other bullshit, I don't buy into it for a second. They are doing it for themselves and don't give a fuck about how it makes me feel. What is the purpose of having money when I am forced to spend every day cooped up in my bedroom? There is no point in going out, making friends, or planning for the future if they are just going to force me to move again. Just once, I want to make it the whole school year without having to pack up my entire life, say my goodbyes and start all over.

The bell rings out across the parking lot, letting me know that I have stalled for as long as possible. I pull the crumpled piece of paper from my pocket and glance down at my class schedule, then back up toward Garda Valley High School. My prison for the foreseeable future.

Taking one last deep breath, I begrudgingly put one foot in front of the other, heading off to find my class.

Lunch couldn't come fast enough. I always hate the first day, hate the feeling that everyone is staring at you. Because well, they are. At least this time I am coming in at the beginning of the school year and not in the middle of it. But I guess no matter when my first day is, everyone still has this obsession with getting a glimpse of the new guy.

Which I find annoying as hell.

I hoped that lunch would be somewhat of a reprieve, that everyone would be too distracted catching up with friends after summer break that I could just fall back into the crowd and disappear. But *clearly*, that is not going to happen. Not in a town as small as Garda Valley, California, which is located just north of goddamn nowhere. When we drove into town for the first time last week, I audibly sighed my contempt when I saw that the population sign read a number consisting of only three digits.

Sitting at one of the picnic tables on the outside patio, I watch another group of students walk away after introducing themselves. I already forgot their names. Not like it matters anyway.

I'm finally alone for the first time since I sat down fifteen minutes ago. I pick up my sandwich, staring at it longingly. There hasn't been time to take even a single bite, not before the next inquisitor came to drill me with the same questions as the last. *And here comes another one,* I think bitterly, setting my sandwich back down.

The guy is around my age. He's also about my height, maybe an inch shorter, but still over six feet. He looks athletic, but he wasn't sitting with the group that's already sporting their school spirit. He has the same brown hair as me, only it's long, hanging down past his shoulders. His eyes are brown, as opposed to my dark blue ones and his tanned skin makes me a little jealous. It seems everyone around here spent a substantial amount of time outdoors this summer, whereas I had been stuck inside, packing up all of my shit for the impending move. *Again.* I figure that the boy must also be a Junior, because we have been in several of the same classes already this morning, but I don't think I've caught his name yet. Or maybe I have, who the hell knows. I have met more people today than I can count and have long since given up trying to keep track of them all.

The boy drops a beat-up paper bag containing his lunch onto the table and for a moment, I think he is going to sit across from me. But he doesn't.

He sits down right. Next. To me.

I stare, unsure of what to do, but before I can say anything, another group of onlookers begin to make their approach. I try desperately not to notice any of them, which turns out to be impossible. I shift uncomfortably on the bench, realizing that I should probably give up on trying to eat. Or maybe I will just go spend the rest of lunch hiding in the bathroom. It wouldn't be the first time.

That's when the boy sitting next to me turns to the oncoming group and, to my surprise, *shouts* at them.

"For fuck's sake, give the guy a break, it's his first goddamn day!"

I have to hold back a smile, finding his boldness amusing. The guy is clearly friends with everyone, because they don't even seem to mind his admonition. They simply shrug, give me a quick wave and go on their way.

"Hell of a day, huh?" the boy says, nudging me with an elbow as he pulls a sandwich from his bag and starts in on it.

I glance down at my side and blink, a little taken aback from this abrupt encounter.

"Um, yeah. It's been... busy," I say, still staring after the retreating group in shock. Snapping out of it, I take advantage of the opportunity and take a large bite out of my untouched sandwich.

"You look scared shitless. First time at a new school?" he asks.

I nearly choke on my food. The way he said it makes me think that the guy could make *anything* sound funny. Not to mention it's the first time that someone hasn't bothered with the perfectly pleasant niceties of a traditional introduction, which I find to be a refreshing change.

"Far from it, actually," I say. "I'm just not used to anyone actually talking to me and here..." I look around warily at the groups of people who are trying their best to stare inconspicuously.

Which they are doing a terrible job at.

"Yeah, well, welcome to the valley. Everyone knows everyone here and they're all going to know everything there is to know about *you* in under twenty-four hours, if they don't already. You're the most interesting thing that's happened around here since the beginning of summer when Sunny stole his dad's boat and took it out on the lake for a joy ride."

"That's what you guys call exciting?" I ask, incredulous.

"Well," the boy says through a mouthful of sandwich, "Sunny, that dumb-ass, swerved to avoid hitting a stump and ended up parking the boat eight feet up on shore. He took out the Baker's fence on the way and it took Mr. Jay, Sunny's dad, and the guys from down at the shop over three hours to get it fixed up and back into the water. Sunny was grounded for a month and everyone still talks about it. I'm Noor by the way," he says, jutting his hand out for an introduction as I ponder where the hell he gets all his energy.

"It's nice to meet you, Noor," I say genuinely, "I'm Steven. Steven Stone." I reach out, firmly shaking his outstretched hand with a smile.

Brash as he is, I like the guy already.

"Well I already knew that," he says, glancing toward a group of nearby students who are obviously gossiping about me. "But it's nice to meet ya, all the same. So where ya from?"

"The last place we lived was Chicago, but we weren't there for very long before moving here," I repeat for the hundredth time today, only this time, I don't mind it.

"*Chicago.* Damn, man! That's pretty cool. I've never been to a city that big. Was it fun living there?"

"Um, not really. But we move around a lot, so I only had to put up with it for about six months," I say with a shrug.

"That's awesome you get to travel. The only times I've ever even left the state were to visit my Grams and she's only a few hours north. Let me tell ya, living in the same town, *hell*, the same *house* your entire life gets real old." Noor says, finishing off his sandwich and starting in on a bag of chips.

"Hang on, you've lived in the same *house* your whole life?" I ask, baffled. I want that life. A life where you have the same house, the same school, the same friends.

I can't even imagine it.

"Yup. Born and raised here, like most kids in this town. But it gets pretty boring. We're always trying to come up with new things to do. Lucky for us, you came along!" he says, knocking into my shoulder.

"Oh, *great,*" I say sarcastically, but I'm actually *smiling.* I find it surprising how easy it is to talk to Noor. I can't remember a time when I got along this well with anyone, let alone so quickly.

As soon as the bell rings, Noor gives me a shove as he gets up from the table. I smirk, shaking my head as I follow after him and the other students heading back to class.

"Hey Steve," Noor says as he walks backward toward the double doors that lead inside. "Me and some friends are going camping down by the lake next week. It's just for two nights, Friday and Saturday. It would be cool if you could make it. I've got a tent, so you could just bunk with me."

"Um, sure. I'll ask my parents tonight," I grin. No one has ever invited me to... well, *anything* before. I love camping and find that I'm already looking forward to it.

"Sweet, we can talk more about it after school. Catch ya later!"

"See ya!" I say with a half wave.

What in the fuck just happened? I wonder as I watch an energetic Noor disappear down the hall. When I turn, heading toward my next class, something on the pinboard catches my eye.

I'm staring at a picture of a girl, about my age. Her long red curls spill over her shoulders, framing her perfect face. She has a small, but sweet smile and freckled cheeks. She also has the most striking green eyes I've ever seen. I'm mesmerized by them.

By *her.*

But it isn't the *picture* of the girl that caught my attention. It's the large bold letters written above it:

MISSING PERSON

Chapter 2

I pull into the driveway after school and park my Jeep off to the side of the garage, knowing that if it were to make a single mark on the custom stamped cement driveway, my parents might actually follow through on their threats and send it to the scrapyard. I don't care that I have to fix the damn thing every other weekend, or that it's an eyesore, as my mother puts it. It's *my* eyesore and it's staying. Back in Chicago, they tried to get me to sell it. In exchange, they offered to buy me something newer after the move, but I wouldn't go for it. I worked hard doing side jobs and saving every penny for two years straight in order to come up with the money to buy it. It is the only thing in my life that wasn't given to me. I earned it. And no one would guess how much money my parents have when I'm driving it, which is precisely the way I like it. The last thing I need is to draw even more attention by showing up at school in a brand-new car.

As I walk through the oversized front door of my parents' *extravagant* house, I mentally prepare for another round of twenty questions. Sure enough, before the front door has even clicked shut behind me, I hear Mom's voice coming from upstairs.

"Steven? Steven, is that you honey?" she says.

"Yeah, mom, it's me," I mutter with as much enthusiasm as I can manage, which turns out to be *complete indifference*.

"What do you mean, *yeah mom*," she says, imitating my deeper tone as she makes her way down the stairs. "Come here and give me a hug! How was your day? Do you like your teachers? Did you make any friends?"

I try ignoring her and her questions as I head down the hall toward the kitchen, but I'm not fast enough. She catches me in a hug and I am unable to escape.

"Mom, oh my god, let me go. Do we have to do this every time? And why are you in such a good mood?" I say, squirming free from her grasp.

"Can't a mom just be excited for her only child's first day of school?"

"Mom, this is like my *hundredth* first day. And I'm not a child, I'm almost seventeen."

"Sorry honey, I can't help it. And quit saying you're almost seventeen. You've only been sixteen for three months," she says, exasperated. After a pause, she continues, "I just can't believe how old you're getting. Look at you, already taller than me." She looks up at me, all *proud* and I roll my eyes, turning toward the kitchen once again.

"And you're right, I am in a good mood," she says, following behind me. "Not only was it your first day," she ruffles my hair and I quickly brush her hand away, annoyed, "but work is going well too. Everyone in this town is so..."

"Intrusive... nosy... meddlesome?" I offer, looking at her with a sideways grin as I drop my backpack onto one of the bar stools.

"I was going to say *friendly*," she says, clearly amused by my apt description. "I really feel like this move was a good one. But enough about me, I want to hear about your day! So come on, spill it!"

"Well, it's another new school..." I say, already done with this conversation. I think about meeting Noor at lunch and realize that it was probably the best first day I've ever had. But I am not about to tell her that. She looks at me all hopeful, with big dark blue eyes that match mine, and I realize that she isn't about to give up the conversation that easily.

"Okay, fine. It wasn't horrible. Not *great*," I add before she can get too excited. "But it wasn't horrible. My teachers are fine. I just wish we didn't have to move all the time."

"Sweetie, your father and I-"

"Yeah, yeah, you just want the best for me, I know," my voice softens. She wouldn't understand what I am going through, so there's no point in trying to explain it.

"So, your teachers are fine and it wasn't horrible. That's certainly a start. How about your classmates? Other than intrusive, nosy and meddlesome, I mean," she says, grinning. I don't appreciate her attempt at humor and I'm even more upset that her ploy to brighten my mood is almost working.

"Well, everyone wanted to talk to me, which is... different. And a guy named Noor invited me to go camping with him and some friends down by the lake next week," I say as I grab a package of lunch meat from the fridge and start eating from it as if it were a bag of chips. "I guess it's kind of a tradition. They always do one last camping trip of the year before it starts getting cold." I shrug, trying to sound nonchalant about it. It's just camping for god's sake, so I shouldn't be this excited. But I am.

"Oh, that's great honey! I'm so happy to hear you've already made a friend," she says genuinely, then snatches the package from my hands, putting it back in the fridge.

"Yeah, Noor seems cool," I say, glaring after my stolen snack. "I also met this guy, Sunny. He and his dad live on the lake and have a lot of property, so they're going to set up camp there, just down from the house. Noor said I could stay in his tent. Is it alright if I go?"

"Well, your father and I would like to speak with Sunny's dad first, just to introduce ourselves and make sure this is all okay with him, but sure, sweetie. I think it would be great for you to get to know some of the other kids. And I know how much you like camping. Heaven knows I won't be participating in that sort of activity, even if we do live in the woods now. And get out of there," she scoffs as I, once again, have the refrigerator doors wide open. "Your dad will be home soon for dinner."

It was a long week of unpacking, and getting familiar with my new class schedule, but it's finally Friday. The second school is out, Noor and I will be packing up our gear and heading over to Sunny's to set up camp. I can't wait to spend the entire weekend out of the house. It is going to be two whole nights with no parents and no curfews. And as wary as I am about hanging out with people I don't know, I figure that I will most likely spend all of my time with Noor anyway, which is just fine with me.

I've only known him for a little over a week, but we already eat lunch together every day, and have been hanging out after school as often, and for as long as our parents will allow. As it turns out, we like the same movies, listen to the same music and play all of the same video games. Noor is easy to hang out with and I'm slowly beginning to feel more like myself.

We are sitting at our usual picnic table out on the patio and I stare off into the surrounding redwood trees, mindlessly picking at the food in front of me. It's always hard to concentrate on school at the start of the year, the warm weather making everyone reluctant to leave summer vacation behind. And here in the valley, it seems like the entire Junior class is either out doing something every day after school, or making plans for the weekends. Noor says it's because the winters here are long, dark and rainy. Which is hard to believe, considering the current temperature.

As I sit in the warm air under the shade of the trees, I feel a wave of nostalgia. Up until I was ten years old, I lived in a small town incredibly similar to this one. Only, it didn't have so many trees. The redwoods overhead appear to be as tall as skyscrapers and outnumber the amount of houses in town by the thousands. The school, my new house and all the roads in between, seem to be cut into the landscape, somehow becoming a part of it. It feels... safe. But it doesn't quite feel like home. Not yet, at least. I don't see the point in calling anywhere *home*.

Nevertheless, I like the valley. I like living in the woods, like the people, and I like how it isn't anywhere near a big city. Hell, the nearest *town* is almost an hour away. Before moving, I thought living in a town this small would be even more insufferable than living in the city had been, *if that was possible*. But so far, I've done more in the short time I've been here than I did the entire six months we lived in Chicago.

Maybe once I am out of the house, I'll come back to the valley someday. I could find a job, buy a house, start a family. Someday, maybe, I could actually have a life.

But not now.

"Hello? Earth to Steve?" Noor says as he waves a hand in front of my face, snapping me back to reality.

"Oh hey, yeah, sorry," I stammer.

"What, you never seen a tree before?" Noor says, chuckling.

"Not like these. I guess I'm just still trying to take it all in..." I trail off.

"Yeah, I can imagine. Coming from a big fancy city, then being dumped into a shithole town like this," Noor mumbles, the last few words barely audible through the handful of chips he is currently shoving into his mouth.

"Trust me, the city is way more of a shithole. And smells like one, too. At least here I'm not being woken up ten fucking times a night by honking horns and sirens. And did I mention the smell? There's air here, it's kinda weird," I say, looking around as if I could actually *see* the quality of it.

"*Air...*" Noor says slowly, staring at me suspiciously. "Ya know Steve, *you're* kinda weird."

At that comment, I jump up quickly, one eyebrow raised. Noor, looking panicked, stumbles as he tries to get up from the picnic bench, his chips flying from the crumpled bag in a mess of crunchy confetti as he evades my attempt at a tackle. We fight over the bag, which is nearly empty at this point, ignoring the complaints from other students until both of us are out of breath and laughing.

I take the stairs two at a time, round the corner at the top and head straight into my bedroom. Noor will be over to pick me up within the hour and I still have to gather the last of my camping gear and toss some clothes into a bag. An hour is more than enough time to pack, but my excitement has me throwing things around the room in a rush.

My parents and I used to go camping all the time when I was a kid and I still have a lot of the basic gear, which I managed to dig out from the boxes in the garage yesterday. Staring at the pile of supplies strewn across my bed, I consider if I'm missing anything. I have a tarp, two fishing rods and a tackle box, several lighters, a hatchet and a pile of miscellaneous items that I, for some reason, deem necessary.

But I guess you can never be too prepared.

No more than twenty minutes later, the doorbell rings, proving that Noor is just as eager to get going as I am. As I gather everything up in my arms, I hear Mom open the door to a very enthusiastic Noor.

"Hey, Mrs. Stone! You're looking dashing today!" Noor remarks and I roll my eyes at his blatant kiss-assery. *Does this guy ever run out of energy?* I think, struggling with my armload of supplies as I make my way carefully down the stairs.

"Hello, Noor. And please, call me Sarah. Now why don't you come in and help your pack-mule-of-a-friend with his bags."

"It's not that much..." I mutter as I try to get a better grip on one of the fishing rods that is already starting to slip.

"Yeah, not much at all for a *freight train*, but for a guy who's only going to be gone two nights..." Noor says with a jesting grin, but makes his way over to the base of the stairs all the same. I answer his jibe by throwing my duffle bag the rest of the way down and into his chest. The muffled, "Holy shit," that comes from Noor's mouth is immediately reprimanded by Mom and I laugh, shoving him out the door.

"Sorry, Mrs. S! Have a wonderful day Mrs. S!" Noor calls back as he stumbles down the front steps.

"Have fun and don't get into too much trouble!" She calls after the two of us, already halfway down the path to the curb.

"Will do! Bye Mom!" I shout back up toward the house.

Noor's truck rattles its way down the pothole-filled road as the redwoods jutting up on either side become more dense. I stare out the window, realizing that we haven't passed any houses for at least the last ten minutes. I wonder how much further we are going.

"Is this janky road the only way to get to the lake?" I ask curiously.

"Nah, there's lots of ways. Some of them are even paved, like the road to the boat launch and to some of the campgrounds. Mr. Jay just doesn't give a shit about their driveway."

"This is their driveway?"

"Sorta. It's also a fire access road to this part of the lake, but the county doesn't give a shit about it either."

"So, there are campgrounds? How big is this lake?" I say.

"Oh, it's pretty huge actually. You can barely see the other side of it when the fog rolls in. During the summer, we do bonfires out on one of the islands whenever someone manages to snag a boat from their parents."

"Does *everyone* have a boat?" I ask.

"Yeah, pretty much. There's jack shit else to do around here, so you either have a boat, or know someone who does."

I am definitely not in the city anymore.

Back in Chicago and New York for that matter, people my age consider walking around the city and gossiping as *fun*. None of them ever wanted to actually do anything, which made me even more inclined to stay home rather than trying to make friends.

Boats, bonfires and camping every weekend are certainly a change of pace. And I couldn't be happier. At least, I would be, if I didn't know that sooner or later my parents would force me to leave it. Which has me wondering if I will ever get the chance to see a summer here.

I stare out the window again. Noor is clearly a good driver, but the speed at which he apparently insists on maintaining has me keeping a constant hold on the side handle to steady myself as the trees blur past. The massive columns of bark seem to jut out from an ocean of ferns and vines, so crowded that you can't tell where one plant ends and the other begins. Bright shades of vibrant green and dark browns give a sense of calm. It makes me want to take a hike and stay out here forever.

"Do you guys get a lot of tourists?" I say, turning back to Noor.

"Oh, for sure," he answers. "The town pretty much triples in size for the summer and most school breaks. It's kind of annoying actually. But dad says it 'keeps businesses open,'" he says in his best old man voice. "So ya know, we deal with it. I guess if I owned a business around here, I would be happy to overcharge out-of-towners to make a quick buck. No offense, *Chicago*."

"Shut the fuck up," I say with a laugh, giving Noor a quick shove. The second everyone found out that I lived in Chicago, they immediately adopted the nickname. But the truth is, I am the farthest thing from a "city boy." I have lived in a lot of places, sure, but I hated every second of it. After growing up in a small town, moving to the valley almost feels like coming home. It feels like I'm back to the time when I was younger, when we would go camping and fishing. A time when I rode quads and learned how to drive a truck when I was only eight years old. But when my parents got this *great opportunity,* off we went. No more camping, no more trees and no more life. Just one city after another, for six years straight. My parents have tried to smooth everything over by taking me on a "camping trip" every summer. But their idea of the great outdoors is more *glamping* than anything. We don't even stay in tents anymore. They will either rent some ridiculously large RV with every amenity you could possibly imagine, or get a cabin for the weekend. Neither of which I even remotely consider camping.

The truck continues on and the underbrush becomes more and more sparse until the woods clear and I'm able to make out a two-story house along with several outbuildings scattered among the trees. Everywhere I look, there is a tractor, car, truck or trailer of some kind. Everything looks well used, but also well taken care of.

"What does Sunny's dad do?" I ask, looking around.

"Oh, Mr. Jay? He owns the mechanic shop downtown, but he also does some construction here and there whenever someone asks him to."

"Huh," I muse as Noor drives around the side of the house. I can already see how close we are to the lake. Through the trees, the sun is shimmering off the gentle waves and I am eager to get a closer look.

When Noor adds his truck to the line of vehicles already parked, I suddenly start to feel nervous. "Hey, how many people are going to be here?" I ask warily as we get out of the truck. Distracted by the scenery, I nearly forgot that I will have to converse with total strangers for this entire weekend.

"Same group as usual, unless anyone else brought along extra baggage,"

Noor says, giving me a sidelong glance of feigned annoyance. I reply with a crude hand gesture that he returns before continuing. "So it's gonna be me, you, Sunny," he says, lowering the tailgate, "Kai, Makena, Zuri, Efe, Ari and-" he cuts off suddenly and it isn't lost on me that his face has lost a bit of color. "And that's it," he says brusquely. "Which makes..." he looks down at his fingers to count, "eight of us."

I have no idea what could have run through Noor's mind to upset him, but it's not the first time I've noticed this particular reaction. Something has been bothering him, but whatever it is, he clearly doesn't want to talk about it. And I won't make him.

"I'm sure I've met all of them ten times at this point, but you're gonna have to help me out. I've had so many names thrown at me since I got here, hell if I can keep any of them straight," I say, then Noor extends his own hand out to me for a formal introduction.

"Hi! I'm Noor!" He smiles widely.

And just like that, he is back to his usual self. I slap his hand away with a roll of my eyes and begin hauling our tent from the bed of the truck. But I can't help but wonder what could have caused someone as lighthearted as *Noor* to carry so much weight.

A heaviness that he is working hard to keep hidden just below the surface.

Chapter 3

After dropping the last of our gear into a pile in the clearing just up from the water, I look up at the lake for the first time. I walk toward it in a trance, because Noor was right, it is *pretty huge*. But it is also calm, like everything in this town. It's as if the valley exists apart from reality. A place where the hustle of the outside world is unable to reach.

The water is impossibly flat, as if a large piece of dark glass has been cut out, and set down among the trees. The water gently rolls up the sand before retreating silently back home. Beyond the surface of the water, I can see the hazy outline of the tree-covered mountains on the other side. I revel in the beauty of it, but deep down, I know that I won't be happy here. *Can't* be happy here, because it isn't home. This is just a pit stop in the endless revolving door of places I am forced to stay. But even so, the beauty of the landscape in front of me is impossible to ignore. It's as if the view has been torn straight from one of my books. The books that I choose to drown myself in rather than attempting to live a normal life.

I take a breath then push back my bitterness, if only for a moment, and try to just enjoy it.

"I told ya, it's huge. But it's also cold as shit, so don't fall in!" Noor says, shoving me toward it. I stumble a few steps forward before I regain my footing, then immediately chase him back up the sandy slope toward camp. Once in the clearing, I finally give up the pursuit. I know from experience that I can't outrun him.

When I look around, I see that there are several other piles of gear that I hadn't noticed before. Then I hear a muddle of loud voices. Looking up toward the house, I see a group of six, all about my age if I have to guess, are heading down the hill toward Noor and I, laughing and talking animatedly. They are all speaking at once, which makes it next to impossible to distinguish what anyone is saying. Among them, they carry an ice chest suspended between two people with cases of soda and water balancing on top, a cook stove, an armful of fishing rods and a few tackle boxes.

Above the cacophony of voices, an older man's gruff voice rings out, silencing all others immediately. I look up to see Mr. Jay and his southern accent shouting from the porch up at the house, beer in hand.

"Don't poke your eye out with those fishing rods, keep an eye on that fire and for god's sake, don't fall in the damn lake, 'cause I ain't comin' down there to jump in after *any* 'a you!" he shouts out, stern, but good natured. I have met him once before, but it still surprises me how similar he is to Sunny. If I didn't already know they were related, then I would have figured it out all on my own. They both have the same black hair, dark eyes, and even though Mr. Jay's beard is speckled with gray, their facial features are unmistakably familial. Mr. Jay even has on the same style of Carhartt overalls that his son wears on most days. Only, Sunny always seems to have one of the straps undone, letting it hang lazily in the back.

"Yeah, yeah, thanks pops!" Sunny shouts back up toward the house with a wave before the chatter immediately resumes.

Beside me, Noor waves up at the group and, seeing that we have arrived, their conversations switch to a barrage of greetings.

"Hey Chicago! Glad you made it!" Sunny says, along with several other acknowledgements that I struggle to make out. I quickly realize that deciphering their conversations is just something I will have to get used to. I also consider that I've never experienced such a warm welcome before. Not anywhere. I immediately feel included and slowly, my nerves start to dissipate.

Noor jogs over to help out the girl with long reddish-brown hair who is struggling to keep a hold of several fishing rods. She is at least a foot shorter than the guys and looks tiny standing between them, as delicate as a bird. I can barely make out their quiet exchange over the sounds of everyone else, but I manage to hear part of it.

"Shay's not coming?" Noor asks the girl in a low tone. She shakes her head with a frustrated roll of her eyes.

"No, she's not," the girl replies quietly.

Following Noors example, I head over to help, grabbing the case of water bottles and soda that is balancing precariously on top of the ice chest between two of the guys, then follow behind as we make our way down to our spot by the lake.

I take a step back and look at the tent. Glancing at my phone, I realize that I managed to set it up in under five minutes. A new personal record. I wasn't particularly *trying* to set it up fast, but I am naturally competitive. And after the last nine days of being primarily addressed as "Chicago," I have something to prove.

"Damn, Steve, I guess I'm off the hook! I'm gonna go take a nap or something!" Noor says as he, not so gracefully, rolls himself onto the hammock that the girl with purple hair just finished hanging between two trees. She responds by grabbing the edge and dumping him out of it, laughing hysterically when he lands with a *thump* in the dirt below.

"Hey Chicago, wanna do mine next?" Sunny says, holding up a pile of knotted polyester, ropes and poles.

"No way man, that mess is all yours!" I say, putting my hands up, then back away slowly, offering out a hand to help Noor up off the dirt.

After everything is set up, I look around and smile, because this is what I consider camping. In the center of the large area between the trees is a circle of rocks stacked three high, making up a well-used fire pit. The ice chest is full of food, soda and we have so many snacks we could probably stay out here a week.

The three tents are scattered among the trees around the outskirts of the clearing. Mine and Noor's is the smallest, but it is still plenty large enough for both of our cots and our gear. Next to us is a slightly larger tent that Sunny and the two other guys, Kai and Zuri, are sharing. On the opposite side of the fire pit is the girls' tent, which is clearly the biggest. It is situated in the only spot large enough to accommodate it, set perfectly between two trees. When I look over, I see that they already have a welcome mat, a big fluffy rug inside and their bed is perfectly made atop their fully inflated air mattress. I also notice that each of their bags seem to have already exploded into a mess covering nearly the entire floor. I shake my head and smile, finding the whole thing amusing.

I recognize everyone here, but I've still had to subtly ask Noor what their names were several times, seeing as the only person I ever really talk to at school is him.

I watch as Efe, the girl with the purple hair, and Zuri crouch over the fire pit, expertly stacking the kindling and logs. They have the fire going in no time at all. I smile, watching the flames flicker to life in front of me. I can't remember the last time I saw an *actual* fire, in a fire pit.

I study Efe for a moment. I talked to her a few times earlier while we were setting up camp and was surprised to find how down to earth she is, considering her short and wild pastel purple hair that suggests otherwise. In fact, she's been eager to lend a hand with everything out here.

Eventually, everyone is settling into their chairs, circled around the fire, and the group talks easily as the glowing light of day begins to fade. Earlier, we all managed to find sticks long enough for cooking the hot dogs over the fire. I found one that is almost perfectly straight and have spent the last ten minutes whittling the end to a point. Noor, on the other hand, is struggling just to keep his hot dog from falling. His stick is bent in three places and has a few branches sticking off the sides in various directions. I notice that one branch still has a leaf on it. I can't hold back my laughter, and neither can the others, as we watch him struggle.

As we eat and the chatter continues, I look around the circle and wonder why this particular group is camping together at all. Even though they all go to the same school, I didn't think that any of them even *knew* each other, let alone that they were this close. Each of them eat at different lunch tables, hang out with different friends and I can't remember a time that any of them had even spoken to each other. But here they are, laughing and joking around the fire as naturally as if they do this every day.

I remember that Zuri and Kai are both pretty quiet in class, but I quickly realize that certainly isn't the case out here. They talk animatedly with each other, along with Efe who is sitting on the other side of them. Zuri has dark skin, his black hair cut short in a fade. His outfits are always tidy, even out here, which is in stark contrast to the rest of the guys, who probably don't think twice about what they are wearing on any given day.

Kai's blonde hair is longer on top and flops carelessly over his eyes when he walks, causing him to occasionally flick his head to the side to sweep it out of his vision. His pale skin is clearly tanned from the summer, more so than the rest of them, and he looks like he would be more suited for the beach and a surfboard than for the mountains and trees.

The two girls who sit on the far side of the fire are Ari and Makena, I remind myself. I haven't had the chance to talk to them much, but figure that anyone who is willing to stay in a tent the whole weekend for fun is probably someone that I will get along with. Ari, the girl Noor was talking to earlier, has dark brown hair, the shade tinted with hints of red that is pulled into a ponytail on the side in a no-nonsense manner. Makena, on the other hand, is clearly wearing more makeup than the other two girls. I was honestly a little surprised to see her out here considering that she normally runs with what I would have considered to be a more... *popular* crowd. She put on a beanie a little while ago and her black coils of hair are sticking out from under it in all directions, as opposed to the pristine look she keeps up at school.

I stare at them, still confused, and wondering again at how this group became friends in the first place. It's as though the usual social constructs based on popularity, money, backgrounds and styles don't exist with them. Like they live in their own world where none of that matters. And every single one of them has welcomed me into their group as if I have always been a part of it.

"So, how did you guys all meet?" I say, because I have to know, and I finally feel comfortable enough to ask. They all smile and look at each other, trying to figure out which one of them is going to answer the question, until all eyes land on Noor.

"Okay, okay, fine," Noor says. He's never at a loss for words and everyone knows it. "We were all born here. The towns not that big, so we grew up together. Daycare, summer camps, school, we did everything together as kids."

"Once we got older," Ari adds, "we sorta ended up going our own ways. But that's why we always do a few camping trips a year."

"Gotta keep the gang together, ya know?" Kai says, looking around fondly. Several other glances and smiles are exchanged, proving that the feeling is mutual.

I find it incredible that after all these years and all their differences, they have stayed friends. It's plain to see how much they care about each other and watching them all together, I realize that they look more like a family.

I suddenly feel grateful to be a part of it, even if it is just for a little while.

The sun sets over the lake, causing the glowing yellow of daylight to fade into shades of purple and blue. The world becomes smaller as the darkness draws in, the expansive view of the lake and mountains disappearing, leaving us encased by a wall of trees and shadows. I look up and admire the stars, framed by an elaborate maze of tree branches in the open space above us. The smoke from the fire billows up as if trying to reach them.

Jackets start to make their way out of the tents as it grows colder and I wish that I could have enjoyed the long, warm nights of summer *here*, instead of back in the city.

"Hey, let's play a game!" Makena says excitedly, bouncing in her chair. Her idea is met with a bombardment of complaints and groans, but in the end, she manages to get her way.

"Alright fine, what are we going to play this time?" Kai says unenthusiastically, prompting a heated discussion. Dozens of ideas are thrown out, shut down, brought up again and discussed in detail, until finally the group mutually agrees on a classic game of "Never Have I Ever."

"Okay, the game is simple, but we do have our own variation," Zuri explains, most likely for my sake, as he walks around with a bag of marshmallows. "Everyone grabs a handful of 'mallows. Whoever ate a piece of pepperoni pizza last has to go first. When it's your turn, you say 'never have I ever...' and then state something you've never done before. Anyone who *has* done that thing, has to put a marshmallow in their mouth, but you *can't* eat it!" he says, glaring at Sunny, who is already chewing, an unapologetic grin plastered on his face. "Once you get enough 'mallows in your mouth to the point where we can't understand what you're saying, then you're out. You spit out your 'mallow, you're out. You eat it, you're out! Got it?" He looks around and is met with a mixture of eye-rolls and acknowledgements.

"Got it," I confirm slowly, still going over all the information that was just hurled at me. My family isn't really into games and I am suddenly terrified.

I'm going to fuck this up for sure.

"Okay people, I need pepperoni pizza dates. And be specific!" Noor calls out, followed by an immediate response of random dates and times, all spoken simultaneously. After a brief argument over the definition of *pepperoni* pizza, it is decided that Kai will go first since he happened to have a slice for breakfast this morning.

"Never have I ever..." Kai starts thoughtfully, fidgeting with the marshmallows in his hands, "...parked a boat eight feet up on land!" He says and everyone bursts out laughing. All except for Sunny, of course, who is glaring at him, his thick arms crossed.

"Hey, that's not fair! And it wasn't quite eight feet..." Sunny mumbles with a smirk and a slow drawl as he shoves the first marshmallow in his mouth, shaking his head in protest.

As we make our way around the circle, asking questions, arguing over answers and laughing at the ridiculous faces everyone is making with their mouths stuffed full of marshmallows, I quickly begin to understand why they are all friends. As different as they are, I realize that I was right. They don't just seem like a family, they are one. The muddled jumble of personalities slowly become defined and I am starting to pick up on the dynamics between each of them, which ranges from quiet admiration to flat out crude vocal bombardment.

When we make it back around the circle to Sunny once again, he already has four marshmallows jammed in his mouth. He looks ridiculous. After a few minutes of mumbling, spitting and laughing all around, he is voted out of the game for being unable to speak. After that, it only takes two more rounds before everyone else is systematically eliminated, leaving Ari to be declared the winner. She is beaming from the revelation and sits there with a smug little smile that seems out of place on her normally too-sweet face. Noor grins widely, shaking his head at her.

By the end, my cheeks hurt. Not only because they are stretched out from the marshmallows, but because of how much I have been laughing.

And that's all it takes, I think. *One evening and a goddamn bag of marshmallows,* for me to realize that for the first time in my life, maybe, just maybe, I have friends.

Real friends.

Chapter 4

I wake up early the next morning to the sound of Noor shuffling around in our tent. I open my eyes, blinking to clear my vision. Then I tilt my head sideways as something above me slowly comes into focus.

A worm.

"Shit!" I exclaim, rolling off the cot and landing on the hard ground as Noor bursts out laughing above me.

"Get up, Chicago! We're going fishing!" he says cheerfully, then makes his way out the open door of the tent before I have the chance to throw something at him. Grumbling, I grab a pillow from my cot and pull it over my face in a futile attempt to save myself from the rude awakening.

When I step out of the tent, I take a deep breath of the sharp, clean morning air and look around. Noor and the rest of the guys are all up by the closest outbuilding which, as I found out yesterday, is actually a garage and workshop. There is a small bathroom inside, which has saved us from having to walk all the way up to the house for that particular amenity. Affixed to the outside of the shop is a storage rack that reaches almost all the way to the roof. It holds several kayaks, some miscellaneous building materials and a small aluminum boat.

I run over to help Kai, Noor and Zuri pull the boat from the rack, which is surprisingly light, especially with all of us pitching in. It doesn't have a motor, but Sunny appears around the corner with a pair of oars and the fishing gear. He tosses it all into the hull as we haul the boat through the campsite.

I hadn't even glanced at my phone when I woke up and I wonder what time it is. But once we are out from under the trees, I see that the sky is still the pastel color of dawn and there is a chill in the air, so I figure it must be pretty early. So far, we haven't heard a word from the girls' tent and I'm a little shocked that our commotion with the boat, along with the usual bantering and profanities as we made our way through camp, hadn't woken them.

The five of us walk down the beach to a small pier then lower the boat carefully down into the water. Noor is the last to hop in and his not-so-graceful efforts almost cause a capsize. Once the small boat is finally steady, we shove off from the dock and glide out into the lake. I take another deep breath. The air is brisk, the water perfectly still.

Or, it *was* until Noor gets ahold of one of the oars. The slapping noises from it hitting the water will almost certainly scare off any fish we hope to catch.

"Noor, who the fuck gave you a paddle?" Kai admonishes.

"Seriously, Noor, give it up. We've been over this before, you're not allowed to row," Zuri agrees.

"Oh, come on, it's not that bad!" Noor argues.

"Yes, yes, it is," I say, then shove him aside to take over. I row steadily, keeping us moving forward easily through the glassy water, then smile over at my friend who is now sulking beside me.

It is nearly an hour later when I notice the first of the girls emerge from their tent. We are floating just past the dock and are close enough to see Ari's bright smile as she waves to us from shore.

"Morning boys!" she shouts, followed by two more enthusiastic waves as Makena and Efe walk up beside her.

"Morning!" I respond, then turn my attention back to the knot in my fishing line. Until I notice that the four other guys are staring at me, holding back their smiles.

"What?" I ask, bewildered.

"Man, how the hell do you do that?" asks Kai.

"Do what?" I say, completely out of the loop.

"You got the three grumpy bears to actually be cheerful in the morning. I swear, it's the same at school. Unbelievable..." Noor responds, shaking his head.

"What the fuck are you guys talking about?" I ask, still confused.

"We're talking about how everyone seems to come up with any lame-ass excuse possible just so they can talk to you. Seriously man, they're all into you," Kai responds.

"Well, except Efe, she doesn't date dudes. In fact, most of the time she doesn't even *like* them, but she's been getting on with you for some goddamn reason," Noor adds, giving me a shove.

I look over unbelievingly at Zuri and Sunny, hoping for some backup on this. No one ever liked me at my old schools, at least, not like *that,* and I'm finding it hard to believe.

"They're right," Zuri confirms. "The whole school's hung on every word you've said since you got here. Especially the girls."

Sunny nods in agreement.

I can't believe this, I shake my head.

"They have not. And even if they have, it's just because I'm the *new guy*, not because any of them actually *like* me," I argue, because there's just no way anyone is actually attracted to me. *Are they?*

"Oh yeah, sure. *That* must be it..." Zuri says dramatically, rolling his eyes.

"Seriously, I'm really not that interesting," I shrug.

At that comment, Noor begins twirling the ends of his own long hair and batting his eyelashes in my direction.

Oh boy, this is gonna be good, I think, my eyes already rolling.

"Oh Steve, you're *so* uninteresting! That's why I stare at you all the time in class and try to talk to you at lunch and wave 'good morning!' and-" Noor's sentence is cut off with an *oomph* as my elbow lands in his ribcage, once again almost tipping over the boat. Everyone laughs hysterically at Noor's bad acting and the consequences he'd just received for it.

"What's the matter Steve, you got a special someone back in the big city who's waiting for ya?" Sunny asks.

"Nope, like I said. *Uninteresting*," I reply, hoping to shut them up.

"So what, you've just been dating 'em and leaving 'em?" Noor jokes.

"Wrong again," I state plainly and under my breath, because I don't want to talk about this.

"Hold up, when was the last time you dated someone?" Kai asks, but everyone's eyes snap to me, equally curious for the answer.

"Um..." I run a hand through my hair and wonder how in the fuck this conversation got so out of control. "I haven't..." my voice trails off with a cringe. I already know what their reactions will be.

"Dude, no fucking way. Seriously?" Kai says.

"Well, not everyone can have *your* rap sheet, Kai," Zuri laughs.

"Damn right they can't," he responds, crossing his muscled arms over his chest, a proud grin on his face.

"*Never*? Seriously Steve? You've never dated anyone?" Noor says, ignoring Kai and Zuri.

"Well, it's not on purpose. No one's ever been *interested* in me," I answer matter of factly.

"That's ridiculous. You're fucking ripped, man. And that hair? The eyes? Come on," says Zuri dubiously, causing Sunny to look over at him, a grin on his face.

"Why, *you* interested?" Sunny says, waggling his eyebrows.

"Nope. *He's* not my type," Zuri responds. "No offense, Steve," he adds as an afterthought.

"Oh yeah? So what is your *type* then?" Sunny jibes incredulously.

"Wouldn't you like to know, *Sunshine*," Zuri replies with a wink, causing Sunny to stand up suddenly, fuming at him. Zuri clearly said it just to rile him up. And it worked. They are both standing now and I'm pretty sure that someone is about to go overboard for real this time, but Noor manages to defuse the situation, clearly accustomed to their outbursts. Kai laughs loudly at the spectacle and I smile, glad that the attention is off me for the moment.

"Okay, so you don't date. What do you even do with your time?" Kai asks once everyone has settled down.

"You're looking at it," I say as my fishing rod begins to bow and I start reeling in my third fish of the day. Which is one more than Noor has caught. I've been counting.

"Oh yeah right, Steve!" Noor scoffs. "All this loser does is *read* about fishing, and about camping, and who the hell knows what else. You should see his room, it's like a hundred-year-old man threw up in there," he jokes as I work to remove the hook from the fish.

"Hey, I do normal shit, too. Like binging shows and playing video games," I defend, waving the pliers at him pointedly.

"Yeah and somehow you make *that* seem nerdy too. This guy's beat like every game imaginable and keeps little notebooks around with all of his tricks and coordinates right next to the console," Noor responds, jabbing a thumb toward me.

"Hey, you do that nerdy wiring thing and I don't give you shit about that!" I retort.

"Um, it's called *soldering* and that's an applicable life skill," Noor defends.

"Oh fucking 'ell, you're both a bunch of damn nerds," Sunny states as he opens up the cooler full of water and I drop the fish inside.

After a long day and an even longer hike around part of the lake, we are finally back at camp. It's late in the afternoon and the guys and I are standing by the shore descaling the fish we caught this morning. I have never actually done this before, dad always used to do it for me as a kid, but I've read up on it and watched several videos, so I quickly got the hang of it.

"Man, I guess we're going to have to stop calling you 'Chicago' after this one," Kai states, holding up a handful of fish innards and looking over at me as I do the same.

"I told you guys, the city really wasn't my thing," I smile, ecstatic that I may have earned the revocation of my new nickname.

"Good thing, or we would have tossed you back like all of Sunny's fish earlier," Noor says, his own hands a mess from our unnecessarily complicated dinner plans.

"Hey, not my fault your loudmouth scared away all the big ones," Sunny shoots back from down the line.

"Hey guys! What are you-" Efe's voice cuts off. Eyes wide, she slaps a hand to her mouth before running back up to camp. I can see all the guys, aside from Zuri, trying not to laugh.

"What was that?" I ask curiously.

"The girl is tough as nails, but she also happens to be a vegetarian," Kai explains.

"*Oh shit*," I mutter, suddenly feeling incredibly guilty.

"It's okay Steve, she's fine with us fishing so long as nothing goes to waste. But yeah, we probably should have given her the heads up not to come down here," Zuri says then stares up after her with all the emotions I imagine someone would have given their baby sister. I watch him curiously, realizing how much more I have to learn about them.

As the sun begins to set over the lake once again, I find my spot by the fire. I think back on the trip so far and can't remember the last time I had this much fun. I don't want it to end. Even though it has only been a day, I feel like I have known all of them for years. Sure, I am still trying to catch up on their inside jokes, but I was surprised to find out how much I already have in common with, well, all of them. I have never felt so included and I'm already looking forward to the plans we're making for the next school break.

"Goddammit! We're out of Doritos!" Sunny's deep voice calls out. He crumples the empty bag and throws it at Zuri before heading over to find another snack from the cache.

"Hey! Don't you fucking dare! Dammit!" Sunny shouts, chasing after Noor who just grabbed the Oreos straight out of his hands. I lean back in my chair to get a better view. Sunny has a hold on the edge of Noor's shirt, stretching it out before he finally escapes. I shake my head, thinking how it's a good thing my friend is faster. Sunny is much taller and bulkier than any of us. He's all muscle and would absolutely win in a fight if he actually managed to get a hold of him.

My friend is out of breath and laughing by the time he circles back to his chair next to me, clutching the crinkled package of double-stuffed Oreos that I had brought as my contribution.

"Oh, hang on, I have peanut butter for those," I remember, running over to our tent to retrieve the jar.

When I come back, it's to a circle of silence. Everyone has stopped talking all together, which is a first, and they look pale as ghosts. I immediately pause, wondering what the hell happened. Noor's face is buried in his hands and Ari looks like she is... *crying*? Before I can say a word, Ari is heading toward the shop restroom, followed by Makena and Efe, who give me quick apologetic glances.

"What did I do?" I ask cautiously, suddenly panicked by their reactions.

Noor lifts his head up slowly, his eyes squeeze shut. He pinches the bridge of his nose, then sits back in his chair, at a loss for words.

I stand there and watch as the guy who always lightens the room with his constant positivity slowly breaks down in pain. I look over at Zuri, Kai and Sunny, searching their faces for some sort of answer.

"Noor?" Sunny says quietly, his deep voice a little gruffer than usual as he asks permission to speak for him. Noor waves his hand in a *go-ahead* sort of gesture as he works to compose himself.

"You didn't do anything Steve, it's just..." Sunny pauses for a moment as he contemplates how to word it, "that was something that Alex used to do. Dip Oreos in peanut butter," he says, a catch of fondness in his voice as he gestures toward the jar in my hand. "We, of course, made fun of her for it, but it's just one of those things that remind us of her, ya know?"

The name sounds familiar, but I can't quite place it. Until... *holy shit*.

"The poster from school. The missing girl..." I say softly. My dark blue eyes, which probably look more purple now that the sun is down, snap up quickly as I put it together.

"Yeah. Alexandra Cutter. She's in our grade, or *was*," Kai confirms as he uncomfortably fidgets with his too-long blond hair, clearly distressed by the conversation as well. I look around, the shock settling in as I take in the fact that they actually *knew* her. I have seen plenty of missing person posters before, but they have always seemed disconnected from my own reality. This doesn't.

They knew her.

"We all grew up together, but her and Noor..." Zuri makes a quick glance over toward him before continuing. "Anyway, she went missing about three months ago, at the end of sophomore year."

Her and Noor.

Suddenly, it all makes sense. This is what Noor has been hiding, why he's been so unsettled. They must have been together. *Fuck*, my stomach drops at the thought. I can't imagine losing someone that close to you. Or *having* someone that close to lose.

"Well, fuck. I'm sorry guys, I didn't-" I start saying before Noor cuts me off, suddenly finding his voice again.

"You couldn't have known. Seriously Steve, please don't feel bad. In a town this small, everything reminds us of her. Alex, she-" he cuts off, choking up.

"Noor, it's fine, we don't have to talk about it," I say sympathetically.

"No, it's okay. You live here now too, so you should know," Noor says, collecting himself. Sunny and Kai stare blankly at the fire and Zuri picks at a loose string on his camp chair. It's plain to see how much they *all* care about her.

"So, what happened?" I ask cautiously.

"We don't really know," Kai answers slowly, clearly haunted by the whole thing.

"All we know," Noor adds, "is that she went down by the river with her notebook to draw, like she always does. *Did*," he blinks, "and she didn't come back. There was no note, no bags packed and no sign of her anywhere. It's like she just disappeared. The police came, and even some FBI guys. They did the whole investigation thing, interviewed everyone in town. There were news vans here for weeks, helicopters, search parties, but they didn't find anything," Noor says, staring off. "I think that's the worst part. That there's nothing. We don't even know if-" he cuts off again.

But I don't need him to finish that sentence to know what he was going to say.

We don't even know if she's still alive.

"The police didn't find anything at all?" I ask, confounded. There is an unsettling feeling deep in my stomach and I realize that it is probably the same feeling that they have all been living with since the day she disappeared. It's the feeling that I've seen behind Noor's eyes countless times and am just beginning to understand.

"No, nothing. But I guess that could still be a good thing," Makena says thoughtfully as she sits back down in her chair somberly, then fiddles with the amethyst crystal that she always wears around her neck. I was so caught up in my thoughts, I hadn't even heard the girls come back.

"I'm so sorry-" I start saying before I am cut off again, this time by Ari.

"It's really okay Steve. I'm the one who should be sorry. You'd think I'd be able to hold it together by now. But really, you didn't know," she says sweetly, smiling at me warmly.

It's at this moment that I realize how *wrong* I was about everyone before coming out here. I dreaded being around people I didn't know and had probably been less than hospitable on my first day at school. And still, they have been nothing but kind to me, even with everything they are going through. These are good people and I don't deserve to be around them.

Then I think of something else.

"Wait, you said her name was Alexandra *Cutter*? Like, our English teacher? Mrs. Cutter?" I ask, suddenly putting two and two together.

"Yeah, Mrs. Cutter is her mom. She's been kind of a wreck. I'm actually pretty surprised she's back at work this year, but I guess there aren't any other teachers in the area to take over," Kai explains.

I stare into the fire, trying to digest everything I just learned. The anonymous girl from the poster has suddenly become *real.* My thoughts begin to hit me one after another.

She was so young. It's not fair.

How could the police not find anything?

Mrs. Cutter is teaching a class that her daughter should be in.

Alex would have been on this camping trip if she were here.

The last thought hits me like a ton of bricks and it isn't until the noise and chaos of overlapping conversations start up again that I snap out of it.

And just like that, the entire group is back to their normal laughter and chatter. Only now, I know the heartbreak they carry.

I am suddenly in awe of them. Of their strength, their friendship, of how they manage to hold themselves together when each and every one of them is in pain, on the brink of falling apart.

Later that night, I lie in my cot, staring up at the shadows of tree branches on the tent, their shapes defined by the light cast from the moon. My mind is racing, thinking about my new friends and how close they all are. I think about how lucky I am to be a part of it, how connected to them I already feel. Then my mind shifts to the person who *used* to be a part of it.

The person who is no longer here.

As I drift off to sleep, I think about the girl with the striking green eyes, the pretty smile and the giant hole she left behind.

Chapter 5

I drop into my chair in the back of the class, exhausted. Looking around, I give knowing glances to Ari, Noor and Kai. We are all in the same class first period on this Monday morning and clearly, they are feeling it too. Staying up until nearly dawn all weekend probably hadn't been the best idea, but it was worth it. Despite the exhaustion, the day goes by quicker than expected.

"See ya, Steve!" Noor shouts as he hops off the tailgate of his truck, slamming it shut as I make my way across the lot to my own vehicle.

"See ya!" I reply with a wave then drop into the driver's seat, forcing the door closed. After a moment of cranking, the engine finally turns over. It's always a struggle getting the damn thing to start and today is no exception. I look down at the gauges and see that the fuel needle is sitting dangerously near empty.

"Shit," I mutter, annoyed that I will have to stop in town on the way back to the house. All I want is to get there, suffer through family dinner and shut myself in my room for the remainder of the night. Because I know that sometime in the next six months to a year, my parents will get the phone call telling them about their next project. The call forcing us to leave. So the way I figure it, I might as well start the brooding now. No sense in wasting time. We have only been living in the valley for two weeks, but I am actually *happy* here. The thought somehow makes me more upset.

Because I don't want to leave.

When I pull into the gas station, I lean against the Jeep, waiting for the tank to fill. Arms crossed, I look around at the disparaged building that somehow passes as a mini mart. Everything in the valley is a little run down, and this building is no exception. Even the sign in the window that used to say, "*Come In,* We're Open!" has fallen and is now lying broken in the sill. In its place, someone has simply spray painted "Open" on a piece of plywood, which now leans up against the building facing the road. I drove past it one night and laughed out loud when I found out that the other side just says, "Buzz Off."

Above the sign is a pinboard covered with an array of local flyers and "help wanted" signs. Something about it catches my eye and I walk over to it slowly. Stepping closer, I realize that it is another missing person poster for Alexandra Cutter.

As I stare at it, the world goes quiet.

This flier has several different photos of her, instead of just the one that is hanging on the pinboard at school. A lump forms in my stomach as I realize that this is the first time I've seen her picture since finding out what happened.

Since finding out who she really is. Or, *was*, I think.

My stomach knots again, because she isn't just the girl on the flier, not anymore. She went to my school, is the daughter of my favorite teacher and an integral part of the people who are now in my life.

She was my best friend's girl.

I slowly reach out a hand, touching her face on the sun-faded poster, as if the gesture will somehow help me understand what happened to her.

Or help me find her...

The handle of the gas nozzle clicks loudly, pulling my attention away from the pinboard. Away from her. I feel a sudden wave of emptiness, like a piece of me is missing. It's a strange thought.

I shake my head to clear it before heading to the house.

After dinner, I fall backward onto my bed and stare up at the ceiling. As tired as I am, I quickly realize that I am not going to be able to fall asleep anytime soon. I'm not exactly sure why Alex's disappearance bothers me so much, but it does. I never even met the girl and yet, she is all I can think about. Her and about the inevitable move away from the valley.

"Fuck it," I say, giving up on the notion of sleep. I get up quickly, grab the AirPods off my nightstand, crank up the volume as high as it will go and pull off my shirt as I head downstairs toward the home gym in order to blow off some steam.

"Help! Someone please help me!" The girl's voice sounds desperate and I immediately know that it's Alex. How do I know that? I have no idea. But I do.

It's her.

Opening my eyes, I move my head from side to side, taking in my surroundings. I am lying on a beach, looking up at the stars. The view is peaceful.

Until I hear her scream.

I shoot up and look around, trying to catch sight of her.

"Alex, where are you?" I say out loud, desperate to find her.

Her voice seems to be coming from behind me, but when I turn to look back, there's nothing but the crowded forest. The only light around is from the waning moon, which causes the branches to cast eerie shadows across the sand, reaching out like claws. I stare into the woods, trying to see anything, but the light just fades into blackness.

And then I see her.

She is out of breath, stumbling through the darkness. She trips on the uneven forest floor, falling to her hands and knees. Then just as quickly, she scrambles up and is back on her feet, moving toward the beach.

Toward me.

I slowly stand as she steps out of the shadows into the moonlight and my breath stops when I take in the sight of her. Her hair is matted and full of leaves, her light green shirt and pants torn up.

And she is covered in blood.

I wonder if it's hers. *God, I hope not.*

It takes all her strength to move forward, dragging one leg limply behind her. A hand fists the fabric at her thigh, helping force the leg forward. I can see on her face the excruciating pain that is caused by each step. She is no more than a few yards away, but still, she hasn't seen me.

I have to help her. Have to save her.

But I can't move.

I try shouting her name, but to my horror, nothing comes out. So I scream silently, my arms waving above my head frantically, until tears of frustration stream down my face.

I have to help her. I have to try.

And it's in that moment I realize that I will never stop trying. Not until she is home.

As I watch her struggle through the sand, I can see that she is crying. The liquid streaks cleaning a path down her dirt and blood-splattered face. I reach out to her as she stumbles past, but she is just out of reach, continuing on as she makes her way down to the water's edge. The tide rolls in, splashing against her mud-stained gray boots. I stare after her, feeling helpless, my heart pounding wildly in my chest. I try again to move, but I can't. My body shakes with the effort as I shout voiceless into the wind.

"Alex!" I scream, desperate for her to hear me.

I have to get to her.

And then she turns to face me. The brief moment of hope is immediately shattered to pieces when I realize that she isn't looking at *me*.

She is looking at something *behind* me.

A chill runs up my spine as I watch the horror flood her face. She's trembling. I try to turn around, to see what she is seeing, but there's nothing. I try to go to her, but even as every muscle in my body tenses, I still can't move. I stand paralyzed in the sand, staring at the girl who is in trouble.

The girl who needs my help.

The girl with the pretty green eyes.

My tears fall again, hot against my ice-cold skin as I watch her standing there in the moonlight, her small frame shuttering from exhaustion. And even now, with her clothes torn, covered in dirt and mud and blood, there's only one thought running through my mind.

She's so fucking beautiful.

All of a sudden, Alex's feet are pulled out from under her and she falls face-first into the sand as the waves break around her. She lifts her head slowly and my heart stops.

She seems to look right at me, those sad, green eyes full of defeat.

I watch as one last tear falls down her soft face, as if in slow motion. Then she is dragged quickly, violently, backward into the ocean. It takes less than a second.

Then she's gone.

The echo of her last scream, and the lines drawn in the sand by her struggling fingers, are all that is left of her. Until the ocean waves roll in and wash away even that.

Leaving me alone in the silence.

I sit up in bed with a start and look around my bedroom, frantic and confused. I'm out of breath and sweating. As reality sets in, I rub a hand over my face, surprised to find it wet with tears.

"Hell of a dream," I say under my breath, then sit on the edge of my bed, placing my feet firmly on the floor in an attempt to steady myself.

I don't usually remember my dreams, so it's strange that this one lingers. I not only remember every detail, but I can't seem to get the images out of my head. It doesn't seem possible that I can see Alex so clearly when I've only ever seen a few faded photographs of her. Which means that my imagination must be firing on all cylinders. Then I remember something.

Today is August twenty-second.

Alexandra Cutter's birthday.

It's no wonder that she's on my mind, *hell*, she's on everyone's mind. She would have been sixteen years old today.

Only three months younger than me. My heart hurts at the thought. At how someone so young, with so much time left in this world, can suddenly have it all taken away.

Just then, my alarm goes off, scaring the living shit out of me and reminding me that it's time to start another day. I stare at my phone, letting it chime for another long moment. Then I shut it off, find the strength to push myself off the bed and start getting ready for school.

A few weeks have passed since that first dream of Alex and, for some reason, I can't manage to get a single night's sleep without seeing her.

Every night, I stand by, watching her run from some unseen danger. Every night, I watch her die. Over and over. And every morning, I wake up feeling hollow. Because I couldn't save her.

Again.

Groggy from another sleepless night, I sit at the bar counter in the kitchen and make quick work of a large bowl of cereal.

"You're up early," Dad says as he walks in the room, heading straight for the coffee maker.

"Yeah, we're going to that museum exhibit today," I say, bringing my bowl over to the sink.

"Oh well that will be fun. I know how much you like that stuff," he says, leaning back against the counter.

I do, in fact, like *that stuff* and I'm more than excited that we get to miss our entire Friday of classes for it. In less than an hour, the entire Junior Class will be loading into a bus and heading a few towns over to visit the Ancient History Exhibit showing there. It's a temporary exhibition touring the globe and is supposedly an impressive display of ancient Egyptian artifacts.

I have always enjoyed museums, but I am especially fascinated with anything surrounding ancient languages and cultures. I even have a few books on how linguists deciphered ancient hieroglyphs and runes. I love reading about how those cultures' languages transformed into the dialects we use today. I've even memorized some of the ancient alphabets, pieces of them anyway, if only for the purpose of being able to write notes or my name in a language that no one else can read.

"Well, here, take this for lunch, or for whatever else," my dad says, handing me a few bills from his wallet.

"Thanks, Dad, see ya!" I say, grabbing the money and my backpack. "Bye, Mom!" I shout up the stairs, but I'm already out the door before she has a chance to reply.

Several hours later, I practically fall out of the bus.

Because Noor shoved me.

We talk animatedly with each other about one thing or another, before we are urged to settle down by our history teacher and chaperone, Mr. Reyes. After a quick but detailed briefing on how we are expected and *required*, to act while in the museum, the group of us are let loose to explore the exhibits on our own in the hope that we might learn something.

The large warehouse style room echoes from the immediate chatter of students. I wander around, wide-eyed in fascination. I have watched a lot of videos online about the recovery of some of these very same artifacts, so I'm excited to see them in person.

Noor, who is already bored, runs off with the group who is clearly only here to goof off, which includes Sunny and Kai. So I wander alone from item to item, reading every single word on each and every plaque. There are ancient tools, plates, jars and several sarcophagi on display, all of which give air to a time and people long past. And then I look up to see the main attraction. In the center of the room, encased in a large square of thick glass, is a giant piece of stone. It is worn around the edges and the face of it is covered with writing. I walk forward slowly, as if *called* to it.

The Rosetta Stone.

I have read about the ancient stone, but can't believe that I'm actually seeing it. Standing in front of me is the key to understanding ancient Egyptian hieroglyphs. Without this stone, modern humans may have never been able to translate the language and wouldn't know nearly as much about the culture as they do now because of it.

The stone has the same inscription written on it in three different languages: Hieroglyphs, Demotic and Greek. Because historians already knew ancient Greek, they were able to use the stone to cross reference the other two, finally deciphering a language that, without the key, would have stayed lost forever.

Even though I know the story behind it, I read the plaque anyway. When I look up from it and back at the stone, I find myself suddenly and inexplicably drawn to the symbols carved there. I lean in close, trying to get a better view. Then, I watch as the letters seem to *glow*. I blink, figuring that the strange flicker is just a reflection from the overhead lights.

But then it happens again.

As I stare, the symbols gleam brighter, a white shimmering light that is almost blinding. The glyphs grow larger and I lean forward further, as if being pulled to them. And for some reason, I get the feeling that they are somehow *important*.

What the-

A whistle blows loudly from somewhere toward the entrance of the building and I jump, pulled from the trance. I turn to see Mr. Reyes waving us all over to him.

Time's up.

I turn back, expecting to see the writing still glowing sharply against the hard stone. But it is solid and unmoving, same as it's been for over two-thousand years.

It's been several weeks since the school field trip and I still can't seem to get what happened at the exhibit out of my mind. Can't shake the feeling that the script had called out to me somehow. I've been telling myself that I need to get more sleep, that the dreams of Alex are starting to take a toll on my mental wellbeing. Or maybe I just need to have my eyes checked. But whatever the case, I feel like those symbols are a part of me somehow.

Which is, of course, ridiculous.

That day, on the way out of the exhibit, I stopped by the gift shop and used the money Dad gave me to buy a book specifically on the Rosetta Stone, desperate to learn everything I can about it, with the urgency to understand why it's so important.

Needing to figure out what happened to me on that day.

I've read the book several times already and have even learned the alphabets of the three languages, practicing them in my notebook whenever I get bored in class. I've been obsessing over it and keep finding myself replaying that strange moment in the museum over and over again in my head.

As I lay in bed, I stare out the window and watch as the rain courses down the glass in long streaks. Now that the downpours have started in the valley, it feels like they will never stop. I put my hands behind my head and stare up at the ceiling, closing my eyes as I listen to the rain falling heavily on the roof. Listening to the wind as it whistles through the trees outside. But even with the gloom of the weather, I find myself feeling a type of hopefulness that I haven't felt for a long time. I've even stopped punishing my parents for making me move again, but only because I got tired of pretending to be mad about it.

Even so, whenever I'm here at the house, and not over at Noor's or hanging out with the rest of the group, all I want to do is close myself off from reality. Because pretending that I get to stay is a whole hell of a lot easier than accepting the fact that someday soon, I will have to leave.

I rub my eyes, surprised to find that I'm sweating. I sit up slowly and look down the long hallway, the floor beneath me a dark crimson colored stone. I reach down, pressing my hands flat against it, but immediately pull them back.

"Shit!" I stare at the red burn marks pulsing in my palms, shaking them in an attempt to assuage the pain.

The walls and high ceiling are the same dark red stone, the tall narrow windows starting above me, reaching up. Then a wary feeling creeps over my skin. Somehow, it feels instinctual.

It's the instinct that tells you to *run*.

"Not again," I mumble, suddenly realizing what's happening.

Standing up, I move slowly toward one of the windows, but before I can reach it, my attention is pulled toward a sound coming from the passageway on my right. The footsteps become louder as they approach and I stand perfectly still, waiting.

I watch the intersecting hallway until I see the flash of a person as they run past.

"Alex," I whisper. Even though I only saw her for a second, I know it's her.

Because it's always her.

Without my permission, my feet begin to move, sending me running down the long hall. Because I have to get to her. I don't know why, only that I need to. She's in danger and I have to find her.

I have to save her.

Turning the corner, I see her again. She's moving quickly away from me down yet another hallway, her long red hair bouncing back and forth as she runs. I go after her, watching curiously as she crouches down, peering around a corner.

I'm only a few yards away from her now, but then she starts to move again. *"Ugh!"* I complain, exasperated and already out of breath, but I follow after her anyway.

I always do.

The corridors seem to have an infinite number of passages splitting off, with every turn opening up to more hallways, creating an intricate sort of maze. Alex stays low as she moves from corner to corner, checking the path ahead before sprinting into the next hall. I wonder what she's hiding from this time, but know that whatever it is, it isn't good. It never is. A pit in my stomach tells me that maybe this time, I don't *want* to know.

"Alex! Can you hear me?" I shout toward her retreating figure. My voice echoes down the hall, repeating itself over and over, but there is no reply.

There never is. I don't know why I even try anymore.

I continue on, my skin sticky with sweat from the heat rising out of the stone walls and floor of this place. Alex peers around another corner, then stands upright quickly, slowly backing away from whatever it is she just saw.

And then she's running again.

"Holy fuck, Alex," I complain under my breath.

I'm usually a pretty decent runner, but this time, I have to sprint to keep up with her. She's been getting stronger lately and is far from the girl I first saw on that beach nearly a month ago, the girl who was shaking and terrified.

I look behind me, trying to see what she's running from, but the hallway is empty. She runs up a flight of stairs and as I follow, the room suddenly opens up.

We're outside.

No, not outside. We are in a giant *cavern*. My eyes widen as I look around. It becomes clear that we are in a castle. One that is... *underground*? The cave walls are the same color as the stone hallways. Only, they have to be miles away because I can barely see them far in the distance through the haze. The air is somehow hotter outside the castle walls, though not as stale. I find it even more difficult to breathe.

Particles float ominously through the air and the *sounds...* like the walls themselves are groaning, a low haunting noise that never seems to stop. I vaguely wonder how my mind came up with this one. Because places like *this,* well, they just don't exist in the real world.

I look over and see Alex, still running along the top of a large castle wall, one of many that intersect, same as the hallways. The parapets lead into various turrets scattered around and before I run after her, I stop for a moment to take a glance over one of the walls.

My eyes grow wide when I see what is down below, and how high up we are.

Shaking my head, I move away from the edge, focusing back on the reason I am here.

She is the reason.

I had only paused for a few seconds, but it was enough time for Alex to be far away from me, running along the top of one of the adjoining walls.

"Goddammit, Alex," I breathe, running after her small frame as it outruns me, *again*.

All of a sudden, she halts to a stop. Her feet slide across the stone and she almost falls over as she turns, running straight back toward me. I have long since given up hope that she can see me, so I know that something must be after her.

Suddenly, a loud shrieking noise comes from everywhere all at once causing both of us to press our hands over our ears.

Fuck! I buckle over as if the motion will help me evade the sound. The noise is loud enough that I can feel it vibrate up from the ground and through my entire body.

"What the hell is that?" I shout.

Then Alex is moving again and I look up just in time to see a giant explosion destroy the path between us. I cover my head with my arms as bricks fly in every direction, falling down around me. The wall shakes violently, knocking me down, and I land hard onto the stone.

"Fuck! Alex!" I shout, scrambling to my feet as I search for her through the cloud of debris. When I finally see her, I watch helplessly as the crumbling ground makes its way toward her. She tries to run, but it's too late.

I know it's too late.

I watch with horror as the ground begins to fall out from under her. When she turns, her sad green eyes seem to meet mine for one brief moment.

And then she falls.

Chapter 6

It's been nearly three months since we moved to the valley, which means that it's been six months since Alexandra Cutter went missing.

Exactly six months.

I stand in the hallway at school, staring at the missing person poster for the hundredth time. It has long since faded from the fluorescent lights, along with the hope that they will ever find her. A feeling of sorrow has slowly spread through the whole school, hell, the whole town, this past week leading up to today. I can feel it whenever I speak to anyone. And I can see it in Mrs. Cutter's eyes, as much as she tries to hide it. Those sad, green eyes that match her daughter's. I imagine they must have once been vibrant, but now seem dull and hollow.

Although unspoken, it's clear that everyone knows what today means. With every day that passes, it becomes more and more unlikely that Alex will return home. But today, six months is going to hit harder than the rest of those days. Because six months is a long time for someone to be missing and still be found. And the chances of her being found alive... Well, no one around here is talking about it.

But everyone is thinking it.

Mrs. Cutter, Noor, along with several other students, have opted to stay at home for the day, leaving the halls feeling empty. Alex's disappearance weighs heavily on those who are here and for some reason, I feel it too.

Later, on my drive back to the house, I catch myself thinking about her again. Which isn't a surprise. The dreams won't let me forget her. I don't even know the girl and yet somehow, I feel this connection to her. Maybe it's because my best friend in the world had been her boyfriend, or because my new friends were once hers.

Or maybe it's because they have started opening up about her more over the last few weeks. I've heard so many stories lately that it would be impossible not to feel like I know her. Even Noor told me that she and I would have gotten along right away if she were still here. And after everything I've heard about her, I don't doubt it for a second.

But I also feel a connection to her because of the dreams. The ones I haven't told anyone about, not even Noor. I'm not sure what the dreams mean, or why I'm having them, but I know it isn't something I need to bring up to anyone who knew her. Because I don't feel like I have the right to miss her, but for some reason, I do.

I miss her every day.

As horrible as the dreams are, watching her die night after night, never being able to save her, I still find myself looking forward to them. I have woken up sweating, freezing cold and sometimes, I even wake up on the floor.

But it's worth it.

Because in my dreams, I get to see her. Get to hear her voice, even though she can't see or hear me. And despite the fact that the dreams leave me with an overwhelming feeling of loss every single time I wake up, whatever is happening to me, I don't want it to stop. Because the heartbreak of watching her die each night is nothing compared to the thought of losing the dreams forever.

Of losing *her* forever.

As I pull into the driveway, I think again about that first camping trip three months ago. It was the night that I learned about Alex. But it was also the weekend that I found my new friends.

I missed them today.

I smile, my mood lifting just from thinking about the new life I have here. For the first time, I'm looking forward to the future. There's no doubt I have grown to love the valley and everyone in it. I've even come up with several good arguments to try and talk my parents into staying.

I'm lost in my own thoughts when I walk through the front door of the house. As I'm heading for the kitchen, I hear the sound of Dad's voice coming from the study. One of the large double doors is open slightly and I can see him pacing back and forth in front of the desk, his cell phone to his ear. I reach out to open the door further, planning to give a quick wave, but my hand stops midair.

Because that's when I hear what the conversation is about.

"Jerry, I don't think that it's necessary to-" his voice cuts off mid-sentence, listening to his boss on the other end of the line. I move quickly, putting my back up against the study door so I can listen without being spotted. "Yes, I understand," he continues. "But," he tries to argue, before resigning himself to agreement. "Los Angeles you said?" I can hear his pen moving across a notepad before he continues. "Okay, got it. Thanks, Jerry."

The phone disconnects and I shoot away from the door, not believing what I just heard.

Los Angeles.

"No," I whisper, backing away from the study as if it were on fire. I drop my backpack to the floor in the entryway and run out the front door, leaving it open behind me. I head straight toward the woods behind the house, the cold air stinging my face as I run. I don't care where I'm going and I'm too upset to even think about it, I just know I have to run. This *pull* in my stomach is urging me to run.

I have to run.

A flood of emotions wash over me and I'm suddenly hot with anger as I run straight into the tree line without stopping. I feel the sting of branches as they bite at my arms, my face, but I just keep going.

I run until my struggling breath finally forces me to stop. Bending at the waist, I put my hands on my knees and work to steady my breathing. I focus on the ground as my head slowly clears, on a vibrant green fern sticking out of a pile of dead branches on the forest floor. Its intricate leaves a stark contrast to its simplistic life. I am suddenly jealous of that plant. I want simple. I want a life that is straightforward.

And I want to stay.

When I straighten and look back, I can no longer make out the shapes of houses beyond the web of trees. I wonder how far I've run, but again, I don't care. My parents clearly don't care about my feelings, so I will stay out here in these woods for as long as I damn well please.

I walk slowly, with no particular destination in mind. I just need a few minutes to myself, a few minutes to think. Mom and Dad know I'm actually happy here, so how could they even consider making me move again? Not only that, but it hasn't even been three months. It's too soon. It just doesn't make any sense.

This is not fucking fair. I have to-

Suddenly, the soft ground collapses beneath me. I land straight on my back and begin sliding down the steep slope, internally lecturing myself for being so stupid. Then, a sudden wave of panic hits me.

Because I am heading straight toward a cliff.

I reach out frantically, grabbing onto handfuls of underbrush, but the small plants pull up from the ground, leaving me with fistfuls of useless foliage, none of which help to slow my descent. My feet scramble as I try to dig into the soft ground, but it's no use. I begin to slide faster, rapidly approaching the edge.

I urge myself to think. Looking around, I search for anything to grab on to. I see a tree up ahead, but it's far to the left of my path, its roots clawing at the cliff's ledge, trying to hang on to the earth as much as I am. I'm afraid that my weight will pull the tree right over the edge with me, but I don't have a choice. There isn't anything else to catch hold of.

I use all my strength to roll to the side, the fallen branches and rocks cutting at my hands and arms. When my torso hits the base of the tree, it knocks the wind out of me. My arms slap around its trunk and I grip it tight just as the ground falls out from under my legs, threatening to pull me over along with it. My hands scrape along the bark and my heart sinks.

I'm going to fall.

No, no, no!

I let go with my right hand, wrapping it around the tree trunk and then gripping it tightly with both arms. I swing like a pendulum, nothing but empty space beneath me. My hands and forearms burn as the scrapes and cuts dig themselves deeper into my skin, until finally, I slow to a stop.

But my sudden relief is short-lived as I dare to look down, finding the fifty foot drop between me and the rocky creek bed below. The hillside has washed away, leaving me with no foothold as I dangle here. I have to try and pull myself back up, but looking around, I find nothing else to hang on to. The tree roots are flimsy at best and my grip on the tree won't last forever.

And then I see it.

No more than five feet to my right, there's a rope. It has knots tied into it, as if someone used it for climbing. And even though I can't understand the purpose for it being here, hanging from a cliff in the middle of nowhere, I'm damn glad it is.

I can't quite see what the rope is attached to or how secure it is, but it's the only way back up, so I have to try. I take a deep breath. Hugging the tree tighter, I reach out toward it. It takes several tries, but I finally manage to hook the rope with my foot, pulling it toward me. I hold my feet right above one of the knots and give it a good shove downward. It seems sturdy enough, but there is no way of knowing if it will hold my body weight until I try. It's a risk, but the muscles in my arms are already beginning to shake from exhaustion and I know I can't hold on much longer.

One at a time, I transfer my hands quickly to the rope, letting myself swing downward. A sudden jarring racks through my entire body as the rope goes taught, but I hold on. It isn't until the second or third swing that I take a breath, my heart still beating out of my chest.

As the rope steadies, I take one last glance down before starting the climb back up. That's when something below catches my eye. There is a ledge jutting out from the wall of the bank. Curiously, the rope stops just above the rocky platform. Whatever is down there, it's clearly the reason the rope was put here in the first place.

I look up toward solid ground. Then, against my better judgment, I climb down.

I hop off the rope onto the ledge and look around. Set within the wall of the rocky cliff, is the entrance to an old mineshaft. It's boarded up haphazardly, but a few planks have been pried from their place, leaving room enough to crawl through, the crowbar still leaning against the stone nearby.

Noor told me once that Garda Valley was originally founded as a mining town and that there are mineshafts running all over underground, but I have yet to actually see one.

During the summer, Noor and the group hike through tunnels like these and I can't wait to tell them about this one. But then a pang of sadness hits as I suddenly remember, *I won't be here for summer.*

I quickly bring my focus back to the present, avoiding the sudden ache in my chest. I study the boarded up entrance, the darkness of the mineshaft lurking beyond. Even though my muscles ache and my hands and arms burn from the cuts, I decide to check it out before making my way back.

I am not particularly eager to go back there anyway. I don't want to hear my parents break the news of what I already know. Don't want the apologies or the reasoning, I just want to block out the reality of it. But now that the adrenaline has worn off, I can't. It all comes flooding back, but this time, it isn't anger that overwhelms me.

It's heartache.

I am about to lose the only friends I have ever cared about, leave the only town that has ever felt like maybe someday, it could be home.

How am I going to tell Noor? I shake my head, not wanting to think about it.

The mineshaft is dark and I reach for my phone to open the flashlight.

"Shit," I say, slapping the pockets of my jeans. I must have left it in my backpack when I ran out of the house. But it doesn't matter. Light or not, I'm going in anyway.

I rub at the cuts on my palms subconsciously as I duck through the boards, under the wooden supports and into the mineshaft. I feel the temperature drop immediately, the cold prickling my skin. Taking a few tentative steps forward, I wait for my eyes to adjust to the dark. Beyond the entrance, it opens up into a larger room. There are several other passageways leading further underground, but they are all boarded up with no easy way through. The ceiling is higher than I thought would be possible, with four wooden pillars, one at each corner, leading up into the darkness. I stare, walking forward to get a better view, but stop when my foot hits something. I watch as it rolls away from me.

A flashlight.

I take a step forward, crouching to pick it up.

Huh, someone must have dropped it. I click the button several times and am disappointed to find that the batteries are dead. That's when I notice something else on the ground. It's dark and looks like water. I reach out to touch the surface and when I do, it starts to *move*. I jump backward, confused. Because it doesn't behave like water. It doesn't just ripple out starting from the point of contact, it actually moves from everywhere, all at once.

As if my touch *woke it up*.

And then, just as suddenly, it stops, the liquid perfectly still. I stare at it, bewildered.

"What the fuck..." I whisper, leaning in but not daring to move any closer. The liquid is matte black, as if absorbing what little light there is in the room. Suddenly, it seems infinitely deeper. Or maybe I just perceive it to be. Looking closer, I watch as a small dot of light appears in the very center, like a pinprick. Then I see another.

And another.

The tiny lights seem to spread from the first point, multiplying outwards until they reach every edge of the dark water.

Stars, I ponder. *They look like stars.*

It feels as though I'm looking down into the night sky, each galaxy a million miles away and impossible to comprehend. I take a step closer, I can't help it. I am being pulled toward it, called to it.

It feels as though my entire soul longs to be part of it.

I crouch down and watch as the stars hold their position, giving off an eerie parallax effect. I reach out my hand and hold it just above the water, watching as the stars pull toward my fingertips, like a magnet. I slowly wave my hand back and forth over the surface, the stars matching my movements.

It's mesmerizing.

I'm so entranced that I don't even notice when the stars float out above the water, wrap around my skin, then slowly pull me down into their sky to join them.

Alex

CHAPTER 7

I'm not sure what made me come all the way up here. Maybe it was a feeling, or a sense, or maybe I've finally gone insane.

Whatever the case, I'm here now. Standing on the edge of the cliff at the top of the highest mountain above my house, I nonchalantly kick a couple of rocks over the edge as I look out over the sprawling view. Below me, the crumble of rocks taper out to the forest below. Beyond that, the sparkling sea.

And then, there's the island.

I can barely even see it through the thick haze of clouds that float around me, but there it is, hiding just off shore.

How long has it been? I wonder, because it's been a while since I thought about it. It feels like years, but here, in *this place*, it is absolutely impossible to tell. I kept a tally for a time, but even that became more of a hassle than it was worth.

A wave of a familiar hopelessness washes over me as I stare out over the ocean and think about my friends. About my mom. I have made a place for myself here, but it isn't home. It will never be home. I miss my life, my *world* and I am determined to find my way back to it. Back to them.

Keep your head up, keep moving, stay strong, I repeat once again in my head, taking a deep breath of thin, cool air.

"Get a hold of yourself, Ali. What the hell are you even doing up here?" I lecture myself out loud, something I have gotten into the habit of during my solitude. I also shortened my name to Ali. Because *Alex*... Well, I don't even know who that person is anymore.

I haven't seen that girl in a long time.

Before I turn to head back down into the mountain, I take one last look at the view. It really is beautiful from up here. That's when something catches my eye. I squint, not sure what I'm seeing. There's something... no, not something.

Someone.

Far below on the tiny island across the sea where I first arrived, is a person.

A person lying in the sand.

It can't be, my breath hitches.

I drop my backpack to the ground with a *thud* then crouch to dig through it. A few seconds later, I extend my spyglass to its full length with a click. It takes a few achingly long moments of searching before I find the island in my sights, then another waiting for the clouds to clear. My anxiety rises as they slowly make their way out of view. As they do, I can clearly make out the shape of a man lying in the center of the island. I pull the sights away from my face with a gasp.

I can't believe it. Someone's here. My brain floods with thoughts. Confusion, panic, joy, *hope*. I hold up the spyglass to look again, realizing that he isn't moving.

Maybe he's hurt. Maybe he knows how to get out, or maybe he's here to get me out. I can't stop my thoughts from cascading down the endless hill of possibilities. That's when reality hits me.

He is unconscious.

And it's getting dark.

"Dammit," I look at my watch, panic flooding over me. Because night will be here in less than a minute.

This is the first moment since I arrived that I felt I had even a chance of figuring out whatever the fuck is going on. I can't risk letting anything happen to him.

I have to get to him, and I have to do it *now*.

"Think, Ali, think," I rack my brain, trying to come up with every possible option to reach him in time. Any option at all.

Anything, except for *that* option.

"Fuck!" I shout to myself and the universe as I look up at the night sky. I'm out of time. *That* option is the *only* option.

And so I run.

Right over the edge of the cliff.

My heart leaps to my throat as soon as the ground is no longer beneath me. It doesn't matter how many times I've done this, it's still terrifying.

Dying is terrifying.

I have also long since decided that *falling* is a juvenile term. It almost gives you the impression that the action is in slow motion, or somehow *whimsical*. This is anything but that. My body feels impossibly heavy, as if I'm being pushed to the ground by some invisible force.

Seconds before I hit the rocks at the bottom, I hold my breath, close my eyes, and brace for impact.

The pain is excruciating. But only for a few seconds. As the agony abruptly cuts off, I open my eyes with a start. Then I kneel down beside the man lying in front of me. He is out cold, but at least he's still breathing.

"Hey! Hey, can you hear me? Wake up!" I shake the collapsed figure as I look around, trying to determine how much time I have.

Not long.

He's just not moving. And that's when I look at him for the first time.

"Oh hell, you're just a kid," I whisper, then scan the water again, my hope slowly beginning to fade as I realize that he might not have all the answers that I desperately long for.

I look back down to study him. His soft messy brown hair is lying off to either side of his forehead, but I imagine it will go right to his eyes when he's standing. My heart makes a funny little jump at the thought.

He's probably several years older than me if I had to guess, is much taller, and is decently fit for someone who just showed up here. I tilt my head, studying his face. The way his head is tipped back accentuates his jawline and my heart does that thing again.

Stop that. I tell it, not sure what I'm stopping in the first place.

He looks helpless. Then the blank expression on his face slowly turns from peaceful to pained. *I know that look.* He's waking up. He moves a hand to his head, letting out a pained moan as he tries lifting it.

About damn time, I think, looking around again. It's starting, and we don't have much time.

We.

It sounds strange, even in my head. That's not a word I've used since I've been here. *We.* I think again, before shaking myself out of it.

What's wrong with you? Pull it together, Ali, this isn't the time.

"I'm sorry, I know your head hurts, but I'm going to need you to help me out here," I say softly to the stranger. I move around to position myself and scoop my hands under his arms, using all my body weight to lift him. He groans at the sudden upheaval.

Shit, he's heavy. Somehow, I manage to drag him up enough for his shaking legs to get beneath him. After a few wobbly moments, he can hold some of his weight on his own two feet. I move around to his side and fling his dead-weight arm over my shoulder, struggling to keep us both upright.

"Hang on to me, I need you to hang on," I urge, because he is in fact *much* taller than me and this isn't going to be easy. Then I try getting him to walk, but he is in too much shock to follow suit.

"Hey, we need to move. Can you walk? We're not going far, but I need you with me," I say, but he isn't paying any attention. He's just staring around, confused as all hell, which is not helpful.

"Hey!" I shout much louder and with authority.

That gets his attention.

"What's your name?" I try again, a little more gentle, but with purpose. It takes him a moment, but he finally replies.

"My name?" He looks around again and his voice is deeper than I imagined. And softer. "My name is Steven," he says.

And then he looks down at me. He studies every feature of my face intently, almost as if he *knows* me, which isn't possible. And yet, he seems *familiar,* somehow.

Then his gaze meets mine and the world stands still.

My breath catches and I'm not sure if it's because of his voice, or his *eyes*. They are a deep shade of blue, almost... purple? They are sweet and striking and...

Ali, he's in danger pull it together, I tell myself, reluctantly breaking the contact that his eyes still have on mine. Because this is most certainly not the time for whatever the hell *that* was.

"My name is Ali," I say, much shakier than I intend. "Steven, I need you with me," I say, forcing the confidence back into my tone. I look straight into those eyes again. *Damn*. "Are you with me?"

He looks directly back at me and his gaze doesn't waver. Not even for a second.

"I'm with you," he replies firmly with no questions asked. And by the way he says it, I believe him.

"Alright, let's move!" I say, regaining my purpose and determination. I can see the wooden barrel in the sand ahead of us, but it's still a good hundred yards away. And I am still supporting most of his weight. We limp forward slowly, putting one foot in front of the other. We have to make it.

And we have to make it the *first* time.

My eyes constantly scan the water around us. I can see a few patches of bubbles, indicating where they are hiding below, but nothing has surfaced yet. Although we are in the middle of the island and far from the water's edge, that isn't going to matter once they get on land. They can easily reach us in a matter of seconds.

Ali, you should warn him, I tell myself, because he should know exactly what he just fell into.

"Steven, I need to tell you-"

Too late.

My voice cuts off as a familiar growl pierces the night air from behind us. The boy just about jumps out of his skin next to me, unaccustomed to the sheer volume of it. He loses what little footing he has and we both go down.

I guess that is loud, I muse. It hasn't phased me for a while. We are sprawled out across the sand, his arms still wrapped around me. I ignore our proximity, looking up toward the noise, seeing the tall burley silhouette. Shoulders hunched, it stands in the shadows just offshore, the water falling from it as it emerges from the darkness.

I look over at the boy. The color has drained from his face and his eyes are wide, locked on the shadow. And he's shaking.

Great. There is no way I will be able to get him up and moving fast enough, not now. Looking back at the creature, I remember the first time I saw one and imagine how he must be feeling.

Welcome to my nightmare, I think sarcastically.

I look toward the barrel, realizing that we made it further than I thought. I put so much focus on moving us in the *forward* direction, that I didn't realize we've nearly reached it. I allow myself a quick sigh of relief, before my body kicks into gear. I leave the boy where he is, sitting petrified in the sand, and sprint the rest of the way to the barrel. I quickly open the latch, throwing open the top, then bend at my waist to reach down inside.

I come back up holding a sword.

I always leave a couple spare ones on the island, just in case.

Can't be too careful out here, I think, watching the moonlight shimmer off the blade. I hear the boy's deep intake of breath and turn to see the creature running at full speed, heading straight for him.

Although its hunched stature and stumbling gait gives the creature an air of weakness, it is anything but. Its rippling muscles and strong form lumbers forward at an alarming speed.

Sword in hand, I sprint around the boy and head straight for it. The creature's snarl widens into a wicked grin, not a hint of fear showing in its glowing turquoise eyes.

Big mistake.

It picks up its pace, but so do I. As I grow closer to the wretched creature, I can immediately smell its stench. A mix of fish, salt and dead flesh, it's lifeless skin peeling. The growling grows louder as its guttural sounds attempt to scare me.

Not this time, asshole, I think. Gripping my sword with both hands, I raise it above my head and leap as high as I can, bringing the sword down with me.

Right into its skull.

Its arms flail and the pained noises it makes are ear-piercing, but soon the gurgling moans slowly fade to nothing as the creature breaks apart into a million pieces. I watch as a pile of ash-like dust drifts away into the night.

I stand still for a moment, looking back at the boy. *Steven*, I remind myself, his name is Steven. He is still sitting in the same spot, staring at me with big eyes that are now filled with horror, and maybe a little concern. His white knuckles grip at the sand, but other than that, he seems alright.

I look past him at the ocean beyond, checking the surrounding water carefully, looking for the telltale sign of their approach. My heart thumps, one, two, three sets of bubbles indicate where the next few will surface. Four, five, six, seven- *shit*.

I stop counting.

"Alright, time to go," I say matter-of-factly, running back to where Steven is sitting. I'm not even halfway there when the first three emerge behind him and these ones aren't wasting any time. The second they are out of the water, they are sprinting.

Steven manages to stagger to his feet and stands facing them. He looks around for a safe destination, but there is nowhere for him to go, not when you are trapped on an island. They are closing in and he wavers, about to run.

"No, stay there, don't move!" I shout above their growing growls.

Come on Ali, get there. Move faster.

Surprisingly, he listens to my warning and stays put, but his worried eyes glance back and forth between me and the creatures. They are almost to him now, but so am I.

Ha! I win! I think smugly.

I toss the sword aside and it lands in the soft sand with a muffled *thump*. Using all my body weight, I tackle Steven to the ground. The force of the maneuver causes us to roll twice and we lay there, a heap of arms and legs and sand. My arms are wrapped around his ribcage and his strong hands grip my upper back, holding me close to his chest.

Embarrassed, I quickly try to push away from him, but he moves his hands to grip my upper arms, holding me in place as he looks straight at me. He is confused and scared, that part is obvious, but it's his eyes that give him away.

He *trusts* me.

I tip my head up and smile sweetly back at him. Because I know something he doesn't. Without breaking eye contact, I pull out the arm that he isn't currently crushing into the sand and reach above my head. With searching fingers, I quickly find the lever I know will be there and with one quick pull, the ground disappears out from under us.

As I fall for the second time today, I can hear Steven's ragged scream as he holds on to me even tighter. I probably shouldn't be laughing at him, but I can't help it. I also probably should have warned him about this too, but there wasn't time. So I just hold onto him, laughing as we fall.

A few seconds later, which I'm sure seems longer to him, we hit the bottom, landing in the giant pile of loose hay I put there ages ago to cushion the fall.

This is nowhere near the first time I needed a quick escape.

The weight of our bodies push us deep into the hay, until it fills in on top of us, burying us in a cocoon of straw. By the time I crawl out of the pile and onto the stone ground of the cave, I am an absolute mess of sand and hay. I don't even have to reach up to know that my hair probably looks like a bird has tried, and failed, to make a nest out of it.

Steven crawls out after me and lays on the floor, terrified and breathing like he just completed a marathon in record time. And somehow, I'm *still* laughing.

When was the last time I laughed? I wonder.

I look at Steven, and laugh harder. He looks like a disheveled scarecrow. There is hay sticking out haphazardly from *everywhere*. From his light blue T-shirt, his hair, even his shoes.

He sits up, staring at me in shock, then slowly moves his gaze up toward the hole above us. The trap doors are hanging down, still swinging back and forth from their sudden release as the sand pours through the opening like water. The cascade begins to slow into a trickle as the creatures loom over the hole, ten glowing pairs of eyes standing out from the dark sky staring down at us, confused and angry. None of them are brave enough to follow us down, so they amble away from the opening and begin to mill around above us, making all sorts of angry growling noises.

Steven looks back to me. I'm still smiling like an idiot, but at least I'm not laughing anymore. Then one edge of his mouth begins to rise just slightly, until it breaks out into a full blown smile, followed by his own laughter. His smile is... well, it's fucking adorable. It lights up his whole face and I catch myself staring at his dimples until my own laughter finds its way back to me.

I'm nearly crying by the end of it.

When we finally settle down, we are both out of breath. I'm lying on the ground, my arms crossed over my stomach and staring at the stone cave ceiling as I work to get my breathing in check. Once I have pulled myself together, I roll my head in Steven's direction. He has laid back into the hay, his eyes close, his hands behind his head.

Taking advantage of his distracted state, I watch his chest move up and down with the motion of his breath, watch his lips twitch with the effort not to smile. A strange feeling comes over me in this moment. I feel... happy. But I also have this unexpected and overwhelming feeling of sorrow. It hits me like a punch in my stomach.

How long has it been since I've seen another human? The thought terrifies me, because I can't remember. But somehow, I am inexplicably glad that it's *him.* I know in my mind that he is just a stranger, but somehow, he feels... familiar.

I lay my cheek against the stone floor, grateful for its cool touch against my hot cheek. All the running and the laughter, not to mention the stranger with the adorable dimpled smile, has left my cheeks flushed.

I'm still staring when Steven opens his eyes, tilting his head to meet my gaze. I am not entirely sure what I'm supposed to say to him and clearly, he doesn't know either. So we just stare at each other.

Minutes pass and I can feel my heart beating unusually fast from the way he is looking at me, until he breaks the silence.

"Okay, what in the actual fuck."

Chapter 8

Steven states the phrase simply. *What in the actual fuck, indeed,* I muse.

He rests his elbows on his knees and knits his fingers together out in front of him in a relaxed motion, once again surprising me not only by his apt description, but by his calmness. As I sit up to face him, he leans forward, anxious to hear what I have to say. I stare at the ground for a moment, trying to figure out what the hell to tell him.

It's clear by his confusion that he doesn't know what this place is. *Dammit, there goes one theory.* I nonchalantly pick a few more pieces of hay from my hair before taking a deep breath, deciding on where to start.

"Steven," I ask cautiously, but full of hope, "do you know how you got here?"

Maybe it was different for him? Maybe he knows how to get back?

Steven stares off into the distance past me and his brows furrow as he contemplates my question. After a few moments, he grabs his head, his expression turning pained.

"No, no I don't think so," he says slowly. "I remember... walking into the house. I dropped my backpack, it was cold, there was a tree and stars and... I can't remember. I'm seeing pieces of it, but none of it makes any sense." He winces again.

The stars from the portal. Shit. I mentally kick myself for getting my hopes up in the first place.

"It's okay," I say to him, understanding. But I'm unable to hide the disappointment in my voice. "The same thing happened to me, headache and everything. Your memories will come back eventually, it will just take a little time. For now, we should get back so you can rest. If you're feeling anything like I did, then you're going to want to sleep for a month."

"Get back?" he says wearily, the fatigue resurfacing now that the adrenaline is wearing off.

I walk over to the far wall of the underground cave and grab hold of the rope that is hanging slack. With one good tug, the trapdoors from overhead slam shut with a *click*, securing themselves back into the latch that was released by the lever above. Steven's eyes follow my actions inquisitively, but he doesn't say a word.

"Yes, get back to the house, about a day's walk from here," I say as I make my way over to him. "It's barricaded, so it's safe. I have an extra room you can stay in. I promise it will be a hell of a lot more comfortable than that heap of hay," I nod my chin toward the pile and offer out a hand to help him up. He takes it gratefully.

Once he's on his feet, I notice how he's clearly concerned by something.

"A day's walk?" he asks in response to my questioning gaze. I let loose a short laugh at his mortified face before regaining my composure.

"A *day* is only twenty minutes around here... so it's not that far. And the first half of that walk is underground, which is safe, so we can stop and rest whenever you need to."

"Wait a second," he shakes his head, confused. "A day is-" he starts to say, before I briskly cut him off.

"Listen, Steven," I say, glancing down and realizing that his hand is still in mine. I drop it immediately. Then take a step back for good measure. Once my brain makes its way back to functioning, I continue. "You're going to have a million questions and I have a million for you, but for now, let's focus on getting back. Once you've rested and your head stops spinning," I say pointedly in response to his obvious fatigue, "then I promise I will answer any and all questions that you can come up with. Deal?"

After a beat, he reluctantly agrees. "Deal."

"No questions, just walking," I say.

"Fine. No questions, just walking. Got it," he says with a deep sigh, a smile tugging at his lips.

"Good. This way," I nod my head toward the dimly lit cave system that tunnels out from the far wall. He eyes it warily, but without a word, follows behind me nonetheless.

As we make our way through the underground subway, I notice again how tall he is. An inch or two more and he would be hitting his head on the lanterns that I have hanging from the ceiling.

We walk side by side in silence and I suddenly feel an incredible amount of energy. I want to tell him everything. Well, almost everything. How I got here and all that has happened since. I want to tell him that I am excited for him to see all that I've built. That I'm sorry he's stuck here. Tell him that I've been stuck here too.

Alone.

I have so many questions and can hardly wait to ask them. But I know that it will all be too much and that he needs to sleep. He will have enough to deal with when he wakes up.

Well Ali, you've waited this long for answers, what's another few days?

A few days. In my house.

With him.

Ali, what the hell have you gotten yourself into? I breathe deep. I don't even know him. For all I know, he could have been the one who trapped me here.

Or he could be a serial killer. I internally roll my eyes at that thought, because I can't imagine him as the villain in this story. In fact, he looks just as lost as I am. And those eyes.

Why does he look at me like that? I wonder. It's almost as though he cares about me, which is ridiculous. Clearly, it's just my imagination, or my desperation for human contact, that has conjured such a wild idea. But desperation or not, there is absolutely no denying that he is incredibly attractive. A fact that is making this situation a whole hell of a lot more... complicated.

I have been lost in my jumbled thoughts for who knows how long, when I notice that he, *Steven*, is staring at me. It catches me off guard. I'm so used to being alone, being unobserved, that I clearly don't know how to act in front of other humans anymore.

"Oh god, was I making weird faces or something?" I say, embarrassed. I have to remember that I have *company* now. Steven gives a weak laugh.

"Weird isn't the word I would use, but I am curious. What were you thinking about just now?"

That you're incredibly attractive and I don't know how to act around you.

"Oh, um, nothing," I blush. "I just... have a lot of questions too."

"Well, I need a distraction from the pounding in my brain. So how about we avoid the hard ones and keep it simple. No questions, just talking?" He smiles, playing on my earlier words.

"Sure, no questions, just talking," I agree and can't help but smile back.

Actually smile. *Me*, smiling again.

God, what is this boy doing to me?

"I like fishing," he says.

"I also like fishing," I reply slowly.

"Really?" He gives me a sideways smile and I flush again.

"Yeah. And climbing," I say hesitantly, wondering if I'm doing this right. I can't remember the last time I had an actual conversation with someone other than myself.

"Climbing..." Steven considers. "Climbing trees? Or mountains?" After a moment he adds, "Ladders?" playfully and I burst out laughing. *If he only knew...*

"All of those, I suppose," I smile, surprised by how easy it is to talk to him. He considers my answer and there's a small grin on his clearly weary face.

"I also like hiking and camping," he adds, surprising me, because he is dressed as though he has never been outside a day in his life. Even though he's a mess of sand and hay, that doesn't hide the fact that everything he is wearing is designer. They are brands I know of, but would never spend that kind of money on. *Could* never spend that kind of money on.

"Interesting..." I drawl and can't hide the smirk that tugs at the corner of my mouth.

"*Ugh*," he rolls his eyes dramatically, tilting his head back at my reaction. "Not you too!"

"What?" I chuckle, genuinely confused.

"You were thinking that it's *interesting* that someone like *me* goes outside at all," he stares pointedly at me, not breaking eye contact. His direct nature makes me feel vulnerable, but I'm not entirely sure if I want him to stop.

"No..." I say slowly, standing my ground and hiding all traces of a smile as I stare back.

But he just keeps looking at me.

Dammit. I suddenly lose all control and start laughing, surprising myself.

"I knew it!" he extorts triumphantly. "It's the shirt, isn't it?"

"And the shoes," I reply through a laugh. He grumbles something that sounds a lot like profanities under his breath. For some reason, this bothers him a lot, and somehow, *bothering him* entertains me.

We continue talking until the cave narrows, dead ending into a ladder that leads straight up to the surface. Steven looks at me, an infectious smile playing on his lips.

"A ladder? Seriously?" he asks.

"Well, I hope you like climbing too," I smirk back at him, then look down at my watch. *Almost there...*

"What is it?" Steven asks in a deep whisper. He is closer to me than I expect and it makes me jump. I hope he doesn't notice my reaction to him.

"Just waiting for daylight," I reply, watching the seconds tick by, approaching dawn. With his weary steps slowing us down, we have to time this just right. I don't want to be caught outside during nightfall. Not again.

A few more ticks and I turn back to Steven. He is running a hand through his hair, looking confused again, but I ignore it.

Focus, Ali.

"Okay, can you climb?" I ask earnestly. He looks up the length of the ladder and then back down at me.

"Yeah, I can. But this doesn't lead to another island, does it? If so, I might just head back to that pile of hay," he says, gesturing a thumb back down the cave behind us.

"No, it doesn't. Now come on, tough guy," I chuckle, beginning the short climb. I don't need to look back to know that he will be right behind me.

Reaching the top of the ladder, I shove open the trap door. It creaks on its hinges, landing flat on the grass with a *thud*. I take a good look around. The sun is out, the birds are chirping and it's all clear. I climb out and look back down at Steven. He's moving slowly, but he is moving.

He must be exhausted. At least his first day is going better than mine did... I think darkly, before shaking away the memories and bringing myself back to the present.

I watch as Steven manages to crawl out, making it just far enough to lay out on the grass, his legs still hanging over the hole.

"Leave me here. I can't go on. Save yourself," he says dramatically between panting breaths. I roll my eyes at the spectacle. After moving his legs out of the way, which he is of no help with whatsoever, I use my foot to shove the heavy trap door shut.

Looking back at Steven, I follow his gaze out across the clear blue water to the desert island in the distance.

"Is that..." he asks, amazed.

"Yup. That's where I found you. You ready to walk?"

"But they're gone. Where did they go?" he asks, confused.

Alright, I'll give him this one, I think, figuring that I can't avoid *all* his questions.

"The sunlight kills them. So, if they're smart, they're back in the water. If not, then they're dead," I reply plainly. "This way!" I gesture toward the winding path that starts at the tree line and heads inland toward the cliffs.

Steven quickly loses interest in the island, finding a new fascination. He gazes up at the towering cliffs. They are speckled with trees and trickling with waterfalls. His jaw drops at the sheer size of it. I look up as well, trying to put myself in his shoes, to see what he is seeing. I find myself staring with a reinstated fondness and wonder. It's been a while since I really *looked* at the mountains, the cliffs. The mass and beauty of them are incomparable to anything back home.

What is it about humans that causes them to become so quickly accustomed with their daily surroundings to the point that they take them for granted? I wonder at the thought.

They really are beautiful, I think, staring up at the cliffs that have become my home. No, not home. *Haven*. Because that is where I've found my place in this crazy world. The place where I feel safe. It isn't home, but I'm proud of it.

And now I get to share it with someone.

A smile catches the corner of my mouth, surprising me again. I have smiled more since finding this guy on my beach than I have the entire time I've been here.

I'm not sure if I should find that comforting, or just depressing.

I snap myself back to the present, because we have to move. It's an eight-minute walk from here and the sun will be down in ten. No time for sight-seeing or dilly dallying, *especially* when I don't have any weapons on me. I don't usually need them for this short of a walk, but I also don't usually have anyone slowing me down. In this part of the woods, I can outrun pretty much anything that comes out at night, but Steven definitely cannot. At least, not right now. Not until he's had some sleep.

Or until you decide to explain to him about all the things that lurk in the dark.

"Okay, Steven," I say, pulling his attention off the mountains and back toward me. "Those things that came after you, they only come out at night. Those things and worse are going to come out again. Nightfall is in ten minutes and my house is about that far away. So we have to move quickly. Can you stay close and keep up?" I ask him, because if he isn't up for this, then we are going back down into the caves until he can.

He looks straight at me and I can tell he is taking my question seriously. After a moment of consideration, he looks toward the trapdoor, then back at me.

"Okay. Let's do this," he finally says with resolve, clearly not wanting to go back down there.

Thank god, I think. I don't want to spend the night down there either. *Been there, done that*. It's not a great place to sleep and I want my own bed.

"Alright, stay close," I say pointedly. He nods in agreement and I quickly head toward the tree line, my eyes scanning the forest for any sign of movement. Just because it's daytime, doesn't mean that we're safe.

Nowhere is safe. Not out here.

The birchwood forest quickly surrounds us on all sides, the leaves stretching out overhead allowing only the faintest of daylight through the canopy. As we make our way along the winding path that snakes through the trees, I can't help but think how serene the forest is during the light of day. You can smell the fresh grass, the flowers are in full bloom, and in the distance you can hear the faint sounds of the waterfalls. I've walked this path a million times, but this time feels different. I suppose everything feels different now.

Now that I'm not alone.

Having someone else here should have provided me with a newfound hope that there's a chance of getting back home, or at least some answers, but some part of me has already accepted the fact that this stranger can't help.

No one can help.

No one can save us.

Now, he's stuck here too. And he's going to have a hell of a time once he realizes it. I'm not sure why, but I feel guilty somehow. Or maybe it's just empathy.

Still, a small part of me hopes that maybe he will remember something, *anything*. Something I've forgotten that can help. But then I remind myself that hope is a fruitless idea. I have already tried everything, done everything. It's been my experience out here that the only thing *hope* gives you is disappointment.

I turn back to make sure that Steven is keeping up and, surprisingly, he is. The fresh air, adrenaline and a set goal seem to be fueling him. And my motivation is to get us back within the barricade without dying. I have already done that once today and I'm not particularly eager to repeat it.

"How ya doing?" I ask, glancing back at him.

"Well, I'm not dead yet, thanks to you," Steven says and I give him a bright smile, a little taken aback by the compliment.

But the truth is, we aren't safe yet. He could still die and it's going to be a rude awakening when he does.

Another thing I will have to explain.

But that particular conversation will definitely take longer than this walk. I can already hear the crashing water from the falls growing louder, which means we're getting close.

Finally, I think drearily. It has never taken so long to get back to the house and it's wreaking havoc on my anxiety. We need to get to safety and *fast*. I look down at my watch, suddenly realizing just how long it has taken us already.

Too long.

"Fuck!" I say, mentally calculating out how much farther we have to go. We aren't going to make it.

"What?" Steven asks, looking around frantically in search of immediate danger.

"The sun. It's going to be down in less than a minute," I say, looking up at the leaves, their edges still shimmering with the golden light of day. As impossible as it is to tell right now, it's about to get real dark, real fast.

"What do we do?" he asks, fear flooding his eyes.

"Run," I say plainly. Steven's eyes widen, but he nods his head and we take off quickly through the forest.

The clear crisp view of the birch trees begin fading to muddied shapes as the daylight retreats, replaced by shadows. The world becomes smaller as our vision begins to fail.

We have to move faster, I think, looking back to see how Steven is holding up. He is lagging behind, so focused on every step that he doesn't even notice when I slow my pace to run beside him.

Until I grab his hand.

His weary eyes shoot up, meeting mine. They are a different color at night. Staring into them, I realize that they have lost all traces of blue, settling into a deep purple that matches the night sky.

"You've got this," I say matter-of-factly, encouraging him with a squeeze of his hand in mine and ignoring the feelings that come with that gesture. Without saying a word, he nods and matches my strides.

"Steven, look," I say, nodding my head toward the faint light glowing through the dark forest. "We're almost there."

Steven looks up from his footfall and a smile of relief flashes across his face. It's pitch black now and the trail is nearly impossible to make out. But I know this road, know the way.

That's when I hear it.

The familiar twang of an arrow being released from its bow.

And then another.

And another.

"Get down!" I shout, pulling Steven to the ground with me seconds before three arrows find their place firmly in the tree next to where we had been standing. I hear the sound of clattering footsteps quickly approaching and drag Steven behind the nearest tree, the one now riddled with arrows.

"You have to follow me. Stay low and stay behind the trees as much as possible," I whisper, staring at him to make sure he understands. He nods and we move quickly from tree to tree in the direction of the light, keeping low and keeping quiet. A volley of arrows continue in our direction as we move, some hitting the trees we hide behind and some whizzing past as they cut through the air. I listen beyond the arrows, focusing in on everything else out here.

Well, shit, I think when I realize what's happening.

"When I tell you to, I need you to keep your head up, keep moving and stay strong. Head toward the light and *don't stop.* No matter what," I whisper to Steven behind me.

"What's wrong?" he asks, concerned, and I decide that it's a good thing he doesn't know what I do.

"Just stay calm," I plead. The last thing I need is for him to panic and run off.

Because we are already surrounded.

"Stay here, wait for my signal. If anything goes wrong, *run*," I say pointedly at him. Seeing in my eyes how serious our situation has become, he agrees.

Up ahead, one steps out from behind a tree, the darkness hiding all but the silhouette of its large frame. I run directly toward it, slamming a shoulder into its hard stomach. It tries to grab at me but I duck low, out of its grasp, and I'm already a few feet away when it starts to stumble backward uncontrollably. I hear the low growl of a second creature and quickly pick up a rock. When it appears, I hurl the stone at its face, hitting my mark.

"Steven, now!" I shout and he runs past the stumbling creatures and toward the light, with me right behind him. By the time both creatures catch their footing, we're already long gone.

We're almost there, I think with relief. But just as the sounds of angry growling and arrows begin to fade, there is another sound.

One worse than the rest.

By the time I hear the loud hissing noise, I know already that it's too late. And so, I do all I can. Moving *quickly*, I place myself between the noise and Steven, shoving him as hard as I can away from the sound.

That's when the blast goes off. Sudden, ground shaking and deafening.

Fuck, I think as I take the brunt of the blast.

Everything happens in slow motion. I see the fear in Steven's eyes as he flies backward from my brutal shove, see him slam even harder into a tree from the force of the explosion. Worried for him, I'm barely even aware of my own shrapnel-riddled body as it's thrown like a doll through the trees.

And then I die.

Chapter 9

"God. Damn. It!" I shout, picking myself out of the sand. *Back on my very favorite island*, I muse sarcastically.

"Dammit, Ali. Stupid. So stupid," I reprimand, ruffling the sand from my hair. As I make my way across the island, I see a creature making a run toward me, but I don't pay it much attention. By now, I know the timing as well as I know my own house. I'll make it in time.

Oh god, Steven, I think.

I just let myself get blown up, and then left him in the woods. Alone.

"*Agh*!" I shout, frustrated. I stand over the trapdoors and, just as a few of the creatures start closing in, I kick the lever with my boot. The ground gives way and I'm falling down into the safety of the pit below the island.

Picking the straw from my hair, I make my way quickly through the cave system, up the ladder and out the trapdoor.

I can't believe I left him like that. I should have explained, I think, urging myself to move *faster* as I make my way through the dark, the cold, desperate to reach him. The growling sounds fade in and out as I move past the creatures making them.

Arrows land in trees all around me.

Hang on Steven, I think. *Just hang on.* I run through the dark, through the night and just hope that Steven made it out. Made it to safety. If he didn't, then he won't have the strength to try again. *If he even can try again...* The thought haunts me. I haven't stopped to consider that maybe it won't be the same for him.

Maybe he can't come back.

Distracted by my own mortifying thoughts, I don't even hear the arrow coming. Don't even try to move out of its way. "Fuck!" I shout, pulling it from where it buried itself in my upper thigh. It stings like hell, but not enough to slow me down. And I've definitely had worse.

As the sounds of the waterfall grow louder, I begin to see the glow of lanterns through the trees. I am almost there, almost to the place I left him.

The place I died.

I scan the forest, looking for any sign of him.

"Steven!" I shout, but hope to god that he isn't still outside the barricade.

The trees open up and I can finally see the waterfall. At night, it appears to flow straight out of the dark sky, crashing onto the rocks below before making its way downstream. The mist swirls around me as I run and the deafening rumble mutes my steps as I pad across the footbridge to the meadow beyond.

To safety.

The soft grass that spreads out along the base of the cliffs is scattered with glowing lanterns. Their flickering flames create a barricade of light, along with the actual barricade which I threw together haphazardly when I first got here. It consists of large tree branches interwoven with thorn bushes which, along with the light, keeps the creatures at bay.

For the most part.

As I search the meadow, I'm surprised to realize how concerned I am for him, for *Steven*. Someone I just met. I know that it's a risk to bring him back here, but for some reason, I feel the need to protect him. To be near him.

I find the thought unsettling.

As much as I don't want to be alone anymore, I've gotten used to it. I'm not sure if I even know how to be around people anymore.

As I run further from the falls, the mist begins to dissipate, floating away into the night sky.

And that's when I see him.

Under the overhang of the cliff face, Steven sits with his back against the stone wall, his arms wrapped around his knees, his face buried in them.

He's alive, I breathe. Once again surprised at how relieved I am. Relieved that he's still alive and... *crying*? *Why would he be cry-* and then it hits me.

He just watched me die.

Great, now you've traumatized him. Way to go, Ali.

But traumatized or not, I can't help but be proud that he managed to make it the rest of the way on his own. He watched me die, then without knowing what else lies beyond those trees, he trusted me and made his way out of the dark.

I know better than anyone, it couldn't have been easy.

I approach slowly and crouch down, gently putting a hand on his arm. His head snaps up quickly, he moves back defensively and his whole body tenses.

Until he sees me.

Those dark blue eyes with their purple edges look straight into mine, a mix of confusion and relief. My heart sinks at the sight of his disheveled state. His face and arms are speckled with small cuts as a result of the explosion, his clothes muddied and stained with blood. *My* blood, probably.

I can tell he wants to be glad to see me, but he's struggling, trying to determine if I'm really here.

"Ali?" he asks hesitantly, *hopefully*, his voice husky from his tears.

"I'm so sorry, I should have tol-" my words are abruptly cut off as his arms suddenly wrap around me. Shocked and confused by his reaction, I have to remind myself again that he just watched me die, not knowing that I would find my way back to him.

My heart suddenly softens and I hold on to him just as tightly as he's holding me. I don't care that this boy is a stranger. I don't even care if he is the one responsible for my imprisonment. I hardly notice the wound in my leg, even as it throbs, or that I'm out of breath from my sprint over here. I don't care about any of that. In this moment, I realize that whatever comfort he needs, I am willing to give it.

Because I need it too.

I realize now how much I've needed someone, needed *him*. I cling to him, reveling in the first human embrace since being trapped here. I pinch my eyes shut, holding back tears that I know won't come. *Can't* come. Not anymore.

Because I am broken.

We just stay here in the damp grass, on our knees, holding on to each other. Holding on to whatever *this* is.

Eventually, I begin to feel the warmth of sunlight as it touches the back of my hair. Steven must feel it too, because he slowly releases his hold, putting just enough space between us so he can look up, his strong arms still locked around me. I study his face and can see the streaks where his tears made their mark.

Tears of fear, or tears for me? I wonder curiously. Either way, he will soon find out that there are worse things than fear out here.

And worse things than death.

Things like the throbbing puncture wound in my thigh.

I try adjusting my weight to the other knee and with that simple movement, a shooting pain racks my whole body. My sharp intake of breath through closed teeth alerts Steven to my indisposition and those big concerned eyes are looking at me again.

Dammit, I think. Because I was hoping he wouldn't notice. He doesn't need to be worried about me, not when his whole life was just torn away from him. *And he doesn't even know it yet.*

"Shit! Ali, you're hurt," he says, holding my shoulders firmly as his eyes scan over me, growing wide when they land on the dark blood stain growing on my right thigh.

"I know, I know, it's fine," I reassure him. "It's not that deep, so it'll heal quickly," I say plainly, looking down to examine it for the first time.

"Oh goddammit!" I shout.

"What?" Seven asks frantically, his voice concerned as he looks around.

"My pants!" I say frustratedly. "That damn arrow put a giant tear in them. Shit!" It is going to be an absolute pain in the ass to fix. I shake my head unbelievingly as I tenderly pull the fabric away from the wound to get a good look at the damage to my favorite pants.

"Your *pants*? What about the giant hole in your *leg?*" Steven points out, still bewildered as to why I'm so unconcerned about it.

"Oh, my leg will be fine," I state plainly. "Now help me stand up, tough guy," I say, smiling at him, because I find his concern endearing. And because I don't need him worrying about me.

I can take care of myself.

Steven gets to his feet and helps me to mine. I test my weight on my hurt leg and although it stings, it's functional.

Thank god, I think. The last thing I need is to be forced to sleep down here, *again.* My thoughts trail back to several unpleasant memories.

"Ali, there's no way you can walk on that."

"Huh?" I say, suddenly realizing that he's talking to me again.

Dammit Ali, you're not alone anymore, pay attention.

"Oh, um no it's okay. I'm fine, really," I say quickly, realizing we are still talking about my leg, which I've already forgotten about.

"We're here anyway," I smile.

"We are? But this is a field? And a cliff... and a river..." Steven says as he looks around, confused.

"Yes, very good. That is a field and that's a cliff and a river," I mock him playfully. "But, if I built my house *down here,*" I explain, "then the creepy crawlies that come out at night just across the river would keep me awake and I'd never get any sleep."

"I would also prefer to sleep far away from the creepy crawlies," Steven says. "And because I need *said* sleep, I'll leave the rest of my questions until morning," he says. Then he steps close to me, *very* close, causing my heart to skip a beat. I look up at him. "Like how in the fuck you're still alive," he whispers, staring down at me with a sort of longing that has chills running uncontrollably over my skin.

"Fair enough," I say, finding my voice barely audible. "It's... um... this way," I mutter.

I move away from him, snapping myself back to reality. I limp over to the cliff wall so I can use it for support, politely shooing Steven's hands away when he tries to help me walk. I run my hand along the surface and after a few yards, I stop. I hold back a clump of the dark vines that scatter the stone, revealing the ladder hidden behind them.

"Huh, I would have never seen that," he says slowly, looking up to where it leads.

"That's kind of the point," I say. Dropping the vines back into place, I start climbing. It's awkward, only using one foot, but I manage. And again, I've definitely climbed this ladder in worse shape.

Standing on the ledge, about thirty feet up from the field, I look back down toward Steven as he makes his way up then stands beside me. Without warning, he grabs my hand, forcing it onto his shoulder and wraps his arm around my waist, pulling me close to him.

"Steven, I-" I begin to protest.

"Nope, just walking," he says, looking down at me with a sideways smile. No, not just a smile. A smile and a *wink*. Or had I imagined that part?

Nope. I definitely didn't imagine it.

My heart stutters and I feel my cheeks redden again. I look away immediately before he notices.

What the hell is happening? Is he doing this on purpose? Whatever it is, I can't think about it right now, not while my leg is making its way past throbbing and into shooting pain. So I concentrate on each step, still brooding, but reluctantly grateful for his help.

Ali, what's wrong with you? Give the guy a break.

"Thank you," I finally manage to say in a small voice, but I'm *not* going to look at him again.

"You're welcome," he says genuinely and I can feel his eyes on me.

As we reach the porch steps, Steven keeps his arm tightly around my waist, but pauses, taking a moment to look up at the front of the house. The dark wooden door is flush with the cliff, the metal handle hammered into shape. Beyond the door frame, are large walls of dark glass seated into the stone and running along the cliff to our left and all the way to the right until it reaches the corner. I spent weeks tearing down those walls with nothing more than my bare hands and a pick-axe, because I was sick of feeling closed in and was desperate for daylight.

The porch isn't the greatest, because I threw it together quickly, but it's sturdy, made from the same dark oak as the door. But the best part is most certainly the view. The house was built right into the cliffs, high up from the meadow, simply for security purposes, but it resulted in a spectacular vantage point. You can see all the way over to the waterfall, to the footbridge and to the start of the path leading into the forest. You can see where the birch trees fade out into a dark oak which quickly thickens, blanketing the mountains beyond. And we're just high enough over the trees that you can see all the way to the glistening sea.

And that's just from the *first* floor.

I smile, watching Steven as he looks around. It's a lot to take in, but it really is beautiful. I will have to take him up to the very top at some point. From there, there is a three-hundred-and-sixty-degree view of this world. The landscape so similar to back home that it's easy to forget where you are. The only difference is that *here*, everything is a whole lot *larger* and a hell of a lot more complicated.

Suddenly, that aching desire to know if Steven can help me get home hits me like a wave. I need to know what he knows. How he got here, and if he has any clues on how we can get back.

"Hey," I say, getting his attention. "You ready?"

Steven pulls his eyes away from the view reluctantly, but I can see the cloud of fatigue as he nods in agreement. He helps me up the steps and across the porch, pulling the heavy door open. I slide my hand from his shoulder and use the door frame for support. He slowly lets go of my waist, making sure that I have my balance, and I immediately miss the feel of his hand on me.

As I walk into the entryway, Steven right behind me, I suddenly feel a mild panic. Because no one has ever *been here* before and I wonder at the state in which I left it last.

"Um, sorry if it's a mess or anything, I've never... had company..." I say, looking around with new eyes, surprised to find that it is pretty tidy, all things considered.

Two short steps down to our right is the living room with a few couches and a chair around the wooden coffee table in the center, the fireplace built into the far wall.

To our left, the stairs spiral up to the kitchen on the next floor. It isn't much, but I've worked hard to make it feel like a real house.

Steven looks around curiously and then at me.

"Really? No one's ever been here?" he asks, astonished.

I don't have the heart to tell him that there is *no one* here, so I simply shrug, then hobble straight ahead and down the hall, using the wall as my new support.

"Okay," I say, leading him into the first bedroom on the left. "You're welcome to stay in here. It's not much, but the bed is pretty comfortable. And the *bathroom* is through there," I say, pointing toward a door on the far wall.

I make my way over to the storage cabinet and try to pull down a fresh set of sheets from the top shelf, wincing from the strain to my leg. Before I know it, Steven is right beside me.

So close. Why is he so close?

He reaches up easily, then looks down at me with that confused but familiar look of recognition once again.

"Thanks," I say quietly, meeting his eyes for only a second before grabbing the sheets from his hands and heading toward the bed.

"Hang on, I've got that," he says in a weary tone that is more of a lecture. And because I can tell he isn't going to take *no* for an answer, and because my leg is starting to hurt again, I let him.

While Steven works to put the sheets on the bed, I grab a hand towel from a lower shelf and set it on the small wooden table in the corner next to the water pitcher.

"If you need anything else, my room is-" Turning around, I just smile, shaking my head.

Because Steven is already lying face down diagonally across the bed.

And he's sound asleep.

Chapter 10

He's going to sleep for at least a month, I think, staring at the boy lying across my guest bed. Well, a month *my* time, which is another thing I'll have to explain.

I mentally add it to the list.

I stare for another moment, wondering if I should move him.

Eventually, I just toss a blanket over him, then throw a pillow in the general vicinity of his head. *He'll figure it out.*

Making my way out of the room, I shut the door quietly behind me and let out a breath I didn't know I'd been holding. I stand in the hallway for a long moment, letting the thoughts of what just happened flood my mind. Until the throbbing in my thigh decides to remind me *exactly* what I got myself into.

I limp my way down the hall and into my bedroom, which is bigger than the living room and entryway combined. *What can I say, I like my space.*

Which is precisely why my house is six stories tall.

I make my way over to the far corner. Grabbing the water pitcher, basin and a rag from one of the shelves, I sit at the table that faces the bay window. Which, unironically, overlooks the bay.

My room is on the opposite side of the mountain from the front door, which gives a completely different view from the one in the living room. Instead of trees and waterfalls with the ocean in the distance, the glass wall in my bedroom gives a sprawling view of the half-moon bay miles below and leading out to sea where the sun is just beginning to set over the horizon.

Another pulsing throb brings my attention back to the task at hand. I gingerly work to remove my pants and, after a few bumps and winces, I finally manage to slide them past the gash in my thigh, letting them drop to the floor then kicking them aside. They are covered with blood, grass stains, mud, hay, sand and who knows what else. I grumble, because cleaning them isn't going to be fun.

I dip the rag into the water, then begin clearing the blood from my skin, revealing the wound. The damage caused by the arrow is deeper than I thought, but it takes a hell of a lot more than a tiny hole for me to pass out, so I continue.

After wrapping the wound with strips of fabric, I lean back in my chair to rest. I stare out the window, watching the moon's reflection dance across the surface of the dark water far below.

Once the pain begins to subside, I try running my fingers through my curls, suddenly realizing that my pants aren't the only thing that's a mess. I know that I should probably stay here and let my wound heal for a few more daylight cycles, but I need a shower. And I doubt that Steven will be awake anytime soon. I limp past my oversized feather bed and into my closet, grabbing a fresh pair of clothes and a towel.

In the hall, I pause at Steven's door for a moment, listening for any signs of movement. When I hear nothing but the soft sound of his breathing, I continue down the hall and out the front door.

Even though it was probably the quickest shower I've ever taken, it feels amazing to be clean. The whole time I was down there, I worried that Steven would wake up and panic finding that I was gone.

Once back in the house, I quickly check on Steven, then find myself pacing, unable to sit still. Although my wound isn't completely healed yet, I can finally put some pressure on it without the searing pain that I felt earlier. So I make my way slowly from floor to floor, keeping myself busy. I put things away, straighten paintings, adjust couch cushions, clean the floors and rearrange the rugs.

After several hours, I realize that there is nothing left to do and that I'm being ridiculous. So I pace some more, wondering when Steven will wake up.

Spending time together with another human being, even if those moments were less than ideal, is making me anxious to see him again. Being alone for as long as I have? Well, it's taken its toll. What I've been through, what I've done to survive, being alone... it changed me.

Those days are over, Ali. You're not alone anymore, I remind myself, still trying to believe it.

Maybe he's not really here, maybe you made it all up. I roll my eyes, because although that is a valid thought, I know it isn't true. Because I've gone in there to check that he's real.

Several times.

Every time, he's still here. He's real. And he is sound asleep in my spare bedroom. I shake my head again, still in shock over all of this.

And then I think, *what if he doesn't want to stay.* My heart sinks. This stranger, Steven, doesn't know me at all. What if, after he does, after seeing who I've become because of this place, he doesn't want anything to do with me?

It's a real possibility.

I can't be alone. Not again. I won't survive it this time, I think somberly.

"Alright Ali, enough of that. You gotta find something to do. Something to pass the time," I say out loud. Then I realize that talking to myself is probably something that I should stop doing. The last thing I want is to scare the guy off.

I just have to act normal.

Yeah right, I mock myself.

And speaking of crazy, I suddenly remember that I left my pack on the top of the mountain. Just before deciding it would be a *great idea* to jump off it.

How long ago was that? I suddenly think, curious. After some crude mental calculations, based on how many times the sun has set and how far along my wound has healed, I decide that it must have been about six hours.

Six hours. That's when my whole life out here changed.

I head over to the nearest ladder, the one that leads directly to the top of the mountain. I stare at it. By now, my leg is almost completely healed, but I'm pretty sure that this climb will be overdoing it. I shrug, then continue anyway, needing something, *anything*, to pass the time. And *sleep* is out of the question. With my mind the way it is, which is currently all over the place, there is no way that's happening. Besides, I'm used to not sleeping. A twenty-minute daylight cycle has a tendency to wreak havoc on your mental clock.

As I climb, I wonder again how Steven is doing. I've considered waking him up over a dozen times, but eventually talked myself out of it, remembering how tired I was when I first got here. And then I wonder what he would do if he woke up right now and found that I wasn't in the house. The last thing I need is for him to start *wandering*. Around here, he could easily get himself lost, or worse. *He could go outside.*

I begin climbing faster.

I reach the top of the ladder and open the trap door leading into the small shack on top of the cliffs. There's a narrow horizontal window that wraps all the way around the small building right at eye level, giving a full view of the outside. I learned the hard way that it's crucial to know what's out there before you open the door.

Thankfully, it's already daylight. The blast of crisp air hits me as soon as I step outside. Climbing the ladder was a little more of a challenge than it usually is, due to my latest injury, and so I welcome the coolness of the wind.

I take a deep breath, then stare out over the world. When I first got here, I would spend as much time on top of this mountain as I could spare. I would sit on the large rock that I stand by now and look down at the little island, hoping for *something*. For *anything*. As time went by, I came up here less and less, until I just stopped coming at all. There is nothing to see, nothing to look for, nothing to hope for. I never imagined that I would stare out over the water and find a person.

Find *him*.

So why did I decide to come up here a few hours ago? I wonder, trying to think of any logical reason for me to be on the top of this mountain when I first saw Steven down on that island. All I knew, was that I *needed* to be up here.

How did I know? My thoughts start going off in all different directions, but it's short-lived, because the sun is going down. I grab my pack from where I dropped it earlier and head back inside just as the sun disappears, shooting colors across the blue sky and bringing with it the sounds of creatures as they crawl out of the shadows.

I swing the pack over a shoulder then wrap my knees and forearms around the outside of the ladder. I drop down quickly until I start to see the markers on the wall, designating which floors of the house I'm sliding past. Squeezing the ladder tighter, I start to slow, then hop off on the third floor leading into the supply room. I yawn and massage the sore spot on my leg, realizing that sleep or not, I should probably try to get some sort of rest before Steven wakes up.

I toss my pack onto a nearby table and start slowly down the stairs to my bedroom, done with ladders for today.

As I walk down the hall, I stop in front of the guest bedroom door, resting my fingers on the handle. I stand there for a long moment, wondering if I should check on him again.

Ali, you're being ridiculous. Nothing can happen to him when he's in the house, I tell myself, letting my hand slide away from the handle as I continue on down the hall.

I hear a noise.

I climb out of bed, then walk the short distance down the hall to Steven's door, putting my ear up against it. Even from outside, I know exactly what I'm hearing.

He's having a nightmare.

Welcome to the club, I think empathetically, then slowly open the door and peer inside. Sure enough, he's tossing back and forth under the sheets. His eyes are squeezed shut, as if in pain, and he's mumbling incoherently.

My heart goes out to him as I approach the side of the bed. I know what it's like to have nightmares, I've been having them nearly every night since I got here.

I wish someone would have been here to wake me up.

As I get closer, I can see that there are tears streaming down his face. *Some dream,* I think, but I'm not surprised. Not after what he went through yesterday. As I reach down to wake him, his words become clear as day, even though I can swear his mouth stays shut.

Alex! No, Alex! No!

My hand shoots back and I can feel the blood drain from my face. I stand there completely still, in shock.

I never told him my name was Alex.

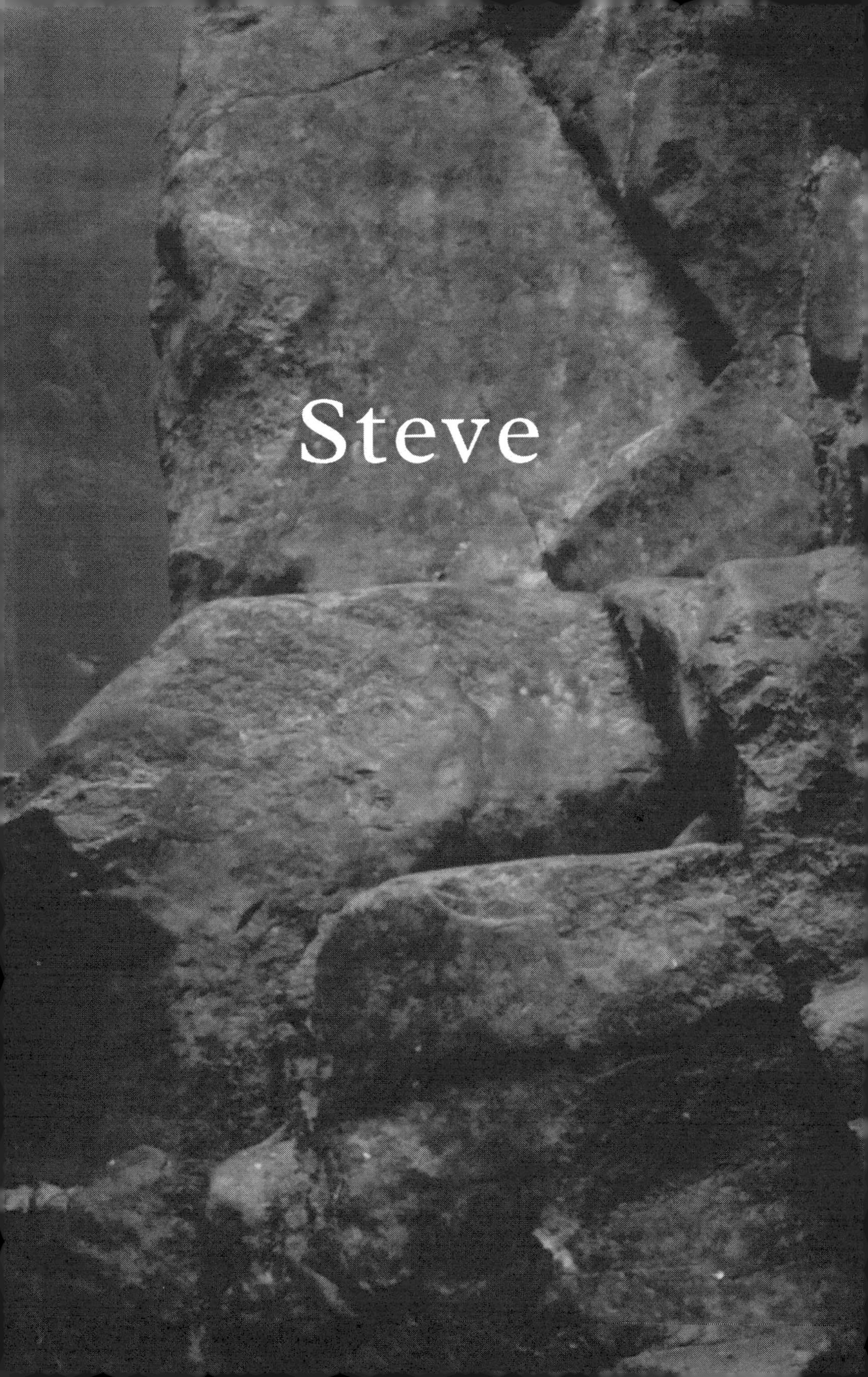

Steve

Chapter 11

I know I'm in a dream, I always do, even when the dreams feel real, more like a memory. Just like every dream, Alex is standing right in front of me, and yet she's so far away.

And just like every dream, I already know how this will end.

I will stare into those big green eyes that are as familiar as my own at this point, and then I will be forced to stand by. Forced to watch her die.

She will be gone, torn away from me, and I will wake up back in my bedroom, that familiar feeling of emptiness hanging over me. But this time, *this* dream feels different. It feels like I know her. *Do I?* I wonder, but I can't remember.

She stands there, the wind blowing her hair wildly around her face. Her sun-darkened skin somehow doesn't hide any of the many freckles and her green eyes shine in the sunlight. She grips the straps of her backpack tightly and I stare at her curiously. Because this dream doesn't just feel different, she looks different too. This isn't the same Alex I normally see in my dreams. *This* Alex is strong and capable. She looks fearless, and *god*, she's beautiful.

I've never seen her so clearly before.

Her brows furrow as she stares off into the distance at something behind me, her hair brushing at her cheeks. I turn to look over my shoulder and immediately feel my stomach leap to my throat.

Because we are standing on the edge of a cliff.

We are high enough up that the clouds drift *below* us and I'm immediately ready to get off this mountain. Even in a dream, I don't want to go over that ledge.

I turn back to Alex, who is still staring straight forward. Without looking away, she slides the pack off her back, dropping it to the ground.

I can see the intention in her eyes.

"Alex! No, Alex! No!" I shout at the top of my lungs as tears start streaming down my face. I try running toward her, try to stop her, but I can't move. The wind stings my hot tears and I stand there, watching helplessly as she runs right past me and off the edge of the cliff.

And then she's gone.

My stomach drops as if I were the one falling. I sink to my knees. I can't breathe. I can't get to her, I can't-

"Steven!" Someone shouts in the distance, but I ignore it. I have to get to her, but I can't move. I have to-

"Steven," the voice says again. I slowly open my eyes, dragging myself out of the fog. My heart continues to race, but I manage to prop myself up on shaky elbows to look around.

Then I see her. And it all comes flooding back. The island, the creatures, falling into the pit, the caves, the woods in the dark.

She. Died.

Or, I thought she did. *Did I leave her there in the woods? Leave her wounded and alone?* I think, the memories coming one by one, like a baseball to the face, each one hitting harder than the last. She was injured on the way into the house and *I. Left. Her.* The thought stabs at me again.

Then I realize why the dream felt so real this time. Because now, I know what she looks like. *Because I found her.* Well, she found me.

She doesn't even know me, and yet, she saved me.

And she's *alive*.

Alexandra Cutter is alive.

The terror of the nightmare quickly dissipates, replaced by an overwhelming feeling of joy as I stare into those green eyes, the one's I've seen a hundred times. Only, *this* time, she can see me. *Finally, she can see me,* my heart races.

She must have showered, because she is cleaner than the last time I saw her. Her red hair is down, falling in gentle waves that frame her face. But there is something in her expression that concerns me.

Something...*feral*.

It's then that I look down and see the sword she is holding to my throat.

"Fuck, Ali! What are you doing?" I say frantically, but I'm very careful not to move. The blade is probably longer than my whole arm and it looks *sharp*.

"That's right, my name is *Ali*. Because that is what I told you," she says sternly.

I suddenly feel like I'm being interrogated.

"What?" I blink, confused and still a little bleary from the dream.

"I told you my name was *Ali*, why did you say *Alex*?" She's almost shouting at this point, the blade firm at my throat, unwavering.

"I didn't, I-"

"You were talking in your sleep and you said *Alex*. That's my name, my *real* name. But I never told you that. So you better tell me right now how the fuck you know my name, or I'm going to get your blood all over my nice guest bedroom."

I stare at her, wide eyed and a little bit in love.

This is definitely not the same Alex I dreamed about. Not in the slightest. After seeing what she did to that creature on the island and the ones in the woods, I actually believe that *this* Alex really wouldn't hesitate before stabbing me.

She holds the sword tighter to my throat and I decide that I better start talking.

"Woah, woah, woah. Okay, I can explain," I say, slowly raising my hands in surrender. She doesn't move. "Do you want to maybe, I don't know, *not* hold a sword to my throat for a minute so I can tell you?"

She doesn't lower the blade, but she does back up to give me some breathing room. I sit up, running a hand through my hair and taking deep breaths as I contemplate where to start.

"Listen, I know your name is Alex because I know you," I say, but I can tell it comes out wrong because she narrows her eyes and looks at me with disbelief, raising the sword up a few inches.

"Okay, okay," I put my hands back up. "You don't know me, but I know you. Well, I don't *know* you, we've never met, but I know *of* you."

I'm rambling. I know I'm rambling.

I take another deep breath. "My family and I moved to the valley after you disappeared," I manage to say quickly. The hard lines in her face immediately soften, but she doesn't lower the sword just yet, so I continue.

"Your picture is all over town. You're on the news, on missing person posters and all over the internet. And then there's that picture of you and your mom on her desk at school and my best friend, Noor, he told me-" I stop talking as the sword slowly falls from her hand, landing on the wood floor with a heavy *thump.* I study her blank expression, unable to read it.

She backs away until she is up against the far wall and, putting her face in her hands, she slowly slides down to the floor and starts sobbing.

I stare at her until the realization of *why* she's crying suddenly hits me. It hits me hard and I have to hold back my own tears. I was so caught up with the excitement of finding her, that I forgot one important detail.

She is still lost.

She hasn't seen her mom, her friends, or even her home, for six months.

Holy shit, it hits me again as I listen to the pain of her sobs, the heartbreak in her tears. Staring at her now, I feel like *this* is the Alex I know. The one who is lost and fragile, not the cold warrior who saved my life back on that island. But *Ali* doesn't know me. I worry how much comfort I can even be to her in this situation, but I can't just sit here and watch her in pain.

I move across the room, slowly stepping over the *sword*, and sit beside her on the floor. I gently put an arm around her and without even looking, she immediately turns into me. My eyes go wide with surprise. The same girl who just threatened to kill me less than a minute ago, is now holding onto my shirt with both hands, like a lifeline, and is crying into my chest.

Not knowing what else to do, I do what feels right. I wrap my other arm around her, resting my cheek on the top of her head.

And I just hold her.

The embrace somehow causes her to sob harder, but I don't let go.

I don't want to let go.

After a while, her sobs become a whimper and I can feel her heartbeat beginning to slow. I can't count the number of times that I have dreamt of holding her like this, of keeping her safe. And now, I finally am. She is soft and warm and I never want to let her go.

And yeah, she has definitely taken a shower, because her hair is still a little damp on my cheek. It smells amazing, like flowers and the woods. Closing my eyes, I take in this moment. *She's so close to me.*

That's when I realize that my pulse is beginning to quicken.

Shit. This is Noor's girl, I think, knowing damn well that what I'm feeling for her, it can't happen.

Reluctantly, I gently pull away, just far enough so I can see her face. *Damn, those eyes.* They catch me off guard and it takes me a moment before I can speak. She is even more beautiful than I remember from my dreams and I'm not sure how that's even possible. As I stare into those big green eyes, I notice the tears resting on her freckled cheeks. Without thinking, I bravely reach up, placing my hands on either side of her small face and wipe them away with my thumbs. Her skin is soft and it suddenly turns a deeper shade of red.

Must be a delayed reaction from the tears.

I hold my hands there for another moment and give her an understanding smile.

"I'm so sorry Ali, I can't imagine what you've been through," I whisper. Those eyes flicker back to mine.

She has got to stop looking at me like that, I think.

"Thank you," she says in a small voice. Then, without warning, her soft smile turns amused.

"What?" I ask curiously, dropping my hands back down to my side and mentally kicking myself for having them there in the first place.

"You," she says, almost laughing. "I may be the one crying, but you're a mess."

I look down at myself and sure enough, the chaotic evidence of our hiking trip from hell is still all over my clothes. You can barely even tell that my shirt is light blue through the dingy shade of brown covering it.

Shit, I really am a mess.

I look back up and give her a lighthearted smile, making a show of an attempt to simply *dust* off the stains, which makes her laugh.

"So where's the bathroom again?" I ask.

She just stares at me and her guilty face tells me that I'm not going to like the answer.

"So... no *showers* out here," she says slowly. "But I can walk you down to the stream. And there's a waterfall," she shrugs apologetically.

I stare at her. *Stream? Waterfall?*

"Um, Ali? Where the hell are we?"

"That's... *complicated*. I'll explain everything once you get cleaned up. And you're probably hungry."

She's right. I feel disgusting and I'm *starving*.

Is this how she's been living for six months? I wonder, but it can't be. She probably just came out here to save my ass and we will be going back into town soon.

Then I look around the room for the first time.

It isn't a *room*, exactly. It's a *cave*. A cave with a door, a crudely put together wooden floor that is covered with brightly colored rugs and, now that I am actually looking, a hand-made bed frame with a lumpy mattress, covered with thick hand-woven sheets.

What the fuck? I think. It's like I dropped back a few centuries. I look over at Ali again, panicked.

"I promise, I'll tell you everything. Here," she says, holding out a piece of fabric that is trying to pass as a towel and a lumpy white stone that I can only assume is supposed to be a bar of soap. *This cannot be happening,* I think, looking at them both cautiously. But waterfall or not, I want to be clean. And I need a few minutes alone to straighten out my scattered thoughts.

"Um, what should I do about these?" I ask, tugging at my muddied clothes.

"Oh, um... I might have something that would fit you. Follow me," she says, heading quickly out of the room.

Damn, she moves fast.

As I step out into the hallway after her, I realize it isn't a hallway at all. It's another part of this intricate cave system that the house is built in. The floor is the same wooden slats as the room I just stayed in, and the stone walls are decorated with what looks like paintings on canvas. They are simple shapes and patterns, and they give the area a warm feeling. Even though it's clearly just a cave, someone went to a lot of work to make it feel like a home. I look down the hall and watch as Alex, or *Ali*, I remind myself, makes her way through the door at the very end of the corridor.

I walk through the threshold and suddenly stop. Because I've never seen anything like it. It takes a long moment before I realize that this is a bedroom, because the room is giant. Although it's still just another part of the cave, with tall ceilings and stone walls, it's even more homey than the rest of the house. The room is dimly lit with candles scattered on every surface and placed on shelves that are carved right into the stone walls. The floors are, again, covered with a variety of rugs.

The large bed is nearly the same size as the room I just slept in and is absolutely covered in fluffy pillows and furry blankets. I smile, thinking of all the fur and pillows that Makena and Ari brought camping, much to Efe's annoyance, on the day I first met them. It makes sense they would be friends.

But none of that compares to the view directly in front of me.

The entire exterior wall is made of a dark glass that wraps around the corner on the far side, creating a bay window of sorts, with a little table and chair in front of it. I stare curiously, wondering how in the hell somewhere so rustic could possibly have such architecture. The glass looks like it melds with the stone seamlessly, with no frame or rail that I can see. It looks like one solid piece, and I want to walk over and tap on it to see if it will fall.

Next to the bed there is a narrow opening in the stone wall, leading into what is apparently a long walk-in closet, because Ali is busy tossing clothes around as she rummages.

She lives here. I suddenly realize, my suspicion confirmed. I'm not quite sure what to make of that information, so I leave her to search, walking over to look out the window.

"Holy shit," I say, not meaning to say it out loud, but *holy shit.*

We aren't just in a cave, we're in a *cliff.* I remember climbing up a ladder in order to get to the front door, but what I'm staring at now is nowhere near that short of a distance. I have been in skyscrapers in cities all over the country, but I'm sure that this is higher.

I hesitantly step a little closer and my stomach drops as I look down. We are suspended above a large half-moon shaped cove far below. Beyond that, is the ocean. The water shimmers an impossible shade of blue and the trees at its edges look no more than toys from up here.

And the landscape... Well, I've never seen anything like it, even in pictures. Everything is too tall, too large, too... *amplified.*

Where are we? I stare.

"Hey," Ali says and I nearly jump out of my skin, so engrossed in the view that I didn't even hear her walk up.

She's holding a jumble of clothes and has several more draped over her arm. She looks amused, maybe even a little guilty. And from her expression, I can already tell I'm not going to like whatever she dug up.

"Crazy view, huh?" she says, making her way over to lay the clothes out on the bed.

"I don't think that *crazy* even begins to cover it.... insane, impossible, preposterous..." I trail off.

"Well, you're not wrong there," she says with a chuckle then gestures toward the clothes with an apologetic smile. "Take whatever you like."

I give her a wary look and start rifling through the clothing in front of me. Most of it is much like the bedsheets and towels, handmade, but all of it is *tiny.* Ali has to be at least six inches shorter than me, barely taller than Ari, and although she clearly works out, she is skinny as a rail.

Which means that so are her clothes.

I pull out one shirt that looks like it would barely fit a doll. Holding it up to my chest, which is much wider, I give Ali an *"are you fucking kidding me?"* look, causing her to blush and burst out laughing.

God, I love it when she laughs.

I start rummaging, but every time I think I have found something that might work, I hold it up to myself and then just shake my head, moving on to the next.

This isn't going well.

Ali has already made herself perfectly comfortable, all perched on the bed next to the clothes as she watches the show with a grin. I glare at her, because this is ridiculous.

Finally, I decide on a gray T-shirt and a pair of black sweatpants that seem stretchy enough to fit. Looking at her small frame, I figure that they are most likely baggy on her, but on *me*, well, this is going to be interesting. But they are far better than the alternatives. I shudder at the thought.

I follow Ali back out into the hallway and she leads me to the front door.

Of course, the waterfall would have to be outside, I realize. Clearly, my brain was not completely awake when we had that particular conversation earlier. As Ali places a hand on the door handle, she pauses, obviously upset about something.

"What is it?" I ask.

"Listen, about before," she says slowly. "With the sword. I'm so sorry Steven, I've just been alone for so long. Then you showed up and I didn't know what to think. When you said my name, my *real* name, I just thought that-"

"It's okay, Ali. Really," I say looking straight into her eyes, because as terrifying as it was, I'm not upset about it. "I'm a stranger to you, so I understand why you would be wary of me."

"I'm sorry, I should have-"

"Alexandra, it's fine, really. I'm not upset," I say the words slowly and with purpose so she will believe me. As I stare into those big green eyes, her expression softens and I can swear she is blushing again.

Did I just use her full name? It seems strange, but somehow, it felt right.

I step out into a world that was once full of darkness and shadows, now shining with beauty and light. The soft grass in the meadow below flows in the breeze and I can hear birds chirping over the rumble of falling water. Looking over, I realize that I must have passed the waterfall on the way here yesterday, but I was too frantic, too heartbroken, to even see it.

But I sure as hell am noticing it now.

I stare up in wonder as the glistening water falls from far above. I've never seen cliffs this tall, not even in pictures or videos online. I wonder again, *where the hell are we?*

"Come on," Ali says, standing on the top rung of the ladder with a smile.

"But," I look around warily and she immediately understands my hesitance.

"You're safe. It will get dark soon, but the creatures don't come within the light barrier, so just stay on this side of the stream and you'll be fine."

I nod, but I still don't like the thought of being outside. Not after last time.

Last time, the memories flood my mind again. The dark. The creatures. Ali shoving me out of the way, the *explosion*.

"Steven?" Ali says softly, breaking me from my thoughts.

"Um, yeah, I'm coming," I stutter, then climb down the ladder after her.

When we are about halfway across the field, Ali stops and points out the browned footpath that leads behind the falls.

"Okay, you can find it from here. Just... don't wander off," she adds seriously.

"Oh don't worry, I won't," I say. She studies me, trying to decide if I'm telling her the truth. "I'll come right back, I promise," I affirm and she seems to relax, warily believing me.

"Okay," she says, then takes one last look at me, as if I am apt to vanish into thin air, then reluctantly turns back toward the house.

"Hey, Ali?" I say, suddenly nervous to be away from her. "When I come back, you and I are going to have a very long chat about..." I look around and gesture toward the forest, then the glorified cave house built into the cliffs. "Well, about a lot of things," I manage to say with a smile.

"Oh, I don't doubt it," she replies, already sauntering back across the field. I watch her leave for longer than I should, studying the strange and beautiful creature that saved my life. Still not believing that I found her.

On the walk back to the house, I ruffle my hair with the makeshift towel and think about everything that's happened. Starting from the beginning, I take myself back to the moment when I heard my dad's voice on the phone. The moment I dropped my backpack, the moment I ran. A sudden fury rises up again with the memories. Dad had gotten his and Mom's next assignment, which means that within a matter of months, I will be forced to leave everything behind. *Again.* Pushing myself past the anger, I try to remember what came next. I start piecing together everything I know, from the moment I woke up on that island until now, mentally keeping track of all the questions I have for Ali. And hell, there are a lot of them.

But there are a few things I know for sure. First, this isn't a dream. This is real. Second, that monsters exist. *Oh,* and for some goddamn reason, the sun goes down *every ten minutes.*

Great, it all makes sense now, I think sarcastically.

I don't have a clue where I am, what this place is, or how to get back. But there is another thing I know for certain.

Alexandra Cutter is *alive*.

And I am going to bring her home.

Chapter 12

After climbing a *ladder* to get up to the porch, I step into the house and can immediately smell whatever it is that Ali is cooking. And it smells amazing.

I look around, wondering where the kitchen is. To my right, there is a large living room. The furniture is clearly *homemade*, like everything around here, but they look surprisingly comfortable.

To my left, there is a wide wooden staircase that winds up to the next floor of the cave. I quickly decide that is where the smell is coming from and head off, taking the steps two at a time. I didn't realize how hungry I was until the scent wafts over me again and suddenly, I'm starving. *How long has it been since I've eaten?* I wonder, because I can't remember a time that I was ever this hungry.

I walk through the small arched opening in the stone wall and into the kitchen, seeing Ali standing over what must be the stove. Her back is to me and I notice that she has tied her wild red curls back with a strip of leather. The kitchen is simple and I am surprised again to find that there isn't a single modern amenity in sight.

One whole wall contains everything that makes up the *kitchen*. The counters are made of stone and look like they have been carved straight out of the cave wall, along with a basin that must be used as a sink. Above that, is a large glass window, showing a view of an outdoor patio, complete with a small herb garden. I stare at the brightly colored curtains that adorn the window and smile.

Because they are hideous.

Above and around the counters are tall shallow indents carved into the walls, fitted with horizontal slats to create open-faced cabinets. Looking around, I find it fascinating. Whoever built this place paid attention to every detail, making the small space as practical as possible.

I look back toward Ali and study the stove she is cooking on. It's a simple metal structure with slats on the top and has an *actual* fire in the bottom of it, which can be seen through a little hinged door on the front.

On the opposite side of the room, there is a quaint wooden table and one chair tucked into a nook. It makes me feel sad for some reason.

What is this place?

It's then I realize that Ali is staring at me, trying hard to stifle a laugh.

What the hell is so funny? I wonder, knitting my brows together. And then I remember my outfit.

Shit.

"Not. A. Word," I say slowly, pointing at her with my handful of dirty clothes.

Well, she doesn't *say* anything, but she's laughing uncontrollably now. I try to be upset with her for as long as possible. The only problem is that her smile is contagious.

Dammit, I think. And after looking down at myself, I can't help the chuckle that escapes me too. I look ridiculous. The gray T-shirt is practically skin-tight, and I'm suddenly grateful that I work out so much, because this could have been a lot worse. The sweatpants on the other hand, are horrifying. They are too tight and too short, landing high up on my calf, rather than down by my ankles where they should be.

I can't wait until my own clothes are cleaned and back on my body.

Speaking of which, I hold up my dirty clothes, my eyes pleading for a good answer to my next question.

"*Please* tell me you have a washing machine."

"Nope," she says with a smile and the horror in my expression has her laughing again. "But I'll show you where you can wash them."

"You're not going to send me down to the stream or something, are you?" I ask, because after showering in a goddamn *waterfall*, I feel the need to ask.

"No, not a stream," she says, then heads through a wooden door leading out to the terrace just outside the kitchen. I follow after her, ducking through the small doorway. The area is small and there are vines crawling up from the bottom of the balustrade. Below the kitchen window is the small planter containing the herb garden and in the corner is another basin, much like the one built into the counter inside. There is a strange piece of corrugated glass inside of a wooden picture frame leaning up against it. I stare at it curiously. It isn't until Ali picks it up and hands it to me that I realize what it is.

A washboard.

"You're kidding." I just stare at her. I've watched enough movies and TV shows to know how the archaic piece of equipment works, but I never thought I would ever have to *use* one.

"Not kidding," she says with an amused grin.

It annoys me how much pleasure she has in teasing me about all this.

"I have a water trap above the kitchen, so you just have to release this here and the water will fill the tub. Just pull the plug to drain it when you're done. And soap's over there," she points, before heading back inside to finish with the food.

I study the strange contraption, once again enthralled. From here, I can't actually tell where the water is collected above, but I can see the thick piece of bamboo that runs down along the cliff, like a water pipe, stopping directly above the basin. Ali had pointed to a small piece of bamboo that is plugging up the *pipe*. I study it for a moment, then pull it from its slot, letting it dangle on a piece of twine. Sure enough, the water flows out and begins quickly filling the basin. As reluctant as I am to be doing my laundry in a *rock*, I can't help but smile at the infrastructure of it. When the tub is almost full, I slide the piece of bamboo back into the slot, effectively stopping the water, and reach for the soap.

After hanging my clothes over the railing to dry, I head back inside, still shaking my head over the fact that I just *hand-washed* them.

My stomach makes an involuntary noise at the mere scent of food and I watch as Ali sets two plates on the table. Another chair has appeared and I smile, taking a seat.

Ali heads back to the counter, rummaging around for what I have to assume is silverware and I can't help but notice her change in demeanor. She seems... *happy*. I watch her movements, suddenly realizing how many different versions of her I've seen since learning of her disappearance.

First, there is *Alexandra Cutter*, the pretty girl with the soft smile and the piercing green eyes who is on the missing person poster. The girl who is lost.

Then I got to know another version of her through stories and memories of her. *She* is the daughter of my favorite English teacher, Noor's missing girlfriend and best friend of my friends. That is the *fun* Alex. The girl who likes to go camping, fishing and hiking. The girl who holds her own, makes people laugh and is down for just about any adventure.

Then there is the Alex who haunts my dreams. The girl who is trapped, the girl who is afraid. *That* is the Alex that I've become inexplicably drawn to. The Alex who needs me, just as I need her. I needed to find that girl, to save her. That is the Alex that I found myself missing during the day. The one who I felt lost without. That is the girl that I would have gladly jumped into a million nightmares for, just for the chance to see her.

And then I met *her*.

I met *Ali*.

The girl who rescued me from that island doesn't need me at all. She doesn't need anyone. The Ali who saved my life, who killed those creatures and then jumped between me and an *explosion* in the forest. The girl who has the strength, the patience and the heart to keep me, a complete stranger, alive. *That* Ali is the strongest person I've ever met. She is a soldier, cold and capable.

And finally, there is *this* Ali. The Ali who is smiling and making me breakfast. The Ali who puts up with me and laughs at every goofy thing I do. But this is also the Ali who broke down and cried in my arms. *This* Ali is full of pain and sorrow, and joy.

Looking at her in this moment, I can't see any other version of her. But I know that they're there. They're *all* there.

It perplexes me.

She is so much more than smiles and breakfast, and there are so many things I don't yet know about her. But I'm suddenly determined to figure her out. As much as I need the answers to where I am and how I got here, somehow, I need to know her more.

Ali sits and I smile, looking down at my plate for the first time. *Not breakfast*. In front of me is a whole-ass dinner spread. The porterhouse steak nearly covers the entire plate. It's accompanied by a separate bowl of roasted potatoes and a salad. I stare at it in awe and my stomach growls again.

"Ali, this looks amazing," I say and her tentative smile broadens into an ear-to-ear grin.

We eat in silence until my plate is practically licked clean. I'm surprised to find that Ali has cleared hers as well, seeing as she's half my size.

When I look up, I find those green eyes watching me curiously. I wonder if maybe she's trying to figure me out too. I lean back in my chair, taking a deep breath as I study her right back, giving her a sideways smile.

"So," I begin.

"So," she repeats, not looking away.

"Maybe we should start with you telling me what the fuck is going on and then we can go from there. Because... *shit*, I have some questions."

"That sounds fair," she agrees, an adorable smile playing on her lips. I quickly look away before my mind has the opportunity to think about those lips too much.

Jesus, what's wrong with me?

"I'm really not sure how to explain this, so I guess I'll start from the beginning," Ali says hesitantly and I bring my eyes back to hers, noticing that they are now devoid of life. Of hope. So I lean forward, lacing my fingers together on the table, and listen.

"I was down in the creek bed behind my house, drawing. I looked up and saw the entrance to a mineshaft. I've been down there a million times, but I'd never noticed it before, which I thought was strange. But we had some heavy rainfall during the winter, so I just figured the hillside must have washed away enough to uncover it. Anyway, I decided to check it out. I got some rope and climbed down. Next thing I knew, I was being pulled into the portal, the one with the stars, and then I woke up in the sand."

I just stare at her, astonished at how *familiar* this is all sounding.

"Yeah, I know," she says, noticing my reaction. "I think we both came through at the same place back in the valley. And yes, I landed in the same exact spot on that beach as you did."

I stare at her, confused. Or maybe I'm just in shock.

Did she just say portal? What the fuck. I run a hand through my hair, because this conversation can't actually be happening, but she continues.

"A lot has happened since then, but I guess the most important thing that you need to understand is that *this place*, well, it's not like home."

"Yeah, I figured as much. So why have you stayed out here all this time? Why haven't you gone home?" With the creatures out there, I can see how she would want to stay in the house, but why not try to get home? Try to contact someone? If she doesn't have a cell phone, then someone else out here must know the way back. Hell, she could have lit a damn signal fire or something.

And then I wonder vaguely if maybe she doesn't *want* to go home.

"Steven," she says, sympathetically. "I'm stuck here. *We're* stuck here." She stops talking so that her words will sink in, but I don't believe it.

I *can't* believe it.

"That's impossible. We can't just be stuck here. There has to be someone out here who will let us use their phone, or give us a ride-"

"Steven," she stops me. "Look around."

"I know there's nothing *here*, but what if we just started walking? We would have to run into a road sooner or later. Then we could just follow it-"

Ali stands up, pacing back and forth, and I realize that her patience has run out. Placing both hands flat on the table, she looks right at me.

"There isn't *anyone*. There are no phones, no cars, no buildings or roads, no electricity, no airplanes overhead, *nothing*. I have walked for weeks in every direction and climbed up fucking mountains so I could see further. I've taken a boat out into the middle of the goddamn ocean and walked up and down the shoreline *hell if I know* how many times. I've screamed at the top of my lungs, lit shit on fire and set off explosions." She sits back down in front of me, rubbing her eyes. Taking a deep breath, she looks up at me and her voice softens. "Steven, you're the first human I've seen since I've been here."

I stare back at her, waiting for the punchline of this ridiculous joke. But it doesn't come. She isn't joking.

She's serious.

No. It's not possible, I think. No place on earth is *that* isolated.

I don't know what to say, what to think. A million thoughts flash through my mind all at once as I work out the possibilities. Because we can't just be stuck here, there has to be a way home.

"What about the island? That's how we got here, maybe it's the way back?"

"It's not," she says matter of factly.

"Or maybe there's another... *portal*?" I say, then can't believe that I just used that word in a sentence unironically.

"There's not. I've looked." Her voice is cold. When her eyes flicker away, I get the impression that I'm missing something.

I suddenly wonder what the hell she went through being alone out here.

Alone.

Holy shit. Has she actually been out here, with those creatures, for six whole months, *alone*? I rub a hand over my face, trying to take it all in.

"When I first saw you," she says softly. "I hoped that maybe you knew about this place, knew how I ended up here, or how to get back. But since that's clearly not the case, why don't you tell me *exactly* how you got here, starting from the beginning. Maybe you will remember something I didn't, something that will help," she says in feign hope.

"Okay," I say, attempting to collect my scattered thoughts. I spend the next several minutes telling Ali everything I remember, starting from my *walk* in the woods. I leave out the part about why I was out there in the first place, and I *definitely* left out the part about the dreams. When I finish, we both sit here in silence.

"Well, shit," she finally says, clearly disappointed.

"Yeah," I agree. She is quiet for another moment and I wonder what she's thinking.

"Steven... How long have I been here?" she asks, surprising me.

How could she not know? I wonder and then look over to the kitchen window, where the sun has come up and gone back down a dozen times just since we've been sitting here. *Oh, that's how,* I think, suddenly realizing how disorienting it is. I take a deep breath, stalling, because I don't want to answer that question.

But, looking into those sad, green eyes, I realize she deserves to know.

"Ali, you've been missing for six months," I say slowly, watching her.

"Six months," she repeats, looking at nothing in particular behind me. "It's... November?"

"Yeah, over halfway through it, actually."

"It feels longer," she says quietly. "But I guess that makes sense. It's just strange, knowing for sure. *Six months,*" she says again. "The whole summer. Oh god, my mom." She squeezes her eyes shut, like she might start crying. Not knowing what to do, I reach out across the table and put a hand over the back of hers, my fingers wrapping nearly all the way around as I hold it. She squeezes back and my heart sinks a little from her pain, then flutters a little from her touch. Her hand is soft, and I don't want to let go. After a few minutes, she takes a deep breath and looks up at me.

"I'm sorry, I just-" she starts to say.

"Don't," I whisper. "You don't have anything to be sorry about."

"I just can't believe I left her, left *everyone*," she says.

"Listen, Ali," I say sternly, surprising myself. "You didn't run away, and you weren't kidnapped, so this isn't your fault. Sure, everyone is hurting from you being gone, but it's because they love you. They don't blame you for it. Trust me," I say and she looks up at me with a small smile. "And besides, you're *alive*, don't you think your mom would be happy for that?"

"You're right, I just wish I could tell her. When I didn't know how long I'd been here, I could imagine that it wasn't that long, or tell myself that the world had somehow stopped spinning when I left. But it didn't. It just kept moving forward without me," she says, her voice trailing off.

"I'm sorry, Ali. I shouldn't have told you," I say.

"No, I'm glad you did. Glad I finally know. Besides, *I* asked *you,* remember?" she says with a smile. "And I don't think I want to know how my mom is doing right now, but I will probably want to ask you about her, and home, later if that's alright?"

"Of course," I say seriously. I can't even imagine what it would feel like to go six months without seeing my family. Or *anyone*. *Shit*, I think again and wonder how she's holding it together as well as she is.

That's when I notice that I've been trailing my thumb back and forth along her soft hand. I immediately let go, then lean back in my chair and cross my arms over my chest so that they stay there.

We sit in silence for several minutes.

"Damn," Ali says, clearly realizing something else.

"What?"

"I guess I'm sixteen now. *Happy birthday* to me," she says sarcastically. "Hey, how old are you, anyway?" She looks at me curiously.

"Sixteen. I'll be seventeen in May."

"Huh," she says, studying me again.

"Not what you expected?" I ask with a sideways smile, my arms still crossed.

"I'm not sure what I expected, maybe eighteen or nineteen? You're tall," she says matter of factly. This girl doesn't tiptoe around anything and I love that about her. And I'm not sure that six foot two is really all *that* tall, but I suppose compared to her it would be.

I find the normalcy of our conversation strange, considering where we are, and decided that it's time for me to get to the bottom of it.

Of *everything*.

"Okay, it's question time. And I'm going to start with the obvious one," I say, gesturing toward the window, where the sun is down. *Again*.

"Oh, that," she smiles. "Well, the sun is up for exactly ten minutes, then it goes down for another ten, then it goes up and back down and so on," she says, mocking me. I stare at her, annoyed. I know how the goddamn sun works and know that she is doing this on purpose, teasing me again.

"Yeah, I got the up and down part, thank you. But *why* in the hell does the sun go down every ten minutes? Last time I checked, a day was twenty-four *hours*, not twenty *minutes*."

"Yeah, I have no idea what to tell you about that. I'm not sure if we're on another planet, in a parallel universe, a dream, or on a spaceship. I literally have no idea. It's just how it is here. There are a lot of things here that are... *different*," she says cautiously.

I lean back in my chair and rub at the back of my neck, because *just how it is,* isn't an answer at all. And neither is *on a spaceship.*

"Okay, so what else is... *different,*" I dare to ask, because I don't like the way she said it.

"Well, I guess I could just give you a quick rundown of the basics," she muses.

"Please," I say, even more confused at this point.

And that was only my *first* question.

"Okay, so there are twenty minutes in the daylight cycle and monsters exist," she says.

"Yeah, I got that part." I mutter, surprised that I actually believe it. But how can I not? I *saw* them.

"The creatures can't survive the daylight. But when the sun goes back down, you better be inside, be ready to run, or be prepared to fight. I'm not sure where the creatures come from, but they show up *anywhere* it's dark. So you will need to get used to sleeping with the lights on."

"Wait, so they can get *in* the house?" I ask, looking around warily.

"No, you're safe here," she says, calming me down. "Just make sure the lanterns stay on," she warns, pointing to one I hadn't noticed hanging from a chain above us.

There are a lot of things I hadn't noticed when I got here. The memories of those first exhausting and terrifying hours come flooding back all at once.

"Shit, Ali. The woods, there was an explosion. You saved my life, but you didn't get out of the way in time. The blast, it hit you. It hit you *hard*. I saw you fly into a tree, there was so much blood..." I shudder at the memory. "I ran over to you and you weren't breathing. I'm so sorry I left you there, I thought you were dead. I could hear something coming, but I should have stayed. I shouldn't have run. Shouldn't have left you there like that. *God*, Ali, I'm so, so sorry. I really thought you were dead," I say, staring at my hands, horrified by what I did.

Needing to bring myself back from those memories, I look up to her face, reminding myself that she. Is. *Alive*. That she is still here with me. She's here. She's safe.

Well, not quite safe, I think, remembering the wound in her leg. Suddenly, I'm confused again. She's been walking around the kitchen just fine, no limp or anything. *How long was I asleep?* I wonder. I can tell she is following my line of sight, and my train of thoughts, because she looks down at the spot on her thigh and answers my unspoken question.

"You were asleep for about ten hours, but yes, my leg is already healed. Another thing that's *different* here. You heal faster. A lot faster."

I look at my own arms, my hands, remembering the deep scrapes from just before I fell into the portal, the cuts and bruises from the explosion in the woods.

"How?" I ask, staring at my skin, where there is not even a scratch left over from the damage that was there before.

"I've kind of figured that it must have something to do with the daylight cycle. You heal just as fast here as you would in the normal world, but based on *this* time. There are around seventy-two *days* here every twenty-four hours. So you were asleep for ten hours, but my leg has healed as though it's been a month's worth of time."

I rub my temples. This is all too much. *Way* too much. I suddenly feel like I'm not sure how much I want to know, because her answers are only leaving me with more questions. But since I already have a headache from all this, I might as well keep the insanity going.

"Anything *else* that I should know about?" I ask reluctantly.

"Well, I don't want you to feel guilty about leaving me in the woods after the blast."

"How can you say that? *I left you there.* Alive and wounded, and surrounded by those... *creatures.* I should have helped you back to the house. You could have *died,*" I say, upset that she could even *suggest* I not feel guilty.

"Well, actually," she says slowly. "I *did* die in that explosion..."

I'm looking straight at her now.

"Steven," she continues, taking a deep breath. "I've died eighty-six times."

Chapter 13

The crazy train has officially derailed and is now flying sideways over the track, destroying everything in its path. And it's taking me down with it.

Eighty-six times? But the number isn't important. She *died*?

I was wrong before, *now* it's too much. And so I just sit here, staring, waiting for her to figure out how in the hell she is going to explain this one.

"So, I can't really die here," she says slowly, trying to judge my reaction. "When I do, I just end up back in the sand on the island. It's really annoying actually, especially when I'm in the middle of working on something and have to walk all the way back," she trails off.

I continue staring. She is talking about dying as if it were nothing more than a mild annoyance.

What the fuck, I rub a hand over my face again. "Ali, you know this is crazy. There's no way that's possible. You survived the explosion, *somehow,* and now you're just messing with me," I say, because it's the only plausible explanation.

I look at her again and realize she isn't laughing. Even in the short time I've known her, I feel like I understand her well enough to judge when she's teasing me and when she is being serious.

She's serious.

And now I'm the one pacing.

It's not possible, I think again. But after everything I've seen... after falling through a *portal*, then running away from the *monsters* that only come out at night which, by the way, is every ten minutes. After finding the missing girl only to have her save my life and then hold a fucking *sword* to my throat, I wonder why this is the one thing that's tripping me up.

Because it's fucking insane, that's why, I decide.

"I can't believe any of this. I'm asleep." I continue my pacing. "I am going to wake up in my own bed, like every other time, and this will all have been some crazy nightmare," I say. When I look over at Ali, she has that expression plastered on her face. The one that lets me know when she's teasing me.

"What," I say, a little harsher than I mean it to be. Everything I know about, well, about *everything*, is being turned upside down. And she is *smirking*. "What is it, Ali?" I say again, this time with a little more composure. She just keeps smiling.

Then I look down at my outfit.

Yup, I'm still wearing *her* clothes and they still look ridiculous. But this is not the time for laughter, I am trying to have a mental breakdown over here and she's distracting me.

"Oh, for fuck's sake," I complain as I stomp outside to see if my clothes are dry yet. All the while, listening to her quietly chuckling behind me.

When I come back into the kitchen holding an armful of clothes, I walk straight past Ali, who's still smiling, and head directly down the stairs, muttering a string of profanities as I go.

Goddamn ridiculous. There is no fucking way any of this is real.

Although I still have a million questions, I need a minute to wrap my head around this. I storm through the hand carved wooden door to the guest bedroom, the *cave* bedroom, built into a *cliff,* and quickly change back into my own clothes. Then I fall back onto the bed and stare up at the ceiling for who knows how long.

Days, I suppose, since every twenty minutes is a new one.

The longer I gaze at the stone ceiling, the more the shock begins to wear off. The more I find myself starting to accept what is happening.

I always know when I'm in a dream.

And this isn't one.

Ali can't fake the daylight cycle, or the monsters, or the cut in her leg healing in only a few hours. I saw all of those things with my own two eyes. And what reasons does she have to lie to me? What reasons do I have not to trust her? As impossible as it seems, if I could believe the things that I've seen, then maybe I can believe what she's telling me too.

Could she have actually been dead when I left her in the woods? Thinking back, I realize that there is no way in hell I would have left her there if I thought there was even the slightest chance that she was still alive.

Not after I finally found her.

Grumbling, I walk out into the hallway to look for her. I'm not entirely convinced that I believe any of this, but I have certainly calmed down enough to be capable of asking more questions.

When I walk down the hall, I see Ali poking at the glowing embers smoldering in the living room fireplace. I watch her toss something into the fire and it's quickly engulfed in flames. *A small book, maybe?* But I probably just imagined it.

I walk down the two short steps and study the room. It has a tall rocky ceiling, with glowing lanterns hanging from it in organized rows. There are two couches arranged in a 'L' shape with an end table at the corner, a coffee table in the middle and a cozy looking chair across from it. The fireplace is built directly into the stone wall and is now flickering back to life as Ali adds piece after piece of kindling. One whole wall is a smooth, dark glass, the same glass as in her bedroom, looking out over the meadow and all the way over to the waterfall.

The one she uses as a *shower*.

The one I used as a shower. I shake my head again and sit down on the larger of the two couches, watching as Ali tosses a log onto the fire.

God, she's adorable, I think, unable to take my eyes off her. At some point she let her red hair down and now it's falling in soft waves down her back. She is small and delicate, but I also remember those first moments on the beach when she saved my life. She swung a sword that looked heavier than her, wielding it as if it were nothing.

It's a good thing that she's already taken. Because I wouldn't have a shot in hell with her, and I would make a damn fool of myself for even trying. She's way too good for me.

Ali turns around and I avert my eyes before she somehow finds out what I am thinking.

"So," I say.

"So," she repeats, smiling. *God*, it's infuriating when she does that.

"Does it hurt?" I say bluntly.

"What?" she asks, confused.

"When you die, does it hurt?" I clarify.

She stares at me, just as surprised by my question as I am.

Even though I'm not completely ready to believe all of this, I'm going to at least try and understand it. She drops into the chair across from me and tucks her feet up underneath her, settling in.

"Um, yeah. It hurts like hell. But it also depends on *how* you die. Some times are worse than others. And sometimes, well, sometimes it takes longer..." she trails off, clearly lost in thought. *Or memories.*

"So, in the woods..." I prompt.

"In the woods, I died quickly." She says it calmly, as if we are discussing the weather. But her eyes flicker to the side when she says it, and I know she's lying.

Because I was there.

I held her small, limp body to my chest, her skin growing cold as she bled out. I knelt there, sobbing, *screaming*, grasping on to her as she was torn away from me.

My body shakes from the memory.

I stare at her for a moment, holding back my tears. That's when I realize something. Her lie is either an attempt to mitigate *my* misery, or to avoid her own memories. Either way, I'm not ready to talk about it either. So I take a deep breath and swallow the lump in my throat before continuing.

"After you... died... you went all the way back to the island?" I ask.

"Yes. And it was a hell of a run to get back. I'm sorry, I shouldn't have left you. Should have *warned* you, but I just didn't want to freak you out. I thought it would be too much. But if you knew, then... god, I'm so sorry, Steven," she says, looking away from me, clearly upset.

"Are you apologizing for dying?" I stare at her.

"I should have been more careful, shouldn't have left you alone. It was stupid," she says. And I can't believe she is actually angry with herself about this.

"Ali, that wasn't your fault. And you did it to save me. *Thank you*, by the way," I say.

"Um, you're welcome," she says quietly.

"And now I feel the need to apologize to you," I continue. "If I hadn't shown up here, then you wouldn't have been in those woods, wouldn't have died. I'm sorry, Ali," I say earnestly, because I am.

"No, it's okay, Steven. I'm glad you're here," she says softly. And I feel my heart leap a little from the way she says it. From the way she is looking at me now.

Then just as quickly, she snaps out of it, lightening her tone just a little. "I've died before, I'll definitely die again. And hey, you should be proud of yourself for making it the rest of the way here alone. That couldn't have been easy," she smiles sweetly.

She's right. Making my way here hadn't been easy. Because I just watched her die.

And it. Was. *Shattering.*

I grit my teeth to hold back the tears threatening to escape again. Watching her die was the most horrible moment of my entire life and even though she is sitting right in front of me now, I can't get the images of it out of my head. I was absolutely heartbroken, thinking that I would have to go on without her. That I would be the one to tell Noor, her mom, that she's gone. *Actually* gone. In that moment, I felt an insurmountable emptiness, like my own soul had been torn out. I had *finally* found her and just like that, she was gone.

I was lost without her.

But I don't say any of that.

"Wait, will *I* come back if I die?" The question comes up out of nowhere, but I have to ask.

"I've actually been wondering that myself. I don't know. That's why I went to find you, I couldn't risk losing the first person I'd seen in six months."

I think about that for a few moments. And then think of something else that doesn't quite add up. The house is far from the island and I can't think of a single reason why she would be all the way out there.

How did she get to me so quickly?

And then it hits me. If dying brings you straight back to the island, and she was nowhere near it... then that means...

Fuck.

"Ali..." I ask hesitantly, not sure if I want to hear the answer. "Were you already on the island when I showed up here?"

Her eyes flicker to mine for a brief moment before she quickly looks down at her hands, which are now fidgeting in her lap. When she answers me, it's hardly more than a whisper.

"No."

I put my face in my hands once again. I can't believe it.

She died to save my life. *Twice.*

"Ali," I whisper, not knowing what to say. And somehow, I believe her now. About everything. No one in my life has ever given a shit about me, let alone done anything like *that*. She *died* for me. Sure, the first time may have been in the hope that I knew the way out. But the second... The second time she had to know I couldn't help her. That I didn't know the way home.

And she still saved me.

I suddenly feel overwhelmed. I'm only a stranger to her and she has already sacrificed herself *twice*. She ran back through those creatures to find me, just to make sure I was okay, and got herself shot in the process. Then, on top of all that, she let me into her home. She gave me a bed and made me an incredible meal. I am overcome with the sentiment of it all. And I don't get sentimental.

What is happening to me?

Alexandra Cutter. That's what's happening. This girl is unlike anyone I have ever met. She is selfless.

And then I think about her being out here, alone. *For six months.* I feel my heart ache. Humans aren't meant to be alone. I wonder how she survived it. How she kept her humanity, *hell*, her *sanity*. She not only survived the creatures, the elements and her solitude, but she is thriving out here. There are so many things I still don't know about her and I find myself wanting to know it all.

"You don't have to say anything, Steven," she finally says, breaking me out of my thoughts. "I'm just glad you're okay and I'm so sorry. I'm sorry that you're here," she says, looking up at me with those sad, green eyes. The silence hangs between us for a few moments and then the reality of it hits me for the first time.

I'm stuck here too.

There is going to be another missing person poster on a crowded tackboard outside of a small gas station in Garda Valley. A poster fading in the sunlight.

Right next to the one for Alexandra Cutter.

I start to think about my parents, my friends, but cut myself off from that train of thought immediately.

"So, what happens now?" I ask, trying to pull myself from the pit I'm suddenly sinking into.

"Well, I guess I could show you around," she says, understanding my need for distraction. I'm grateful for that. "That is, if you're wanting to stay," she adds hesitantly. Her words make me realize that I don't even know if she wants me to stay. It isn't like this was a planned visit. I dropped in on her life unannounced, and so far, I've been nothing but a burden. She might not even want me here.

"Would it be okay with you if I stayed here, Ali? At least... until I figure something out? I know you didn't sign up for this, I don't want to intrude," I say honestly, but I can't imagine where else I would go, or how I could survive out there.

Not to mention the fact that I don't want to leave her. But I would, if that's what she wanted.

"Of course it's alright, Steven. And you can stay... permanently... if that's what you want. There's plenty of room here," she looks at me and I realize she seems... *hopeful.*

She doesn't want me to go, I think, relief washing over me.

"I'd like to stay," I whisper, meeting her eyes. And for a moment, I completely forget about everything and find myself smiling again.

Damn, how does she always manage to do that?

She smiles brightly back at me, then quickly looks away, changing the subject.

"So, first rule of the house: Stay within the barricade. You'll see where the light stops when you're outside. Even if you *do* come back when you die, I don't want to have to go get your ass off that island again," she says, looking at me sideways from under long eyelashes.

"I don't think I'll be going outside anytime soon, but thanks," I return her smile.

"Fair enough. Well, you've already seen most of the first floor," she says, pushing herself out of the chair and walking up a couple of small steps to the attached area.

The space is about the same size as the living room and there are shelves filled with books covering one whole wall. There is a large wooden table in the center of the room, clearly used as some type of workspace, and a few potted plants scattered around. Then, pinned to the walls and covering every available wall space, are maps. They look old. I can see even more of them piled up on side tables or rolled up on shelves.

"This is the map room," Ali says, watching me as I step closer to see them. Around the edges of several is a border of symbols. It looks like some type of ancient language. Only, it's one I've never seen before. *And that's saying something.*

I move to the other wall, studying the largest map in the room. I quickly realize that it's an aerial view of a large area. There are mountains, trees and rivers winding their way across it and out to the ocean. The parchment looks old, but not the ink. And it doesn't contain any of that weird language. The bold black lines define the landmarks more than the rest of the maps do and the colors are in some type of watercolor. I am surprised how detailed it is. As I study it, I realize that the map is divided into perfect squares, some of which are scribbled over.

"What's this?" I ask curiously, pointing at the shaded areas.

"Well, I've been searching for a way out. Or... *any* type of clue to why I'm here, really. That's how I've been keeping track of where I've looked."

"Wait, you drew this?" I ask, noticing the difference in style from the rest.

"Um yeah, that one, I did," she says shyly. Or maybe... *embarrassed?* But she shouldn't be, because the artwork is incredible. "In case you haven't noticed, it's a little dicey out there, so I like to keep track of where I've been so I don't waste time searching the same area twice."

"Makes sense. You've searched all these areas?" I say, suddenly realizing how many sections are shaded in.

"Yeah, I have," she says and I can hear the disappointment in her voice. The fact that she is still *here,* not back in the valley, clues me in to the fact that the search hasn't been going well.

"Wait a second, how do you search this big of an area without, you know, *dying*?" I say. Our little ten-minute walk through the woods had been a nightmare. And every one of the shaded areas look larger. Much larger.

"I've figured out how to survive it, how to fight them. You also get good at finding places to hide," she says nonchalantly as she wanders the room, studying the maps as I study her.

She just keeps surprising me.

Here I am, freaked out just thinking about going outside after our last jaunt through the woods and here she is, surrounded by maps that prove just how much time she's spent out there.

"So how did you find this place?" I say, gesturing to the house in general.

"I um... I found the cave, but I... built everything inside," she says.

She has got to be joking.

"Very funny, Ali," I say, looking back to the maps.

"No, I'm serious..." she says.

I look back at her and then around the house again. Everything is hand built, that much is obvious, but by her?

"Ali, you built all of this? The furniture, the doors, the *windows*?" I stare at her.

"Yeah, I guess I did," she looks around too, as if seeing it for the first time.

"What about the floors? The rugs?" This is insane. I begin to mentally calculate how long it would take to build something like this.

Six months... I suppose.

"Yeah, those too. What can I say, I have a lot of time on my hands. Keeping myself busy seemed like a good thing to do..." she trails off.

I imagine that if I were stuck somewhere, alone for six months, I probably would have done the same thing. *But how did she do it?* I think, studying the windows on the far side of the living room again.

"You ready to see the rest of the house?" she asks with a big smile.

"Wait, there's more?" I ask unbelievingly. I've already seen the first floor, the kitchen and the terrace. That's already more square feet than most people's houses back home. How much more can there be?

"Come on, I'll show you upstairs," she says.

"Upstairs? Haven't I already seen upstairs?" I ask, confused.

"Um no..." she says slowly. "There are actually six floors."

Six floors? And I've only seen two of them. I stare at her, dumbfounded.

"What in the hell do you need six floors for?" I smile at her, suddenly incredibly curious. She just stands there with that smug little smile on her knowing face, before turning to run out of the room and up the stairs.

I stare. Then I take a moment to push down whatever the hell this girl is doing to me before shaking my head and running after her.

In the kitchen, past the door leading out to the terrace, is another staircase I didn't even notice before. Ali stands at the bottom of it waiting for me, and I wonder how she managed to get up here so quickly. She isn't even out of breath and I'm trying desperately not to be. I follow her up the narrow spiral staircase to the next landing, then through a large wooden door.

"This is the storeroom, so if you need anything, it's probably going to be in here," she says, walking down the center of a long rectangular room. The ceilings are tall and on either side of the wide hall are four long shelves, running the length of it. On every shelf, there are rows of ancient-looking chests made from wood and bound with leather straps. They look more like something you would find on a pirate ship rather than in a home.

I notice that on every chest, there is a little wooden placard nailed to the top of it. On the closest one, the word *seeds* is written in bold, perfect handwriting, which I have to assume is Ali's. I open the chest and find dozens of little fabric bundles, each tied shut with a piece of twine. I toss one in the air and then catch it. Sure enough, it feels like a pouch of seeds. Shrugging, I drop it back inside and let the chest fall shut, realizing that Ali is already leaving me behind.

I walk quickly in an effort to catch up, but can't help but try and count how many chests are in the long hall. After a rough mental calculation, I realize that there have to be *hundreds* of them.

Nearing the end of the hall, I sprint the rest of the way until I'm walking right beside her.

"Okay, I have to know, did you make the treasure chests too?" I ask. She smiles up at me and laughs. I love it when she does that. I smile back, beaming.

"Well I don't know about *treasure* chests, but yes, I made those too," she says.

"So what, did you take wood-shop back home or something?"

"No," she chuckles, "but I needed somewhere to put all my shit." She smiles and I shake my head, running a hand through my thick hair, still wondering how she figured out how to do all of this.

"Hey, Ali?" I ask as we start up the staircase to the next floor. "Why was I so tired when you first found me? I could barely walk and now I feel just fine, did that happen to you?"

"Yeah, it did. When you go through a portal you get... *fatigued*. But every time gets a little easier, I don't even notice it anymore," she shrugs.

"Huh. Portal fatigue..." I muse, unsure of how else to respond. Ali looks over at me and chuckles.

And then I think about what she just said.

"Hold on, *every time* you go through a portal? You've been through it more than once?" I suddenly feel hopeful, *can we get back?*

"Don't look so excited," she says, catching my meaning. "There is another portal, but it doesn't lead back home."

"Where does it lead to?" I ask.

"Um, it goes... somewhere else," she says darkly, furrowing her brow.

"Somewhere else?" Now she's being purposefully elusive, and I'm not going to let her get away with it.

"Yes..." she starts slowly. "You know all the things that go bump in the night out here?" I nod in confirmation, waiting for her to continue. "Well, imagine a place where they don't just come out at night. They're out. *All* the time," she stares right at me with a look in her eyes, one I have only seen in the dreams. It's a look that alludes to something worse than fear.

I know immediately that the conversation is over.

"So, be sure to tell me where that portal is so my dumbass doesn't fall into it," I smile at her sideways and give her a wink, trying to lighten the mood. And it must work, because she is smiling widely at me now and I could swear she is blushing again.

Must be from all the running.

"Don't worry, you won't just stumble into it, I promise. And besides, it's probably best that you stick close to me for a while. Try not to wander off," she says pointedly and I agree.

However, I have to admit that my self-preservation isn't the only reason I want to stay by her side.

On the next floor, we walk through two heavy looking double doors and into a large open room with even taller, vaulted ceilings. It reminds me of a factory work room. Unlike the rest of the house, the floor is made of stone, giving it more of an industrial feel. There are large wooden tables set up in rows throughout the room. There are tools and-

"No fucking way," I say, staring around with an idiot grin on my face. Because every inch of every wall is covered with weapons.

I ignore the part of my brain that tells me I should be terrified that she has a goddamn *armory* in her house and look around as if it's already my birthday. There are swords of every size, bows and arrows, spears, crossbows, daggers-and then my eyes fall on Ali.

God, this girl. She is sitting on one of the large wooden workbenches in the middle of the room. Her ankles are crossed as they swing casually off the edge of the table and she is looking at me with that smug little grin again. The sheer size of this room makes her look even more tiny as she sits in the center of it. This room feels dangerous. But not as dangerous as her, I realize. The girl probably knows how to use all of these. *Little warrior,* I think.

I move toward her, but continue to survey every single weapon systematically. I know they aren't toys, but *damn.*

I want to play with them.

"Ali, this is the coolest shit I've seen in my entire life. Can I hold one? Can I?" I ask excitedly, unable to wipe the stupid grin off my face. And although she is laughing at me again, she gestures her arm out casually, giving me the *go ahead.*

"Just don't stab yourself!" She shouts after me.

I am so excited, I don't even know which one to pick up first. I finally decide on the largest and meanest looking sword I can find. I grab the hilt and pull it from its hook on the wall, smiling wider as I feel the weight of it in my hand.

I hold the large blade up in front of me and stare up at it wide-eyed. Yeah, this is definitely not a toy. The handle is wrapped in an intricate weave of corded leather, its iron blade as shiny as glass and it's long. I set the tip of it carefully on the stone ground and realize that the hilt is level with my eyes.

Shit, I smile appreciatively.

And then I lean to the side, looking past it and over at Ali.

"What in fuck's sake do you do with this? The smaller ones make sense, but shit, Ali..." I say unbelievingly, staring at the weapon again. The weapon that is definitely taller than her.

"Well, I don't actually use that one very often, it's too heavy to haul around. But I have used it a time or two, you know, for posterity," she smiles. I stare after her as she hops down from the table and begins to nonchalantly wander around the room, rearranging tools on tables here and there.

Posterity. Unfuckingbelievable, I think, watching as she grabs a pickaxe that is leaning up against a table, then hangs it back in its place on the wall. The image of her small frame wielding any of these weapons would have seemed impossible, if I hadn't seen it for myself.

Memories from my first moments on the island come flooding back. She was the most beautiful thing I've ever seen, and she saved my life. But she also wielded a sword as if it were nothing. And then I picture her wielding *that* sword, I glance back to where I hung it back on the wall.

Ali may be little, but she *is* a warrior. She doesn't have all of these weapons just for posterity, she has them because she needs them to survive out here.

The truth is that I'm in awe of her.

I'm sure that I don't even know half of what's outside the barricade. If she didn't come to save me when she did, god only knows what would have happened to me. When I arrived, I was in absolutely no condition to even run from the creatures, let alone fight them off. *So how did Ali survive when she first got here?* I wonder.

And then it hits me.

She didn't.

Chapter 14

The fact that Ali has died *eighty-six times* keeps replaying over in my head. And I can't help but compare it to my dreams. The dreams where she died, *over and over.*

Could it be just a coincidence? Maybe. All of this is impossible to comprehend. There is so much I don't understand that it's starting to make my head hurt.

As I continue my appraisal of the armory, my eyes land on the area toward the back. And just like that, I'm smiling again. Because this isn't just an armory. It's also a *forge*. There are several large furnaces along the back wall, with an anvil sitting in front of them. There are tools scattered around, but it isn't messy. It just looks well used. And that's when it becomes clear that Ali has not only converted a cave into a home, but that she made all the weapons too.

Of course she has, I think and wonder if there is anything this girl can't do.

"I am coming to the conclusion that my capacity for surprises is starting to dull," I tell her as I hold up and survey another smaller sword. But when I glance over at her, I can tell by the look she is giving me that this tour isn't over yet.

Ali makes her way over to one of the far walls, pulling what looks like a dagger from her boot. I follow after her, watching curiously as she digs the knife into the stone, making one small vertical mark. I stare at her in question.

"I figured we should start keeping track of time out here. Can't count by the daylight cycle," she answers before turning and heading for the door.

I grumble as she leaves the room, because I am nowhere near done in here. I take one last longing look around before following her out the large double doors.

When we are nearing the top of the next spiral staircase, I mentally count how far up we've climbed. *Five floors? Yeah, that's right,* I determine. I am, once again, trying my best to hide the fact that I'm out of breath. Because it annoys me that she isn't.

I stand next to Ali and stare at the single painting hanging in front of us. It's large enough to cover almost the entire stone wall. And instead of having no particular design like the paintings downstairs, this one has a large skull in shades of blue nestled in a bed of thorns and roses. It's... ominous.

"So, don't freak out. This will just be easier to show you, but I promise I'll explain everything," she says, looking up at me warily.

"Don't freak out about wha-" my voice cuts off abruptly.

Did she just? Nope. Not possible. This has to be some sort of trick, or maybe I *am* actually dreaming.

Or going insane.

Ali was standing right here facing me only a second ago, then stepped backward *through the painting.*

Not around it, *through* it.

I just stand here, in shock, not sure what to do. Thankfully, I don't have to decide. Ali comes back through the painting with an understanding look on her face, which surprises me. I half expected her to tease me for my bewilderment, but she seems genuinely sorry for my confusion. It's then I realize she knows exactly what I'm going through. After all, she was new to this place too, once upon a time.

"Come on," she says softly, grabbing my hand and pulling me toward the painting. My eyes go wide, and I try not to think about how her hand feels in mine. I watch her slowly sink through the canvas, pulling me along. Holding my breath, I close my eyes and take a step forward.

When I feel her hand slide from mine, I open my eyes. I'm standing in another room, but it's nowhere near as large as the armory. It's a similar size to the living room, but the lack of windows makes it feel smaller.

I quickly turn back to the painting I just *walked* through, surprised to see that it looks exactly the same from this side. I'm not sure what I was expecting, but it seems... normal, unmoving, like my entire body didn't just pass right through it.

I look down to make sure I'm still in one piece and haven't somehow turned ethereal. I put my hands on my chest and find that I am, in fact, still here. I stare curiously back toward the painting, then reach out until my fingers touch where it *should* be. My hand goes right through the facade and I quickly pull it back, staring at it curiously.

"What is it? Some type of hologram?" I ask Ali, hoping that this new surprise is easily explainable.

Her facial expression tells me it isn't.

Looking past her, I study the room. It's similar to the rest of the house, with the same stone walls and wooden floorboards, but somehow, it feels different. I can't put my finger on it, but there is something about this room that makes the hair on the back of my neck stand up. But not with fear.

This is something else.

It's almost as though I can *feel* the room, like I'm a part of it, connected to it. Connected to the girl standing in front of me. I wait for the feeling to fade, but it doesn't, it only grows stronger.

There is a workbench style counter, about waist high, that continues around the walls of the room and beneath the bench are even more books. Scattered neatly on the shelves above are a variety of empty glass jars and bottles and in the center of the room, is a square table with a dark maroon tablecloth. Sitting in the middle of the table, is another book. A *big* one. It looks like it might weigh as much as Ali.

And then I realize that maybe it isn't the room, but the *book* I'm inexplicably drawn to. I can't take my eyes off it.

"What is this place?" I finally ask after taking it all in.

"It's not just this place, Steven. It's this *world*. It's... different from ours. Nothing quite works the same here," she tries to explain.

"Yeah, I'm still trying to come to terms with that," I say as calmly as possible, but I'm sure my voice is heavy with veiled panic. I have a strange feeling that this room is affecting my emotions somehow because everything seems... heightened.

"I don't know how to explain it, but it's not just the daylight and the monsters and the whole not-dying-thing, it's more than that..." she trails off.

"*More*, like..." I prod slowly.

"Like... *magic*," she cringes, anticipating my reaction.

"*Magic*." I stare at her incredulously. "Like broomsticks and wands and owls that deliver your mail?" I ask sarcastically, because this really is too much.

"No, not like that," she chuckles and messes with her hair as she figures out how to continue. "The magic here, well, it's not wands and spells, it seems to be *in* everything. You just have to know how to pull it out. Once you do, you can control it. You can feel it in here more than everywhere else because the book... amplifies it somehow. Or maybe it's a conduit, I'm not sure."

I give her a blank stare. She's definitely lost me, and she knows it.

"*Ugh*, I'm not explaining this right. Here, let me show you," she says, heading over to one of the counters.

I can feel this room is different, can feel there is something about that book, but *magic*? I don't understand any of this.

Ali walks over to stand in front of the large book. I follow, gravitating to whatever it is that she's about to do. I step close enough so that I can peer over her shoulder, but quickly realize *that* was a mistake. Her hair smells like flowers and now I'm imagining what it would feel like to touch it. I clench my jaw, resisting the urge to lean in closer. Whatever this room is, it seems to magnify *all* my feelings. My fear, my confusion, my excitement and whatever it is about this girl that makes my heart beat a little faster than it should.

I shake my head and try to focus. As she flips through the book, I notice it isn't in English. It's written in the same strange symbols that I saw on the maps downstairs. I've always had an affinity for written languages, especially ancient ones, but the symbols on the page are nothing like the ones I've studied. The language reminds me of ancient runes, but they're not.

This is something else entirely.

The strange writing looks like it was hand painted onto the aged paper. The borders of each page are decorated with an enchanting weave of symbols and vines. Even though I can't read it, I still appreciate the details with a growing fascination as Ali delicately flips through the pages. Whatever this book is, it looks old.

Finally, Ali seems to find the right page and glances back at me, making sure I'm paying attention. She averts her eyes quickly, giving me the impression that she's also acutely aware of how close I'm standing.

I should move back. But I don't.

"Okay," she says, almost apologetically as she holds up a little burlap bundle I didn't realize she had. It looks similar to the one I saw downstairs, but I have a feeling that this one doesn't have seeds in it.

"You ready for this?" she asks.

"Nope. But by all means," I say, giving her the go ahead as I move closer. When I accidentally brush up against her, I notice that she's biting at her lip and her cheeks are flushed with that adorable shade of pink.

Fuck. Is she feeling... whatever the hell this is, too? I back up, reminding myself that she has a boyfriend. I decide to blame the room for my unbridled emotions.

Ali unties the twine holding the fabric closed and tosses it aside, then takes another glance back at me before continuing. I'm not sure what the big deal is, or what could possibly be in that little pouch that will somehow *magically* solve all my questions, but whatever it is, I'm suddenly desperate to find out. She holds up the little pouch until it's as high as she can reach. And slowly, she begins to pour out the contents. Right over the book.

Alright, now I know she's lost it.

Why would she risk ruining- my thoughts suddenly cut off as my brain tries to grasp what I'm seeing. *Sand*? No, not sand. It looks like tiny fragments of glass, each grain impossibly small and falling from the pouch like a trickle of water. But right before the grains hit the surface of the pages, they. Stop.

I just stare at the scene for the longest moment, as if my gaze will give the tiny specks permission to continue on their journey. But they don't continue. They scatter across an invisible surface and are left hovering no more than three inches above the page.

Ali looks over at me hesitantly, trying to gauge my reaction. Apparently, I'm not freaking out enough, because she continues. Leaning over the book, she stares down at the asteroid field of floating particles. I study her face, watching her concentrate. She holds out her hands and makes a motion through the sand-sized grains. It looks as if she's trying to scoop them up, but they evade her grasp. The particles float around all on their own like a cloud.

I see a flicker of green light flash behind her eyes, but it's so quick, I'm not entirely sure if it was real or if my own eyes are just playing tricks on me. Ali concentrates on the specs, until I notice a small, accomplished smile touch the corners of her mouth.

Then the particles start to move on their own.

They spin around in a clockwise motion until they are mixed up together in a turbulent whirl. The pile becomes increasingly more compact as they twirl around and suddenly, there's a bright flash of light, causing me to look away.

When I glance back, the grains are gone. In their place floats a small, clear sphere, hovering just above the book. If not for the slight distortion caused when you try to look through it, I might not have seen it. It just bobs in the air, as if it were floating in water.

What the fuck? I don't even get the chance to voice the thought before Ali grabs the sphere out of the air and starts flipping through pages again. I just blink at her.

Maybe I didn't get enough sleep?

When the shuffling of pages stops, she gingerly places the clear ball back in its place, hovering several inches above the book. I can tell she's doing that concentration thing again, but I can't take my eyes off the sphere. Because it's moving.

No, not moving, *morphing*. I watch it intently. My brows furrow as I wonder what it will do next. After only a few seconds, the ball starts to take on a more deliberate shape. I stare in amazement as it transforms into some sort of glass container, somewhere between a water bottle and a beaker. I finally tear my eyes away and look around the room, realizing that it's exactly the same shape as the ones lining the shelves.

I look back toward the book, mystified. Ali grabs the bottle from its suspended state and holds it out to me. I look between her and the object, asking permission. She gives a slight nod and I reach out and take it.

Ali is clearly grinning, but I can't pay attention to anything as I gape at the delicate glass bottle I'm holding gingerly in my hands. I've seen videos online of glass blowing or bending, but it always takes an immense amount of heat. The glass I hold now is cold as ice. Turning it in my hands, I realize how small it looks compared to when Ali was holding it. Everything about her is so small and delicate that I marvel again at how she survived all of... *this*. Because it's *insane*.

"Ali, this is..." I begin, shaking my head.

"I know," she says excitedly.

"This is crazy, you know that right?" I say.

"Yeah, I know," she says, obviously thrilled to have someone else experience this world alongside her.

"So..." I begin, rubbing my free hand across the back of my neck in contemplation. "Magic?" I look up at her.

"Magic."

Chapter 15

Ali's bright, excited eyes are the only thing keeping me grounded at the moment.

Reality and this new world of magic and monsters are currently battling each other inside my mind. The common sense part of me is trying its best to claw its way to the forefront, but the part of me that wants to believe everything Ali is telling me, showing me, is unfortunately winning. The mayhem of thoughts are tearing at my mind and my head is beginning to ache. This room makes me feel like I'm suffocating in my own emotions. I can't breathe.

"Steven, are you okay?" Ali says, concerned, but I don't answer.

I just stare at her.

I think I'm in shock.

Slowly, she takes the glass bottle from my hands, setting it on the table. I watch her motions robotically, unable to make my own body move in response.

"Okay, let's get you some fresh air. You're pale as a ghost," she giggles.

I make some sort of insane chuckle at that. *Me,* a ghost. Isn't she the one who's died eighty-six times? Suddenly, I can't decide what's harder to believe. That magic exists, or that she can't die. My noise must amuse her, because she lets out another small laugh as she leads me by the arm through the magical wall painting and back out into the hallway.

My vision blurs and my ears are ringing. When I look down, I find her fingers grasping my arm. *When did those get there?* I wonder. They burn, like fire and ice igniting my skin. But not in a bad way. Because I don't want her to let go.

I don't remember walking up the stairs. But we must have, because we're on the next floor. We're standing in front of a large glass wall and I feel a sudden wave of relief, realizing that there is actually fresh air up here. Only, we aren't exactly *outside*.

I follow in a daze as Ali drags me through the doorway and into the largest greenhouse I've ever seen. I take a deep breath as I look around, my nerves already settling just from being out of the mountain.

Out of that room.

Looking up through the angled glass ceiling, I realize that we aren't anywhere near the top of the mountain, evidenced by the snow dusted peaks looming high above.

The greenhouse was built on a large flat spot cut into the hillside, the long rectangle structure built entirely with glass. The walls are crystal clear, like the glass bottle Ali just *made,* with no visible means of how it's being held together. Vibrant green vines cling to the walls, continuing up to the peaked roof and hanging down, the glass shimmering through their leaves in the daylight.

There is row upon row of wooden tables supporting potted plants. Long wooden planter boxes hold various types of herbs, vegetables and flowers, their rich colors glistening with water droplets. At one end of the greenhouse, there's a small orchard. And the air smells like morning mist and flowers.

As I climb my way out of the fog, coming back to my senses, I realize that Ali is no longer beside me. Instinctively, my heart shutters at the loss. Until my searching eyes find her about halfway down one of the long rows. She's walking leisurely, touching the soft petals of flowers and leaves as she goes. When she turns to look at me, her soft smile melts away what little anxiety I have left. She's clearly at peace here. And I can tell by the way her face lights up, the way she walks a little lighter than usual, that this is her favorite place to be.

I stare after her as she seems to float through the room. I smile, seeing yet again, a completely different side of her. A lighter, more carefree side.

I follow her to the opposite end of the greenhouse. This area of the large structure is set up more like a park. The stone ground is covered in a bright green moss, sprouting sprigs of grass and flowers. There are raised flower beds up against the glass walls, giving the area a landscaped feel. It reminds me of a roof-top garden, similar to the ones back in New York.

An oasis of color in a sea of stone and glass.

There is an intricately carved stone table in the center, surrounded by matching benches. It's large enough to accommodate ten people easily. Ali is sitting on the table, her boots on the bench, and is leaning back on her palms casually. Her soft smile lights up the already bright room and her long hair falls over her shoulders, hanging down her back.

God, she's beautiful. I know I shouldn't think that about her, but I can't help it.

She watches me curiously as I join her on the table, trying to match her relaxed state.

"Feeling better?" She smiles over at me.

"Yeah, I think so. I don't know what got into me back there. It's just a lot to take in and that room..." I trail off, still unsure if I imagined the whole thing.

"It's not the room, it's the *book*," she explains. "But I know what you mean. You can *feel* it."

I stare at her, surprised and relieved to know that she felt it too.

"So, the book. It's... magic?" I say tentatively.

"Well, everything here has some type of magic and it's all connected, but the book just helps channel it in a way. I'm nowhere near understanding it, or figuring out what all it can do, but I've picked up a few tricks here and there," she says. I let that sink in for a minute.

Magic, I think again.

I stare out over the room, realizing that she's right. It is in everything. The plants, the glass, the stone, this entire room. Hell, even the *air* is pulsing with it.

I don't know how I didn't feel it before. I suppose I just didn't know what I was looking for. Now that I do, it's impossible not to notice. Not to *feel* it.

"So, do you like it?" she asks in a small voice, looking around at the greenhouse with pride.

"How can I not like your favorite place?" I whisper back.

Shit. Did I really just say that? I cringe at my own words, stealing a glance in her direction.

And she's staring right back at me... Fuck.

"How do you know this is my favorite place?" she asks so quietly, I'm surprised I even heard it.

"Um," I begin stupidly. "I can just tell," I say quickly, wishing that I could bury my head in one of the nearby planters. "So, are there any more surprises? I'm already in shock, you might as well get it over with," I ask, changing the subject.

"No, I think we've covered all the basics. There's still a lot more for you to learn about this place, hell, I'm still learning it myself. But I wanted you to know everything right from the start, instead of-" she suddenly grows somber.

"Instead of what?" I ask, urging her to continue.

"Instead of how I found out," she whispers, looking down at her gray boots as she fiddles with the laces. "I don't know, maybe I should have waited to tell you. I'm sorry, I don't know how to do this," she looks up at me with a small apologetic smile.

"Ali, it's okay, really. At least now I don't have to keep guessing what the fuck is going on." I lean over, nudging her shoulder with mine playfully. "Now I know for a *fact*, I don't have a clue what the fuck is going on," I say, finally getting a genuine smile out of her.

I smile back, watching her.

Suddenly, the purple shades of twilight start to reflect off the greenhouse for the first time. I look at Ali, worried that we should be getting inside.

"It's okay, this room is safe at night," she says nonchalantly. She lowers herself back until she's lying on the table, her hands folded on her flat stomach, her hair spreading out around her.

I stare at her for a moment, one eyebrow raised at her relaxed state. I wonder if I will ever be as comfortable as she is in this place.

After one last wary glance around, I resign myself to join her.

We lay in silence, watching the blue sky darken to night. I lace my hands behind my head and then struggle to breathe at a normal pace. Not only are there monsters outside, and the little fact that *magic* exists, but I can also feel everything around me. Feel how *close* Ali is to me.

I can feel exactly where she is, can feel every movement. Like we're connected.

Because I want nothing more than to look at her, I force myself to focus on the changing colors of the sky instead. But as peaceful as this moment is, I feel anything but *at peace*. Now that I'm sitting still for the first time, there isn't anything to distract me from thinking about... well, everything.

And my brain can't decide what to freak out over first.

I feel as though I'm watching my own thoughts in fast forward. As soon as one memory appears, it disappears just as quickly, replaced by another. My mind jumps back and forth between waking up on the island, watching Ali's small body being thrown against a tree, her wound healing, seeing *magic*, the daylight fading to dark every ten minutes, the creatures, then back to watching Ali die. And not just in my dreams.

Actually. Physically. *Dying*.

Right in front of me. I squeeze my eyes shut.

Then I think about home. About the fact that *I* am the one missing. That I'm trapped here. My stomach drops and the blood drains from my face. For a moment, I think I'm going to be sick. None of this is possible, but I don't have a choice but to believe it. I've seen firsthand how dangerous it is out there. If I don't get a grip and adapt, I could put myself, or Ali, in danger.

And that's what terrifies me the most. Putting *her* in danger.

She's already died twice for me. There is no way in hell I'm letting that happen again. I know now that I have to do whatever it takes to keep her safe, even if that means accepting all of *this* as my new reality.

"Are you doing okay?" Ali asks quietly and I realize she's staring at me. I wonder how long she's been watching. What she's seen on my face.

"I don't know." I answer honestly, returning her gaze.

"I'm so sorry you're stuck here, Steven. No one deserves this. You're going to be confused and angry and I'm sorry for that. I don't know if there's anything I can say or do to make it any better, but I'm here if you want to talk about it. Or, if you want me to leave you alone, that's okay too. Whatever you need," she smiles over at me and my face immediately softens. She is so genuine and I feel my building panic start to subside.

"I think it's just going to take some time to wrap my head around all of this. But thank you, Ali," I smile. It's curious how she manages to calm me down so quickly. How she seems to know exactly how I am feeling.

"What is this place, Ali? Why are we here?" I add after a moment.

"And that's the question of the year, now isn't it," she says softly, turning her head to look back up at the night sky meditatively.

We sit in silence for another couple of minutes. And then, I decide what I need to do.

"Ali, I think I want to go back to the island," I say.

"You do?" She stares at me curiously.

"Yeah. Not now, obviously, but I think I just need to see it again. See how I got here. I'm not sure if it will help me accept all of this or not, but I was so tired and confused before. I want to see it with a clear head. And I know it's dangerous, so I'll just go by myself, I'm sure I can find my way," I say confidently, even though I feel anything but confident.

I just don't want her going back out there.

"Steven Stone," she laughs. "There's no way I'm letting you go out there alone. But I understand why you need to go, so we'll go."

"No way, you're not coming. Last time-"

"*Last time*, I was a little distracted. It was the first time I had seen another human in six months, remember? And you were walking *really* slow," she turns her head to give me that teasing grin again.

"Hey!" I scold playfully. "It's not my fault that I fell out of a fucking portal and straight into the land of *crazy*. But you're still not coming with me."

"Crazy is right, but I am going with you," she says firmly. "The path splits in several spots, there's no way you would find your way, especially before nightfall. And besides," she adds before I can argue, "once you get your strength back, we can easily make the run during daylight. And last time I didn't have any weapons on me. We'll be more prepared next time."

I sigh, realizing that she's right. Remembering all those marked off sections on her maps, remembering her goddamn *armory*. She knows her way out here, and I would most definitely wind up getting myself lost.

Or *dead*.

As much as I hate the idea of going outside, of *her* going outside, my mind is made up. I need to see the island again. I'm not sure what I expect to find, but it's the only thing I can think of that will help me accept all of this.

I need something to convince myself once and for all that this isn't a dream.

Chapter 16

The sky above us deepens into blackness, but somehow, the greenhouse is still illuminated with the soft green touch of light. My hands are behind my head as I lift myself up, trying to see where the hell the light is coming from. I look down the length of the greenhouse and can't help but feel awestruck by the sight.

Everything is *glowing*, as if it were luminescent. I glance around curiously, but don't see any of the usual lanterns that are scattered through the house. It's as if the light lingers in the air all on its own.

"Um, Ali?" I ask quietly, bewildered.

"Yes?" she says, sitting halfway up on her elbows.

"How is this room glowing?" I look at her.

"Oh, it's the vines," she states plainly, looking around with a smile. I look around as well.

After a moment, I finally see it. The vines that crawl up from their planters and cling to the glass, are *glowing*. It reminds me of those fish who give off a similar bioluminescence.

I stare at the plants in awe.

The light is subtle and yet it consumes the whole room, surrounding us in a dreamlike radiance. I notice that there are tiny particles floating through the air, refracting the light and making it look like the room is filled with floating stars. Droplets of water fall from the vines and land on the plants below, forming tiny crystals that refract the light.

And then I become increasingly aware of how close I am to Ali. I've been doing just fine pushing back whatever feelings I have for her, but the atmosphere in here isn't doing me any favors. All the worries of the day, how I got here, how we will get back, suddenly drift away. In this dreamlike room, sitting next to her, I can't think of anywhere else I would want to be.

And then I remember.

Noor. Goddammit, I think, angry at myself for feeling anything for my best friend's girl. I have to get a hold of myself.

"Steven?" Ali asks.

"Yes?" I answer, but can't look at her, not right now. Not in this place.

"Can I ask you about home?" she asks shyly. The question is so full of longing it makes my heart break for her all over again.

"Of course," I say softly, looking right at her.

But looking at her is a mistake. I knew it would be. Because she somehow looks even more beautiful right now, her green eyes more vibrant in the dim light.

I quickly look away, concentrating on literally anything else.

"What has everyone been up to since, well, since I've been here?" She asks and I can tell it's hard for her to get the words out.

"Well, I haven't lived there that long, just a few months, but I'll tell you everything I can," I say, realizing that any piece of home will probably mean the world to her after being away for so long.

"I would love that. Anything," she says, her eyes full of hope.

So I tell her everything.

I tell her about my first day at school, how Noor saved me from the endless barrage of questions and how we've been best friends ever since. I tell her how her mom is doing, that even though she is hurting, she still shows up to work every day with a smile. How she quickly became my favorite teacher.

When I tell her about how Sunny crashed the boat during the summer, she nearly falls off the bench laughing. I can't hold back my own laughter, because after getting to know Sunny, I find it even more hilarious. I smile, watching Ali's enthusiastic grin and the way her head tips to the side when she laughs.

I love seeing her like this. Seeing her smile. Seeing her laugh.

And it's strange, talking about the *real* world, but no matter how boring the subject, Ali hangs on every word. The conversation seems to bring a new kind of light to her eyes, so I just keep talking. I can't remember a time that I ever talked this much to anyone. But somehow, I want to talk. I want to talk to *her*, want to see her happy, even if it's just for a few minutes.

At some point we moved to sit on the table facing each other. We're sitting crisscrossed, our knees nearly touching as I tell her about all of my classes. I tell her of every break-up, new couple, and every funny thing that Noor or the guys have said or done over the past three months that I've lived in the valley. I tell her everything about the camping trip and how close I instantly felt with everyone.

And then I tell her how much everyone misses her. How they've been spending more time together since she disappeared. How they've been there for each other.

She grows quiet for a few moments, letting it all sink in.

I watch her silent contemplation and I can't believe that we've only known each other for less than a day.

It feels like we have always known each other.

Because it is always her, I think. The involuntary memory making its way back up from one of my dreams.

It's always been her, I think again, before shaking my head.

"*Huh*," she muses after a while. "The girl who couldn't wait to escape the valley and the boy who never wanted to leave it..." she smiles.

"And just look at us now," I smile over at her, shaking my head at the irony.

"Thanks so much for telling me," Ali says softly. "I miss them all so much. I just wish I could have been there."

"You know this isn't your fault," I say, because I can tell she has been beating herself up over it.

"I know it's not. But I still feel like a failure. I should have found a way back to them by now. Sometimes, I get so busy just trying to survive, that I find myself going days or even weeks, without thinking about them. It feels like I'm betraying them, like I don't care about them," she hugs her knees, resting her chin on top of them as she looks at me. Seeing her pain is heart-wrenching. I can't even imagine what she must have gone through over the past six months.

As the sun goes down again, I look into her sad eyes. They are illuminated by the glow of the vines, making them an even sharper shade of green once again.

"Ali," I begin softly. "You aren't betraying them. They know you would never forget them, never leave them on purpose. And it's not your fault you can't find a way back to them." I take a moment and a deep breath before continuing, because I don't want to fuck up what I'm about to say. "Whatever is happening, I want you to know that you don't have to deal with it alone anymore. I'm here, and we're going to figure this out. *Together*," I whisper, knowing that the words are just as much for me as they are for her.

Her eyes fill with tears and she looks away, trying to hide them from me.

Reaching out slowly, I brush my fingers against her chin, turning her face back to me. Letting her know that whatever she is feeling, she doesn't have to hide it.

Not from me.

As she looks at me, her tears begin to fall. I brush one away before pulling my hand back. I stare into those eyes and I'm surprised to find *relief*. Like a weight has been lifted from her shoulders. I smile, because I meant what I told her.

We're in this together now.

And we are going to find a way out.

It's abundantly clear that I need her. Need her experience, her skill, in order to navigate this world. But I also know that this feeling is more than just self-preservation.

Inexplicably and undeniably, I need *her*.

And by the way she is looking at me now, eyes full of hope for the first time, I realize that maybe she needs me too.

My heart pounds, a lingering side effect from touching her, of being so close. I don't know what to say and the silence hangs between us.

Suddenly, Ali closes the space and is in my arms. My body goes rigid with the contact, but as soon as the shock wears off, I relax and allow my arms to wrap around her.

I close my eyes, realizing how comfortable it is to hold her. It feels like she belongs here, belongs this close to me, belongs in my life. I feel it with every part of my soul. And in this moment, I realize something else.

This girl is my whole world.

My own thoughts surprise me. I wonder if it's just the adrenaline causing the overreaction and I have to remind myself that I barely know this girl.

So why is it that I'm so drawn to her? I wonder. But whatever it is about her, I'm sure that it isn't going away anytime soon. And that's when I realize that maybe I do know her. She's been a part of me, even before we met. Her life has been entwined with mine since the first moment I saw her on that missing person poster.

Since that first dream.

Why am I dreaming of her? I wonder for the thousandth time.

At the mere thought of dreams, my own body betrays me and I yawn. Noticing, Ali slowly draws back. I feel a sort of emptiness wash over me as she leaves my arms.

Because I don't want to let her go.

The short gap between us now feels miles long and I stare at her, desperate to close the distance again. But I force myself to stay still.

"You're going to be tired for a few more days, that's normal," she explains. She steps down off the bench and I let out a breath, shaking off whatever it is this girl is doing to me.

As we walk together down one of the long rows of planters, I run my hand along the leaves. Something suddenly occurs to me and I stop, wondering why I didn't think of this before.

"So," I begin, looking around. "No grocery stores. Which means all of this..." I trail off.

Amusement tints her smiles as she watches me slowly put together a more complete picture of how she's been living out here.

"You grow your own food," I say, amazed. "How did you know how to do that?"

"Well, mom's a teacher, so she has the summers off. She works at the greenhouse in town during the breaks. When I was a kid, I would go with her. I still do. Or, *did*," she says.

Suddenly it makes sense. *That's* why it's her favorite place.

Because it reminds her of home.

I can't breathe.

I try to inhale again, but my lungs fill with water instead. My eyes shoot open and I realize that I'm underwater. I also realize, with relief, that I'm dreaming again.

Being aware that I'm asleep has actually made the nightmares a little more bearable. Instead of drowning, like I'm doing now, I've figured out that I can calm my mind and simply stop struggling. Once I stop trying to breathe, my body instantly calms, realizing that it doesn't actually need to.

As I float here in the darkness, I look around, trying to figure out where I am. Trying to find *her*.

I'm suspended somewhere deep in what looks like the ocean. I look up, the surface of the water high above me. The distorted rays of sunlight pierce through the darkness, but they don't reach me.

It's cold. *So cold.*

I look down and the infinite darkness below me causes my stomach to turn with fear.

Suddenly, it feels like I'm falling.

I hear the deep muffled sound of something, or *someone*, plunging into the water. It only takes me a second of searching before I see her. She's sinking downwards quickly, no more than fifty feet away. Her arms and legs float up, as if she is being dragged down by her waist. Her long red hair floats around her, curling around her face.

I need to get to her, *need* to be close to her.

Need to save her.

I realize with panic, that she isn't moving. She's unconscious.

"Ali!" I shout, but my voice is muffled by the water, barely making a sound.

She can't hear me.

She never can.

I swim toward her until the muscles in my arms and legs burn from the effort, but I ignore them, pushing myself forward.

I begin to panic. She's sinking too quickly.

I swim down, trying to get to her.

And then she wakes up. Her terrified eyes shoot open and look around. I reach for her, begging her to swim toward me but suddenly, I feel like *I'm* the one drowning, sinking. I try to take in a breath, but I can't. My lungs burn and my body convulses with panic.

She is directly under me now, but falling away so quickly. She reaches a hand up toward me, but it's no use.

She's too far away.

I'm losing her. *Again*.

My tears mix with the ocean in silent sorrow as I watch her disappear into the darkness.

Alex

Chapter 17

I stare at the stone ceiling above my bed. I don't know how long I've been lying here awake, but I have seen the shadows of night dance around the room several times so far. As exhausted as I am, I just can't make myself close my eyes. So much has happened in such a short time and it's replaying over and over in my head, leaving me restless.

I know that it's a horrible thing for anyone to wind up here and yet, I can't help but smile. Because *he's* here. Even though Steven has been confused and terrified, he has also been kind. Which, coming from a complete stranger, is the last thing I expected.

Then I remember how it felt to be in his arms.

Another thing I hadn't expected. *Ever*, actually, let alone out here. I think about how he bumped my shoulder, giving me that sideways grin that somehow makes my heart melt. I think about how he touched my hand, holding it while my heart was breaking and how his fingers gently turned my face back to him, not allowing me to hide my tears. My own fingers linger in the same spot now, wishing his were still there.

God, Ali. What the hell is happening? I think, rolling over with a sigh as I try to ignore the memories of the last few hours. Because I have to get some sleep.

Then I remember that moment in the greenhouse. The moment he told me that he's here with me. That I don't have to be alone anymore. I'm afraid to believe him. Afraid that it's too good to be true. But a warmth passes over me as I find myself giving in to the possibility that maybe he's right.

Maybe I don't have to be alone anymore.

Because like it or not, he's here with me. I suddenly feel a new resolve, a new type of strength, as I consider for a moment that maybe we can survive this place.

Because we are going to do it together.

Suddenly, I wake with a start.

I don't even remember falling asleep, but I must have, because my heart is beating fast and I'm sweating from whatever nightmare had graced me with its presence this time. I can't remember the last time that my dreams weren't flooded with horrific memories.

As I lie here, trying to decide if I should attempt to fall back asleep or give up and find some menial chore to do instead, I hear his voice. *Is he calling my name?* I sit up, tilting my head toward the door in an attempt to hear him better. But there's nothing. I lie back down, but then I hear it again, this time a little louder.

"Dammit, so much for sleep," I grumble. But it's not like I was getting much anyway. I grab the top blanket and my pillow off the bed and make my way down the hall.

I knock on the door, but he doesn't answer. I open it a crack and quickly realize that he's having another nightmare. My heart goes out to him as I make my way over to sit on the edge of the bed. I can see the pain wracking his face and he's sweating. I stare at his clenched jaw and hear him say my name again, which for some reason, makes me smile.

I reach out and gently shake his shoulder. He wakes in a panic, looking frantically around the room, until his eyes find mine. Seeing me, he immediately relaxes and rubs a hand over his face.

"Shit, I'm sorry, Ali. Did I wake you up?" he asks, concerned. It gives me the impression that maybe he isn't a stranger to nightmares either.

"It's okay, I couldn't really sleep either. I have nightmares too," I say with a small smile and he gives me an understanding look.

"Do you... want me to stay in here until you fall back asleep?" I ask, because evidently, I'm an *idiot*.

What the hell are you going to do, Ali? Sleep on the floor? I mock myself, because this is a horrible idea.

His tired eyes look straight into mine, making my heart jump a little.

God, I wish he would stop looking at me like that, I muse as I work to keep my breathing steady.

"Would you?" he asks quietly, once again surprising me. I didn't think he would say *yes*, let alone look afraid that I would leave him.

"Move over," I say, tossing my pillow at him, which earns me a smile. I climb up onto the bed next to him.

What in the fuck, Ali. I admonish myself again, because apparently, I have completely lost my goddamn mind.

Steven slides over to the far side, giving me plenty of room, which I'm thankful for. I steal back my pillow and lay on top of the covers facing away from him, pulling my own blanket over me. As I stare at the stone wall, I wonder how long it will take for him to fall asleep.

It's only a few minutes later that I hear an unmistakable sound coming from Steven's side of the bed.

He's crying.

I bite my lip and squeeze my eyes shut. The sound of it breaks my heart.

I'm actually surprised that he hasn't broken down and done this sooner. God knows I did when I first got here.

Finding out that you are in a land full of magic and monsters and that everything you've ever known is gone, replaced by a world that doesn't make any sense, is a lot to take in. And then realizing that your family and friends will be out looking for you. That they will never find you... well, that's impossible to bear.

I know that better than anyone.

"Ali?" Steven says, his voice deeper and a little scratchy. I turn slightly toward him in acknowledgement. "Would you stay? Not just until I fall asleep," he whispers. "I don't want to be alone."

"I can stay," I whisper back. I close my eyes and take a long, relieved breath.

I don't want to be alone either.

When I wake up, I find myself looking around the room. I can't even remember the last time I slept in here. It's disorienting. Before I built my bedroom, or the rest of the house for that matter, this little room was all I had. It was my safe place, my shelter.

And now it's his room, I think, slowly turning to look over at Steven. He is still sound asleep in the bed next to me. My stomach does a little somersault, but I quickly push that feeling aside, knowing that I'm only in here because he was upset and that this will probably never happen again.

I'm not sure how long we slept, but I suddenly realize that it was the best night sleep I've had since... Well, ever since I got here. I feel... rested.

I get out of bed slowly, then stand perfectly still when the motion of it prompts Steven to roll over. When I am sure that he's still asleep, I relax and decide to take advantage of the opportunity. As I slowly work to gather up my pillow and blanket, I study his face.

He really is attractive, I notice and *god knows* not for the first time. Even asleep, I can see the dimples in his cheeks, remembering how they become even more defined every time he laughs. His brown hair is hanging over his eyes and his lips-

Ali, stop it, you're staring. What if he wakes up? Blushing, I quickly make my way out of the room, unsure what the hell has gotten into me. I remind myself that I barely know him and that more likely than not, there is a special someone, probably a blonde, waiting for him back at home. But even as I close the door, I suddenly feel the urge to stay.

I stand here in the doorway, fighting my own feelings. After spending so much time alone, six months alone, I have become accustomed to it. Gotten good at it, in fact. I never thought I would find myself getting used to being near people again so quickly, let alone wanting to be near anyone. At least, not like this. And I don't just want to be near him, I feel as if I need to be with him. Like somehow, he's a part of me. Every second I'm away from him, I feel like I am alone again.

And I don't want to be alone anymore.

It's barely a half hour later that I hear a knock on my bedroom door.

"Um, come in?" I say awkwardly as I finish lacing up my boots. It's strange having someone else in my house.

"Hey, um, good morning," he says hesitantly, stepping only part way into my room.

"Good morning," I smile.

"So um, thank you... for... well, for last night. And I'm sorry, I thought I could hold it together a little better than that," he says in that deep sheepish voice as he looks down at the floor, rubbing a hand over the back of his neck.

He is kind of adorable when he's being shy and awkward. It makes me feel more comfortable, realizing that I'm not the only one who doesn't know how the hell we are supposed to act in this situation.

"Actually, I would say that you are holding it together pretty well, all things considered," I say as I finish tying my boot and stand up. "You are definitely holding up better than I did."

"I am?" he asks, unbelievingly.

"Oh yeah. When I realized that I couldn't get home, I broke more than a few things around here. Including my hand. And then there was the daily ritual of ugly crying myself to sleep, so ya. I think you're doing great," I smile at him genuinely, because he has no idea what I went through.

"You broke your hand?" He smiles, looking relieved by my honesty. He leans against the doorframe casually and my heart does that thing again.

I could get used to having him around.

"Well, I broke pretty much whatever I could find, but when that wasn't good enough, I punched a tree. Broke my hand in at least three spots... not the best idea I ever had, but it's how I figured out that you heal faster here. So I suppose it was worth it," I shrug.

"Well, I'll do my best to not break anything," he smiles.

"I would appreciate that. At least, not in the house. If you do decide that you want to break something, let me know, and we can go outside," I smile widely back at him. "So, what do you want to do today?" I ask, wondering how he is feeling about everything.

He thinks for a moment before responding.

"I think I want to go back to the island. I know it's soon, but I just can't get it out of my head."

I study him carefully, wanting to make sure that he is actually up for this. I can handle myself out there, easily, but last time caught me completely off guard. I'm not about to let that happen again. I know that I can protect him, so there's no reason not to go.

"Okay," I finally say. "But first, breakfast."

I sit across from Steven at the small table in the kitchen, unable to hide the smile on my face.

It's nice to have company.

Steven seems to be enjoying the breakfast I made, which I find flattering, considering I had never cooked a day in my life until I found myself stuck here. And cooking here isn't exactly... easy.

Steven stuffs another large piece of bacon in his mouth. I watch with amusement as realization dawns on his face, his eyes going wide with mortification.

I nearly choke on my food.

"Yes?" I inquire playfully, because I know where this is going.

"Ali... where did you get the bacon?" he asks hesitantly before raising a hand to stop me. "You know what, don't tell me. I am going to finish this meal and you can explain that to me later."

"Wow, you really are a city boy, aren't ya, Chicago?" I say, laughing, which earns me a glare from across the table. He told me about his nickname back home and how happy he was to be rid of it. So naturally, I am going to slip it into every conversation that I possibly can.

"Just let me eat my little piggy in peace," he says, waving a piece of bacon at me with a smile.

While Steven helps himself to a third serving of breakfast, I run upstairs to get my backpack and a sword for our little adventure back to the island. For a moment, I consider grabbing a weapon for Steven too, but eventually decide against it. The last thing I need is for him to accidentally stab himself, or me, trying to fight off one of the creatures in a panic.

When I make my way back down to the kitchen, Steven has just finished drying the last dish and is reaching up to put it away on one of the shelves.

"Oh, he cleans! Alright, I guess you can stay," I say as he turns to lean back against the counter.

"Well, that settles it then. Sorry Ali, I guess you're stuck with me," he says with a wink and I brush past him quickly so he doesn't see the red flooding my cheeks.

As I walk down the stairs to the first floor, I casually wonder if Steven does this on purpose just to tease me, or if he is completely clueless to the effect he has on me. Either way, I'm not happy about it.

When we approach the front door, I work to compose myself. Focusing on the mission at hand, I turn to face him.

"You sure you're ready for this?" I ask.

"I'm ready, prepared, up for it..." he says as convincingly as possible and I pretend to believe him.

"Okay, ground rules. I need you to stay close to me. The monsters can't live in the sunlight, but that doesn't mean they won't be hiding in the shadows, so you can't wander off. If something comes after us, just follow my lead. I've got the sword and I know how to use it. We don't know if you will come back if you die, so don't try and be a hero. If I get killed, I need you to just keep running until you find somewhere safe. Stay hidden until daylight and then stay on the path until I come to find you. Any questions?"

"Uh... nope," he stares at me wide-eyed and I can already see the terror finding its way back to him.

Ali, you probably could have handled that a little more delicately, I mentally lecture myself.

"Listen," I say, softening my tone. "I've made this run a million times, there's really nothing to worry about. As long as you stay close, you'll be fine. It only takes about eight minutes until we're back in the tunnel, so we'll make sure and leave right at dawn," I say encouragingly.

"Okay," he says, a little more sure of himself. But when I open the door to the night sky, he immediately takes a wary step back.

I shake my head.

This is going to be a long walk.

"So, if the light hurts the um... *creatures*, then why don't you just always carry one with you?" Steven asks curiously, pointing to one of the lanterns that is hanging on a hook along the path as we make our way slowly across the meadow toward the footbridge.

"Well, the sunlight hurts them, but lanterns and torches don't. So carrying one around won't stop them from killing you. And it certainly won't stop an arrow. But I have found that most of the creatures are too stupid to realize what is casting the light, so if an area is lit, they will generally avoid it," I explain.

"So, that's why they stay away from the house. Away from the barricade," he ponders, looking out beyond the light toward the darkness of the forest.

"Exactly. And once we're outside of the barricade, you're going to have to pick up the pace. Not only are you going to drive me insane, but you're also going to get yourself eaten."

"Wait, there's things out here that can *eat* me?" His face pales and he stops walking, staring at me intently.

"Like I said, you're safe as long as you stay close to me," I smile. "But you better get used to moving quickly. I've found that it's best to stay on your toes out here."

"I've noticed. It's been hell trying to keep up with you," he says, looking over at me with that adorable smile.

I wish he would stop doing that.

"Soon enough, you'll be keeping up with me without even realizing it. Out here, you can move... *faster* than you think, but you also have to eat a lot more to keep up your energy."

"Is that what's happening? Damn, I've been hungry every second since I got here, I was beginning to think that there was something wrong with me."

"Nothing is wrong with you," I chuckle. "You just burn more energy here, so your body needs that much food. In case you didn't notice, I ate just as much as you did this morning."

"Shit, you're right," he says, eyeing me up and down unbelievingly. I punch his arm in response, but can't hide my grin.

When we make it to the footbridge, which is pretty much the only break in the barricade, I look down at my watch. After a moment, I notice that Steven is standing close behind me. *Too close*.

"Yes?" I ask, looking up at him.

"Your watch... it... it doesn't have any numbers on it?"

"Well, lots of clocks don't have any numbers on them," I tease.

"You know what I mean," he says, giving me a look. I smile, because I do understand his meaning.

The tiny gold chain around my wrist holds a delicate quarter-sized watch. Looking at it now, I realize that it resembles something more like a compass than a traditional analogue watch. And it doesn't have twelve notches.

It has *twenty*.

"Is that?" Steven asks, figuring it out as I hold my wrist out for him to see it.

The disk inside the gold framed glass is painted with two colors, a turquoise blue to represent the daylight and a deep black for the night.

"Yes, it rotates every twenty minutes. So when the little arrow is in the darker section-"

"Then it's the night," he finishes for me, smiling.

"Exactly. It's easy to lose track of time out here, so this helps."

Steven seems fascinated by it. He takes my wrist in his large hands to examine it further and I feel... proud. I worked hard on that little trinket and it has saved my life more than once. As he studies it, I feel his thumb brushing against the skin on my wrist, sending a chill up my arm.

I can't breathe.

Steven is so focused on watching one minute tick to the next that I don't think he realizes he's doing it. And he definitely doesn't realize what that subconscious gesture is doing to my heart rate. I dare to look up at his face and as his eyes meet mine. Then I see his panic. He quickly drops my wrist and turns away. I try to determine what is going through his head. Is he *embarrassed* to touch me? Or does he somehow feel the same electric charge that I do when we're this close?

I dismiss both thoughts immediately.

"So, how much longer?" he asks awkwardly.

I look back down at my watch, because clearly, neither of us bothered to notice the time.

"One minute," I say.

"Okay," he responds. But he seems distracted, almost upset.

After the longest minute of my life, we make our way across the footbridge and into the forest, keeping a steady jog.

As we continue along the path in the shaded sunlight of the birch trees, I think about how unsure I felt about having someone else around. As grateful as I am for the company, I've worked hard to survive here, to build some resemblance of a life. I wasn't sure if I was ready to share it. And I definitely wasn't ready to take care of someone else, or listen to them complain when things got hard.

But he hasn't complained, I think. Not once. It surprises me to find that Steven is easily able to keep up with the pace I set, that every time we come to a turn, he studies it, mentally keeping track of which way we are heading.

As I look over at the man running alongside me, I realize that he isn't someone I will have to take care of. He's not a burden and he isn't a liability.

Maybe, just maybe, he's everything I need.

Chapter 18

As we make our way through the tunnels and into the hidden cave beneath the island, I realize that it's still scattered with hay from the day Steven arrived. I smile at the memory of our first conversation and find it impossible to believe that it's been less than two days since he got here.

Yesterday, he was a complete stranger. I didn't know if he was here to save me, to kill me, or if he was the one who trapped me here. Since then, everything has changed. He is just as lost as I am, and somehow, it feels like I know him.

Like I've always known him.

It could be because he lived in the valley, but it feels like so much more than that. I feel as though I can tell him anything, just like I used to with Noor.

Well, not quite like Noor, I muse. This is *definitely* different.

I keep telling myself that whatever it is I am feeling toward Steven, it's easily explainable. I have been completely alone for six months and humans need companionship. It's as simple as that. No matter what I *think* I feel for him, it's been pretty clear he doesn't feel the same. The fact that he immediately pulls away every time we get close, looking either embarrassed or angry, puts everything into perspective. I quickly came to the conclusion there must be someone waiting for him back home. Because there is no way in hell that someone who looks like *him* doesn't already have someone. The thought saddens me, but facts are facts. And that is one that I will just have to live with.

Because having a friend, having someone, *anyone*, after being alone for so long? It's more than I could have ever hoped for.

I kick the hay out of my path and check my watch, waiting for the darkness to fade back to light, then head toward the ladder that is attached to one of the far walls.

"Hang on, there's a ladder?" Steven accuses me. "You're telling me, that you made me fall down into a pit with no warning, scaring the shit out of me, when there was a *ladder*?"

"Oh, but scaring the shit out of you was so much more fun for me," I say, grinning back down at him as I climb.

"Unfuckingbelievable. A ladder..." he mumbles, climbing up behind me.

I open the trap door outward and it thuds into the sand. After a quick glance around, I pull myself up and out onto the island. Steven makes his way after me and I watch as he takes in his surroundings warily.

I wander over and hop up to sit on the barrel. I make myself comfortable, figuring that this will most likely take the whole ten minutes.

"There's nothing here," Steven says dismally, turning in a circle.

"I know. I've been keeping an eye on it, but I've never seen a portal, a person, or anything. At least, not until I saw you," I say, staring over at him curiously. Wondering again why and how he's here. Why either of us are here.

Steven walks over to the place where he first woke up, clearly remembering it, and stares down at the sand.

He stands there for a long time.

Suddenly, he picks up a rock and, with a frustrated shout, throws it as hard as he can into the ocean before dropping to his knees and punching his clenched fists into the sand, yelling again.

There it is, I think knowingly, remembering my own anger that came just before hopelessness.

Watching Steven take this all in, really take it in, is a surreal feeling. I feel like I'm watching myself. The same confusion, frustration and anger that I had during those first few weeks are plastered on his face now. But I leave him alone, knowing that he needs to work this out on his own. At least, for right now.

Steven sits in the sand on the far side of the island facing away from me, his posture defeated. He rubs a hand over his face and then stares out toward the ocean.

And that's when I can't watch him anymore. Can't see that familiar pain. Knowing that if I did, my own emotions would find their way back to me. I haven't cried in months. Thought I lost the ability to. Until him. Now, I've already broken down several times and I'm not about to let myself go there again.

It's my turn to be here for him.

I wait as long as possible, but too soon, time is just about up. I reluctantly make my way over to him.

"Steven, it's time to go," I say softly, breaking him out of his thoughts.

He stands, turning toward me with a vacant expression and is about to follow when something clearly crosses his mind. He looks around, searching for something.

"Ali," he says warily, "how did you know that I was here? There isn't anything for miles?"

"Oh, um... I was up there," I say pointing high above the house. My stomach involuntarily drops from the memory of the fall.

"Wait, where?" He looks to see where I'm pointing, confused.

"The cliffs... I uh, have a spyglass, so I could see all the way down here," I say sheepishly. Then hope he won't figure it out.

He does.

I can see it on his face. He knows now how far I fell to save him. And he looks horrified.

Then his face quickly changes to something unexpected, a mix of confusion and determination.

"Ali, I need you to take me up there," he says firmly.

"But... why?" I ask, confused.

"Just, please. I have to see it," he says. I can tell that there is no talking him out of it, so back into the tunnel we go.

As soon as daylight breaks, we head straight into the birchwood forest. What had started off as a jog, Steven quickly turns into a run.

What is he expecting to find? The way out? I wonder.

I know for a fact there's nothing up there and nothing you can see either, even with a spyglass. So whatever it is that he's hoping to find, he is going to be extremely disappointed when we get up there.

Once we are back inside the house, I lead Steven to the ladder entrance on the first floor. I turn and wait for him to complain, but he doesn't say a word. And so we climb. Rung after rung, past all six stories of the house. We continue on and I become increasingly concerned by his silence. This ladder is practically the height of a skyscraper and there have been no comments or clever sarcastic remarks. In fact, he hasn't said a word since we left the island.

When we're standing in the little shack on the top of the cliffs, I check my watch.

"Less than a minute before we can go out," I say, looking up at Steven, trying to gauge his strange behavior.

"Okay," is all he says in response, but he doesn't even make eye contact. He hasn't been this quiet since he got here and I would give anything to know what he's thinking right now.

The sun finally comes up and I stand on my toes to check out the windows, making sure it's clear. Before I can say a word, Steven is out the door and standing on the cliff, looking around frantically. I run out after him. He clasps his hands behind his head and takes a deep breath, turning slowly.

That's it, he's completely losing it, I think.

"Steven, what-"

"I saw you," he says frantically, turning to look at me.

"What?"

"I saw you. On the cliff, *this* cliff. I saw you, I watched you jump," he says.

His face is serious, and I'm hopelessly confused.

"Steven, you aren't making sense. You were passed out on the beach, there's no way that you could ha-"

"No, not from the beach. I saw it from *up here,*" he says with a frustrated sigh. "I dreamed about it, about *you*. The first night I was here, when I said your name, that's what I was dreaming about. This was the place, *this* was that dream," he says, gesturing around the hilltop.

"Steven, that's impossible."

"I know. I don't know how I saw it, but I did. *I saw you,*" he says definitively, waiting for my reaction. I just stare at him, because it doesn't make any sense.

"Look," he says, walking back toward me. "You started right here. You went to go back inside, but then you stopped and turned around... right about... here," he says, pacing out my steps perfectly. A knot slowly forms in my stomach.

This is impossible.

"Then you dropped your bag right... here, then pulled out a telescope looking thing and looked toward the island, you set it down... here. Then you... you... stepped off the ledge. Ali, it was so real. I watched you fall," he says it all in one breath and I watch in horror as he replays my own memory, step by step.

I don't know what to say, what to think, but I believe him. Whatever this is, I have to believe him. Even if he had been awake on that island, there was no way in hell he could have seen any of that from way down there. And certainly not in so much detail. My eyes meet his and we stare at each other for a long moment, the silence hanging between us.

And then it gets dark.

Dammit.

"Steven, inside!" I shout, upset that I got distracted, *again*. The panic on his face is clear, but I'm already at the door, holding it open for him. Steven runs inside and I am right behind him, slamming the heavy door shut with a *clang* just as the noises of the night start on the other side of it.

Ignoring the sounds, I pace back and forth in the small room, trying to figure this out.

"Steven, what is happening? How could you have seen me?"

"Actually," he says quietly, taking a deep breath. "That wasn't the only time," he says slowly, lifting his eyes to mine.

"What do you mean?"

"I mean... I had a lot of dreams about you, before I got here, I mean. I know that sounds crazy and I thought it was just because you were missing and I was worried about you, like everyone else. But the dreams, they all..." he trails off.

"Steven, they all what? What else did you see?"

"The dreams were all different, but they all ended the same," he looks down at his fidgeting hands. And he seems... *sad*? No, it's more than sad.

He looks *heartbroken*.

"How did they all end?" I ask slowly, afraid that I already know the answer.

"They all end... with you dying." He reluctantly meets my gaze and I can see his eyes are brimming with tears. I stare at him, in shock.

How is this happening? I wonder.

"God, Ali. Were those all *real*? I know you said you died a lot, but... fuck-" His voice cuts off and he starts pacing the room, a hand over his mouth.

Is he... concerned? For me? For what I went through? His reaction is so severe, I'm afraid that maybe he actually did see me die.

My mind floods with my own memories, flashes of the eighty-six times that I died. None of them were pleasant, but some were definitely worse than others.

There are several that I hope to god he hasn't seen.

"Well, what did you see? I can tell you if they happened or not," I offer hesitantly, because even though I don't want to, I need to know for sure. Steven stops his pacing, sitting down on the floor and I slide down the opposite wall facing him.

"I had a lot of dreams. Nearly every night, actually. Sometimes they were new and some of them kept happening over and over," he pauses for a moment, considering. I wait for him to continue.

"The first one was probably the worst, because I didn't know I was in a dream. After that, I could bear it a little more, but they were still... *awful*. They felt *real*, more like a memory than a dream. I remember every second of them as if I were there. And some of them..." he looks at me, as if he *knows* what I've gone through. "Sometimes I felt like those things were happening to me."

I just stare at him, trying to take this all in.

"The first dream," he continues. "I woke up on the beach, just below the tree line. It was so dark, I couldn't see anything. And then you stumbled out of the woods holding your leg. You went right past me and I tried to call out to you, but you couldn't hear me. You went into the water... and then looked back toward the woods, but I didn't see anything. And then..." he breaks off, clearly horrified by the memory.

"And then it knocked me down. I grabbed at the sand, but it dragged me under," I finish for him, my voice soft, remembering my first day here like it was yesterday. He looks at me and I meet his gaze, because we both know it.

He watched me die.

But how? I wonder. The monsters and magic are one thing, but *this?* I can't wrap my head around it.

"Then I saw you in that hallway maze, in a dark crimson... *castle*. There was an explosion... you fell..." he searches my eyes, looking for confirmation.

"Yeah, that happened too," I answer softly.

"Fuck," he says, burying his face in his hands.

"I know, *silly little girl,* always getting herself killed," I say as an attempt to lighten the mood. But it's also something that I truly believe. I am not cut out for this. If I were, then I would have found a way home by now.

His eyes shoot to mine and they're *serious*. More serious than I've ever seen them.

"Ali, I saw you die dozens of times and no matter what, you kept fighting. Even when you were hurt, you didn't give up. I never saw what was after you, but I saw your fear. I *felt* it too. I don't know how you did it. No one could go through what you did and still keep trying to find a way home. Most people would have given up and stayed inside, but *you* didn't. Even when I got here, you jumped off a fucking cliff for me. And then you were laughing and joking, trying to keep my spirits up during the scariest moments of my life. Now that I know that what I saw was *real*, knowing what you've gone through... dammit Ali. You're not a *silly little girl*. You are the bravest, *strongest* person I know," he says. Those big dark blue eyes with their flecks of purple meet mine, looking out from under waves of dark hair.

I stare back, holding my breath.

I don't know if I want to smile, or cry, so I just sit here, my gaze lost in his.

Without breaking our eye contact, Steven stands and offers his hand out to me. I take it and before I can blink, he is pulling me up against him. He wraps my arms behind his head and moves his hands down to my lower back, holding me close. He buries his face into my neck and squeezes me tight, as if he never wants to let me go.

And I don't want him to.

I'm barely aware that my feet aren't touching the floor anymore. I feel him breathing heavily, as if he is relieved that I am finally safe in his arms. The comfort of his embrace is overwhelming and I melt into him, never wanting this moment to end.

And then, just as quickly, he lets me go.

I almost whimper in protest.

He stands as far away as he can in the small room and turns away from me, locking his fingers behind his head and taking a long frustrated breath.

"What's wrong?" I ask, concerned by his abrupt change in attitude.

"Nothing's wrong. I'm sorry. I just..."

"What?" I ask.

"I just... shouldn't... hug you like that," he breathes out.

"Why not?" I ask, and then I remember. "Oh, you have someone back home." I stare at the ground, ashamed that I let my own feelings get so carried away.

He stares at me, confused, but only for a moment.

"Like, a girlfriend?" he lets out a slight chuckle. "No Ali, I don't have a girlfriend. But Noor would kick my ass."

"Why would Noor-" I start to say, but then I see it in his expression and I understand. "Wait a second, you think that..." I burst out laughing, because it's *insane*. "You think that Noor..." I laugh again. "*Noor...* and *I...* are..." I am really losing it at this point.

How could he think that?

"Well, aren't you?" he says, making eye contact once again.

Shit, he's serious. I quickly compose myself before continuing.

"No. Noor and I are *not* together. We never have been and never will be. He's been my best friend since we were *babies* and I miss him like crazy because there's no one else in the world that I'm closer to. I do love him, but like a brother," I say, hoping he gets the picture.

"Oh," he stares at me in shock, a blush flooding his cheeks.

I'd been too busy laughing to really understand what this revelation would mean.

Until now.

I suddenly grow just as quiet, thinking back on all the times Steven has cut our contact short. All the times he purposefully avoided sitting too close. He was keeping his distance, *for Noor.*

He was just trying to be a good friend, I realize, still staring at him. And then I replay his words in my head and suddenly, I can't breathe.

"No Ali, I don't have a girlfriend."

Chapter 19

My cheeks flood with red and I'm angry at them for it. Steven being single shouldn't cause this type of reaction. He's still a stranger. And we are still stuck here. Together. For god knows how long. I can't think about him like… *that,* not when we should be working on a way to get home.

He doesn't have a girlfriend, I think again. And then I realize that we are still staring at each other. He must realize it too, because he quickly breaks eye contact and the awkwardness of the conversation hangs between us.

"So, um… What do we do now? About finding a way home, I mean," Steven adds quickly. "You said you've been looking for another portal? Like the one we fell into back in the valley?"

"Um, yeah," I reply quickly, happy to be talking about *anything* else. "I can show you on the maps where I've searched so far and then maybe we can figure out where to look next?"

"Shit, this means we have to go down that damn ladder, doesn't it?" he whines playfully, smiling. And I laugh, grateful to have him back to his normal self.

As it turns out, climbing down the ladder is even more insufferable for me than it is for him.

"Can you climb any slower? Jesus Christ, Steven," I tease. I'm hanging by a single hand several feet above him, trying to keep myself entertained while I wait for him. I am so used to just sliding down, that actually *climbing*, one rung at a time, is absolutely unbearable.

"I'm climbing as fast as I can! And who the hell uses a fucking *ladder* as their primary mode of transportation?" he retorts.

As annoyed as I am, I find myself smiling down at him.

When we finally make it all the way back to the first floor and into the map room, I immediately start rummaging around through the stacks of parchment on the table. Steven watches as I lay out several of the maps and then steps closer to get a better view.

"Okay, this map shows the entire area around the house and part of the way to the island. And this," I run my finger along a marked path that goes from one map to the next, traveling through the wooded area and out into the ocean, "is the path to the island. So that kind of gives you an idea of the scale," I say, looking over to see if he's following.

He leans over, crossing his arms on the table to study the two adjoining maps.

"Okay, so that was about a twenty-minute walk and it covers only... half of each map. So, the maps are roughly twenty minutes from one side to the other? Same as the daylight cycle," he says.

I look over at him, surprised that he caught on so quickly. It took me ages to figure that out.

"Um, yeah, that's right. So based on that, it should take around seven hours to search the entire area on each map. But that isn't exactly *possible* most of the time."

"What do you mean?" he asks.

"I mean that some areas are an easy walk, but most of the time you are stumbling through thick woods, or climbing over mountains. Some sections are solid cliffs, or you have to tread through water, so those take even longer to search. Not only that, but-"

"You have to deal with the sun going down every ten minutes," Steven says, finishing my sentence as he looks over the maps once again.

"Exactly. So you might as well just double that estimate right off the bat. I don't think I've ever searched an entire map in less than sixteen hours. And when you do go out, you better be prepared for anything. It's not just the creatures that you have to worry about. There's also good 'ol mother nature who likes to take her turn at trying to kill you every chance she gets."

Steven thinks for a long moment, taking it all in. Then he looks around the room. I only pulled out a few maps to spread out across the table, but I have hundreds of them. He walks over to the largest map on the wall, the one I made, and studies the areas already shaded in.

"You've really searched all of these?" he asks, amazed. There are dozens of sections with diagonal hash marks, and each section is the equivalent to one of the maps on the table.

"I probably could have searched more, but I don't like being away from the house for that long. It kills all my plants."

He gives me a quick, amused glance before staring back at the large map on the wall.

"God, Ali. I was freaking out over a ten-minute walk and you've spent... *months* out there," he says in a trance. I smile at the compliment.

Steven walks back over to the table and fumbles through another stack of maps.

"What do these symbols say? The ones around the edges? It looks like the same language from the book you have upstairs," he asks, holding up one of the parchments.

I take a step closer, studying the familiar language. Honestly, I forgot they were even there.

"It is the same language, but I have no idea what it says."

"Wait, didn't you *make* the maps? And if you can't read the big book upstairs, then how did you figure out how to do... what you did? That thing with the glass?" he asks.

"Well I made the big map on the wall, but the smaller ones... those I found. And as far as the *big book* upstairs... I figured that out by accident. I have no idea how to read it."

"Okay, hang on," he says, rubbing his temples. "You *found* them? So someone left them here?"

"Must have. And I know what you're thinking, but there's no one here now. *Trust me.*"

"But there must have been at some point?" he says hopefully.

"Yes, there were definitely people here before. They left the maps and all these books behind," I say, gesturing from the table to the bookshelf that covers the entire wall behind us. "Which is why I keep searching. I can't help but think that if we can figure out what happened to them..."

"Then maybe we can find how they got out," he looks at me brightly.

Or if they got out...

"Um, yeah," I say quietly, keeping my thoughts to myself. It's too early to crush all of his hopes and dreams. That will happen all on its own soon enough.

"Okay, so what about the big book upstairs? How did you figure that out?"

"Well, when I found it, I obviously couldn't read it, so it just kind of sat around for a while. And then one day, I had it open outside and it started raining. Only, the water didn't touch the pages, it just... *hovered*, just like with the glass. So I started experimenting. I dropped random objects onto the pages, just to see what they would do. Pretty much everything hovers, but it took me a while to figure out that I have to drop the right object onto the correct page before I feel that connection to it. Once I could *feel* it, then I found I could manipulate the object." Listening to myself, I realize how crazy this sounds.

"So how did you figure out that you could make the objects... *change* into something else? Something specific?"

"I don't really know how, exactly, but I felt *drawn* to it. Like it was an extension of me? I just knew what to do, almost like an instinct," I look over at him and wonder if he experienced the same feelings when he was near the book.

"I think I know what you mean..." he says, lost in thought. "Ali, this is insane," he drops down into one of the chairs against the wall.

"I know. I'm not really sure how any of this works, but once I figured out that I could manipulate objects using the book, then I was able to make all sorts of things. I haven't even come close to figuring out what all the pages can do, but it certainly has made life a little easier out here."

"What about all of the smaller books?" Steven says, pointing to the wall of them behind me.

"As far as I can tell, they don't *do* anything. But they're all in that same language," I consider, wishing that I could find a way to translate them.

"Ali," he says, looking serious. "Do you think that one of those books could tell us how to get home?"

I sigh, because of course I've thought about that. Lot's of times.

"If one of those books has the answer, we wouldn't even know. I've stared at them for hours, but I can't seem to make any sense of it. There's no way to translate them," I say dully.

Steven walks over to the shelf and takes out a small book with a brown leather cover. He flips through the pages, studying each one carefully.

"You need a key," he says plainly.

"A what?"

"A key. Something you can compare this text to in order to translate it. Have you found anything else since you've been here? Something that has English *and* these symbols on it?"

"So what, you're a linguist now?" I laugh, not taking him seriously.

"No, but I have some books at home that talk about how they translate ancient languages. They usually have some type of key. I've studied a lot of different languages, Hieroglyphs, Greek, Demotic, Sanskrit, but I've never seen anything like these. I think I would remember it if I had..." his voice fades out as he runs a finger over the delicate page curiously.

I stare at him, recognizing that feeling. The language seems... familiar. Like something you used to know, but have long since forgotten. It is a somber feeling, almost... reminiscent.

After a moment, he breaks himself out of the dreamlike state and looks at me.

"What about the book upstairs? You said certain pages match specific objects, like water, or glass. I bet there is a word on the page that is the translation for the object, right?" He looks hopeful.

"You're right, that word has to be on that page somewhere. Only problem is that there isn't just one word per page, there are *hundreds*. I've tried going through it systematically, but I can't seem to cross reference the pages and symbols in a way that makes any sense."

"Well, now who's the linguist?" he says with a smile, but his face drops a little, realizing that there are no simple answers. Not out here.

"Not a linguist, I've just been here for a while..." I say, looking around the room, my mind flooding with the memories of everything I've been through.

Steven looks at me then, like he has so many times before, but this time, it feels different somehow. He looks at me with a sort of sadness, but not pity. And somehow, I know that he's also thinking about what I went through. *Because he saw it.*

Some of it, anyway. If he saw *everything*, I know his reaction would be different.

He looks away, then thoughtfully flips through the pages of the book he's still holding.

"Ali, what do you think the books say?" he asks whimsically.

"I have no idea. But I have a feeling that they're important."

Chapter 20

It's been nearly a week since the day Steven appeared on my beach. As we sit in the kitchen, finishing off another meal, I smile, realizing how comfortable it is to be around him.

Ever since he got here, we've spent nearly every second together. He has been telling me stories about back home and I've been guiding him through everything he needs to know about living out here. We've spent our days laughing and talking as I show him around the place that has been my life for the past six months.

Aside from the everyday chores, I've also shown Steven around the mountain, the cliffs and all other areas within the barricade.

And I've shown him all the ways to get back inside the mountain just in case something gets through the perimeter. It doesn't happen often, but it's best to be prepared.

The six-story house in the cliffs not only has a main entrance, but countless tunnels, all hidden underground or within the cliffs themselves. Back before I made the barricade and filled it with light, it was necessary to have a quick way back inside. Some of the tunnels I found, but most of them took me quite a bit of time to dig out. I find myself almost... *giddy* to be able to share them with someone.

With *him*.

"Ali, we have to stop eating like this," Steven moans, leaning back in his chair to stretch.

"Trust me, living here means that you *do* need this much food. But not the way we've been doing it... Which means vacation is over. I guess it's time to get back to work," I smile over at him. I know that he's up for the challenge, even if he pretends to complain about it.

"This is what you call a *vacation*? Ali, we've jogged halfway across the world, *twice*, up the Eiffel Tower of ladders and we've been running all over this mountain and through your super secret passageways for days. What the hell do you *normally* do?" he smirks.

"*Normally*, I do all those same things, but I don't walk. I run. And I've never spent so long on that damn ladder," I tease.

"It's always about the ladder with you isn't it," he gives me an equally teasing grin and a half smile that melts my heart.

And with that, I immediately stand to clear our plates.

It makes my heart beat and breath hitch when he looks at me like that and the last thing I need is for him to notice my ridiculous reaction.

"So," I say, turning back to face him. "I was thinking tha-" I pause, and it takes me a moment to register what I'm looking at. Sitting in the middle of the table is something that looks like a cake. It's a little lopsided and has a layer of crudely spread white frosting all over it. I take a step closer and find that there are tiny pink flowers decorating the top.

"Happy birthday, Ali. I figured, since you missed it... I know it's not much, but I-"

"You made me a cake?" I gape at him.

"Um yeah, I hope you don't mind, I used some of your supplies. And it probably doesn't taste very good, because well, I couldn't exactly look up a recipe out here..." he looks down shyly.

"Steven, it's.... perfect," I say, bringing his eyes back to mine.

He baked me a birthday cake, I think, blinking back tears.

"Yeah well, like I said, it might not taste very good. And it took me a few tries to get it right. Well, a lot of tries actually..." he looks away.

When did he even have time to do this without me noticing? I think, realizing that no one has ever done anything this nice for me before.

"It's okay if you don't like it-"

"Thank you, Steven," I say sweetly, cutting off his sentence with a broad smile. It takes substantial effort not to hug him. But I know if I did *that* right now, I would completely lose it.

"You're welcome, Ali," he replies in that deep voice of his, an adorable smile playing at his lips.

I immediately turn, heading over to find us two forks.

No more than ten minutes later, we finished off the entire cake. It was dry and the frosting tasted a bit like chalk, but I didn't care. I hadn't even thought to *bake* anything since I'd been out here and the sugar rush is a welcome comfort.

"Okay, now we really can't just sit around here all day. Like I said, vacation's over," I smile at him slyly.

"Oh god, what fresh hell do you have in store for me today?" he asks, looking concerned, yet decidedly amused.

"Well, I was kind of thinking that it's time you learn how to handle yourself out there..." I say slowly, unable to hide my smile.

I already know what his reaction will be to this and, just as expected, I have his full attention. Suddenly, he's no longer slouching in his chair.

In fact, he's already standing.

"Fuck yes! Can I have my own sword? Can we go now?" he rambles excitedly.

"I guess we can go now if you're-" I stop talking. Because he's already up the stairs and out of sight.

Oh yeah, he's definitely going to stab himself at some point, I think, entertained by his enthusiasm. I head toward the ladder rather than the stairs, because what would also amuse me, is how I'm going to beat him up to the armory.

It is, in fact, *very* enjoyable to be sitting on the top step of the fourth floor and casually picking at my shoelace when Steven comes running around the corner, breathing heavily.

His face drops when he sees me.

"Goddammit it, Ali. How... did... you..." he breathes out between gasps, his hands on his knees. I simply point to the ladder behind me and smile as he lets out an annoyed sigh. He sits down next to me, lying back onto the floor to catch his breath.

I laugh because, well, it's hilarious. He turns his head just enough to glare at me, his scraggly brown hair brushing his forehead with the motion.

Deciding to have pity on him, I offer to help him up as I stand. As soon as his hand grasps mine, strong and yet incredibly gentle, I feel a shiver run through my body. Like it always does when I touch him. I let go as soon as he is standing, looking anywhere but at him as I make my way past and into the armory.

Steven follows me through the double doors and immediately heads for the *giant* sword against the wall.

"Hey!" I say, stopping him in his tracks. "Do you *want* to lose a leg?"

He looks over to see the two wooden practice swords I'm holding, then reluctantly makes his way back to me. Because he knows I'm right.

Looking around, I realize that there isn't much space in here to practice. Steven must notice too, because he's already dragging one of the worktables to the outer edges of the room. I help, and several minutes later, we have moved enough of the tables out of the way to create an open space large enough for training.

Aside from some fencing lessons as a kid and childhood games with Noor, I had no idea how to use a sword when I first got here. But being here, I learned quickly. *Had* to learn quickly. I have no doubt that Steven can do the same and, by the looks of it, he's excited to. I couldn't share that same enthusiasm when I first got here, but *now*?

This is going to be fun.

Steven stands opposite me in the training area, holding up his wooden sword, a giant grin on his face. And that's when I realize just how much I'm going to enjoy beating him.

"Alright, let's go through how you stand and some of the basic motions. We'll keep training simple at first, but you have to remember that once you're out there, nothing is simple. Out there, the creatures don't fight by any set of rules, so you can't hold back. They're a hell of a lot stronger than either of us, but you can learn to be *faster*. It's just going to take a lot of work," I say.

Steven meets my gaze with his own and twirls his sword around, a giant grin spreading across his face. "Then what are you waiting for?"

Chapter 21

The warming sunlight streams in through the glass of the greenhouse. I look over toward Steven, thinking back to the day when I first brought him up here. He immediately recognized that this is my favorite place. I'm still surprised by how well he reads me, even back then.

And now, we know practically everything there is about each other.

The daylight cycle makes it next to impossible to know how much time has really passed since he arrived, but based on the daylight marks we've been carving in the armory, we figure that it's been over a month. But out here, a month feels like a year. In that time, Steven has become so much a part of my life that it feels strange to imagine a life without him.

I don't want to imagine a life without him.

Slowly, I'm beginning to forget about the nightmare of a world I was living in before he was here.

The world where I was lost.

The world where I was alone.

Steven and I have settled into somewhat of a routine around here, and I find myself actually *smiling* again. Every day we talk and laugh as we take turns making meals, working in the greenhouse and tending to the animals that we keep in the pastures downstream from the house.

And every afternoon, we train.

Steven has been getting stronger every day, both with the swords and in hand-to-hand combat. But he still has yet to beat me. And, being that I'm half his size, it's been driving him crazy, much to my amusement. But even with my constant need to tease and annoy him, Steven has hung on my every word. Even though we've stayed safe within the light barrier, he understands that there are certain dangers that come with living out here and has been eager to learn everything he can.

I've been teaching him everything I've learned and shared what I know about the creatures I've encountered before. How they move, how to fight them, and when to run.

When I began to show him some basic survival skills, I was surprised to find how much he already knew. But knowing is one thing, doing it because you have to, is something else entirely.

I was also surprised at how quickly he acclimated to living out here. He has even come to embrace the magic side of things as well. But using magic takes a lot out of you when you aren't used to it, so he practiced with the book nearly every day until he could make everything I know how to do with ease. And his exhaustion from using magic has lessened to a manageable state. He finds it particularly fascinating that we can create large panes of glass. How we can meld them together to make seamless walls of it, fusing them to the stone with little more than a thought and some energy as long as the big book is around to amplify what seems to be our own powers. So, naturally, he found great pleasure in taking a pickaxe to a few of the exterior walls.

Now our house in the cliffs has several new, and *unnecessary* windows.

But even with magic at his fingertips, Steven still prefers to spend his time in the armory. He has spent hours upon hours in there pounding away on that damn anvil, making his own swords, tools, and modifying the ones I already had. Everything I made in the time I was here alone was simply a necessity for my survival, but Steven spends his time there simply because he enjoys it.

I quickly came to realize that the armory is *his* favorite place in the house.

But as much as Steven would love to spend all day in there, he still makes time to follow me around and help out, like he's doing right now. I glance over at him, watching as he picks berries from one of the plants a few rows over. He returns my gaze with a smile and those dimples still make my heart skip just as much as the first day he fell into my life. Well, maybe not *just as much.*

It might actually be getting worse.

But it seems Steven always has a smile on his face.

Except for at night.

At night, I can easily hear his nightmares from down the hall, just as he can hear mine. We have also settled into a routine of waking each other up. Some nights we try to go back to sleep and others, when the dreams are particularly horrifying, we give up on sleep entirely. On those nights, we sit together on the rug in front of the fire for hours, talking until we eventually fall asleep right there on the floor, waking up in a heap of limbs and pillows.

But even though we are both lost, both hurting, we manage to push forward.

I look over at Steven again, his strong features defined under the soft glowing light of the vines above. And I realize that his presence is something that I need. It's something that, now that I have it, I don't think that I can ever live without. As much as I long to get back home, I can't think of anywhere that feels more like *home* than with him.

He's my home.

The thought is so abrupt that it startles me. Then I realize, I'm staring at him. Again.

Shit.

I quickly look back toward whatever it is that I'm supposed to be doing, embarrassed. I don't know what comes over me when I'm around him, but I have long since realized that it's something I can't control.

Maybe I should just avoid looking at him until we find a way home, I think. *Because that's a practical thing to do.* I roll my eyes.

I want nothing more than to be with him all the time and yet, every second I'm in his presence is an endless torture. Because he is clueless of the effect he has on me.

And there is no way in hell I'm going to enlighten him.

Later that day, we lay head-to-head on one of the long benches in the armory, out of breath and covered in sweat. It only took Steven a few sessions of us training together before he realized that he doesn't have to hold back when it comes to me. Now when we train, he comes at me with full force. There have been a few incidents involving broken bones or bloodied fists, on top of the usual bruises, but they heal quickly enough with the daylight cycle that we are usually back at it within a day's mark or two.

Even Steven heals just as quickly out here, which had been a relieving discovery. Knowing that makes me hopeful that maybe he can survive if he dies. Still, I hope never to find out. Getting hurt while training is one thing, because we both know that we need to be ready for the very real dangers that lurk outside, but watching him *die*.

That's something I'm not sure I could bear.

"God, Ali, you're killing me," Steven says through a panting breath. "I'm going to need the longest shower of my life to get the smell of *defeat* off me."

"Hey, you almost had me on that last one," I say through my own struggled breath.

"Yeah, *sure* I did," he says sarcastically.

"But as far as the shower goes, I think I have a better idea..." I say, and I'm not sure why I haven't thought of this sooner.

I bounce up, excitement in my eyes.

"Ali... what are you up to?" he says, pushing himself up onto his elbows, looking concerned.

I grab his hand, dragging him out of the armory and over to the ladder. I slide down quickly, with Steven right behind me. And once again, I'm overjoyed that he finally got the hang of this little trick. It's nice not having to wait around for him all the time.

Without stopping, I hop off the ladder and run straight out the front door. Steven grumbles at the sudden exertion, but keeps up with me all the same.

Instead of heading toward the usual waterfall, which is nestled in the corner of the cliffs upstream, I run downstream along the river, through the makeshift gate in the barricade and just keep running. Once we are far beyond the pastures, Steven finally speaks up. He hasn't been this far from the house or been outside of the barricade since those first days here.

"Ali, where the hell are you taking me?" The concern in his voice is apparent.

"We're almost there!" I shout back lightheartedly and no more than a minute later, the river to our right comes to an abrupt end.

As I slow, Steven steps up beside me and takes a long look at where we're standing.

"Absolutely not. No fucking way," he says definitively.

"What? You said you wanted a shower," I say, teasing him again.

"Yeah, a *shower*. Not a goddamn forty-foot waterfall. Ali, you're crazy if you think I'm jumping off this," he says, looking over the edge and down at the large basin of water below.

"Oh, come on, it's plenty deep enough. I've done it a million times. You know, before I was stuck with this *burdensome* roommate." I jab his ribs playfully with my elbow and he glares down at me. But I know he will give in eventually. Because like it or not, he always makes a point to keep up with me and whatever bullshit I'm up to that day.

"Not going to happen, Ali," he says.

"Okay, suit yourself. But *I'm* getting clean," I say as I back up toward the ledge, taking my boots off as I go. I keep the rest of my clothes on, they need washed anyway, and give him one last look before I quickly do a backflip off the rock, landing in the water far below with a splash. The water is cold, but not freezing. It's a welcome relief after hours of training.

"Show off!" I can hear Steven shout from the rocks high above.

"What's the matter, *Chicago?* You scared of a little water?" I yell back and can hear several inaudible, presumably curse words, as Steven reaches down to take off his own shoes. After taking one hesitant step closer to the ledge, he gives me a mischievous smile, then jumps. By the time I realize his intentions, it's too late. He lands in the water within a few feet of me and I barely have time to hold my breath before a torrent of water invades all of my senses.

"Hey!" I yell as he resurfaces.

He flicks his head to the side, clearing the hair from his eyes and laughs loudly as I spit water from my mouth. Brushing the wet curls from my face, I try to be mad at him, but his laughter, his wet hair, *that smile*... I can't hold back as my own laughter escapes me.

"Well, you survived," I say, amused to see that he's clearly enjoying himself, despite all the grumbling.

"Yeah, I guess I did," he says, looking up toward the top. "I've never jumped from that high before."

"So, ready to go again?" I say, smiling. He stares at me and his eyes narrow, as if he's *really* thinking about it.

"Race ya to the top!" he yells suddenly, splashing me in the face again in a futile attempt to slow me down as he quickly swims to shore.

"Oh, no you don't!" I yell, following after him.

Although the cliff is practically straight up and down, there are plenty of rocks and footholds, making the climb to the top an easy one. When I realize how rapidly Steven is scaling it, I pick up the pace, because there is no way in hell I'm letting him beat me.

"Goddammit, Ali, I won and you know it!" Steven says once we are at the top.

"No you did not! Just because your *hand* reached the top first, doesn't mean you won. I was *standing* up here before you," I argue, as we walk over toward the edge to jump again.

"Give it up, I win," he smiles crookedly. Which I find adorably infuriating.

"Did not!" I laugh and try to shove him over the ledge. He loses his balance, but grabs my hands at the last second, pulling me over with him. I scream and he laughs as we fall the distance, then hit the water together. The sting of our awkward landing spreads across my skin instantly, but I don't care.

When we resurface, we're both laughing uncontrollably, until Steven notices the purple hues of the twilight sky above us.

His face goes rigid.

"It's okay," I'm quick to say as my laughter dies down. He calms immediately. It's then I realize how much he truly trusts me. He doesn't ask how, or why we're safe, he just takes me at my word.

Like he always does.

I watch him look around as the sunlight fades, then watch his slow smile when he discovers *why* I'm not worried. Around the edges of the pool, there are lanterns scattered everywhere, reflecting off the calm black surface of the water. Keeping us cocooned in a soft glow of safety.

"But, won't the creatures *outside* of the lights see us?" Steven asks, still a little wary. The few lanterns that are down here are nowhere near the same scale as the light that floods the area within the barricade up by the house. And he hasn't been this close to the darkness since his first night here.

"Yes, they'll see us. But they won't step into the light. As long as we stay out of arrow range, then we're safe," I say.

"How do you know how far *arrow range* is?" he asks, glancing over at me before his eyes dart back to the dark. I slowly swim backward, heading toward the very center of the pond, then climb up onto a small smooth rock in the middle.

"*This* is out of arrow range," I say, settling in as I wring the water from my long hair.

"Do I even want to know how you figured that out?" he asks, swimming toward me.

"Probably not," I smile. Then he lifts himself out of the water to sit next to me.

Very close to me.

His shirt clings tightly to his body and I quickly look away, thankful that he is too distracted by the night to notice my reaction. It's dark now, so I can't be sure, but that quick glance gave me the impression that maybe he's more fit than I realized.

I push that thought aside immediately.

"What was that?" he asks frantically, hearing a sound coming from somewhere in the forest. I listen for a moment before replying.

"Well, which one? There are eighteen," I state plainly.

"*Eighteen*? Creatures?" He looks at me wide-eyed and I'm close enough to see how purple his eyes look at night. Close enough to see the fear behind them. "How the hell can you tell how many?"

"Here, close your eyes and just listen," I say, curious to find out if he will pick up on this little trick as easily as he's picked up everything else I've taught him. He seems to be good at *everything*, which I find infuriating.

But he doesn't close his eyes, he just looks down at me skeptically.

"Nothing can get to us out here. Just trust me," I say.

"I trust you," he whispers, before turning his head back toward the dark and closing his eyes. Once he does, I find myself studying every feature on his face, unable to help myself. His jaw flexes and his brows furrow as he concentrates. I memorize the sight of him for a moment before dragging my eyes away.

"*Listen*, but don't try to hear everything all at once," I say, closing my own eyes. "Pick one noise and focus on it. Once you've isolated it, then move on to the next one and then the next, until you can hear them all separately."

We sit here completely silent, listening to our own heartbeats and the sounds of the night. Something about this world, about the magic in it, allows you to hear and *feel* everything around you in a way that shouldn't be possible. Once you are able to focus, it's almost as if you're a part of it.

"Twenty-three," Steven says, opening his eyes wide to me. "There's twenty-three of them now," he says excitedly, obviously proud that he can hear them so clearly.

"Twenty-four, but you were close," I say, pointing to an area high up in the trees to our right. "You have to listen *everywhere*, not just for what's on the ground," I whisper.

"Wait, I don't see anything?" he says, concentrating on the darkness.

"Just watch, it's there," I say.

After a few silent moments, several adjoining sets of dark red eyes blink all at once, then shifts, just as an entire section of tree branches start to *move*.

"Those aren't branches," I whisper, watching for Steven's reaction. The massive creature blinks again, then crawls away from us, disappearing into the darkness of the treetops.

Suddenly, Steven takes in a sharp breath, loses his balance and is back in the water with a splash. He comes up quickly, gasping and scrambling to get back onto the rock.

He is terrified and I'm, once again, laughing my ass off.

"*Shh!* Ali, they'll hear you!" he whispers.

"So what if they hear me," I continue laughing at full volume. "I told you, they can't get to us out here," I smile, still entertained by the display.

By *him*.

"Dammit, Ali. You knew that was there and you knew it would scare the shit out of me. A little warning next time?" he says as he runs a hand through his wet hair, flicking water all over me. I just smile, because I probably won't warn him next time either. It's just too much fun to tease him. He must glean as much from my face, because next thing I know, *I'm* the one in the water.

"Okay, okay," I say as I climb back up onto my perch, from where he just shoved me. "I guess I probably could have given you a little bit of a heads up about that one," I say, but I'm still smiling.

And I'm not sorry.

Steven looks over at me, exasperated. "God, you kill me," he finally says, defeated, as a small smile tugs at the corner of his mouth.

"I know," I say.

Several minutes later, the sun comes up over the trees, flooding the dark water with its light and warmth. Steven watches the shadowed silhouettes move through the dark on shore and lets out a small gasp when he sees the first one disintegrate. One by one, the sun touches the fleeing outlines and the dark figures break apart into a million ash-like pieces, floating away in the morning breeze.

I always find it strange, watching him discover something new out here. I feel as though I'm experiencing everything for the first time again, through his eyes. Seeing him take it all in, I can almost feel his fear and bewilderment. Because it's the same fear and bewilderment that I once had.

When the sun has completely risen above the trees, I take one last look around, making sure there isn't anything else lurking in the shadows nearby, then slide off the rock and into the water.

"Well, I don't know about you, but I'm starving," I say as I float on my back, paddling leisurely toward shore.

"You're always starving," Steven mutters, then looks around warily before eventually following after me.

Stepping up onto land, I'm surprised by how warm it is already. I wring out the bottom of my shirt the best I can and then sit on the grass, enjoying the sun on my face.

I watch as Steven makes his way to shore. He's still keeping an eye on the tree line, but it seems more of a precaution than actual fear, which I consider a step in the right direction. He hasn't left the house much in the last few weeks, so it's probably good we made the short trip down here. But as much as he needs to get used to this world, there is always that lingering thought that I can't seem to shake.

What if he doesn't come back when he dies.

I can't even think about that.

I watch as Steven lifts himself up from the water and onto one of the rocks along the shore. As he walks toward me, he does that thing where he rubs his hands quickly through his messy brown hair in an attempt to dry it. That *thing* that, for some reason, drives my heart rate up. The weight of the water makes his brown curls lie casually over his dark blue eyes. And his clothes are clinging to his body in a way that has me staring again. I try not to most of the time, but *sometimes...* I think, biting at my lower lip.

Suddenly, before I can look away, he grabs the hem of his shirt and with one quick motion, pulls it over his head and off.

Oh. My. God.

I knew that he worked out back at home, he told me as much, and I've seen the muscles in his arms put to work when we train. But this is the first time I'm getting the *whole* picture.

And I can't breathe.

I can't even move enough to take my eyes off him.

Sure, I've seen boys with abs, but at our age, most of them can barely manage a four-pack, let alone a six-pack. And most of them are pretty scrawny.

Steven is *anything* but scrawny.

Standing there, soaking wet, he reminds me of a Greek god, all hard lines and confidence. My heart beat begins to quicken.

His toned muscles ripple as he wrings out his shirt. I know in my head that I should stop staring, but he hasn't exactly noticed me yet...

God, he's beautiful, I muse.

I've told myself dozens of times over the last month that I'm not attracted to this man. Not in that way at least. That my feelings for him are simply due to our proximity.

That I'm fine with us just being friends.

But looking at him now... *fuck*. There's no denying what I feel for him. And no matter how much I've tried to convince myself, I've never seen him as just a friend. My attraction for him has been there from the very first second I saw him on that beach. And *now*? There's absolutely no denying it.

Not when the image before me is seared into my mind for all eternity.

Steven turns away from me, heading over to lay his shirt out to dry, and I have the absolute pleasure of discovering that his back is equally as muscular as the front had been.

Of course his back is beautiful, what were you expecting? I think, rolling my eyes.

And then, I see it.

He has a tattoo starting at the base of his neck, running between his shoulder blades and straight down to his pant line. It looks like some sort of language or symbols, but I can't read it. All I know is that it is sexy as hell. I bite my lip again, thinking about what it would feel like to run my fingers down it.

Just then, he turns and looks right at me.

Shit, I think, snapping myself back to reality with a jolt. I quickly look away, embarrassed. But if my eyes don't happen to give me away, then the color of my cheeks most certainly will.

I watch out of the corner of my eye as Steven studies me curiously, then looks down at his shirtless chest. When his eyes wander back up to mine, he has a half smile playing at the corner of his mouth. He looks at me intensely and I look away again, mortified.

The last thing I want is to have to explain what was going through my mind a second ago.

Steven walks over and sits beside me on the grass, then leans back, lying down to enjoy the sun. After living together for a whole month, we've become closer than ever and the feeling of him this near to me *usually* feels natural. But not right now it doesn't.

Not when he looks like *that.*

So I lay back as well, trying to act *normal.* I force myself to concentrate on the clouds floating by as I work to get my heart rate in check.

After several minutes, I realize that lying mere inches from him when he has his shirt off is making my heart rate do anything and everything besides calm down. So I decide to break the silence, hoping that talking will help bring my brain back to reality.

"Hey Steven?" I say shyly.

God, when was the last time I was shy around him? Get it together, Ali.

"Yeah?" he answers easily, and I find it frustrating that he's always so calm. I turn my head to look over at him. His hands are behind his head and his eyes are closed, his face perfectly at ease. I look back at the sky before my eyes can wander further.

"I um... like your tattoo. What does it mean?" I struggle to get the words out.

"What tattoo?" he says plainly.

"Um, the one down your entire back?"

Does he have more than one? I think, smiling at the thought.

"Ali, I don't have a tattoo. My parents would absolutely *murder* me if I got one before I turned eighteen," he chuckles.

I sit up quickly, drawing his attention.

"Steven Stone, you have a giant tattoo down your back. It's in another language, so I can't read it," I say, confused that I have to explain this.

"What?" he says, then shoots up into a sitting position as he tries to see behind him. My eyes wander over him again as he turns. Because *apparently,* they have a mind of their own today. I quickly look away.

Frustrated, Steven gets up and jogs over to the water's edge to stare at his reflection. I watch his concerned eyes grow wide as he gazes at the symbols embedded on his skin in a thick black font.

"You really didn't know that was there?" I ask quizzically, because *how could he not know?*

"No," he says, eyes furrowed as he continues staring at his reflection with an intense gaze.

"How is that possible? Did you have some sort of wild party or something back in the big city?" I tease, but then realize something. As well as I know him *now,* I have no idea who he was back in the real world. Maybe he is the type who parties and finds themselves out until all hours. Someone who comes home with new tattoos and no memory of how they got them.

"No, I didn't. I don't... do... *parties.* Ali," he says, his voice rough as he turns to look at me. "I've never seen this before in my life."

"Steven, tattoos don't just magically appear-" I start to say, but my voice cuts off at my own words. We stare at each other for a long moment, and I know we're both thinking the same thing.

Magic.

"Ali, do you think this could have appeared when I got here? I know for a fact that I didn't have a fucking tattoo back in the valley. We have *mirrors* there, I think I would have noticed. Or at least, someone would have," he considers, looking at his reflection again.

I vaguely wonder who else has a habit of seeing him with his shirt off... *Jesus, Ali. You're unbelievable,* I lecture.

"Here, let me see it," I say, standing and making my way over to him.

He turns his back to me, allowing me to get a better look and I have to take a moment to catch my breath. Because being this close to him is suddenly... unsettling.

Keep it together, Ali, I admonish. I reach my hand up hesitantly before giving in and reaching out to trace the symbols. As soon as I touch the intricate design, I feel a spark race through my fingertips and up my arm. Steven's body reacts as goosebumps spread like wildfire over his skin. Suddenly, my mind involuntarily wanders back to that first moment. The moment when I found him on the beach.

Steven, I need you with me. Are you with me?

I'm with you.

"What did you say?" Steven asks curiously.

"Um, I didn't say anything." *Did I?* I wonder, then shake my head to clear whatever the hell just came over me.

"Steven," I say, promptly backing away from him. "That's definitely a permanent tattoo."

"Seriously? What the fuck..." he wonders. "Did you get one when you got here?" he asks hopefully, trying to make sense of it.

"No," I laugh. "I think I would have noticed in the, what, seven months I've been here?"

"Well I've been here a month and neither of us noticed mine," he says plainly. He has a point. This is the first time he's taken his shirt off around me and there are no mirrors here.

Do I have one? I wonder, my panic rising. I take one long, concerned look at Steven, then quickly turn around, moving my thick hair over one shoulder and out of the way so he can check. His hands gently tugged at the neckline of my T-shirt, pulling it down just a little. The second I feel his fingers brush my skin, I freeze, feeling lightheaded.

"No fucking way," he whispers.

"What?" I say frantically, turning my neck to try and see.

"Ali," he starts to say, but I'm already standing over the water, lifting the bottom of my shirt to stare down at my reflection. "You have one too," he says quietly, but I barely hear him.

"I can't believe it," I gasp, staring at the writing that flows down my spine in the same way as Steven's. I stand perfectly still, my mind going fuzzy as I wonder if the words have always been there.

Or were always meant to be there.

"Wait a second... Steven! Turn around, let me see yours again," I say quickly, realizing something that I was too *distracted* to focus on the first time. He turns and I study the symbols down his back. Only, more clinical this time.

"Yours is different from mine... Steven, I recognize it! Yours is the same language from the books," I say excitedly, because this is something new. And new things just don't happen around here.

"Really?" he takes another look at his reflection. "Holy shit, you're right," he says, unbelievingly. "Here, let me see yours again," he grabs me by the shoulders and turns me around as I lift up the bottom of my shirt high enough for him to see my lower back.

Then I close my eyes and try desperately to ignore how strong and warm his hands feel on my upper arms.

"It's Demotic," he says excitedly.

"What the hell is that? Are you sure?" I say.

"Yeah, I'm sure. It's one of the languages used on the Rosetta Stone, the artifact that helped to translate Ancient Egyptian Hieroglyphs for the first time," he explains. I remember him telling me about the field trip he went on to that exhibit back at home. I wonder, not for the first time, if that strange experience was somehow connected to this world.

"So, now we have *two* languages that we can't read. *Great,*" I say hopelessly, lowering my shirt as I turn to face him.

"No. Ali," he says with a slow smile. I watch him curiously. "I can read it," he says.

I just stare at him. Then, gradually, I realize what this means.

"So... if our tattoos are the same..." I say slowly.

"Ali, it's the *key*."

Chapter 22

The key.

Can our tattoos really be the *key*? The one thing we need in order to translate the books? *Can this be how we get home?* I wonder.

As Steven and I stare at each other, I realize that I haven't felt anything even remotely resembling hope, since.... Well, since *he* got here.

And now we have *this.*

I can see the same flicker of excitement in Steven's eyes as he realizes what this could mean for us. After all, he's been stuck here long enough to know the hopelessness of our situation.

And then it starts to get dark.

"Ali?" he asks without even looking up to the sky.

"We can make it, but we have to run," I say, nodding toward the path back home.

Without skipping a beat, Steven grabs his shirt off the rock, throws it over his shoulder and is climbing up the cliff alongside me as we head toward the safety of the barrier.

Just as the sun makes its final descent behind the trees, Steven and I are stepping into the softly lit field below the house. Knowing that it's safe within the barricade of light, we both slow our pace to a casual walk.

When Steven first arrived, I wondered how he would adjust to this fast-paced world of magic and monsters. And now, it seems as natural as breathing to him.

Just like it is for me.

Once we are in the house, Steven makes his way through the living room and directly into the map room, quickly finding one of the homemade pencils and a piece of parchment. I watch him and smile, realizing how at home he is here.

Because it's his home too. I warm at the thought.

"Alright," he says, turning to me, "let's see if this is what we think it is." He hands me the pencil and parchment and pulls out one of the chairs, sitting in it backward. He still has his shirt off, giving me a clear view of his tattoo.

And of his ridiculously toned back.

Damn. Why does he have to be hot? This would be so much easier if...

"What?" Steven asks.

"Nothing," I say quickly.

Did I say that out loud? I wonder, but I'm one hundred percent sure that I didn't.

I blink, then examine the language once again. Pulling up my own chair, I begin to copy down the symbols, one by one. Once I'm finished, I study the parchment, making sure that I got all the dots, lines and strokes correct.

Not bad, I muse. It's been months since I drew anything and I'm secretly relieved that I haven't completely lost the ability.

"Let me see," Steven says, turning in his chair to face me as I hand him the paper. He stands, studying it, and I try desperately not to stare at him. Because he is still shirtless. And the way he *moves*... strong and confident and-

"Ali, this is great," he says, smiling at me. I blush, and not just because of the compliment.

"Your turn," he says, gesturing to the chair.

I stare at him, suddenly realizing what I have to do for him to see the *whole* thing.

"Um... here," he says, sensing my hesitation. Going over to the couch, he returns with a large fluffy pillow, which I take gratefully.

Cute, and a gentleman, I muse as he turns away from me, giving me the privacy to remove my shirt and settle in the chair, hugging my pillow. My back is mostly bare, aside from my bra strap, but I figure that he can see around it well enough. And there's no way in hell that I'm taking *that* off.

"Okay, ready," I say as steadily as I can manage. I take in one long breath and wait until I can hear him settle into the chair behind me, hear the pencil moving across the paper, before I let it out. I sit there, closing my eyes, and trying to focus on anything but the silence and my bare back between us. It could have easily been an hour later, or maybe only a few minutes, when Steven finally speaks up.

"Ali, I'm almost done, I just have to... um... I just have to move this a little," he says awkwardly. But before his warning fully sinks in, I feel his fingers gently brush my skin, pulling my bra strap down so he can see the symbols hiding beneath it.

I freeze, pulling in a sharp breath and holding it, annoyed that the chills running across my skin could betray me. I muse over my body's response and vaguely wonder about Steven's own reaction by the swimming hole. When I touched *his* tattoo, his bare skin. I quickly dispelled the thought.

As his warm fingers leave my back, I find that I'm as equally relieved as I am forlorn.

Get your shit together, Ali, I lecture.

"Okay, done," Steven manages to say, but without his usual confidence. He hands me my shirt from the table and turns away as I quickly put it back on, thankful that whatever *this* was, is over.

Sitting down at the table together, I realize that Steven has put his shirt back on too. Which, thankfully, gives me the freedom to breathe normally for the first time since he took it off. I've nearly forgotten the point of all of this, until Steven begins writing out the letters of the English alphabet on a new piece of parchment.

That's right, the key, I think. Then I force myself to focus on what Steven is *doing,* so that I will stop focusing on *him*. As he concentrates, filling in the symbols letter by letter to create his own sort of key, I realize that this project is going to take him a while. And I'm starving.

"Food?" I ask.

"God, yes. Thanks, Ali," he says softly, glancing up to me for a split second, just long enough to flash me that dimpled smile, before getting back to work.

Running up to the kitchen turns out to be a welcome distraction. I desperately need some time alone, time to think about everything. I start by talking myself down from being excited over the prospect of being able to translate the books. Because I have rules against optimism. As compelling as it all is, I refuse to let myself think that this could help us get home. Ever since I got here, any spark of hope has been immediately and *overwhelmingly* met with disappointment. And I am not about to open myself up to that.

Not again.

I also can't believe that I have a tattoo. Well, that *we* have tattoos.

Matching ones. I smile at that, but I'm not sure why. We didn't choose to have them.

As I mindlessly move the food around on the stove, I try to forget about how my *roommate* looks with his shirt off. Try to ignore the fact that the delicate line I have drawn between us being friends and how I actually feel, has been completely obliterated.

As it turns out, trying *not* to think about those things is impossible, so I'm grateful when the food is ready and I'm finally heading back downstairs with two wooden bowls in hand.

I find Steven still hunched over his project in the map room, his brows furrowed as he concentrates. I sit down beside him and as we eat, I watch anxiously as he continues to write down the corresponding Demotic symbols below the letters of our English alphabet, then crossing them out and moving them around when he realizes that it's wrong.

I watch the sun come up for the third time. I've been busying myself by reorganizing the maps. When that activity runs its course, I decide to start poking at the fire in the living room.

Steven leans back in his chair to stretch and looks over at me. The smile on his face tells me that he's made some sort of progress. My excitement brims as I make my way over to him. I lean over, staring at the page. I quickly notice that there are a few letters missing from the alphabet. A lot of letters, actually.

"What about the missing ones?" I ask, confused.

"Um, they don't exist. Or, if they do, I don't know them. The book I have back in the valley explains which symbols are *most* equal to the letters they correspond to in English, so we are just going to use what I can remember and go from there. If we can figure out most of it, hopefully we can just fill in the blanks," he says with a shrug, rubbing a hand over the back of his neck.

I look at the paper again.

"There aren't any vowels?" I notice immediately.

"No, there aren't. Ancient Egyptians didn't use vowels in hieroglyphs, Hieratic or Demotic scripts. I think that some consonants were assigned to act as vowels, but I don't really remember. I just hope that we can match up enough of it..." his voice trails off as he studies it again.

I hope so too.

Using the English to Demotic key that he just created, Steven begins translating our tattoos, symbol by symbol. I watch eagerly. If he can translate what is now permanently affixed to my body, and his tattoo is the same, then we can create a new key.

One that will translate the shelves of books surrounding us.

Again, I quickly remind myself of the futility of hope.

Why Steven decided to learn how to translate ancient languages is beyond me. I stare at him curiously, because I thought I knew everything about him. *What else don't I know?* I wonder.

I continue to watch with fascination as he jumps around the script, filling in letter after letter. Watching him think and write should bore me to death. But I'm on the edge of my seat. I have to know what our tattoos say. This could be the key to figuring out everything. How we got here, why we're here and most importantly, how to get home.

Suddenly, Steven sits back, glaring at the page with furrowed eyebrows. I lean over him, studying the letters closer. We knew that there wouldn't be any vowels, but *jeez*. I thought I knew my own language well enough that I could figure it out without them, but nothing seems to make sense. I look over at Steven, who is unconsciously chewing on the end of his pencil looking just as confused as I am.

For the next fifteen minutes, we systematically go through every possible combination of vowels and consonants, until there is a heaping pile of crumpled papers scattering the table in front of us.

"This isn't getting us anywhere," I say, defeated.

"It just doesn't make any sense," he mumbles.

"Are you sure you translated it right?" I offer, not sure where to go from here. He gets up from the table and starts pacing the room, his hands clasped behind his head, like they always are when he's frustrated.

"No, of course I'm not sure. I just thought I could remember it," he huffs, upset with himself.

"Are you sure it's in the right order?" I ask.

"Ali, what are you talking about?" he says, not slowing his pacing.

"Well, aren't some languages written backward? Like, from right to left, or bottom to top?"

He stops immediately and stares at me.

"Ali, you're a genius!" he says, rushing over to the table and scribbling frantically on the paper, reversing the order. I sit beside him and watch intently.

He looks up at me and I smile widely back. Then, without warning, Steven is on his feet, dragging me up with him. His arms wrap around me, cutting off all circulation. I try to laugh, but it comes out more of a wheeze.

He did it.

"*We* did it," he says, holding me at arms-length and giving me another broad smile before letting me go and easily filling in the missing pieces.

SOUL BELONGING TO TWO WORLDS

I just stare at the parchment, wondering how one simple phrase can mean so much.

The fact that those particular words are permanently a part of me, makes me realize something. Whatever the reason for us being lost here, wherever *here* is, suddenly, one thing is clear.

We *belong* here.

Chapter 23

It's always been difficult to calculate time in this place. But now that we aren't sleeping, it's been next to impossible. It could have been two weeks, or maybe even three since Steven deciphered our tattoos and created the key for translating the books. Since then, we haven't had any more than two or three hours of sleep at a time.

The key is simple enough to follow, sure, but taking the time to translate every word has been nothing less than time consuming. Day after day, we rush through training and our chores, then sit right back down at the large table in the map room to translate the books until we can't stay awake anymore. Then, we force ourselves to get a few hours of sleep and do it all over again.

We started translating the big book upstairs, which turned out to be extremely helpful. There are so many more things we can make now that we know which items to combine and what pages to use. But as eager as we are to translate the whole thing, it's a daunting project. After some simple math, we realized that to translate the whole thing would take months. And because the big book doesn't seem to contain anything even alluding to a way out, Steven and I decided to spend our time translating the books downstairs in the hope to find something, anything, that will help us get back.

I lean back in my chair and look around the map room. It's an absolute disaster. Steven and I pulled all the books off their shelves and they are now stacked all over. On the table, the chairs, and every other available surface in sight as we systematically go through and attempt to organize them.

We quickly realized that the first few pages gave us a pretty good idea of what the book was going to be about, so we have since narrowed down our translations to only that, categorizing them into sections and piles to go back through later.

But even just *that* has been nauseating.

I've threatened to throw myself off the balcony on more than one occasion. But Steven reasoned that the walk back would be counterproductive.

So far, we have several categories figured out. There are books on herbology, astronomy, cartography, as well as weapons and potions. All of the books seem to be lessons or accounts of how to survive out here. They're all fascinating, especially the ones on herbology, and I can't wait to translate more of them. But the one subject that we haven't come across yet, is the "how to get the hell out of here" category.

Even though Steven and I have spent every waking moment we could spare over the past few weeks translating the books, all we've come up with is a whole lot of *nothing*.

I pull my focus back to where I'm sitting at the table, at the books piled high all around me. I stare down at the page until the handwriting becomes blurred. Exhausted, I rest my cheek on the table, pencil still in hand, and close my eyes for just a moment.

I feel like I am on a boat, the motion of it rocking me deeper and deeper into a state of unconsciousness. I am drifting, floating, and at peace.

I slowly open my eyes, blinking until the world comes into focus.

My world.

A sudden warmth floods my entire body, because he is holding me.

Why are you holding me? I think, trying to pull myself from my groggy state.

"*Shh*, it's okay Ali, I've got you. Just sleep," he whispers. His strong, deep voice is soft and it makes me want to fall back into my dreamworld. But I can't take my eyes off him.

Not when he's holding me in his arms.

I study his face. He has stubble lining his jaw. I want to reach up and touch it, but I can't seem to move my arms. Overcome by exhaustion, I'm barely even aware that he's carried me down the hall and to my bedroom. He gently lowers me onto the bed, covering me with a pile of soft blankets. I sink deeply into the feather mattress, surrounded by its warmth.

"Good night, Ali," I hear him whisper as I drift away, back into a cloud of sleep.

I know I'm dreaming, I always do. It's never an actual *dream* per say, but a memory. A nightmare of a memory. The same memory that I've already experienced a thousand times before.

I'm running through the halls of the dark fortress, checking every corner before turning down another endless corridor. I have my sword, but that won't help me here.

Nothing can help me here.

I'm on the rooftop now, running along one of the walls, but I know it's already too late. It's always too late. I'm not getting out this time.

No one can help me here.

Then I turn around, and see him. Those normally deep blue eyes, with their shades of purple dancing around the edges are now only one color. The crimson hue that permeates the air causing one vibrant shade of purple. The light behind them shines through the dark.

He's afraid. Not for himself, no, but for me. I don't know how I know that, but I do. I want to go to him. I know I will never make it, but I have to try.

I run across the top of the long wall, but then I hear it.

The explosion.

It tears apart the ground and I shield my face with my arms, falling backward onto the hard, hot stone. Lowering my arms, I see him through the dust and the falling rubble.

He's looking at me, terrified for me.

I get to my feet and try to run, but it's no use. The ground falls out from under me. As I fall, all I can hear is my name shouted desperately from his lips.

I call out for him too, but he can't hear me.

No one can hear me here.

I watch as shards of stone fall alongside me. I look up toward the ledge, seeing it become further and further away, and know that I will never see him again. He's gone.

I'm gone.

I feel the heat, the unbearable temperature, surrounding my entire body, filling my lungs and growing hotter. Everything is brighter as I fall closer and I can feel it *burning*. I raise my arms in front of my face, squinting in the light to see them. Then I watch in horror as my skin turns a deep red, then boils, until it is peeling from my bones. I try to scream, but I can't as molten liquid fills my lungs.

Then, everything stops.

I shoot up in bed with a gasp.

I'm sweating and my heart is threatening to pound out of my chest. And then I see them. *Those eyes*. Those deep blue eyes barely have any trace of that purple left, letting me know where I am. I'm here, not *there*. I'm with him, looking into eyes that are sad and scared and... *relieved*.

"Steven," I breathe. He's here, in my room. My body is still shaking violently, not just from the horrible death, but from the memory of leaving him there, in *that place*.

Of losing him.

"Hey," he says softly, more than used to my wakeful nights at this point. "I um, I couldn't sleep either. I hope this is okay?" he says sheepishly. Looking over, I realize that he's dragged his entire mattress into my room.

I smile as he places it on the floor beside my bed.

"Of course," I whisper back, and wonder why we hadn't thought of this sooner.

I lay back down, overwhelmed by emotions and relieved by the realization that I haven't lost him. He's right here with me.

We're safe.

I look over the side of my bed just as Steven is tucking himself into his own blankets and I notice that he's sweating too. Living in the side of a cliff means that the temperature stays cool at best. Which makes me wonder... *Did he have a nightmare too?*

"Are you okay?" I ask softly, my voice still shaky from the dream. He looks up at me and his sad eyes and sweet smile hit my soul.

"I am now," he whispers, his eyes lingering on mine for a long moment.

And then he rolls over and falls asleep.

I wake up groggy and every muscle in my body aches. I look over the side of my bed and see that Steven's makeshift bed is still right there on the floor.

I didn't imagine it, I smile.

There's no denying that I sleep better when he's around and so I hope he will leave his mattress in here again tonight.

As soon as I step out into the hallway I no longer have to wonder where

Steven ran off too, because the smell of something amazing is wafting down from upstairs.

When I walk into the kitchen, Steven is just dishing up the second plate. Each one is piled high with eggs, bacon and topped with a slice of toast. He's made me breakfast plenty of times before, but I'm still trying to get used to it. After living alone for so long, it's kind of nice to have someone taking care of me, even if it's only for breakfast and nightmares.

"Good morning," he says with a bright, dimpled smile.

God, he's attractive, I think for the hundredth time.

"Morning," I say, rubbing my eyes once again.

"So," he says, setting a plate in front of me. "I think we need to take a break from staring at those goddamn books, what do you think?"

I think back to the night before... me falling asleep at the table, him carrying me to bed, my nightmare, him sleeping on my floor...

"Yeah," I chuckle. "I think we could definitely use a break," I say, digging into the gourmet dish in front of me.

"I was thinking," he says warily. "What if we hit the next section of your maps? I know it's dangerous out there, but... I think that I might *actually* go insane if I stay in this house for another minute. And I swear, if I have to look at one more book," he says dramatically, stabbing something on his plate with a little more aggression than necessary.

"I know what you mean," I laugh, recalling a memory. "When I first got here, I stayed cooped up for god knows how long, too terrified to go out there. But once I started talking to myself, out loud and in the third person, I decided it was time to figure out how to defend myself," I say, shoving half a piece of toast in my mouth.

"Wait, you're telling me that you don't currently talk to yourself, out loud and in the third person?" he teases. I give him a pointed look and a feign aggravated grin as I chew my food. It wasn't easy adjusting to the fact that I have *company* and I definitely slip back into my old habits now and then.

And Steven just loves to remind me about it.

We haven't really talked about my first days here, but after realizing that Steven's dreams back home were somehow *real*, I didn't feel like we needed to. Him seeing some of the things I went through firsthand is enough. And some things, well, I'm just not ready to talk about. And he hasn't asked me to.

"Okay," Steven says when we finish eating. "Ready to go?"

"Huh?" I say, confused. "Go where?"

"*Out*," he says. I just stare at him.

He's serious.

"You want to go, *now*?" I ask, bewildered. Personally, I don't care when we go, it's just *business as usual* for me, but I'm surprised at how quickly he made up his mind about this. Because he's right, it's dangerous out there.

More than he knows, I think.

"Yup," he says confidently. I give him a wary look, but eventually give in with a shrug.

"Alright. Well I guess we have some bags to pack."

After spending a few hours gathering anything and everything we could possibly need for the trip, Steven and I stand in the armory, backpacks packed.

I pull my sword and sheath from the wall and watch as Steven grabs his own. He spent hours in here making that sword and, I have to admit, he's getting pretty good with it. We've only practiced together with the wooden swords, but a few weeks back, Steven managed to drag an entire *log* all the way up to the fourth floor. Then, he somehow secured it upright in the middle of the room and has been hacking away at it ever since.

And I find the pleasure he gets from destroying it endlessly amusing.

I watch Steven secure his sword at his side and I do the same. There's no need for me to grab a dagger, because there's already one in my boot.

Like there always is.

I follow Steven out of the room and silently wonder how this is going to go. Sure, I've told him as much as I possibly can, but some things can't be explained. Not until you're out there. He has no idea what he's getting himself into and there's nothing more I can do to prepare him.

But I guess he will figure that out soon enough.

I've gone on map runs and explored new areas of this world all on my own countless times before, but somehow, this time feels different. Even though Steven and I have been training, and I know undoubtedly that he can take care of himself out there, I still feel some sort of responsibility for him. We just don't know for certain if he will come back after he dies and the thought of losing him, *really* losing him...

I can't even think about it.

I knew the day would come when we would have to leave the house. But as excited as I am to be getting a change of scenery, I still have this undeniable feeling of uneasiness. Even though the area we are heading to looks easy enough on the map, it isn't a section I've explored before. And if past experiences have taught me anything, it's that every new area comes with its own new variety of horrors.

Who knows what we could be walking into.

After spending days pouring over the maps, Steven and I decided on a section that's mostly flat. There's only one small part of it that will take us up a mountain. We can't tell how steep of a climb it will be, or how rough the terrain, but my hope is that our first trip will be a relatively easy one.

Yeah right, I shake my head. I've set out for areas before thinking that they would be a walk in the park, but once I was actually out there... they turned out to be a living hell. The truth is that I have no idea what to expect, so I have no idea what to warn him about. I told him as much in an attempt to talk him out of this little excursion, but he hadn't gone for it.

And so here we are, standing by the front door.

I look over at him again and ask the same question I've already asked a dozen times before.

"Are you sure you're ready for this? Because we can-"

"Ali, I'm ready. I can't just stay inside forever, so we might as well check off another area on the map," he says.

"Alight," I say, giving in for the last time. "While we're out there, keep your eyes peeled not only for creatures, but for anything out of the ordinary. Any structures, holes in the ground, weird looking trees, mineshafts, anything that might lead us to another portal. And at the very least, maybe we'll find another clue to who was here before us, maybe another book."

"Oh boy, another book," Steven says dryly.

I look up at him, shaking my head at his sarcasm. But I don't blame him. I've seriously considered lighting the whole bookshelf on fire.

And then I notice something, *did he shave?* The stubble that I saw last night is completely gone, and I actually find myself a little sad. Even in my groggy state, I remember that I liked it.

"What?" Steven asks, looking down at me quizzically.

"Um, nothing. You sure about this?" I quickly mutter, changing the subject.

After one more gigantic eye roll and an exasperated breath, he strides out the front door. I stare after him sorrowfully, taking in my own deep breath. Because he has no idea what we are in for.

But I do.

Chapter 24

Holding up the map in one hand, I rest the other on the hilt of my sword as Steven and I run side by side along the coast heading up-shore. We're already long past the trapdoor entrance that leads out to the island and keeping a good pace.

The area we are planning to explore is two maps out from the island, which means that based on how far we've already gone, we could reach the new section in a little less than an hour, assuming that we stop each night.

And we are absolutely stopping at night.

Before Steven arrived, I already had mapped out the connecting areas, so I know this terrain well enough. I've even marked on the maps all the places that we can hide.

As the sun sets, Steven and I duck into a small lean-to shelter, one that I built ages ago. It's made out of nothing more than a few driftwood sticks leaning up against a crudely built A-frame.

I honestly can't believe it's still standing.

After draping a blanket over the entrance, we hurry inside. I light the lantern that I have strapped to my pack, setting it in the sand between us as we hide from the night. Steven and I sit close together, whispering quietly and using our sleeves to muffle our laughter as the sounds of creatures resound around us outside.

Before I know it, the sun is already rising.

Several nighttime cycles later, we're walking through a meadow of thick grass, heading away from the ocean and moving inland. As we walk, I think about how different this trip has been from the previous ones.

The ones I ran alone.

Back then, sitting around for ten minutes felt like an eternity. I sat in silence, with nothing to do but listen to the sounds of the night and pray that nothing would find me. But this time, with Steven, the time flies by like it's nothing. Even after spending every second together over the past two months or so, we still, somehow, haven't run out of things to say to each other. I find myself smiling more than I ever have before. More than I did even before this place.

I know that Steven is aware of the dangers out here. And I know that he's more terrified than he lets on, but so far, he's been calm, collected, and has stayed alert. He's even managed to crack as many jokes as I do. I'm more than a little impressed by him.

I always am.

As we approach the beginning of our designated section, I smile, realizing that we've made good time. But *now* is what I was worried about. I don't know the terrain here, or what dangers it holds. There are no pre-made hideaways and no telling what lies ahead.

I look up from the map and notice that Steven is close behind me, reading over my shoulder. He gives me a look, confirming that he also realizes where we are.

"Okay, this is it," I say, starting to move again. "We have to find or build a place to hide. And we only have," I look down at my watch, "nine minutes."

"Got it, let's go," he says affirmatively, but I can hear the hint of nervousness in his voice. And he should be nervous. Because nine minutes isn't a lot of time.

Not out here.

As we move forward, I look around, trying to get a lay of the land we're about to explore. But the thick forest of pine trees and oak isn't doing us any favors. There's a gentle breeze that rolls through the trees, making the leaves flutter. Tiny white flowers nestle in the grass here and there and it makes the forest look peaceful.

But I know better.

As we trudge deeper into the woods, the grass turns to a thick underbrush that tugs at our clothes as we struggle through it. I keep my head up, scanning the area constantly, searching for anywhere we can hide.

The clock in the back of my mind begins to tick faster.

Tick, tick, tick.

We've been running for a solid five minutes and as the flat ground slowly starts to incline, so does my panic. I don't care if I die. Sure, it would be a long and inconvenient walk back here, *but Steven...* I worry at my bottom lip as I search the woods. As the trees begin to break, I can see the mountain beyond, stretching up into the sky. It isn't as tall, or as harsh, as the cliffs back home, but it's still going to be a hell of a hike.

If we make it that far, I think, and the hopelessness of not finding a shelter by now starts creeping in. I look at my watch again. We have to find somewhere to hide.

And then I see it.

A large pine tree has fallen, taking two more down with it. The larger landing on top of the others in such a way that its trunk is suspended at an angle. Its branches curve down to meet the ground, creating a large hidden area beneath it. I look back at Steven and he smiles, seeing it too.

"Grab your torches, we need to make a perimeter," I say, dropping my pack to the ground and reaching for my own stash. "An arrow will go right through those branches if they see us, so we need to make the area large enough to keep them back," I direct.

I tuck a pile of torches under one arm and crouch down, scraping one against a nearby rock. Sparks fly out from the end for just a few seconds, before it settles into a flickering glow. I walk over to Steven, holding the torch up to one of his until it ignites.

"Head left and space them out, same as mine," I say, already stabbing the first one into the soft ground, then using it to light the next. Steven gives me a quick nod and moves in the opposite direction, placing his first torch. We create a large circle around the fallen trees, meeting up on the other side, then make our way back to where we left our packs just as the twilight begins creeping through the forest. The light cast from the torches slowly illuminates the entire area, glowing brighter as the sun goes down. I look around, trying to find any gaps in light, but I don't see any.

"Hey," I say, looking over at Steven. "Nicely done."

"Thanks," he smiles.

I take another deep breath, because this was a close call. *Too close.* The woods here aren't like the ones back by the house. On the trails by the cliffs, you can run through the darkness for several minutes before the creatures catch up with you. Out here however... we wouldn't have lasted more than a few seconds.

Steven holds back the branches of the fallen tree and we duck into our newest hideaway. Once inside, the ground slopes down enough that even Steven is able to stand up straight in some spots. And between the light barrier and the surrounding tree branches, we're completely hidden from the outside world. He pulls out his sword, then hacks off a few branches, tossing them aside. And after a few of our previous hiding places, I'm grateful for the extra space. Especially since we will most likely be staying here for several daylight cycles. Because of its central location, we should be able to search most of this section without having to find a new place to hide.

Lighting the lantern, I hang it from an overhead branch and sit down, allowing myself to relax for the first time.

And then the sounds start outside.

Twigs snap all around us and the growls, hisses and clattering seem to come from everywhere all at once. I can hear that the light barricade is working, because none of them are any closer than the perimeter, but when I look over at Steven, I have to hold back a chuckle.

He looks petrified.

The trees are thicker out here, which means the night is darker. And the noises are louder. Out here, there are simply more of them.

A *lot* more.

That first time down at the swimming hole, the number of creatures lurking in the dark was in the twenties. Out here, it's in the hundreds.

"Hey," I say calmly to Steven when I realize what he's doing. "Counting them won't help right now, it will only freak you out. We're safe here."

Although I can see him physically relax, I can tell his mind is somewhere else.

"Ali, how the hell did you survive out here?" he says softly, but it isn't a question. It feels more like a complement, shrouded in bewilderment and a tinge of sorrow. I take my time before responding.

"You know that I didn't," I reply quietly and can't make myself meet his eyes. It isn't something that I want to admit, but I can't let him underestimate how dangerous it is out here. Secretly, I want him scared.

Because I need him safe.

I can feel Steven's eyes on me as he thinks about that, but he doesn't say anything else. And so we sit in silence until the noises start to die down and the soft rays of morning light begin to reach through the branches.

"Okay, you ready?" I ask, noticing that in the ten minutes we had to sit here, his attitude has completely changed. There's no trace of fear left in his eyes, only cold determination.

"Let's go," he says confidently.

Leaving our bags where they are, we grab our swords and the map, then head off to explore the region around us.

Holding the pencil between my teeth, I stare at the map and at all the markings on it. We have systematically checked every square inch of this section.

Everywhere, except the mountain.

I lost count of how many night cycles we've spent in our little hole beneath the tree. But after looking over at Steven, I realize that it's time for a break. The thick undergrowth between the densely crowded forest has made searching the area take longer than it should have. And I am beyond frustrated.

Because we haven't found a single thing.

No portals, no maps or books and no sign of human life whatsoever. We're both discouraged, dirty, exhausted, and this has been a complete waste of time. *Again.*

"Dammit," I say, kicking a pinecone hard enough to send it flying as Steven and I make our way back to the hollow under the tree. I don't know why I still let it upset me, but it does. After searching as many sections as I have, you would think I'd be used to the disappointment. But I'm not. This has been just as unbearably infuriating as every time before.

I shove the branches aside and duck inside, plopping down on the blanket with an exasperated sigh. Steven follows, sitting down beside me.

"We should go back, there's nothing here. There's *never* anything out here," I say disparagingly.

"We still have the mountain, there could be something up there?" Steven says hopefully, but I don't believe his attempt at optimism. He's just as worn out from stomping through this forest as I am.

"No, it's too dangerous. We would barely have enough time to hike it, let alone find a shelter in time. If we can't find a place to hide, we wouldn't have enough time to get back down here before nightfall. So, no. We're not going. We're going back," I say definitively.

"Ali, we made it all the way here, we can't just leave this section unfinished. Let's just try," he looks straight at me. "Please, we have to try."

I turn to tell him that it's not happening, but when I meet his eyes, I understand. He needs to see if there is anything out here. Just like I did on my first few map runs. He needs to know, and to give up now would haunt him. I swallow my frustration. After seeing those eyes so full of waning hope, how can I say no?

"Okay, fine. But we are going to *sprint.* If we don't find a place to hide immediately, we're heading straight back down here and going home. Deal?"

"Deal," he says with that slow crooked smile. He's all weary and optimistic, and incredibly gorgeous, even in his disheveled state. And that's when I know it.

This man is going to be the death of me.

Chapter 25

I open my eyes and I'm immediately aware that Steven's back is pressed up against mine. I blink, staring at the wall of tree branches in front of me.

Oh, right, I think, the memories coming back as I realize that we're still in our little hiding place in the woods. I know I didn't start the evening off this close to him, but I'm not about to complain. Sometime after we fell asleep, it got *cold.* I think about shifting away from him, but he's all warm snuggled up against me and I'm reluctant to pull away. Normally, I would have just built a fire. But considering that we're sleeping in a tinderbox, it didn't seem like the greatest of ideas. So I hug the blanket closer, lean into the man behind me, and try to fall back asleep.

Just as I'm beginning to drift, I feel Steven stir. Feel the muscles in his back flex as he stretches. Then I feel him tense, his body going rigid, presumably noticing our proximity. He sits up quickly and I immediately miss his warmth.

I also feel a little... heartbroken.

Is touching me really that terrible? I wonder, secretly wishing that we could stay here, back-to-back, safe and warm. Instead of what we are about to do.

Because today, we're going to hike a mountain.

Fantastic, I think sarcastically, dragging myself up to a sitting position. By the time I am upright, Steven is already gone. I can hear him building a fire in the clearing outside the shelter and, as I watch him through the branches, I consider, not for the first time on this little outing, that he's avoiding me.

When he decides to spend the whole ten minutes working on that fire, only coming back in once the sun is completely down, it has me thinking that maybe I'm right.

Even though I'm impressed that he was able to get the fire started so quickly using only the flint and my dagger, he knows as well as I do that a fire is completely unnecessary when we will be leaving soon. Which means yes, he's definitely avoiding me.

Several minutes later, I watch him reorganize his pack for the *third* time.

Okay, something is definitely bothering him, I decide. Then wonder what I'm supposed to do with that information.

After we eat, Steven puts out the fire as I re-pack my own bag. He's barely said a word all morning and when he comes back inside, he quickly puts on his pack and then stands restlessly beside me.

Well, not *beside* me, I realize.

He's as far away as the tiny shelter can accommodate. I feel that pang of sadness once again.

I check my watch and can't believe he talked me into this. Sure, the mountain looks fine from down here, but I have no doubts that the climb will be brutal, even with all our training.

As I mentally prepare myself for the journey, I realize that I am going to have to keep track of time down to the second. If we don't find shelter within the first seven minutes, max, then we are heading right back down. I would rather face a minute or two of the creatures down here, where we have some place to run to, than face them on the mountain with nowhere to go. I shiver at the thought, hoping it won't come down to either one of those scenarios.

As my watch ticks toward daylight, I give Steven a quick nod. We run from our shelter, swords drawn. Hopping over logs and slashing through shrubs, we quickly make our way through the trees, until they open up to a wide view of the mountain.

The grassy slope quickly turns to loose slate and a wary feeling creeps over my skin as we start the climb. Between the loose gravel rocks and the crumbling slate, the path is slippery and difficult to climb. My palms are already hatched with deep cuts from catching my own near falls, as are Steven's, but we continue on.

I check my watch again.

Six minutes. Shit, I think. I continue scanning the terrain, looking for anywhere that we can hide. There are a few rocky outcrops that look like they could have a cave, or some type of shelter, but they are still far up ahead. Glancing back down the hill, I suddenly realize that the slate will make it next to impossible to run back down without slipping.

My stomach drops. Because we don't have a choice anymore. We have to move forward. I look toward the rocks up ahead.

It's too far, I realize with horror.

"We need to move faster!" I shout back toward Steven and we both pick up the pace. I pull a torch from the side pocket of my pack and light it on a passing rock.

I curse under my breath at how stupid I am to let this happen.

As the darkness begins to close in, so do the sounds. When I start hearing arrows hitting near our feet and the hillside beside us, I urge myself to move a little *faster*, but not so much that I leave Steven behind.

Then suddenly, the light is gone.

I can no longer see the rocks we are heading toward, no longer see beyond the glow of the torch. But I just kept moving, trusting that I can keep our heading.

"Steven, draw your sword," I say quietly, doing the same. I can hear them getting closer, the gravel disrupted under their feet.

Finally, the rocks come into view. We run alongside them, waving our torches into every crevice, searching for a place large enough to hide in.

"Ali! Over here!" Steven whispers from nearby. When I run to his side, I see that he's found a narrow space between two rocks, one that's wide enough we may be able to squeeze through.

"Here," I say, handing him my torch. He throws it into the gap and we both watch as its glow illuminates a hidden cave in the hillside.

"Thank fuck," Steven mutters. Then he quickly begins lighting more torches, surrounding the entrance with their light just as the low growls of creatures come rumbling out from the dark nearby.

Steven stands watch outside, sword in hand, as I quickly toss my backpack inside, turning sideways to follow after it, sword first. If there is some creature hidden inside, then I'll be ready for it.

After a quick but thorough look around, I call back out for Steven, satisfied that we will be the cave's only occupants. I step aside as his backpack is thrown through the narrow opening, followed by Steven, who is out of breath and a little shaken.

The cave opens up into an area that is about three times the size of our last hiding place. Which I figure will come as a welcome relief for Steven. Since he clearly doesn't want to be anywhere near me at the moment.

He waves a torch around and then settles his eyes on me.

"Alright, look at this," he admires and I glare at him.

"Yeah, it's great, but that was cutting it a little close, don't ya think?" I lecture.

"But we made it," he says with a shrug, smiling.

"That giddy expression that's all over your face, that's called adrenaline and it happens when you talk me into doing something incredibly stupid."

"Yeah, this was incredibly stupid. Why didn't you talk me out of it?" he snarks back.

"You're unbelievable. Next time, I'm using you as bait," I huff. Sliding my sword back into its sheath, I sit down and wait for daylight.

With every daylight cycle, I become more and more frustrated. The hillside is slippery and hard to climb, so our search is turning out to be even more infuriating than the last one. All we've ended up with so far is more scrapes and more bruises. And just because they heal quickly, doesn't mean I enjoy getting them.

Not only that, but it's starting to get colder.

Every time the sun goes down, we are forced back to the shelter of our cave where we shiver in silence.

Then we do it all over again the next day.

After god knows how many daylight cycles or how many hours we've been searching, Steven and I finally make it to the last area at the top of the mountain.

We look around the sprawling view of landscape before us. Pulling out my spyglass, I look beyond what my eyes can see, but find nothing more than an endless world of wilderness.

Just like I always do.

I look over to see Steven standing there. See the expression on his face. As much as he's tried up until this point, there's clearly no hiding his discouragement anymore. It's one thing to tell him that there's nothing out here, but now that he's seen it for himself, he's finally starting to believe it.

I step over to stand beside him. We're at the end of our search, staring out over a world as empty as our hope.

"I don't think I really believed you when you said that there wasn't anything out here. I thought if we walked far enough, or looked hard enough, that there would be something. *Anything*," he says thoughtfully.

"I know. That's what I keep thinking too. It's why I keep coming out here. But this clearly isn't getting us anywhere. There has to be something back at home, something we're missing. We didn't end up with matching tattoos for no reason," I muse.

"Yeah, you're right. I'm ready to get back," he says, standing to his feet.

"Me too," I say. The longer we're out here, the more I miss our life back at home. Because with him, that's what it's become.

A home.

I miss laughing with him, training with him, and I miss the quiet moments in front of the fire when neither of us can sleep. Being out here, we have to be on our guard at all times. There's no time for quiet moments. Out here, we just have to survive.

As we start our trek back down the mountain to the cave, Steven and I stop dead in our tracks.

Because it's getting dark.

"Um, Ali, how long have we been up here?" Steven asks, panicked. It's a four-minute run back down to the cave and I thought we timed it perfectly.

"Not long enough for it to be dark," I say. I look at my watch, confused. And then I look up at the sky. "Dammit! It's the clouds. Looks like a storm is coming," I say.

"Ali," he looks at me, frantic. "Please tell me the creatures only come out at night..."

"No. They come out whenever the sun is gone," I meet his terrified gaze and we take off running across the top of the mountain.

Chapter 26

The darkness comes on so quickly, we don't even have time for our eyes to adjust. I light a torch as we run, but it's short lived. A second later, the rain comes down to extinguish it, along with our hopes of getting back.

The wind is blowing the rain sideways, hitting us with such force that it's difficult to stay upright. Steven and I stay close, not wanting to lose sight of each other. Swords drawn, we practically slide down the mountain, until the ground levels out and we make our way along the path that leads horizontally across the mountain toward our cave. The heavy rain drowns out all sounds, which means that even though the creatures can't hear us, we can't hear them either. I don't like not knowing what's lurking in the dark ahead.

"Keep your head up and keep moving!" I shout toward Steven.

"Okay," he calls out, not taking his eyes off the darkness as we move quickly along the path.

Minutes later, I realize that I can hear my own footsteps. I immediately stop, looking around warily. The sun must have actually gone down by now, because the darkness is all consuming, leaving us in a world of shadows and silence. It's eerily quiet and it takes me a moment to understand why. A chill runs up my spine as I realize that the harsh rainfall is turning to snow. The thick white flakes are falling with a type of delicacy that is unfitting for the cruel darkness surrounding them.

And then we can hear them. *Dozens* of them.

They're all around us.

I hear a *whoosh* and grab Steven's arm, pulling him to the ground. The arrow lands in the hillside next to us and I see Steven's eyes widen.

That was a close one.

We pick ourselves up and keep moving, staying low and staying quiet. As the trail narrows, it forces us to walk one in front of the other instead of side by side. I follow behind Steven, letting him lead as I keep an eye on the path behind us, the hillside on our left and the cliffs to our right. Knowing that they can come from anywhere.

The sound of arrows piercing the night air begins again, rapidly increasing. I'm so focused on pinpointing where the creatures are at, I don't even notice that Steven has stopped.

Until I run into him.

"Ali... what the hell is that thing?" he whispers, eyes fixed on the path ahead. I grab his arm and lean to look past him. I can barely make out the figure through the darkness, but I don't need to see it.

I know what they look like.

The creature could have once been a man, but there's nothing human about it anymore. Unlike some of the other monsters who are solid muscle and decaying flesh, these look like they have starved themselves until there is nothing left.

As I look closer, the one standing in front of us now is no exception. Its rib cage is clearly visible and several broken bones are protruding out at unnatural angles. Its bony fingers are horrifyingly long, the lack of skin elongating them as they wrap around the bow held at its side. It cocks its head like a bird, listening for any signs of movement. And even with its acute hunch, it's still taller than Steven.

The white of its skull can clearly be seen through the thin layer of skin that's stretched tightly over it and there are holes where its eyes may once have been. I know it can't see us, know that it can only hear us, but that doesn't stop the shiver from running up my spine when it suddenly fixes those empty sockets straight toward us, sensing our presence.

Still leaning around Steven's shoulder, I look up at him, putting one finger over my mouth, silently telling him to keep quiet. I bend down slowly and pick up a rock, my eyes never leaving the creature. If it hears us, we're done for.

The creature cocks its head again, listening in a different direction. I freeze.

Despite its decrepit form and hunched shoulders, it can move quickly. And it would be deadly accurate with that bow from this close range.

I slowly recoil my arm and throw the rock down the hillside, away from our path. I hear the sound of stone hitting stone and watch as the creature immediately turns toward it, twitching its head to the side to listen again.

Suddenly, the skeletal creature pulls the bow over its head, securing it to its back. When it moves, the sounds of bones rubbing together and the cracking of joints make my skin crawl. It leans down until it's on all fours, twitching its head frantically. And then it crawls down the mountain so quickly that the white of it blurs into the darkness, disappearing in less than a second.

I feel Steven start to move, but I grab his arm, signaling for him to wait. A moment later, at least fifteen more of the creatures crawl down from the hillside to our left and across our path, continuing on toward the sound. Their heads twitch sickly back and forth, listening to the movements of the others and listening for *us*.

After they're out of sight, I wait another moment just to be sure, then step in front of Steven. I move forward slowly along the path, my sword out in front of me. Steven walks close enough behind me that I can tell he's shaking. But all things considered, I think he's holding it together pretty well.

Finally, I can see the cave up ahead, the moon and the snow highlighting the edges of the rocks in the darkness. But I also see something else.

There's something in our way.

Just outside the entrance to the cave, the tall muscular figure turns toward us, its shoulders hunched. I can tell by the malice in its eyes that it's seen us. Even if we can outrun it, which we can't, *not on this hillside*, there's simply nowhere else to go.

We need to get into that cave.

I look back toward Steven and he understands. He gives me a quick confirming nod and we're moving.

I run straight at the creature and Steven draws his sword, staying a few paces behind, just like we trained to do. The creature runs toward me and I use its own momentum to shove my sword into its chest. It grabs at me with long arms, but I use my leg to shove it off my sword, causing it to lose its balance, falling backward down the hillside. Just as it disappears into the dark, its growls growing distant with its descent, I hear the sounds of three more coming from the darkness. Two stumble down from the hillside, landing on the path between us and the cave.

Great, I think. Not only am I soaking wet from the rain and cold from the snow, but now I'm also annoyed.

I quickly sprint up the hill to my left, gripping my sword with both hands. I jump on top of the first creature's back, burying the blade straight down into its neck, all the way to the hilt. It screams, a deafening sound that leaves my ears ringing.

The second one starts after me. I let go of my sword, dropping the distance to the ground and landing in a crouch. I pull the dagger from my boot and, as I stand, jam it into the creature's stomach, slicing upwards. I jump backward as its innards spill out onto the path at my feet and shake the dark blood off my dagger.

The creature that's been twitching on the ground behind me, my sword still in its neck, finally stops screeching and its body stills. It quickly turns to ash, blending into the fallen snow surrounding it.

I pick up my blade, then turn back to the creature that's hunched over, clutching its stomach. It moans stridently, until I chop its head off.

It disintegrates immediately.

Where's the third? I think, because I could have sworn I heard another. But there's nothing now. Only the eerie silence of snow as it falls around me.

As I turn back toward Steven, I find him standing on the path, looking at me with wide eyes. His hair and clothes are dripping wet from the rain and his stance is tense.

Then I look down to the sword in his hand.

It's dripping with blood, and he is covered in ash.

Steve

Chapter 27

I can't remember squeezing through the narrow entrance into the cave, but apparently I did.

Because I'm here.

I can't believe I killed one, I think, staring blankly at the cave wall. I look down at my sword, still wet with the shimmer of blood, in shock. It shouldn't disquiet me, or even phase me, because *this* is what we've been training for. Ali taught me how to defend myself, *how to protect her* and that's what I did.

So why do I feel like this? Why do I feel like a part of me has changed forever?

I can't believe I killed one, I think again, still looking at my sword. I feel a small hand touch my arm and it makes me jump.

"Hey, it's okay. I'm sorry, I didn't mean to startle you," Ali speaks softly.

Why is *she* consoling *me*? She scared off dozens of those terrifying skeleton creatures. And then, she single handedly took down three more bone crushing man-creatures three times her size. She is the reason we made it back here safely. And she is consoling me? I barely took down one of them and I'm sure I'll have nightmares about it for the rest of my life.

"No, no... it's okay," I stutter in response. "I'm just... it's just that... oh, I don't know," I give up, sitting down. I let my sword clatter to the ground and bury my face in my hands.

"I know," she says, sitting down beside me. "I still remember the feeling of the first one. It gets easier, I promise."

I look over to her, still replaying what just happened in my mind. "I saw it heading for you and I just... *reacted*. It felt natural and I knew I had to do it, but somehow I still feel... guilty," I trail off. And then a thought occurs to me and I chuckle a little to myself. "I've just never killed anything bigger than a fish. This was a little different," I say quietly.

Ali gives a little laugh as well. "Yeah, killing a monster that could tear you to pieces in seconds is a little different than a fish."

Tear. You. To pieces.

I look over at her, realizing *how* she knows that particular detail. *Fuck*, I push the thought out of my mind immediately.

"I know we've been training for it, but I didn't *know*, not really. Not until..." I stare at the wall again.

"I was hoping that maybe you wouldn't have to," Ali says, a hint of regret in her tone.

A mental image of the eyeless skeletal creatures dropping to all fours and *crawling* across the path in front of us flashes into my mind, along with the sounds of their bones cracking and creaking as they move.

The way their heads twitch as they try to sense us. To hear us.

A chill runs up my spine and I put my face in my hands again, squeezing my eyes shut as if that will dispel the horrifying memory of it.

"God, Ali. How do you sleep after something like that?" I say, my voice muffled.

"Well," she says slowly, determining how to answer. "At first you don't. Because closing your eyes just brings everything back. But you have to sleep eventually. That's when the nightmares start. And I'm sorry to say that they don't ever go away. But they do get better. At least, for me, they're starting to," she says and something in her tone makes me glance over and look at her. She averts her eyes quickly, but I catch something in her expression. Something she's trying to hide.

Am I helping with her nightmares? I wonder, hopefully. But I figure that not being alone anymore, no matter *who* it is, would help anyone not be as afraid.

"And Steven," she says, changing the subject. "Thank you. That last one, I didn't see it. So thanks for having my back out there." She looks so genuine and her small smile melts my heart.

"I guess we make a pretty good team, don't we?" I say, realizing with relief that I am capable of smiling again.

"Yeah, I guess we do," she looks at me for a long moment and I find that

I'm already forgetting about the monsters. I'm lost in those eyes. Eyes that I have very *purposely* been avoiding lately. But I can't avoid her anymore.

Right now, I need her.

She stands up suddenly, breaking the contact. I avert my eyes as well, looking around.

How is she so damn distracting? I wonder, because for a moment, I somehow forgot that we're trapped in an ice cave and I'm still soaking wet from the rain. A sudden chill runs up my spine and it's cold enough to see my breath. Now that the shock of the whole ordeal has worn off, I realize just how cold it's getting.

I look over at Ali, who's already dumping an armful of wood in the center of the cave. We have a good sized stockpile in the corner that we brought back during our last several trips out. I'm grateful that Ali had the foresight to do so. She always seems to be one step ahead out here.

Ali makes quick work of the fire. Watching her now, I realize that I have a lot more to learn about surviving out here. I can make a fire, sure, but she makes it look effortless. I also notice that even after slaughtering several creatures and saving our lives, she doesn't even seem phased by it. She is calm and meticulous, sauntering around the cave as if today is no different than any other. And then it dawns on me.

That *this*, all of this, is just a part of life out here.

I shake my head, realizing just how lucky I am that she found me. Living in the house is one thing, but out here? I wouldn't have survived it. But this is her life now. This is *our* life now.

I didn't see it before, but now I have the whole picture.

Once Ali has the fire crackling in front of us, I move closer, trying to warm my icy fingers, but I can't really feel them. I shake violently all over and my body aches from the inside out. My wet clothes feel as though they are turning to ice and I realize that the temperature is still dropping.

And it's dropping fast.

Needing my clothes to be dry, I kneel in front of the fire and pull at my shirt in an attempt to get it closer to heat. I try to turn, warming the side of me, but that leaves the rest of me freezing and so I turn back. I have almost burned myself twice already and still, I just can't get warm.

"Alright, mountain man, you ever had hypothermia?" Ali says from behind me as she rummages through her oversized bag.

"I can't say that I have," I say, continuing my rotation. "Wait a minute, have *you*?" I stop turning to stare at her.

"Twice. Now strip," she says, throwing a blanket at me. Catching it, I stare at her wide-eyed. She *cannot* be serious.

And... she's serious, I realize.

This is no longer the shy, sweet Ali who goes swimming with her T-shirt on. Nope, this is the survivalist Ali. The no-nonsense, *don't mess with me*, Ali.

And I don't plan to.

Well, maybe just a little... I think mischievously. *God,* I love messing with her.

"Okay," I draw out the word as I stand. Staring directly at her, I start to slowly unbutton my pants. Her eyes go wide and her face turns a cute shade of pink. She stands perfectly still, unsure of what to do. She looks *horrified.* I chew on my lip to hold back my laughter. When her eyes wander up to my face, she understands immediately what I'm doing.

"Oh, goddammit, Steven! Stop that! Now turn around. Fuck," she mutters, exasperated by me once again. I burst out laughing, turning around. I laugh even louder when her boot hits me square in the back of the head.

I smile, because all is right with the world.

Chapter 28

We sit by the fire and stare outside, waiting for the snow to stop. It's already been at least five hours since the storm started and we both know that attempting to run down the hill in the dark isn't even an option.

And so we wait.

As the snow continues to fall, I'm at least grateful that our clothes are finally dry. Sitting here in a blanket, staring across the fire at her sitting there in a blanket, had probably been the longest two hours of my entire life.

I can appreciate that the awkwardness of earlier has finally worn off and we're back to our usual selves.

I watch as Ali pokes at the fire and think again about how incredible it is that she survived out here. She seems to have an endless amount of stories about all the places she's gone, the creatures she's fought and all the insane hiding places that she found. She told me about a time when there was nowhere to go, nowhere to hide, and how she wound up throwing a rope over a tree branch high overhead and hoisting herself up, staying just out of reach until daylight. Hearing her stories is fascinating and I can't stop asking about them. Because I want to know everything about her.

Or maybe I just like hearing her voice.

Watching her now, I realize just how close we've gotten over the past two months since I've been here. There's just something about her that makes me open up more than I normally would, makes me feel like she's a part of me.

Like she's always been a part of me.

I often think about how my feelings toward her could simply be because of what we're going through. Lost together in the wilderness, away from everything you once knew, and being forced to survive would give anyone a certain type of bond. But somehow, I know that it's more than that. I feel connected to her, and no matter what happens, I know we can do anything together. She has become my best friend and I'm sure that nothing in this world, or the one we left, could ever change that.

Ali sits down beside me and leans her head on my shoulder, exhausted. I tense, because she is *too close*.

"We should probably try to get some sleep," I say to her. As soon as the snow stops, we're going to have a hell of a run back down the mountain and we need the strength.

"Mmhmm," she hums. It's adorable, which makes it infuriating.

There's an ice-cold breeze coming in through the narrow cave entrance and even with the fire burning in front of us, it's still freezing. The stone cave floor doesn't help the situation and the cold brings about a sudden thought, filling me with panic.

Ali and I have already slept in this cave several times, but so far, we've been sleeping on *opposite* sides of the fire. Tonight, in order to combat the windchill coming from the doorway, it's inevitable that we're going to end up on the *same* side. And probably under the same blanket.

Fuck. This cave is already too confined a space for comfort and having her curled up next me, asleep and adorable, is the last thing I need right now.

The whole reason I wanted out of the house in the first place is because being cooped up with her, in that mountain these past months, has been insufferable. Every time I look at her, I want to pull her into my arms. I find myself holding my breath whenever she walks past, whenever she's near me.

The tension has become excruciating.

I know in my mind that she doesn't have feelings for me, at least, not like *that*. But *god,* I want her to. Every second of every day is becoming harder and harder to avoid my feelings for her. I want to tell her that I don't want to just be friends. To tell her that she's changed my life and that I don't want to live without her. I *can't* live without her. The need to say those words have been suffocating me and I'm not sure how much longer I can stand it. Not knowing if she feels the same, or worse, that she doesn't, is driving me insane.

So I wanted out of the house. I needed to get out of that house. Needed some fresh air and some space. Some space from her.

Yeah, because that's been going great, I think sarcastically, thinking back on the trip so far. I've tried to keep my distance, to not notice her in that way, but I can't help it. I can't help but notice the excitement in her eyes when she's teaching me something new. Or the way she walks, strong and confident, her hand resting on the hilt of her sword as if this is how she's always lived. The way her hair moves in the breeze, or how she surveys the area around us constantly, even when we're talking. The way she's able to keep us alive so easily, so naturally, all the while joking and smiling, has given me a new picture of her. And I love it.

I love everything about her.

And then there was that tiny little excuse for a shelter in the forest. Waking up to find my back up against hers had put me somewhere between miserable and *more* miserable. Touching her just makes everything worse.

Now we are in a cave.

And it's freezing.

She'd been sitting over there in nothing more than a blanket, for god's sake and *now?* Now we are going to have to *cuddle up* to keep warm.

Fuck, I think, shaking my head. Because I'm not sure how much more of this torture I can take. This trip was supposed to give me some space, some fresh air, or *hell,* maybe just some perspective. But nothing has turned out like I'd planned.

I watch as Ali curls up on the ground in front of the fire, huddling up in *all* of the blankets. Then she looks back up at me with hopeful eyes.

Goddammit. This girl is going to be the death of me, I think miserably.

I take a deep breath, then settle in behind her, trying desperately not to touch her. But before I know what's happening, Ali grabs my arm and wraps it around her, forcing me to give in. I take a deep breath, then reluctantly pull her small shivering body up against mine.

It's been six days since the snow started.

Four days since we ran out of food.

With the sun perpetually hidden away, the daylight cycle impossible to make out, we've started counting the days the same way we do back at the house. Based on when our bodies tell us it's time to sleep. So it very well could be longer. Or shorter. Who the hell knows at this point.

Thankfully, the snow has offered an infinite supply of water. Ali showed me how to boil it over the fire, not only to melt it, but also to remove any pathogens that may linger. The last thing we need is to get sick with some weird magic-land bacteria when we're stuck in an ice cave. Trudging out into the snow with a torch whenever nature calls is risky enough.

Going this many days without food would be bad enough in the real world, but out here, where our bodies require more calories than seems possible, four days feels like a week. I've never in my life gone this long without eating.

I'm fucking exhausted.

Every muscle in my body aches and my head pounds in protest. I can tell Ali is feeling it too, because we hardly even talk anymore. We take each day an hour at a time, a *minute* at a time, just trying to keep ourselves strong enough to push through this.

We both know that we can't hold out much longer without food, but running down the hill in the snow, in the dark, still isn't an option. The darkness caused by the storm is as black as night and the creatures would be on us within seconds. There hasn't been a single moment in which we haven't heard them clinking around outside the cave. And so we either have to wait it out, or wait until *that* is our only option.

Knowing that Ali can *come back* if she doesn't make it is one thing, but we still don't know if I can. I dared to ask if she wanted to leave me here and try her luck on her own, but she shot that idea down immediately.

I know better than to bring it up again.

I stand in the cave entrance and look up toward the dark sky. The snow is deep enough that it completely covered the entrance days ago, but we've been taking turns keeping the passage clear so we will know when the sun comes back out. But so far, the storm is relentless. We keep waiting for the daylight comes back to us. The moment that will allow us to make a run for it. But it hasn't come.

Another sharp pain stabs through my stomach. And all I know, is that we are running out of time.

I lay on the cold stone ground and wonder how much longer my body will hold out before betraying me to the endless sleep it longs for. By day five, I wondered if we would survive this. And now, on day ten?

I know that we won't.

It's been a week since we ran out of food. It's a struggle just to lift my head, but I manage, eager to watch as Ali makes her way over to the entrance of the cave. She stands on her toes, peering out for about the tenth time already today. As I watch, I can tell by her body language that it's still dark. That we're still trapped.

And then I hear the *woosh* of an arrow.

I shoot to my feet just in time to see Ali duck down. The arrow clanks hard on the rock beside her, then falls to the ground with a clatter. Relief washes over me as I watch it roll across the floor by her feet.

"Dammit!" she shouts, kicking the arrow as hard as she can, sending it skittering across the floor. "God, this is all my fault," she says frustratedly, pacing the room. "We shouldn't have come out here. We should have just stayed at home. I've never found anything to help get us home before, why the fuck would it be any different this time," she says. She's exhausted, hungry, angry and on the verge of tears.

I know the feeling.

"Ali, this isn't your fault. Neither of us could have known about the storm. And besides, it was *my* idea to come out here," I tell her, because it's ridiculous for her to blame herself.

"But *you* didn't know. I did. And chose to do it anyway. I always *choose* to come out here and I never find anything," she paces the room, and not for the first time. "This is so stupid. *I'm* stupid for even thinking there's a way out of here," her voice falters, defeated. And I know she isn't just talking about the cave.

"No, you're not *stupid*. And I wasn't completely oblivious. I knew this was going to be dangerous, but I signed up for it anyway, because-"

"I know, I know, finding a way home is important," she grumbles.

"No. Finding a way home isn't important," I say, my tone serious. It causes her to stop the pacing and stare at me.

Looking back at her, I realize that I need her to see what I see. She needs to know how strong she is. She survived out here, alone, for six months. In all that time, she didn't give up.

"Well, it's finally happened. You're just as crazy as I am," she says and there's a deep pit of hopelessness in her eyes. I would do anything in this moment to take it away.

"Finding a way back isn't important. What's important is that we keep looking. We owe it to our families to not give up." My tone softens and I stare at the ground before continuing. "Even if we never find a way back to them."

That's when the tears she has been holding back finally fall. She stands in front of me, so lost and so tired, and all I want to do is hold her.

She slowly collapses to sit on the floor, weak with exhaustion, and starts sobbing. The sound of her crying breaks my heart and all I want to do is take her away from this place, to take her somewhere she feels safe.

Somewhere that we can just be.

"Ali," I whisper, my weak voice raspy as I kneel down in front of her. "Look at me." My own tears threaten to fall, but I manage to hold them back. She looks up, her lips quivering with sorrow. I push back the hair from her face and gaze into those sad, green eyes.

"I don't think we have to be lost to this nightmare. When I'm with you... I feel like I'm lost to a dream... and... I don't want to wake up."

She stares at me and I watch as another tear falls.

Why did I say that? I know I shouldn't be so bold, but I need her to know that I don't blame her for this. That I'm not upset. Not at her. I need her to know that I will go hungry for any number of days, so long as I am with her.

But she's still crying.

What I said is either lost on her, or she doesn't feel the same. I tear my eyes away from her and stand up, frustrated.

"Dammit, Ali. I'm so sorry I dragged you out here. This is all my fault," I say, storming to the other side of the cave and turning away. Because I can't look at her right now. Not with my own tears on the brink of falling.

"Steven," she says softly. "Steven, this isn't your fault either."

I turn around and see that she is standing, staring at *me* with sympathy.

She just isn't getting it, I have to make her understand.

"No. It *is* my fault. I made you come out here because-" I cut off, anger in my voice, but not at her. I'm angry because the pain that she's feeling, the tears she cries now, they are all my fault.

"Because what?" she asks softly.

"Because... because I couldn't stand to be in that mountain with you for another second," I blurt out, my teeth grinding with frustration. I turn around again, away from her, rubbing a hand over my face. The room is silent.

And then I realize what I just said.

Fuck.

I slowly turn and see the sorrow in her face. A sorrow that sends a shooting pain straight through my heart. Because I caused it.

No, no, no, what have I done? Her tears are flowing freely now, her eyes averted, unable to look at me.

"Fuck," I run my hand through my hair. "That's not what I meant," I say frustratedly.

"Then what did you mean?" she asks slowly, her voice barely audible. Her eyes on the floor.

"I meant..." I take a deep breath. "I meant that if I stayed in that mountain with you for another second, I would end up doing something else incredibly stupid."

"Like what?" she whispers as her confused eyes lock on mine. I stare at her for a long moment and suddenly, I can't hold back any longer.

"Like this." I take three long steps toward her and within a second, I have my fingers buried in her hair and my lips pressed against hers.

Her lips are soft, *incredibly* soft. I wait for her to pull away, but she doesn't. She just stands there, in shock. I know this is a bad idea, but I don't care.

This moment is everything.

She. Is. *Everything.*

I move one hand to her cheek, gently brushing it with my thumb. I part my lips slowly and my heart leaps to my throat when she mimics the action.

Is this actually happening? All I've wanted since I got here was this. Was *her*. I need her.

And then my mouth moves against hers, as if all on its own. Her lips respond to mine, sparking something in me that I didn't know was there. And so I deepen the kiss, holding her face like it's the most precious thing in the entire world. Because it is. She is.

I'm afraid that my heart will pound out of my chest and it takes my brain several moments to realize what's actually happening. When it does, I can't breathe.

Because *she is kissing me back.*

I know I should probably pull away, know that because we are stuck here together, that this will only complicate things. But I can't let her go.

I can *never* let her go.

I slide my hand out of her hair and trail it down where I know her tattoo is hiding beneath her shirt. My fingers stop at the small of her back. Then with one quick motion, I pull her body against mine. She lets out a quick gasp and I pull my lips away from hers, just far enough to look down into those eyes, searching them for her reaction.

We just stare at each other for a long moment, our labored breaths in sync.

Her hands, which were previously flat at her sides, hesitantly move to my shirt. Her eyes still locked on mine. I feel her small fingers slide up my chest and she wraps them behind my neck. I close my eyes, fearing that I might pass out from the sensation of her touch.

Steadying my breath, I dare to look down at her. I find that she is studying every detail of my face with an adorable little half smile. My breath hitches, because she's never really looked at me before. Not like this. Her fingers gently explore the back of my neck and it sends a new wave of chills through my body.

I can't move.

Suddenly, those hands are in my hair and she is pulling my mouth back down to hers.

Chapter 29

"*God,* Ali," I mumble against her lips before kissing her deeply once again.

I'm intoxicated by her.

It doesn't matter that we're near death from starvation, stuck in a cave, or lost in a world of magic and monsters with no way out.

None of that matters.

All that matters is this moment. That I'm here, with her.

I don't know how long we've been standing here, but I never want to move. I'm afraid that maybe this really is a dream, because this is too good to be true.

"*Incredibly stupid,* huh?" she asks, her lips barely leaving mine, her breathing heavy.

"Like I said..." I respond, before taking back the lips that nearly escaped me.

"So why didn't you do something stupid sooner?" she asks against my mouth.

That catches my attention and I pull away just enough to steady my breath. I lean my forehead against hers and close my eyes before answering.

"I... I didn't think you wanted me to," I answer honestly.

"Well, what do you think now?" she teases, biting at my lip. I laugh at her playfulness, but secretly hope that this girl isn't about to give me a heart attack.

"I think..." I say, kissing her again. "That I could get in the habit of doing incredibly stupid things more often."

She wraps her arms around my neck, holding me tighter, and I pull her body against mine. Our kiss becomes frantic, desperate, as if the whole world depends on it. On this moment.

Right now, there is only her. Her breath, her lips, how she feels in my arms.

She is all that matters.

We lay by the fire, keeping watch outside for the storm to pass. I am happier than I've ever been in my entire life, but that doesn't stop the pain of starvation that is racking my entire body. I know that humans can live for a few weeks without food, but if this is what eight days feels like? Then *weeks?* I can't even imagine.

And I hope I won't have to.

I look down to the equally exhausted girl lying in front of me, the flames of the fire illuminating her delicate face. Every night in this cave, I've slept beside her. I've held her to keep her warm, to keep *me* warm, trying to get us through the long, cold nights. But lying next to her now, *this* time is different.

Because now I can breathe.

Before, sleeping next to her caused my heart to ache and I would hold my breath until morning, fighting my feelings for her. Now, it's like a weight has been lifted. Now, I can hold her in my arms, knowing that she wants me the same way. And not just for warmth. She actually *wants. Me.*

At least, right now she does.

We haven't talked about what will happen once we get out of here, but Ali has made it abundantly clear that my attraction isn't one-sided. And for now, that's enough. *More* than enough, in fact.

I am beside myself with overwhelming joy.

I prop myself up on one elbow, my eyes fixed on the flames. I gently run my fingers back and forth over Ali's arm, just below the line of her T-shirt. It's a simple gesture, but I've stayed awake for hours in this cave, staring at that arm, imagining what it would feel like to touch her like this. Now that I finally have the freedom to, I'm having a hard time believing that it's real.

God, she's beautiful, I think as my eyes follow the path my fingers are languidly tracing along her bare skin. Considering her small frame, I'm surprised to realize how strong she is. Even relaxed, the muscles in her arm are clearly and impressively defined. I suppose I should have known, the way she handles a sword and herself when we train, but still. I've never noticed. Which is probably because I have spent most of my time actively trying *not* to notice her.

I wasn't sure what I expected her reaction to be when the sleep deprived, hunger stricken, out-of-his-goddamn-mind version of me decided that it would be a *great* idea to kiss her, but it certainly wasn't this. She not only let me kiss her, but she kissed me back.

A lot. I smile, lost again to the memory of those moments.

Looking down, I realize that Ali is smiling up at me. I study her face and can't help but think that maybe, just maybe, she's been wanting this as much as I have.

Or maybe I'm fooling myself and this will all be over as quickly as it started. But for now, I bury my face in her neck, causing a giggle to escape her, thinking again how I really am lost to a dream. And as much as I long for this to be real, I know in the back of my mind that once we get out of this cave, once the fatigue wears off and she has some perspective, then this dream will be over.

My heart aches at the thought.

"What are you thinking about?" she asks, rolling to her back so I can see her face.

"I was thinking... about how good Oreos with peanut butter sounds right now," I look down at her, giving her a smirk.

"How did you..." she stares up at me quizzically. "Oh, Noor. Of course. But that's not funny," she says, hitting my arm. "If you talk about food again, you're sleeping outside in the snow. Now, tell me."

I think for a moment, wondering what to say to her. I could easily make up some bullshit answer to her question, but find that I'm too exhausted, and too hungry, to lie to her.

So I tell her the truth.

"I was thinking that... once we get out of here and things go back to normal, you might not feel the same about me," I stare anywhere but at her, because the last thing I want is to hear the answer to my unasked question. I'm not sure why the hell I even said anything in the first place.

"Steven," she says quietly. "I don't know how to say this..." she trails off and I look down at her. For some reason, I need to see her face when she breaks my heart.

I'm in love with you. Her green eyes flicker with light as the unspoken words flood my mind.

Only, those words aren't *mine*. I know they aren't, because those are not the words I am currently thinking. *Those* words interrupted my thoughts. I furrow my eyebrows and stare at her.

It was *her* voice I just heard in my head, but her lips hadn't moved.

What the fuck was that?

"What?" she asks, concerned by the sudden change in my expression.

"You.... you love me," I whisper. It isn't a question.

I *heard* it.

"*Um,* what? Steven, I didn't say that," she says, panicked, sitting up quickly.

"I know you didn't say it, but I heard you. Did you mean it?" I ask, sitting up as well. My desperation to find out if it's true overshadows everything else.

"You couldn't have heard me, Steven this is crazy. I didn't say anything."

"But do you?" I ask again, my eyes fixed on hers. I can't give up this opportunity to find out. I have to know if she feels the same way that I do. Because *not knowing,* has tortured me every second since I woke up on that beach.

She looks into my eyes and must see the hope in them, because her concerned gaze softens and she lets out a relinquished breath.

"Dammit, Steven. Yes, I meant it. Steven Stone, I'm in love with you. I've been in love with you. When I'm away from you, even for a second, it feels like I can't breathe. I don't want to live without you ever again, I *can't* live without you. Now, are you happy?" She looks at me, exasperated from her declaration, eyes full of fear.

I just stare at her, completely in shock.

Did she really just say that?

And if her fear is that I don't feel the same, well, then she really has gone crazy. And I'm still staring. Because she just keeps surprising me. If she would have answered my question with a simple *yes,* then I would have been over the moon. But she didn't *just* do that, she gave her heart to me. And I'm suddenly desperate to give mine to her.

"Happy," I laugh. "That's not the word I would use."

"What word would you use, then?" she says warily.

"Hmm... I could use... elated, delighted, rapturous-"

She punches my arm, because she hates when I do that. I smile at her, my gaze growing serious. I lean in closer, then tuck a loose hair behind her ear. I trail my thumb over her freckled cheek, letting it linger there as she stares back at me with those worried eyes.

"Alexandra Cutter, I'm in love with you. I've been in love with you and I'm never letting you go. *I'm with you,*" I whisper, relieved and terrified to have finally said the words out loud.

Now *she* is the one in shock. I can tell she isn't breathing as her big, green eyes stay locked on mine. I move my thumb over her soft cheek again and her hand finds the back of mine, pressing my palm to her face. She leans into it, her eyes welling with tears.

"*God*, you're beautiful," I whisper. Not believing how confident she makes me.

Suddenly, her hands move to either side of my face, drawing me in. She kisses me desperately, frantically and it lights my whole body on fire. My lips respond with their own desire and I wrap my arms around her, my hands holding her, grabbing her, clinging to her, needing her closer to me. She moves her hands up into my hair, gripping tightly and pulling my lips harder against hers. I let out a groan. I feel her lips smile against mine for a moment, before they continue their relentless torture.

My head is spinning, my mind a complete blur. I don't know where we are and honestly, I don't care. It takes me a moment to realize that her lips aren't on mine anymore.

All I know is that my world has been turned upside down and I am completely and wholly okay with it.

"Did you know that's one of the first things you ever said to me?" I hear a small voice say, bringing me back to the present.

"Huh?" I blink slowly, focusing on her. She smiles at my dazed state.

"That first day on the beach. '*I'm with you.*' That's what you said to me. Do you remember?"

"Yes, Ali. I remember it," I smile, but my tone is serious. "Because that's the moment I knew I was in love with you."

"What?" she says, disbelievingly. "Steven, you didn't even know me when we met on the beach. How can you say you loved me then?"

"I did know you, in a way," I say plainly, because I've given this a lot of thought.

"What are you talking about?" she asks.

"I knew all about you from our friends and then... and then the dreams started. I watched you face death, over and over. But even as you struggled, you always got back up. Always kept fighting until the very end. I admired you for that. I got to know every expression on your face, when you were tired or concentrating, and that little smile you get when you figure something out. I thought about you every second of every day and couldn't wait until I fell asleep. Because in my dreams, I got to see you, even if you couldn't see me back. I felt like I was drawn to you, like I needed to find you. I knew I was falling for you, even when I knew I shouldn't. And then I woke up and saw you on that beach," my mind takes me back there.

"I saw you and I had *finally* found you. You were so beautiful and strong and you saved my life before you even knew me. I tried not to love you, especially when I still thought you were with Noor, and it took me a while to come to terms with it, but yes. That's the moment I knew that I had fallen in love with you. And then getting to know you, *really* know you... *god*, Ali. I love everything about you."

She looks up at me with those big eyes and I fall for her all over again. Because after all those times she couldn't see me, all these months of fleeting glances, she is finally *looking at me*. *Really* looking at me. And I don't have to guess what's behind those eyes anymore. She told me.

She loves me, I think, still trying to convince myself that it's true. She can tell me a million more times and I still might not believe it. Because how could someone as amazing as *her* love someone like me?

Whatever is happening between us, I'm almost certain that I don't deserve it. Never in my life have I done anything as incredible as her surviving out here. In fact, my life before was as easy as it could get and yet I spent the majority of my time complaining about it. But being out here, where every day is a struggle to survive? Watching how Ali takes it on day after day has caused me to reevaluate everything.

How can I complain about anything ever again after seeing what she went through?

What she's endured?

Back in the real world, I put off any thoughts and aspirations for the future, simply because I was unhappy with how my life was going so far. And now, with this beautiful and strong girl in my arms, I feel like I owe it to her to be better. To try harder. And not just for her, but for myself too. Even in this world of chaos and death, I find myself looking forward to the future. To having a life.

A life with *her*.

"Can I tell you something?" she asks, hesitant.

"Of course."

"I think I might have loved you on that beach too," she muses thoughtfully. "I think we were meant to find each other. I can't explain it, but I feel like you're *a part* of me. Like I've been waiting for you... and whatever happens, I'm with you too."

Chapter 30

I wake up slowly and try to shake off the dream that must have been brought on by starvation or delirium.

And then I look down to the girl sleeping in my arms.

Could that have been real? I wonder, hope rising inside my chest. My head is spinning and my stomach aches. Between the sudden chills and fatigue, who knows what's real anymore?

I still, because Ali is waking up. Holding my breath, I wait for her response to us waking up like this. Blinking, she looks up at me and a bright smile spreads across her face. She looks at me with none of the usual awkward evasive maneuvers that we've both grown so accustomed to and it all comes flooding back.

It was real. She's in love with me.

I smile, deciding to take a chance. Slowly, I lean in and brush my lips against hers.

But apparently, *slow* is not her plan. She grabs the front of my shirt, pulling me down to deepen the kiss.

God. If I die in this moment, that would be completely fine with me. I melt into her, losing myself.

"Steven? Have you checked outside yet?" she says, breaking our contact. I grumble.

"No, have you?" I say, letting more of my weight press into her, pinning her beneath me.

"No," she laughs. "Let me up, I want out of this cave."

I give her a look, acting aggrieved.

"Oh fine, I'll bring you with me when I leave," she smiles, but I don't move. She rolls her eyes, then shoves me off her, heading toward the entrance of the cave.

"Well, it's still dark. And it's still snowing," she says, frustrated. A pain shoots through my stomach at the thought of spending another minute being trapped here.

As much as I am, *now,* enjoying this little cave along with her company, we need food. And *soon*. I've lost track of how many days we've gone without, and it hurts to even think about it.

As Ali sits down beside me, I wrap my arms tightly around her, pulling her close. We stare at the fire for a long time.

"Steven?" she asks and her tone causes me to look down at her curiously. "How did you hear me?"

"What do you mean?" My brain is a fog of exhaustion and I don't have a clue what she's talking about.

"Why did you ask me if... or, how did you *know,* that I love you," she blushes. "I didn't say anything."

Oh yeah, that.

"Oh, um. I don't really know. I heard your voice, same as I hear it now, but it was in my head. You were looking at me and I just... *heard it.* Which saying out loud, sounds crazy... I must have just imagined it."

"What *exactly* did you hear?" She stares up at me intently, waiting for my response.

"You said that you didn't know how to say it... and then you said, 'I'm in love with you.' But I know you didn't actually say it. I'm sorry if I forced you to..." I look away, suddenly embarrassed.

"No, Steven, you didn't force me to say it. I think I *did* say it. I said those exact words in my head."

"Ali, there's no way I could have *actually* heard you," I say.

"No, I think maybe you could," she stares off. "Because... well, maybe I wanted you to."

I look at her skeptically. It's *definitely* time to get out of this cave.

"Steven, I don't think that this is the first time that it's happened..." her voice trails off.

"What do you mean?" I stare at her, because now I'm really confused.

"I thought about it more last night. There's been several times that you responded to something I said, only, I hadn't said anything *out loud*. I only *thought* it. I didn't think much of it at the time and just assumed that I was accidentally talking out loud again, but now... now I'm not so sure..." she looks away, thinking again.

"Ali, I think I would have noticed if I could read your mind," I give her a playful look. Because even after everything I've seen since being out here, this one would make it pretty close to the top of the crazy list.

"I don't think it's like that. I don't think you can hear me all the time but if I want you to know something, even subconsciously..." she looks away, deep in thought. "I think the first time it happened was when I saw your tattoo. And then again back at the house," she says, concentrating. Clearly trying to figure something out.

I think back to that day by the swimming hole, trying to understand what she could be talking about. But I have other memories from that day that are suddenly distracting me. Flashes of moments that, as much as I've tried, my mind won't let me forget. But I suppose, I don't have to forget them. Not anymore. Secretly, I wish Ali could see them, because then she would know how long I've felt this way about her...

I splash her and she smiles at me, her laughter fills me with warmth, despite the chill of the water. I love the way she looks with wet hair, how her red curls are framing her perfect face. I take off my shirt, not only because it's soaking wet, but because I want her to see me. It's stupid, I know, but I don't want her to picture me as a friend anymore. And her reaction... my heart is nearly beating out of my chest as I try to decide if her blush is because she's embarrassed, or because she's attracted to me. Either way, I can't waste the opportunity to tease her. I never can. So I sit down a little too close to her. Her body goes rigid, and I'm struggling to remain calm. Because I want to be this close to her. Always. Even though it drives me insane. Her fingertips touch my back and a spark ignites my skin, sending chills up my spine. I never want her to stop. I sit down behind her, my breath shallow at how sexy that tattoo is running down her bare back. Her skin is soft beneath my fingertips. I let my eyes wander. God, I want to touch her everywhere. I want to...

"Steven, stop! I can hear you!" she says quickly, interrupting my reverie. A blush is blooming across her face and her eyes are wide. I see a quick flicker of light behind them.

When have I seen that before?

Then the reality of what she just said sinks in and embarrassment floods my own cheeks.

"What... what do you mean you heard me?" I ask hesitantly, my eyes growing wide with horror. But I'm afraid I already know the answer.

I *wanted* her to hear me. I just didn't think that it would actually work.

"I knew it!" she shouts, hitting me in the arm with a teasing smile that tells me she isn't actually upset.

"Hey, watch it with that," I say, trying to defend myself.

"You *were* doing it on purpose, I knew it! You are always hovering way too close, or sitting too close, or touching my arm... you were messing with me *on purpose!*" she says.

I just stare at her, in shock. Because she did hear me.

Fuck. What else has she heard? I wonder, panicked by the thought.

"Ali, how is this possible?" I ask.

"I have no idea. I guess we'll add that one to our list of unanswered questions," she shrugs. And I wonder how she always manages to stay so calm whenever the sky is falling.

"Hang on, so have you been able to hear me the *whole time* I've been here?" I look at her, mortified.

This cannot be happening.

"No, I haven't heard you at all actually... I think that was the first time. Except maybe..."

"Oh god, what. What did you hear?" I ask.

"No, no," she chuckles. "Nothing bad. When you first got here, when you said my name-"

"And you held a *sword* to my throat? Yeah, I remember it," I smile and she glowers at me. Because we've been over this.

More than once.

She glares at me again before continuing.

"When you said my name, I'm not entirely sure that you said it out loud, because I didn't see your mouth move. I thought I was just tired and not paying attention, but it makes me wonder how many times this has happened and we just didn't know it."

"What about my dreams? Do you think that they are somehow connected to this?"

"Maybe, but I don't know. This feels different somehow. Whenever I've accidentally said something to you and just now, when I could hear you, I get this feeling. It's almost like a tugging deep in my stomach. Like it's pulling at me. Like I *need* to tell you something, or *need* to know what you're saying."

"That's exactly how I feel when I'm in the dreams. Well, most of them anyway. Like I *need* to get to you. But I also get that feeling whenever we're around the book, only, it's not as strong," I say as my mind slowly pieces it together.

She looks up at me suddenly, realizing it too.

"Steven, you're right, it's the same feeling. Which means that..."

"Which means that it's *magic*. Except, I didn't feel anything when you heard me just now."

"But *I* did," she says seriously. And then I remember something else.

"Ali, it's *you*. *You're* doing it. It's in your eyes... it all makes sense."

"What are you talking about?" she stares at me curiously.

"Your eyes. They have this flicker of light behind them when you are using magic with the book. I saw that same light just a minute ago when you heard me. I saw it when you said that you love me. Whenever you use magic, I can see it in your eyes. So whatever this is, it's coming from *you*. It's *your* magic."

"Steven, this is crazy. I've never been able to do anything without the book. How is this possible?"

"I have no idea. But try it again," I say, staring at her. Now I'm just plain excited.

Steven, can you hear me? Her faint voice floods my head. It sounds a little different from her speaking voice, but it's definitely *her* voice.

"Holy shit, Ali! I can hear you!"

She's staring at me with wide eyes and I stare back.

Can you hear me? I ask her.

Yes, I can hear you, her soft voice responds.

"No fucking way," I smile. "Ali, this is insane. And your eyes, I can see it. It's so subtle, I probably wouldn't notice if I wasn't looking for it."

"Your eyes didn't do anything," she says curiously.

"Because it's all *you*, Ali," I say. She thinks about that for a moment before responding.

"I feel like it's me. Like it's a part of me," she smiles, looking like someone who just found something that was lost. "But I've definitely seen your eyes too, back at the house I mean, when you've used the book. I thought it was just the light playing tricks on me..."

"Seriously, mine do that too?" I ask and then stare off, my mind racing.

Soul belonging to two worlds. I've never questioned that *Ali* belongs to this world. But *me?* I don't feel a part of it. But maybe that's because I haven't opened myself up to the possibility that I already am.

"Steven!" Ali says, sounding frantic.

"What is it? Are you okay?" I say, suddenly concerned.

"Steven, listen," she says, her eyes filling with unspilled tears. I still, listening carefully.

"Are those?" I question, because it's too good to be true.

"Birds!" She smiles as happy tears begin to fall.

The storm is over.

We both run to the entrance of the cave and I squeeze out, sword first. I squint, shading my eyes from the sun, seeing it for the first time after nearly two weeks in the dark.

"Is it over? Steven, can we go?" Ali says, making her way out of the cave behind me. I turn to her, unable to wipe the smile off of my face. I pick her up, then spin her around in circles in the fresh, powdered snow.

We're out, I think as her laughter fills my heart. I set her down slowly then hold her face gently in my hands.

"You ready to go home?" I say, looking down into those big green eyes.

Home, I think. Because I've never called it that before.

I've never called anywhere home before.

"Let's go home," she smiles sweetly back up at me.

And then I kiss her. Long and slow, and full of relief.

God, Ali, I love kissing you.

"I heard that," she whispers against my lips.

"I know," I smile, realizing that talking to her like that and kissing her like *this*, are two things that I'm looking forward to experiencing more of.

But not now.

Now, we have to get the fuck out of here.

"What time is it?" I ask her and she checks the little golden watch on her wrist.

"We only have two minutes until nightfall, we're going to have to wait," she says, heading quickly back inside.

Everything is packed. I stand, taking one last long look around the cave. Somehow, this small stone room holds the worst moments of my life, and the best. We nearly froze, practically starved to death and had mentally gone down so far past hope, I thought we would never find our way back.

But then there were those moments with Ali. *She loves me,* I think again, and I smile.

Looking over at her now, I realize that I get to take the best parts with me.

The rest I'm going to leave behind.

Ali pulls on her pack and gives me a knowing nod as the sun touches the tops of the trees in the distance.

"Let's go," I say, taking a deep breath as we make our way out into the world once again.

Trudging through the snow, Ali and I look around at the world of white. We know there is a shelter waiting for us at the bottom, we just have to get there. But as we begin making our way down the familiar slope and back toward the woods, we realize that nothing is *familiar* anymore. The trees are bare and the path we took to get up the mountain is long gone, buried somewhere under a few feet of powder. Even without the trail, we know that we have to go in the downwards direction. So we continue on, wading as quickly as we can through the thick snow.

When we come to the edge of a cliff, one we haven't seen before, Ali and I give each other a knowing look.

We've been going in the wrong direction.

Looking down, I can see the path leading into the woods, but what I don't see, is a way down.

"Steven, there isn't time to go back up to find the right trail. We have to find another way," Ali says, her voice trembling from her exhaustion.

"Well, then this way it is," I say, because there has to be a way down eventually. It's just a matter of *when*. And time is running out.

As we make our way along the ridge, the snow begins to thin. I scan the landscape, searching desperately for a way down. For a place to hide.

And that's when I see it.

"Ali, look! There's a cave, right up ahead," I say just as the sun begins making its way back down to the horizon. We both pick up the pace.

"We're almost there," I say, turning to look back at Ali, who smiles at me, relieved.

We're going to make it.

And that's when everything starts to happen in slow motion.

I watch as Ali's face turns to horror. Can see her mouth screaming my name.

But I can't hear it.

The rumble of crashing snow has drowned out all other noises and the ground shakes beneath me. I watch Ali's face as it grows smaller and smaller, the distance separating us. And then slowly, I understand what is happening.

I'm falling.

I shout out to her, but she doesn't hear me. I see her pained face as she stares over the ledge and I see the look in her eyes.

A look that tells me what she's about to do.

Don't. Ali, it's okay. Don't follow me, I say to her from my mind, hoping that she will hear me. Her eyes meet mine and she shakes her head, letting me know that she isn't willing to listen.

She is going to jump.

Suddenly, something knocks her down. I can see her arms hang lifelessly over the edge. Whatever it is drags her away with so much force that she's torn from my view in a split second.

"Alexandra!" I scream her name. I *need* to get to her. My whole body shakes with the effort, but there is nothing I can do. I look up, defeated, as the walls of the ravine rise above me at a dizzying pace.

I stare up at the night sky.

It's peaceful.

A few twinkling stars emerge from the darkness, shining through the black veil. It's as if they came to tell me that everything will be okay.

I love you, Ali, I think one last time, before my world goes black.

Chapter 31

The pain is excruciating. Sure, I broke a few bones as a kid, but *this*. This pain is beyond anything I've ever felt, or ever thought I could feel.

I need to breathe, but I can't.

The pain won't let me.

My mind isn't attached to my body anymore, because my body is broken.

And then everything stops.

I'm floating in an endless pool of darkness, finding myself gasping for breath. I choke on the air that now fills my lungs. Until suddenly, it's cut off once again.

I feel as though I've lost the knowledge of *how* to breathe. When I open my eyes, I see why.

The blueish glow of the creature's eyes shine above me through the dark. Its large cold hands are wrapped completely around my neck.

The noises it makes are deafening.

My ears ring and the sick smell of rotting flesh assaults my nose. My head begins to spin and I know that the lack of oxygen is going to make me pass out at any moment.

And then I think of her.

I have to get to her, I think desperately. *Something took her. She's in trouble.*

A new resolve breaks me from my hopelessness. I manage to pull my legs up, placing my feet on the creature's stomach and shove.

Hard.

It stumbles backward and my hands fly to my neck, as if the action will somehow help bring back the air to my lungs. I roll over, trying to cough as I scramble to get to my feet.

I turn to see the creature running straight for me and somewhere in the back of my mind, I remember what Ali taught me.

They're a hell of a lot stronger than either of us, but you can learn to be faster. You can be smarter. Keep your head up, keep moving, stay strong.

I stand face to face with the creature, then hold my ground as it runs for me, repeating the words out loud.

"Keep your head up. Keep moving. Stay. Strong," I pant, my throat burning with every word. As soon as the creature is close enough, I duck low, darting past it. The motion catches it off guard and it stumbles forward.

By the time it finds its footing, I'm out of reach. Running across the sand away from it, I see the barrel, and recognition finally dawns on me.

The trapdoor. I can make it, I think, smiling that this nightmare is almost over.

But then something causes me to stop.

A stabbing pain originates from behind my ribcage, moving outward through my entire body. My legs give out and I drop to my knees.

I look down.

My palms are already pressed against my chest. And they are covered in blood. I hold my hands out in front of me and watch the crimson drops fall from my fingertips.

A second arrow pierces out from just below my collar bone. My mouth fills with the taste of metal and rust.

I feel the blood as it pours from my mouth, hear the sound of it dripping on the sand.

My vision blurs, and I lose consciousness.

I gasp for breath. *Again.*

Ali was right. I'm more annoyed than anything at this point.

I have been strangled, shot with arrows, drowned in the ocean, shot again and this last time? I don't know what the fuck happened, but somehow I *exploded.*

I actually exploded.

My body shivers with the memory of my body being blown to pieces and I can swear that my ears are *still* ringing. I look around, frantically searching for the next thing that wants to kill me.

I'm getting really tired of this shit.

Three more creatures are heading toward me quickly, fresh out of the ocean and smelling like dead fish, but I don't pay them much attention. They are easy enough to handle at this point.

I'm just really trying not to get shot this time.

Or explode. That hadn't been very much fun either.

My senses are in tune with everything around me to the point that I can *feel* them coming. I hear the bone-chilling sound of cracking knuckles and bones before I see it.

I stay perfectly still, then barely move as I look behind me. The creature slowly stands up onto two legs, its skeletal form long and sickly. It pulls the bow from its hunched back and racks an arrow. Its head twitches around.

Listening.

I hold my breath. If it hears me, I'll be dead instantly and my long thought-out plan will be fucked.

I stand perfectly still, waiting for the creatures to close in around me. Right when the three ugly piles of decaying muscle get close enough, I make my move.

"Hey! Over here!" I shout, then duck behind one of the massive monsters just as an arrow lands square in its chest. It howls its unearthly gurgling groans, as four more arrows find their marks in the creatures beside it. They let out their own bellows of pain.

Using their bodies as a shield and their howls to drown out my footsteps, I make a run for it. By the time the three creatures fall, shaking the ground beneath me, and the twitchy skeletal creature fixes its empty eye sockets on me, I'm already standing over the trap door.

"Sorry, not this time!" I pant. With a triumphant smile, I kick the lever and drop down an instant before an arrow pierces the air where I just stood.

I laugh as I fall, and it makes me think of Ali. The day I first fell into this pit feels like a lifetime ago.

I land in the hay, then crawl out of the pile. Looking back up at the trap-door, I realize something. *Ali's not here with me. She's not here. She's still alive,* my mind races.

I have to find her.

Then I think about how long it took me to get off the island. *Too long.* A pit forms in my stomach. *I have to get back to her, have to save her.*

I can't waste time going back to the house for supplies. Looking around the cave, I see a large chest in the corner. When I open it, I nearly laugh out loud. My smile broadens as I stare down at the ridiculous amount of weapons inside.

That girl is always prepared.

I pull out a sword, and a pile of torches, then take a deep breath before I'm sprinting through the cave.

Ali, I'm coming to find you. Tell me where you are. Ali! I shout in my mind as I run, but she doesn't reply.

Maybe I'm too far away? Or maybe she's...

Ali, goddammit, where are you? I shout again, pushing myself to run *faster*.

I slam open the trapdoor and take off running along the familiar path toward where I left her. Jumping over rocks and logs, I realize that it's a good thing that I paid close attention to our route the first time.

Getting lost out here would be hell.

Ali and I jogged the distance in a little over an hour, stopping each night. But this time, I'm not jogging.

I'm *running*.

And I'm not going to stop at night.

When I make it to the thick woods below the mountain, the sun begins to disappear again, casting long shadows across the forest floor. Within a second, I can hear the sounds of the night already beginning. I listen carefully, trying to determine how many are out there.

Too many.

Fuck.

I shake my head, knowing there's no way I can make it through this part of the map section in the dark. But I remember a nearby hideaway where Ali and I stayed before.

Even though I know where the small cave is, the woods look different in the twilight. I run along the rocky hillside, striking a torch on a nearby tree as I go. It sparks to life, lighting my way. Just as the sky turns to absolute darkness, I find the cave.

If you can call it that. It's more of a dugout in the rocky hillside and I have to scale the face of it for several feet before I reach it. Lifting myself over the ledge, I stand, backing into the nook and out of sight. I breathe heavily, dropping the torch down next to me as I try to catch my breath. I sit down and look out over the trees, into the blackness, already knowing what will be there when the sun comes up.

The mountain where I lost her.

The ravine where I fell...

The pain and memory of falling away from her, of needing to get back to her, suddenly floods my whole body. I feel that *pull* again, just like in the dreams. I squeeze my eyes shut and every muscle in my body tenses. I ball my fists and let out a frustrated shout.

And then suddenly, I can see her.

I blink, unsure if this is real.

Ali is right in front of me and I watch as she slowly makes her way back to consciousness. Which explains why she didn't hear me calling out for her before. I look around.

My heart sinks when I realize where she is.

I watch the horror spread across her face when she sees it too.

The long hallway is dark and there is a flickering light coming from a nearby torch somewhere down the hall. Water drips from the ceiling and the sound of it hitting the stone floor echoes down the long corridor. Wooden supports are holding the stone ceiling in place every so often. *Like a mineshaft.* But what causes the pit in my stomach are the walls. Because every inch of them is covered with cobwebs.

Cobwebs, and dark stains. Stains that look like dried blood.

My mind races back to that day by the swimming hole, how seeing a spider the size of a horse added a terrifying new element to my nightmares.

And now Ali is in their den.

She is suspended a few feet up on one of the cave walls. I watch her struggle, trapped in their thick webs.

Ali! I shout in my mind, trying desperately to reach her, but she can't seem to hear me. Nothing I'm looking at gives me any clue as to where these tunnels are located, so I keep my mind focused, trying not to lose the fleeting images I finally have of her. She fights against the webs that encase her hands and the lower half of her body in their prison, but she can't break free. As she looks around, I realize that she doesn't quite seem *awake*. Her struggles are weak and her eyes look foggy.

It takes her several minutes before she finally manages to get one hand free. She tiredly reaches for her ankle, wrestling with the thick webs there. It only takes me a moment to realize what she's reaching for.

Her knife.

I know she always keeps a dagger in her boot, and she is determined to get to it.

Come on, Ali. You can do this, I think as I stand by, watching helplessly. She finally manages to widen a hole large enough to maneuver the dagger out of its sheath and begins cutting herself free.

That's my girl.

After a few minutes, she's finally out and stumbling down the narrow passageway. She seems incredibly off-balanced, made even worse when her feet stick to the webbed floor. But she just keeps on going.

Ali, what happened to you? I wonder.

I keep watching, my jaw tight with frustration as she makes her way down hallway after hallway through the mineshaft, searching for a way out. The passageways present her with endless options, creating an impossible sort of maze. Every once in a while she hits a dead end and is forced to turn back around. There are torches mounted above the wooden supports every so often, but they are too high up for her to reach. So she continues on.

In the dark.

I hate being this helpless. At any moment, the creatures could come for her and there will be nothing I can do to stop it. I need to know where she is.

Ali! Tell me where you are! I scream at her in my mind.

No response.

She keeps moving and I follow right behind. No way am I letting her out of my sight now that I found her.

I hear something coming from the darkness, and a sudden shiver runs up my spine. The sound is faint, but unmistakable. Ali stops, hearing it too. She turns slowly to look down the long hallway and then, I see it.

Something is *moving*.

I stare at the motion, forcing my eyes to focus in the low light. When they do, I see one long jointed appendage wrap around the edge of an intersecting passageway. Three more legs join it, before pulling the rest of its body around the corner and into the hall, high up on the wall. The hairy creature has an assortment of beady red eyes and they are all scanning the hallways, *searching*.

I scream at Ali to run, but she can't hear me. The spider slinks toward her in the dark and she slowly backs away from it, trying not to disturb the webs she's actively stepping on.

And then I hear a *crack* as Ali steps on something. *A bone,* I realize. Then the giant spider-like creature fixes its too-many eyes directly on her.

"Ali, run!" I shout, but it's no use. She can't hear me, but I can see in her face that she knows what's happening.

She has to get out, and *fast.*

She takes off running through the endless dark, her boots sticking in the webs with every step.

Come on, Ali. Show me where you are, I urge as I follow behind her, angry that I'm not actually here to save her. And suddenly, I realize how familiar this all feels.

I desperately hope this ends differently than it always does in my dreams.

And then I see the light up ahead. It's just a pinprick, but it's there. Ali must see it too, because she runs faster with a new type of resolve. The creature crawls quickly along the ceiling, getting closer every second. It's legs tapping with every step, it's hiss reverberating off the stone walls.

Then I watch as another creature appears and then another. Until suddenly, there are too many to count. The webbed walls have turned black with hints of bluish green, covered with undefinable hair and eyes and legs moving so quickly that it's impossible to focus on a single one.

I look ahead, watching the light as it gets closer, gets brighter, as Ali and I run toward it.

Suddenly, she stops.

I step up beside her and lean out. The cave opens up to a hole in the side of a mountain, the sheer cliff offering no footholds or path. Looking over the edge, I can see that the nearest ledge is at least fifty feet below.

There's no way down.

Ali turns to face the creatures. She reaches for her sword, but it isn't at her side. She stares at the small dagger in her hand for a long moment, before placing it back into the sheath in her boot and stepping backward off the ledge.

"Ali! No!" I scream, trying to reach for her, but it's too late.

A few seconds later, she lands on the rocky ledge below. I squeeze my eyes shut as I hear the sound of her body hitting the stone. I hear the loud *crack* of breaking bones. My eyes well with tears. I know too well the pain she is going through.

When I find the courage to open my eyes, I force myself to look down.

She's still alive, I breathe.

Ali lets out a cry of pain, reaching for her leg.

I hear the deafening hissing and tapping sounds of the spiders coming up behind me. I crouch, covering my head with my arms as they crawl past me and pour down the cliff toward her.

Suddenly, they stop dead in their tracks.

I stare, confused. They seem hesitant to move any further toward her, then they quickly scramble back up the cliff past me, and back into their hole.

A second later, the sun peaks over the horizon.

Looking down, I watch Ali lie back in relief. But she's clearly in too much pain to move. And definitely too injured to climb the rest of the way down.

But it doesn't matter.

Because now, I know where she is.

Chapter 32

I shake my head, breaking the connection that I have with Ali and find myself still sitting in the little dugout cave in the hillside. I can't wrap my brain around what just happened, but whatever it was, it doesn't matter right now. Because I know where she is and this time, I'm going to save her.

I hop down from my alcove in the cliff and take off running toward the mountain.

When Ali and I traveled through this part of the forest before, I saw that cliff. I noticed the peculiar shadow high up on its face and mindlessly wondered if it was the start of a cave system. After watching Ali fall out of it, I know exactly where she will be. But even though the sun just came up, I'm going to have a hell of a time reaching her.

And an even harder time getting her back.

Once I make it to the base of the mountain directly below the ledge, I don't even stop for a second before climbing. I move quickly, scaling it with ease, realizing that I've never been so determined to do anything before in my entire life. Because after all those times I couldn't save her, this time I have a chance to save her. *I have to save her this time.*

After a few minutes, I let out a grunt as I pull myself over the ledge. And then, I see her. She's lying on her back, one hand holding her side. Her broken leg lying limp at an awkward angle. She's barely breathing, but she manages to roll her head to one side to look at me. She stares with wide, unbelieving eyes.

"Steven?" she asks in a small voice. "You're alive. You found me," her eyes well with tears. "I thought... I thought that you... that you..." she sobs.

"*Shh*, it's okay Ali. I'm here," I say, moving toward her. I press my hand against her cheek and she leans into my palm.

"How?" she whispers through her tears.

"I saw you. In the mineshaft. I watched you fall and knew where to find you. Now, are you ready to get out of here?" I say, trying to smile.

"Steven, I can't move. My leg and... and the poison..." she says tiredly.

Poison?

"Don't worry about any of that. I've got you," I say, removing my sword and tossing it over the ledge to the ground a hundred feet below. "Get on my back, I'll carry you down."

"No, Steven, it's okay. We won't make it if you carry me. Just leave me here, you have to get back before the sun goes down," she says urgently, looking around.

"And do what, leave you here as spider bait? No way. You don't think I climbed all the way up this cliff just to say 'hi,' do you?" I smile at her sweetly and watch as more tears fall.

"I didn't know if you could come back. You fell and I thought..." she sniffles, her eyes going vacant.

"I know, but it's okay. I can come back, I promise. Nothing's going to happen to me. Now let's get you out of here," I say quickly, looking up at the sky.

We are running out of time.

When I go to help her up, I realize that she can barely move. I pull her onto my back, being careful of her injured leg. I hold her arms tightly around my neck and glance back at her.

"Can you hold onto me?" I ask, because I'm going to need both hands to climb down.

"Yeah, I can try," she says softly.

I stand and take a deep breath, walking over to the ledge. Carefully, I find my first foothold and then the next. And then I begin to climb down.

About halfway down the cliff, I can feel the burning from my bleeding fingers, feel the sticky liquid running down my arms. But I don't care. The half-conscious girl whose small arms are wrapped around my neck is all that matters. Still, the exertion of the climb has every muscle in my body shaking and I can feel Ali's grip starting to lose its hold. As her arms begin to give out, my hand shoots up, holding on, pulling her tighter to me.

"We're almost there, Ali, hold on. Hold on for me. You can do this," I whisper back to her.

"Steven, I can't. I can't hold on much longer."

"You *can*. Just hold on. Stay with me, Ali. I need you with me," I say, turning my head to press my forehead against hers, the contact a welcome comfort after being away from her.

"I'm with you," she says. It's barely audible, but she manages to tighten her grip.

A few minutes later, despite her efforts, I can tell she's about to pass out.

I climb down faster.

Just as my foot hits solid ground, Ali's arms give out and I have to catch her from falling the rest of the way down. I turn, helping her collapse slowly to the grass. She winces from the pain.

And I am out of breath.

I look up toward the sky, realizing that the sun is almost down. It isn't far to the cave, but this is the last place I want to be when it gets dark. The forest is no joke. Especially when you're standing directly under a spider den.

"Steven, just go," Ali says in her dazed state, making a pathetic attempt to wave me off.

"There's a cave not far from here. We can make it," I smile reassuringly. She doesn't know that running through the dark doesn't scare me anymore. Hell, *nothing* scares me anymore.

Except the thought of losing her again.

I look around and quickly find my sword a few feet away. I buckle it back around my waist, then scoop up an almost-unconscious Ali into my arms, relieved to discover that it's a whole lot easier to carry her on flat ground than it was while scaling down that cliff.

"Steven, you can't just carry me the whol-"

"You know, for someone who's getting a free ride, there's sure a lot of complaining going on here," I say, giving her a crooked smile. She wraps her arms around my neck and smiles warmly back up at me.

I'm happy to see you too, she whispers in my mind, too tired to speak. It fills me with so much warmth to know that she hasn't lost this *ability*, or whatever it is. I missed her voice. Missed the way it feels when she speaks to me like that. Because I don't just hear the words, I can *feel* them too. *Feel her.*

But now, it's time to get that voice, and the rest of her, to safety. I hold her closer to me, and run.

Just as the sun goes down, I step out from the tree line far from the mountain. I know that the cave isn't too much further, and I left a torch burning so I will be able to find it easily. But I also know that this part of the forest is crawling with creatures. And I won't be able to outrun anything while I'm carrying her.

Which means that things are about to get... *interesting*.

As I'm running, I feel the urge to stare down at the girl in my arms, but I force myself to stay focused. I keep my eyes trained on the forest, searching for any sign of movement.

It doesn't take long before I see one.

A huge hunched figure steps out from behind a tree ahead. It's moving slowly, but only because it hasn't seen us. *Yet.*

Then five more appear. I freeze. Looking past them, I can already see the glowing light coming from the cave. My abrupt stop brings Ali's focus back to the present and she looks over at the creatures with anxious eyes.

Steven... we have to go back before they see us, she says frantically.

I look down at her and give her a mischievous smile, elated that I'm about to save her for once.

Steven... what... what are you doing... she says, the concern in her voice apparent. Even more so inside my mind. I casually wonder if I will ever get used to our new form of silent communication.

Gingerly, I set her on the ground hidden behind a large rock and kiss her forehead sweetly before standing and drawing my sword. *Don't move,* I say and even though her eyes are beyond concerned, she nods, knowing that she won't be any help in her current state.

I run across the open space and sneak back into the tree line, quickly making my way up to the first creature.

Its head is rolling at its feet before it even sees me. Within seconds, an ash-like dust scatters across the forest floor where it once stood.

The commotion draws the attention of the other five creatures and they are now running straight toward me in their lumbering fashion. I spin my sword around and wait patiently for the first one to get close enough. Then I lunge forward and slash at its legs, severing both of them just below the knees. The creature falls forward, helpless, and lets out an ear-piercing screech that I'm all but used to at this point.

I glance back to check on Ali. Sure enough, a pair of wide green eyes are peaking over the rock, watching intently.

The next four come at me all at once. I quickly swap my sword to my off-hand and pick up a fist-sized rock. I throw it hard at one of the creatures, hitting it square in the face and knocking it off balance. It trips and slams into the creature next to it. They both go down, shaking the ground beneath my feet with their fall.

Two left, I think to myself, smiling.

I toss my sword back to my dominant hand as I run at them. I jam my blade deep into one creature's chest and lift myself up by the hilt, using my momentum to slam both my feet into the other one, knocking it to the ground. The first creature explodes into ash, releasing my sword. I twirl the blade around, landing it straight in the stomach of the one lying in front of me, creating another dust pile in the grass.

I hear two loud growls from behind me and know that the ones that stumbled are now back on their feet.

And they are *mad.*

I quickly grab Ali's dagger from the waistband at my back and, with a blade in each hand, duck below the creature's grabbing hands, slicing their sides as I run between them. They buckle over and I whip around, slamming a blade into each of their backs. They thrash, but I stand my ground until they explode into clouds of ash.

I look around, making sure no others have appeared from the dark, then head back toward Ali, scanning the trees as I go.

The one with no legs has been dragging itself along the ground toward me, leaving a trail of blood behind it. I drive my sword through its head, shattering it to tiny pieces as I pass.

I use my pants to clean the blood off my sword, and Ali's dagger, as I make my way back to her. I slide my sword into its sheath as I crouch in front of her, looking into those beautiful and now shocked eyes. Without breaking contact, I smile, then casually tuck the dagger that I stole from her earlier back into her boot, letting my hand linger on her good leg.

She just gapes at me, her mouth wide open. I gently close it, brushing my thumb over her lips before leaning in, kissing her slowly on that perfect mouth.

"I get the feeling we have some things to talk about," she says, still staring at me and a little breathless from our kiss. I give her a knowing look, but this isn't the time to talk.

I'm not entirely sure if it will ever be the time to talk. Not about that.

I slide a hand behind her back, then her knees, and she lets out a small gasp of pain as I lift her. I wince at the sound. She manages to wrap one arm around my neck, but leaves the other clutching at her side. The sound of her in pain makes my heart ache, but at least she is back in my arms.

At least she's safe.

Suddenly, the memories of *why* I didn't get to her in time come rushing back. I hold her closer to me, kissing the top of her head, finding my own comfort in the gesture.

Her eyes are already closed from fatigue, and I'm grateful for that. Because I can feel the tears escaping from mine, sliding down my face. But these tears are not from relief.

And they are ones that she will never see.

Chapter 33

By the time we reach the alcove, Ali is unconscious in my arms. I drape her over my shoulder and somehow manage to climb the few feet up without waking her.

I lay her gently down on the stone and sit with her, moving her head to rest on my thigh. Her eyes are pinched shut in pain, but she's still out, struggling through a restless sleep. I gently brush her hair from her face before running the back of my hand over her cheek. I smile when I see her visibly relax from my touch.

I study her, realizing what a mess she is. I'm sure I'm no better. Her red hair is a tangle of waves, her face covered with dried blood and dirt. Her clothes are filthy and torn, and that makes me smile. Because I know how pissed about it she'll be when she wakes up.

But even so, she's still breathtaking.

She always is.

But seeing her like this makes me feel even more protective of her. She's the strongest person I've ever met, has saved my ass god knows how many times, so it's strange to see her this... *vulnerable.* For the first time, she actually *needs* me. Just like I've always needed her. I want to take care of her and I'm resolved to do so. Because I owe it to her.

I owe everything to her, I think.

I never would have survived out here by myself. Not the way she did.

I stare out of the alcove, taking in a deep breath of the cool night air. I wondered what it would feel like to be around Ali again after our time together in that cave. Some part of me worried that it was all a dream, induced by delirium. I worried that once we were out, she would suddenly realize it was a mistake. That us being together would only complicate, or *compromise*, our survival.

That fear has eaten away at me during the long days away from her.

Because I don't want to go back to how we were before.

Before, was unbearable.

When we were in that cave, shut off from the world, I felt like all the walls between us had broken down. And I don't want that to change. The fear that I would lose that connection with her was scattering my brain to pieces.

But when I found her on that cliff, and her eyes met mine? I knew it instantly. The way she looked at me told me everything that I needed to know.

That she still loves me.

A pinching pain grips my stomach and I suddenly realize that I still haven't eaten. And most likely, neither has Ali. With everything that's happened, there hasn't been a single moment to even *think*, let alone find something to eat. But now that I've stopped moving, the truth of that fact is making itself known. All the way down to my bones.

Looking around, I realize that neither of us have our packs anymore. Mine ended up at the bottom of a ravine, and hers is most likely lost somewhere in a maze of cobwebs. Which means the only things we have left are my sword, her dagger and a couple of torches. Without any supplies and without food, I know we can't survive out here for very much longer.

And there is no way Ali will be making the trip back anytime soon.

I look back down at her, trying to gauge how bad her injuries actually are. Her leg is clearly broken, that much is obvious. And I saw her gripping her side earlier, but if she has any broken ribs, I won't have a clue how to fix them. If Ali were awake, she would know exactly what to do. But she's in too much pain for me to even think of waking her.

And what did she say about poison? I brush my hand over her forehead and can tell immediately that she has a fever. And I'm not sure what to do about that either. Knowing that our bodies heal quickly is a relief, so I figure that the best option is just to wait. Hopefully, by the time she wakes up, the pain will at least be bearable enough for her to tell me what I can do to help her.

I consider for a moment, just *carrying* her home. But then I think back on my journey here. It only takes a moment to realize that we would never make it. Navigating through the rough terrain was hard enough, but doing it while carrying someone would be next to impossible. We would never make it to each hiding place before dark. So we will just have to bide our time here until she is up for the journey.

Hours later, I stare out toward the trees and watch as the rising sun chases away the shadows, the remnants of ash floating away in the breeze. Ali is still asleep in my lap, unaware of the brightness of day that surrounds her. She's shaking now and her fever seems to be getting worse. Not knowing what else to do, I decide that I can at least find her food and water. Her body is weak, and I want to give her the best chance to fight off whatever this is.

My own stomach growls audibly and I realize that *I* won't make it very much longer either.

Ali whimpers in her sleep as I move out from under her, but she doesn't wake. I grab my sword, then bend down and gently unclasped the little gold watch from her wrist and press a kiss to her forehead.

After taking one last look at her, I jump down out of the cave and take off running.

"Well, good morning," I say as Ali slowly opens her eyes.

"Steven? Where are we?" She looks around the little hole in the hillside, confused and groggy. Her fever finally broke a few hours ago and I was so relieved that I nearly woke her up to tell her the good news. But as much as I wanted her back with me, I knew she needed as much rest as she could get. It was bad enough that I had to wake her every few hours to force her to drink some water. She was barely even conscious for those times, which did nothing to assuage my worry.

"Well, the bad news is that we're in another cave. Good news is that this cave doesn't have any snow. Or spiders. I checked," I say, smiling over at her.

"Well that's a relief. I'm not a huge fan of either these days," she says slowly as she struggles to lift herself into a sitting position. She winces from the pain and her hand shoots reflexively to her side.

"Ali!" I say moving closer to her. I've been keeping a close eye on her leg, which seems to be healing fine, but I didn't realize her side was still in pain.

I should have checked, I think, worry furrowing my brow.

Ali manages to lean back and pulls up her shirt just enough for me to see the wound right below her ribcage.

Two wounds, actually.

The large punctures are several inches apart, the entire area is swollen, and there are purple tree-branch-like marks spreading outwards from each.

"Shit," I say slowly, because it looks painful as hell.

She touches the area delicately, then winces. It takes me a minute to figure out what could have caused the injuries. And then it hits me.

A spider bite.

A *big* one.

"Well, I've had worse bites than this. It's almost healed anyway," she shrugs, pulling her shirt back down over it carefully with a wince.

"You've had a worse spider bite than *that*," I stare at her, unbelievingly.

"Well, yeah. This one didn't kill me," she smiles, still weary, but just as feisty as always. I shake my head at her.

Unbelievable.

"*Hell*, Steven, how long was I out?" she says, looking past me to the make-shift camp I set up.

"I lost track of the daylight cycles, but probably a couple of days. I figured you would be hungry. And we lost our supplies, so it's not much..." I say, wishing I could do more for her.

"Not much? Steven, this is great," she says, looking toward the food cache. She tries to get up, but the pain in her side prevents her from reaching it.

"Oh sit down, Wonder Woman. I'll bring it over to you," I admonish.

This girl, I roll my eyes, unbelievably happy to have her back with me.

"Thanks," she grumbles, clearly annoyed that her own body is betraying her. I smile, shaking my head at her stubbornness as I hand her a piece of bark that's piled high with berries.

When I went out in search of food, I was elated to find the berry bushes nearby. I knew immediately that they were edible, because Ali has the same ones back in the greenhouse. And after not eating for the better part of two weeks, a few berries was all I needed to keep going. And I can see that they're doing the same for Ali. The color returns to her cheeks immediately, and she slowly seems more alert.

"Steven?" she asks a few minutes later. "How the hell did you get a fire going?"

I look over at the flickering flames and smile, then playfully hold up two sticks.

"No fucking way. How long did *that* take you?" she asks.

"*Eh*, like five... ten minutes, tops," I say nonchalantly.

"Bullshit. How long did it take you?" she asks again, stuffing another handful of berries in her mouth.

"Okay, okay. I just finally got it going a few hours ago," I admit, scratching at the back of my neck. "But, I was pretty determined, because I wanted to cook these," I hold out another piece of bark for her, which has several small, slightly burnt, fish piled on it.

Okay, so they're mostly burnt.

But I couldn't just let them go to waste after I spent all that time catching them. I was so desperate for protein, that I cooked them with the head, tail, scales and all. But damn they tasted good. I've eaten several already and if Ali hadn't woken up when she did, then I would have had no choice but to wake her before I ended up finishing off the rest of them.

When Ali sees the tiny fish, those big green eyes get giant as she stares back and forth between me and the pathetic meal. She looks shocked, delighted, and a little bit like she might gladly kill someone over them.

I hand them over before she has the opportunity.

She takes the platter hesitantly, unbelievingly, and it warms me to think that I could do this for her, as small a thing as it may seem.

"What about you? You have to eat too and I just ate all of the berries," she says, suddenly looking remorseful.

"I already ate my fish, and I can pick more berries. Those are all yours. And sorry, they're probably a little cold, I cooked them a while ago. But I wanted to let you sleep," I smile at her.

"I don't care if they're cold. Thank you," she says sincerely.

As I watch her expertly pick apart the fish, I'm once again confronted with how long she's been out here. It took me nearly an hour to get all of the meat away from the tiny bones on mine. But within seconds it seems, she's already finished off the first one and is on to the next.

The reminder of the time she spent alone is sobering. She was only out of it for a few days, and I was already to the point where I was about to start talking to myself. Out loud, and in the third person.

As I tend to the fire, I keep sneaking glances over at Ali, realizing how much I missed her. The time between when I fell and now has been the longest we've gone without being together since I got here.

It felt like a lifetime.

And after everything I went through to get back to her, finding her nearly dead, then having to wait out her fever, hadn't exactly been part of my *heroic* plan. But now that she's safe, now that we're here together, I can't stop staring.

Not only did I miss the girl, but I had finally confessed my love to her.

And then *I died*.

I internally chuckled at the irony.

"What are you thinking about?" She smiles at me sideways.

"I don't know, you tell me," I tease her.

"I don't think it works like that. Believe me, I've tried," she says.

"Oh really?" I smile coyly at her. "So why do you think it worked that one time?"

"I have a theory about that," she stares at me mischievously.

"Oh yeah? And what's your theory?" I look at her from across the fire, holding back a smile.

"I think that you wanted me to hear you," she says, challenging me.

Shit.

"And why would I go and do a thing like that?" I fix my eyes on her, a smile playing at the corner of my mouth.

Why would I purposefully open up my thoughts to you... letting you know how much all this being stuck with you... in small spaces... makes me want to...

Why don't you stop teasing me and get that smart mouth over here, she says, her eyes fixed on me.

I've never been bold, or even remotely confident when it comes to girls. But somehow, with her, I find myself saying and *thinking* things that I never thought I would. I find that letting her hear my thoughts is easier than coming up with the words I want to say to her. It's almost as if we have a language all our own, a *world* all our own. And in our world, there's no line between emotions and words, because in our minds, they're intertwined.

I feel like I can say anything to her.

Be everything to her.

"What, this smart mouth?" I ask, placing a gentle kiss on her forehead before sitting down beside her.

"Yes, that-" she starts to say, but I cut her off immediately, covering her lips with mine.

I move one hand to her face and place the other on her back, gently pressing her into me. I feel her body relax, letting me hold her weight in my arms.

I close my eyes and realize how different this kiss is from the ones we shared before. It isn't shy or hesitant, or full of fire that threatens to ignite my whole body. This is more intimate.

This kiss is full of relief, contentment and love.

"Ali, I think I missed you," I whisper, gently nudging her nose with mine. I allow some space between us before this turns into that familiar fire and I get carried away.

"I... I think I missed you too," she replies, breathless. "But I also think that I was poisoned and unconscious for most of it," she looks up at me, concerned. "How long was it?"

"Well, including the time we've been here?" I look away, pushing back the images that are trying to claw their way back. "I think it's probably been around five days."

"Five days," she says, thinking out loud. "Three days until you found me..." her voice trails off, then she looks up at me quickly. It's then I know she understands.

Her eyes fill with a mix of horror and sympathy.

How many times? she asks quietly in my mind, unable to hide her aching heart with the intimacy of our mental connection.

"Counting the fall?" I say quietly, not looking at her. My mind floods with memories, ones I don't let her see.

Nineteen, I think, because it's too difficult to say the word out loud.

Her eyes shoot to mine, immediately filling with tears.

"Nineteen times? *Oh god,* Steven," her hands involuntarily move to my chest and she looks me up and down, as if checking to see if I'm still in one piece.

"Um, yeah. Not gonna lie, I don't recommend it," I try to joke, but the memories are so fresh in my mind that I know it's a weak attempt to assuage her concerns. When I finally look at her, I notice that her tears have started to fall. Holding her face gently, I brush them away, unable to stand the heartbreak in her eyes.

"It's okay, Ali. Really. And besides, I think that I should be thanking you," I say.

"Why would you thank me? If I would have gone down that mountain first, if I saw the ravine in time, then maybe I could have-"

"Ali, there's nothing you could have done, you know that. And I have to thank you. Because without you, nineteen times would have been a whole lot more." I move to sit behind her, wrapping my arms around her in a comforting embrace. "I used to think that how we train is a little overkill. And, as much as I enjoy it, I couldn't imagine actually using those skills. Not really. But you were right. You were right about everything. When I was out there, I just kept going over everything you taught me in my head. You saved me. And from now on, I'm going to take training a lot more seriously."

She turns to look up at me and smiles a little, but it doesn't meet her eyes.

"Besides," I continue. "If I didn't have all that first-hand experience, I probably wouldn't have been able to drag your ass back here."

"You were kinda great out there," she admits, peering back at me from under those dark lashes, letting a real smile escape her for the first time.

"I was, wasn't I?" I smile proudly and she tries to slap my shoulder, but winces before she can. I just shake my head.

"Hey, Ali?" I ask, remembering something. "When I was... on the island, and after, when you were in the den, I tried calling for you, but you didn't hear me, even after you were awake. Do you think it was the poison? Did it somehow affect your ability?"

"It could have been the poison. But I also think that I just wasn't listening. This is still so new to me, I can only hear you when I'm trying to. I was so groggy, I wasn't even thinking about it. I'll have to work on keeping my mind open to you. That way you can reach me anytime," she smiles sweetly. "That is, unless you're annoying me, then you're on your own."

I look down at her, giving her a smirk.

"Well, I think I've had enough fun for one map run. Ready to head back home?" she asks, trying to get up. I tighten my arms around her, pinning her to me, and she leans back against my chest with an exasperated groan.

"*You* are not going anywhere," I say, kissing her temple. "*I* can go out and get food when we need it and you can just sit your stubborn ass right here and heal."

She gives me her best glare and I laugh.

Beautiful and stubborn, I think amusingly, allowing her to hear. She lets out an adorable huff of annoyance, but finally relaxes, tipping her head back against me and closing her eyes. I hold her close to my chest, enjoying the feel of her.

I stare out into the world, then rest my cheek on the top of her head, letting out a long relieved breath. I lean up against the stone wall behind me, finally allowing the exhaustion to take hold, tucked away in our own little hideaway in the hillside. Knowing that she's going to be alright.

"Steven?" Ali says sleepily.

"*Hm*?" I say, closing my own eyes.

"Thank you. Thank you for coming back for me. For not leaving me on the ledge. For keeping me safe," she says in a small voice.

"Ali, I will always come back for you. I will never leave you. And I will ceaselessly do everything in my power to keep you safe," I whisper.

Then we drift off to sleep, safe in each other's arms at last.

Chapter 34

The rain comes down outside, turning the world to gray. I'm suddenly grateful that we are in *this* hideaway and not in one of the previous ones that were prone to flooding.

"How's your leg?" I ask, then watch as Ali stretches it, trying to determine for herself.

"Still hurts. But I think I can probably walk on it soon," she says.

"How about your side?" I ask.

Her aching body struggles with the hem of her shirt. I lean over, gently moving her hand away.

"Here, let me," I say, looking to her for confirmation. She nods, relieved, then leans back as I carefully lift her shirt up enough to see the wound.

The two punctures from the bite are slightly smaller and the area around them is only a little red and swollen. I notice, with relief, that the angry purple lines that previously spread across her entire stomach, are completely gone.

I also notice, as I let my eyes wander, her perfectly toned abdominal muscles.

My breath hitches.

Fuck, I draw out the word in my mind, wondering how in the hell I've been living with this girl and never noticed... *that.*

Clearly, I was too preoccupied with her wound last time she raised her shirt to notice, and then there is the fact that she's always worn a T-shirt whenever we've gone swimming. The last time she had her shirt off, I only saw her back.

Her handmade shirts are incredibly practical and don't exactly give anything away.

But now… *damn.*

I've always found her attractive, but this new image of her sends a wave of desire through me. It makes my head spin. I clench my jaw, trying to hide the emotions that are suddenly running rampant through me.

Okay, she is definitely going to catch me staring if I don't pull myself together.

I clear my throat and try to act *cool.*

Yeah right. I feel anything and everything but *cool.*

"It… um, actually looks… um… a lot better," I mutter, then dare to look up at her with a strained smile. She seems confused by my reaction, but only for a moment. When she looks from the wound, then up to the awkward as fuck smile plastered on my face, I know that I've been caught.

I panic, but I hold her gaze. Then suddenly realize that *she* isn't thinking about her injury anymore either. I try to control my breathing and know that whatever this is, I need it to stop. Right. Now. *She's injured for god's sake. This is not the time.*

I begin slowly sliding her shirt back into place, being careful of the wound, but I casually let the backs of my fingers run down her bare skin as I do. I marvel at how *soft* she is. And I don't know what it is about this girl that drives me to do things like this, but I can't help myself. I just have to touch her. I can feel under my fingers that her breathing is a little faster than before and I watch her face as her eyes flicker down to my hands.

Once the fabric is back in place, I regret it immediately.

I gently slide my hand back under her shirt and press my warm palm against her waist. I allow it to linger there, not ready to let her go just yet. My hand is large on her small frame, my fingers wrap all the way around to her back. I gently rub my thumb back and forth over her stomach for a few moments, feeling her soft skin, before realizing what I'm doing.

Dammit. I have to keep it under control. She's. Hurt. I remind myself again.

I take a deep breath, resolving to let her go. Maybe I will go make myself busy by tending the fire or something. *Anything*, to keep my mind off of her for a few minutes. But just as my fingers start to pull away, her small hand keeps them in their place.

Ali, I don't want to hurt you, I say, looking up into those big, green eyes.

She gives me that crooked little smile again, the one that drives me crazy. Hell, all her expressions drive me crazy.

Then be gentle, she whispers in my mind.

And how in the fuck could I ever say no to *that.*

Giving in, I lean toward her, moving my hand to the bare skin of her back. Without breaking eye contact, I brush my lips against hers as gently as possible, barely letting them touch.

Like this? I tease, doing it again.

She lets out an annoyed groan and I smile, pleased at how much I enjoy making her feel the way I've felt these past months. But what little control I thought I had over the situation doesn't last long.

Our lips are suddenly moving together frantically, like we can't get enough of each other. I use the hand on her lower back to pull her closer to me, and use the other to cup the side of her face for a moment before quickly moving it back and into her long hair. Grabbing hold, I deepen the kiss. Her own hands reach up, and I can feel her wince under me. I back my mouth away from hers and she whimpers her complaint.

No, come back, she pleads.

Then. Be. Gentle, I lecture, slowly lowering her back to lie on the stone.

I firmly grasp the arms that tried to escape, pinning them down at her sides so she won't attempt that again. Then I take back her mouth, starting over at a more leisurely pace, closing my eyes as I melt into her.

When I wake up in pain, I decide that I never want to sleep in a cave again. Well, aside from *our* cave in the cliffs. But that doesn't count. Because it has *curtains*. Even if they are ugly as fuck.

And even though I know that my body will heal in under an hour, stone floors are definitely not my favorite thing right now.

I want my own bed.

Looking down, I realize that Ali has been using my bicep as a pillow. So on top of being sore, I can no longer feel my fingers either. But she looks so peaceful when she's asleep. I don't want to wake her. Until I feel another shooting pain run up my back.

Okay, I'm waking her.

I try to free my arm, but it's no use. I'm trapped.

"Ali," I whisper, shaking her just a little. "Ali, I need my arm back."

"No you don't," she mumbles and moves a hand up to hold it in place.

"Yes, I do," I laugh, gently rolling her off of it as she grumbles her complaints. Once free, I stand, stretching out my aching body.

Ali sits up, watching stoically as I place a few more logs on the fire.

"What are you thinking about?" I ask, because she's never this quiet.

"Nothing," she says, but I know better. And even if I didn't, the way she's currently using a stick to push around a small rock would have clued me in.

Ali, you know you can tell me anything, I say in our minds, so she knows I'm sincere. She looks up at me and I see the sadness in them, but then she goes back to playing with her rock. I leave her alone for several long minutes. I'm about to bring it up again, when she finally speaks.

"Fifty-two," she says so quietly that I barely hear her.

"Fifty-two?" I ask curiously.

"I've died eighty-six times. But fifty-two of those times... the *first* fifty-two... were in the first few days."

I stare at her.

Fuck, I think as the realization of what she's saying sinks in.

I suddenly feel sick to my stomach.

Dying nineteen times over the course of three days left me exhausted, hopeless and well, *traumatized*.

And I already knew about the monsters. I knew about this place and I knew how to fight them. I knew that I would just come back if I died. I knew where to go for safety on that island and I had a *purpose*.

Because I have Ali.

As horrible as those days were for me, I just kept repeating everything she taught me and used it to my advantage. I stayed strong because of it. I knew that I could survive, knew I had to find her. She was the only thing that kept me going.

But Ali didn't have any of that.

When she woke up on that beach, exhausted and confused, she had no memory of how she got there. She didn't know why she was here, or what would happen when the sun went down. She was a fifteen-year-old girl who didn't have a chance in hell against these creatures.

She didn't know how to fight.

She didn't have a hidden trap door, and she didn't have anyone there to save her. She tried to run, tried to escape them. And she failed.

Fifty-two times.

I put my face in my hands, the thoughts of what she must have gone through leaving me in *pieces*.

What I went through was nothing compared to what she did.

After a moment, I look up, not bothering to hide the unspilled tears welling in my eyes. I can't even imagine her going through any of that *now*, let alone back then. And she went through it *alone*.

"I'm so sorry, Ali. I knew that your first days were rough, but I couldn't have imagined... not until I..."

"I know. I wasn't sure how to explain it, but when you said you died nineteen times... Well, I just wanted you to know that I understand what you went through. And if you need to talk about it, I'm here," she says.

I look at her again, dumbfounded. After all *she* went through, here she is, comforting *me. Again*. That is the moment that I realize what Ali is to me.

She is my strength.

Whatever I'm feeling about my first nineteen deaths, it's time for me to face it. Because if fifteen-year-old Alexandra Cutter could survive *worse,* then come out the other side being the caring and selfless person she is, with no complaints, no remorse, then I know I can survive this. Because I have her.

And now, it's time she lets me in. Lets me be that strength for her.

"Ali, there's plenty of time to talk about what happened to me. Tell me about when you got here."

"You really don't want to hear about it," she says, not making eye contact. And I get the feeling that she's needed to speak to someone about this for a long time.

"You're right, I don't want to *hear* about it." Sitting in front of her, I reach out, clasping her forearms as she instinctively holds mine, creating an unbreakable bond.

I want you to show me, I tell her.

"Steven, no. That would be so much worse. You would feel everything I felt and see everything I saw if I shared my memories with you."

"I know," I say seriously, because I've already made my decision on this. And I'm not backing down.

Ali, I can handle it. You don't have to carry this alone anymore, I say, meeting those big, sad, green eyes that are already brimming with tears.

No way, it's out of the question, she argues.

Ali, you know I'm with you, I say, my gaze unwavering. *Let me be with you on this too.*

She gives me one last long look and then I see the unmistakable flicker of light behind her eyes. An instant later, I'm staring at those same green eyes as they wake up on the beach for the first time.

We've shared flashes of our thoughts before, but never have we shared a memory, not like this. Everything seems to happen in fast-forward. Scattered flashes of moments flicker in front of my eyes, until Ali focuses in on one memory and it plays out in front of me as if I were there. I see everything that she sees, feel what she feels when she wakes up on the sand that first day. And I experience the excruciating pain of her death up until the breath leaves her body.

And then her eyes open and it starts all over again. And again.

In every memory, I feel her confusion, her fear, her anxiety.

Her pain.

And ultimately, I feel the incurable despair as she slowly realizes that the nightmare doesn't end when you die.

I feel it all, carry it all, right alongside her.

I feel my breath stop when she drowns for the first time. Feel the blood dripping down my skin every time she's shot with an arrow. My body breaks when she's thrown against a tree, and my skin tears when she is pulled to pieces by sharp teeth and large hands.

I feel her freeze.

And fall.

And *burn*.

I feel her die.

Fifty-two times, in rapid succession.

And then, it's over.

Ali drops our joined hands and I slowly open my eyes, my mind becoming my own once again. Reaching up, I feel that my face is wet with tears. My hands are shaking. Looking over, I see Ali isn't doing any better.

"I'm so sorry, Steven, I shouldn't have-"

"*Shh*... stop that. Ali, come here," I whisper, pulling her into my lap and wrapping my arms around her, letting her cry into my chest.

I just wish the memories would fade as quickly as the scars, she says. I squeeze my eyes shut, because now, I understand.

Knowing that she has gone through hell and then actually seeing it, *feeling* it, are two very different things. My mind is weighed down with the horror of those images, but when I feel the warmth of the girl who is gently sobbing in my arms, I know that it was worth it.

I hope that me knowing, trying to understand what she went through, will help alleviate some of her pain. Or at least, prove to her that she isn't alone anymore.

That she will never be alone again.

I hold her even tighter and rest my cheek on her head, grateful that she's no longer on that beach, in the woods.

She is here with me, safe in my arms.

And I am never letting her go.

But I didn't just see the relentless cycle of blood and death, she also showed me how she broke out of it. After nearly a dozen tries, she eventually managed to *swim* to shore.

Swim.

I mentally calculate the distance. I'm not sure if I could have done that.

By then, she already figured out the daylight cycle, already learned how to hide at night and make a run for it during the day.

I watched her in her memories as she ran along the base of the mountain, looking for somewhere to hide. She climbed nearly thirty feet up a cliff with shaky hands until she pulled herself over the ledge, then lay there, exhausted. In that moment, I wondered why she chose to show me that particular memory. But when I looked around, really looked, I understood. She was sprawled out on the ground of a large cave. A cave, which I immediately recognized.

Because it's our living room.

I couldn't believe how different it looked. The cave was cold and dark, nothing like the warm and inviting space full of light, furniture, paintings, books and memories that I know it to be. Seeing our home back before it was built was a surreal feeling. Before Ali got there, the space was completely bare. There was no floor, no lights or windows, nothing. It was just a cave. I hadn't realized my lack of appreciation for it until now. But after seeing how much work went into building it, I'm suddenly proud of her all over again.

In the corner of the cave was an old chest, covered in dust and cobwebs. Inside of it was the big book from upstairs and several torches. The book left Ali confused and entranced, but without knowing what to do with it, she quickly turned to the torches. She figured out how to light them, then illuminated the space, keeping the creatures at bay.

When Ali showed me that memory, there was one question that kept replaying over and over in her mind.

Who left this here?

I wondered the same thing, until more pressing, more *concerning* thoughts tore at both of us as we relived her memory.

What happened to them? And, *Will the same thing happen to us?*

"Okay, your turn," a soft voice says from my arms. I was so lost in my own thoughts, I didn't even notice that she stopped crying and is now looking up at me.

"What?" I ask.

"It's only fair," she says, holding my arms tighter as they wrap around her. I stare down at her, confused for a moment.

And then I realize what she wants me to do.

"No way," I say adamantly.

"Steven, I've died eighty-six times. Think I can't handle your nineteen?" she says.

I sigh heavily, knowing damn well that I've already lost this argument.

"Ali, if I didn't already know that you could handle anything, I sure as hell do now. But are you sure you want to?" I ask.

Am I sure *I* want to?

She nods against me and I hold her closer. *I can do this. I can face it. I know I can. Because she's here with me.* Closing my eyes, I let my mind go back to that moment.

I'm falling away from her now, the ravine rising up around me.

I feel Ali's body tense in my arms when I hit the ground, but I continue.

I take her through every death on that island. All nineteen of them, feeling her shudder for some of the particularly gruesome ones.

I let her see my journey back to her. How I *fought* my way back to her.

And then I show her how I found her. It's something that's been eating away at me ever since. I wonder if maybe she can make any sense of it. She stands by, watching as I see her waking up in that cave.

How I was *miles* away from her at the time.

My hope fades when I can feel in her mind that she's just as bewildered as I was. But hey, it was worth a shot.

I also let her see the moment when I found her on the cliff. Because I want her to *know*. Finding her had made my broken world complete again. I love her, and not having her by my side had suffocated me more than my nineteen deaths. When she tells me to leave her there on that ledge, I let her hear my thoughts, my feelings, my entire soul, so that she *knows*. In that moment, there isn't a single part of me that considered it.

Not even for a second.

And then I break the connection.

She opens her eyes and immediately turns into me, wrapping her arms around my neck. I breathe her in and run my hands over her back. After reliving what I went through, knowing that she saw it too, has me grasping at her as if she were the very air I needed to breathe.

And then I remember her injuries. Realize how tightly I'm holding her to me. She could barely lift her arms yesterday, and now she has them around my neck. *Not that I'm complaining.*

"I'm sorry Ali, are you okay?" I ask.

"Shut up, I'm fine," she says into me, her voice muffled as she holds me closer.

I know she's lying, but I give it up. Because her mouth is on mine and I've lost all capability for coherent thoughts.

When she kisses me, every concern or worry in the world disappears. She kisses me deeper and when her tongue touches mine-

"Ali," I say, reluctantly breaking our connection. "I think that you might be okay to walk back now," I say.

She's still sitting on my lap and it's starting to make my head spin.

"What gave you that impression?" she smiles against my mouth.

Your hands in my hair, for one thing. You definitely couldn't do that yesterday.

But can I do it tomorrow? she asks.

"Tomorrow, I would like to not be sleeping in this fucking cave. And if you don't get off me now, I might never leave," I say, smiling widely at her.

"True. I would also like to not be in this cave, or *any* cave, ever again."

"Well, except for the one with those hideous curtains," I tease her, recalling my earlier thoughts, then dumping her softly off my lap before I get any bright ideas to take this further.

"Hey, I love those curtains," she grumbles and I roll my eyes. Because this is not the first time this particular argument has come up.

I walk over to the edge of our hideaway and lean against the stone wall, arms crossed. I'm pretending to look out at the night sky, but really, I just need some fresh air on my face. If I thought that being cooped up with her in a six-story house had been insufferable, then boy did our last few hiding places prove me wrong.

Thinking about the cliffs, I suddenly can't wait to get back. I want to be *clean* and to sleep in an actual bed. Not to mention the food. As soon as we're back there, I am going to eat. *A lot*.

I also wonder how different it will be. Everything feels different now that I've died and now that Ali and I are...

"Hey, that's a cute watch," she says behind me.

I'm confused for a moment, but then I look down at my wrist and laugh. It does look *cute* on me. The girly trinket is way too small for my large wrist and looks ridiculous. But I have to admit, it was a lifesaver, literally, when I was out gathering supplies.

"You know you're going to have to make me my own. This one doesn't match my eyes," I say playfully, dangling the little golden chain near my face, batting my eyelashes.

"I don't know what you're talking about, I think it's *adorable*," she says, holding back a laugh.

"Yeah, *adorable*. My point exactly," I smile, helping clasp it back around her wrist, taking my time so my fingers linger on her skin as long as possible. Ali checks the watch and then stands against the opposite wall, looking out over the dark forest sprawling beneath the night sky.

"You sure you're feeling up to this?" I ask.

"Trust me, I've made it back home in *way* worse condition. And I'm ready for *food*. And I mean, *a lot* of food."

With Ali's injuries and stopping each night, it takes us nearly three hours before we're at the footbridge.

I couldn't be happier to see it.

I smile broadly at Ali as we stop, looking up at the cliffs ahead. The rocky face is scattered with windows, illuminated from the lights within. I can even see the little balcony off the kitchen and part of the greenhouse high above. I can see the waterfalls crashing down and I'm surrounded by a strange feeling.

It almost feels like *home*.

I smile, thinking about how it looked in Ali's memory. The cliffs loomed over her, like another creature ready to attack.

And then she turned that cold edifice into *this*.

It's warm, inviting, and even the rocks seem to glow not only from the light, but from the comfort that I know waits inside.

Ali steps up closer to me, intertwining her fingers with mine. The gesture catches me a little off guard, sending shivers up my arm.

Have I held her hand before? I'm sure I have, but not like *this*. It makes my heart race and I can't hold back my smile as I look down at how our hands look interlocked together. I stare into the beautiful eyes of the amazing girl standing by my side. I gently stroke the back of her hand with my thumb, not wanting the moment to end. She smiles sweetly up at me, then playfully drags me along behind her.

Hand-in-hand, we cross the bridge and pass the barrier, into the safety of the light. Feeling her hand in mine, it's then that I know it for certain...

I'm home.

Chapter 35

I close my eyes, letting the cold water from the falls run over my face and down my body. The map run left me exhausted. Sleeping outside, living outside and well, *dying*, has left me with more layers of grime than I care to think about. I'm relieved to finally be getting clean and even more relieved to be back here.

Ali and I ran straight up to the kitchen, laughing and joking over what a mess we were as we scarfed down whatever food we could find.

Then we quickly decided that showers were the number one priority. Even though I was beat down from the whole journey and couldn't wait to crawl into my own bed, I insisted that Ali come down here first to clean up before me. *She's probably sound asleep by now,* I figure, then decide that I should probably drag myself to bed before I end up passing out right here on the stone ground of the grotto.

I step off the wooden platform that Ali built under the falls and quickly dry myself off, sliding on a clean white t-shirt and gray sweatpants. Ali showed me how to use the book to make new clothes using the wool we got from the sheep down in the pasture, so I was finally able to put together my own wardrobe. Because wearing *her* clothes is something that doesn't need repeating.

Ever.

I pick up my old clothes. They are torn, dirty and smell *horrible*. I can't wait to wash them, or maybe burn them, but I can't be bothered to do anything right now. Right now, I want to get some sleep. Some actual, in-a-bed, not on the stone floor of a cave, *sleep*.

Just the thought of it has me yawning again.

As I walk barefoot across the meadow back toward the house, I run my hands through my hair, suddenly realizing how long it's getting.

I climb the ladder, make my way into the house and walk straight into my room, looking forward to falling into bed.

Only, there's no bed.

Shit. The bed frame is completely empty, reminding me that my mattress is still on the floor in Ali's bedroom. I've already said goodnight to her and the particular *nature* of our goodnight caused me to forget that one minor detail.

I think for a long moment if I really even *need* a bed.

Stepping out into the hallway, I look over toward the couch, considering. But after one long sigh, I turn and walk down the hall toward Ali's room, hoping that she isn't already asleep.

I knock sheepishly and wait for a response.

A few seconds later, she opens the door and I immediately lose track of why I'm here in the first place.

Why does she do this to me?

Her hair is still wet and she has her head cocked adorably to one side as she attempts to dry it with a towel. Her skin is clean, soft, and *god*, she probably smells amazing too. Like she always does fresh out of the shower.

In an attempt to avoid her eyes and my thoughts, I look down at the floor. Which unfortunately, turns out to be a big mistake. Because I can't help but notice her outfit on the way down. She's wearing a baggy t-shirt, *one of mine?* that stops about mid-thigh. And it's clinging to her damp body in all the right places.

And that's it. That's all she's wearing.

Her little outfit gives me a full view of her long legs, all the way down to her bare feet. Staring at her, I clench my jaw and have to take a moment to focus on my breathing. For as long as we've lived together, and as many times as we have slept in the same bed after one of us had a nightmare, I have never seen her dress like *this* before.

Suddenly, I have a sneaking suspicion that she did this on purpose. *Touché, Alexandra*. If this is how she is going to play it, then *game on*.

But not tonight.

"Did you forget something?" she asks sweetly. But I know what she's doing. And it isn't going to work.

We already talked about this, and decided to sleep in our own beds tonight.

Because we need some actual sleep. And we need it *without* distractions. But here she is. Standing there. Like *that*.

Distracting me.

"Um... yeah... my bed seems to be missing and I would like it back. So if you don't mind, I will just grab that and get out of your hair," I say, squeezing past her, trying not to make eye contact and trying even harder not to touch her. I go to the side of Ali's bed and pick up the corner of my mattress. I'm about to drag it out the door, but glancing back at her, I notice she looks... *sad*.

Dammit, Ali, I think to myself. I don't doubt that the emotion is genuine. We're so used to sleeping in the same room at this point, it would be strange not to. Especially after everything that happened.

I take a deep, frustrated breath, giving in.

"Ali, would you like me to sleep in here tonight?" I ask, staring at the ceiling before glancing over at her.

She nods her head enthusiastically and I drop the mattress back to the floor with a *thump*.

"Fine, but no funny business, I mean it. We had a deal, remember?" I admonish, crossing my arms.

"Got it. No funny business here," she says, putting her hands up in surrender. But I can tell by her smile that she's already up to something.

Sure enough, she walks over to her bed and then *crawls* up to her pillow before plopping down onto her stomach playfully right in front of me. Her *night-shirt* has risen up and is now lingering just below her butt.

Yup, that's definitely mine.

The curves of her body are fully outlined under *my* shirt and although it isn't see-through, *thank fuck for that*, I can still make out a hint of the dark lines of her tattoo through it. I follow the letters down with my eyes, taking in the sight of her.

And then I realize what's happening.

Goddammit.

The smug little smile on her face tells me that she knows *exactly* what she's doing. I glare at her, but two can play at this game.

And I intend to.

We've always been competitive. Why would this be any different?

I take a deep breath to clear my head, deciding on my strategy. Staring straight at her, I pull my shirt up and over my head with one hand, tossing it to the floor. And then, just for good measure, I put my hands behind my head and flex my arms as I yawn, stretching out every muscle in my chest and abdominals.

Her expression gives nothing away and I worry for a moment that my ploy didn't work. But then I notice how her cheeks have turned a rosy shade of red and I smile. Putting both of my hands on the bed in front of her, I lean in close, letting my lips linger a few inches from hers.

"Now be good, or I'll have to come up there and take my shirt back," I whisper. I don't miss that her mouth drops open just a little.

Then I immediately draw back, quickly tucking myself into my own bed on the floor, not saying another word. I put my hands behind my head as I lay there, *waiting*.

Hearing only her breathing and mine, I stare at the shadows dancing across the ceiling. I watch as the night turns to day, then back to night and although I can't actually see her, I'm acutely aware of her presence.

We can never sleep in the complete dark, because for some unknown reason, the creatures can appear *anywhere*, not just outside. So when the sun goes down, Ali's room is lit with the soft glow of candles. They are scattered on the floor, the dresser, the table and in little nooks and shelves dug into the stone walls. Before, I found the soft light soothing. *Now*? I find that the ambiance is making it straight up impossible not to climb into bed with her. If she doesn't break soon, then I'm going to.

Steven... she finally says, her voice soft in my mind.

Finally, thank god, I think only to myself, relieved. *Yes, Alexandra?* I reply coolly.

I give up. You win. Now get your ass up here, she says, frustrated as all hell to have lost this battle.

But she doesn't have to ask me twice.

Within a second, I'm throwing back the covers and climbing under them with her. I slide my hand over her tiny waist and pull her close to me. She laughs as I nuzzle my nose against her cheek and let my damp hair tickle her face.

And I was right. She *does* smell good.

When we were out in the wilderness, I thought that sleeping beside Ali was the happiest I could ever be. But I was mistaken.

Because those nights were nothing compared to *this*.

Tonight, we aren't shivering by a fire, or lying on a stone floor that makes your body ache every time you move. We aren't constantly on guard, or worried about what the next day will bring. There are no monsters, no birds, no bugs, rain or snow. In here, in our home, we are safe. I feel like my body is sinking into the mattress and the sheets that wrap around us feel impossibly soft.

She feels impossibly soft.

I hold her small body tight against my chest, not wanting to succumb to exhaustion, but knowing that it's a battle I'm about to lose. The emotions of having her finally safe in my arms, of having her be mine, is overwhelming.

I close my eyes, letting every muscle in my body relax. I can't remember a time that I was ever this happy, or this at peace.

"Goodnight, Ali," I whisper.

"Goodnight, Steven," she whispers back, just before I fall into a deep and nightmare-free sleep.

Chapter 36

When I wake up, I breathe in a sigh of relief, realizing that I'm home. Not in a cold, damp, cave. Not on the island, *home*.

And in Ali's bed.

I am lying on my back, one arm behind my head, the other around Ali. She is tucked into my side, her cheek resting on my bare chest, still fast asleep. Her arm draped lazily over my stomach. My heart leaps at the sight of her pressed flush against my skin. I stroke her arm lazily and, without waking up, she snuggles in closer.

I hold her tighter, wondering what in the hell I ever did to deserve this.

To deserve *her*.

I run my fingers through her long, silky hair and think back on how much we've been through together. I know that I've only known her a couple of months, but it feels like a lifetime. We live together, train together and have become best friends. On the map run, we fought together, protected each other.

Admitted that we are in love with each other.

We died together in our memories and finally made our way back home after all of it.

Living out here in this crazy world, there's no telling what our future will be like. Or if we will ever make it back to the world we left behind. But even with the constant uncertainty, after everything we've gone through, moments like *this* make it all worth it.

I feel Ali stir in my arms. Slowly, she looks up at me with those big, green eyes, still sleepy and incredibly adorable. My heart melts again and I wonder if she could ever truly know how much I feel for her.

"Good morning," she says brightly, a smile spreading across her lips as she peeks up at me.

"Good morning," I smile back.

She rests her head back on my chest and I feel her body stiffen, like she's afraid to move.

"Ali, what is it?" I ask.

"Oh, um... No, it's nothing..." she trails off, still tense.

"Ali..." I urge, trying to get a glimpse at her face, but she stays still and quiet. I nudge her a little, prompting an answer.

Your shirt's off, she finally admits and I can feel in her thoughts that she is embarrassed to have woken up like this.

And whose fault is that? I remind her.

Well, you didn't have to be so competitive about it...

"Well, I guess I could just put my shirt back on..." I say teasingly, making a half-hearted effort to get up.

"No! Um... I mean... it's okay, you don't have to," she says, the arm she has around me holding a little tighter.

I don't need to see her face to know that she's blushing.

As we continue to lay here in silence, I can feel her heart rate steadily start to increase. Glancing down, I realize something.

Is she checking me out right now?

Sometime during the night, the blankets ended up pushed down and are currently bunched at my waist, leaving my chest and abs bare. I've been working out more since I've been here, so I don't have any shame in the toned muscles that are currently on display. And from where Ali is lying, she has a clear and up close view of them.

But she can't actually be checking me out, can she? I wonder again. No one has ever really looked at me in that way before.

Then again, no one has ever been this close.

I can almost feel her eyes wander over me, and hope that she doesn't notice the effect she is starting to have on *my* heart rate. But, as I soon realize, there is no way I can hide the unsteady beat of my heart.

Not when she has her cheek resting on it.

I stare back up at the ceiling and wonder if she is going to have the courage to do or say something about this little situation, because I sure as hell won't.

You would think that I would be used to her presence by now, but I'm absolutely not. I don't know how to act around girls. Never have.

Kissing Ali had been my first kiss and I'm still baffled at how I managed not to fuck it up completely. And even though I somehow found the courage to say, or *think* about my feelings toward her when we were out running around in the woods, this is something entirely different. This isn't driven by adrenaline or the severity of our situation. We are home and we are safe.

And I am *petrified.*

Lying here, I'm suddenly sure that my actions before, when we were out on the map run, could be easily explained. The fear of losing her, of wanting to protect her, had spurred me to act on my feelings when normally I would have sat around overthinking everything.

Like I'm doing right now.

I don't know how to be with someone. What if I totally fuck this up? My thoughts spiral and I am starting to panic. *What if she doesn't like this version of me, what if-* my scattered thoughts are abruptly interrupted, cut off with a sharp intake of breath.

Because she is touching me.

She found the courage after all, but it's anything but confident. Her small hand slides from my side onto my stomach, splaying out over me. With hesitant fingers, she starts to slowly trace the lines of every muscle on my naked stomach.

I tense, but she doesn't stop.

I watch her delicate fingers move over me, exploring every inch. I can't breathe. She's barely touching my skin and the intimacy of it is driving me insane.

Once I am finally forced to take a breath, it comes out much too quickly and keeps speeding up from there. And I know that I'm not going to be able to handle her slow torture for very much longer.

Suddenly, I realize something.

That I'm not overthinking this anymore.

I know exactly what I want to do.

Grabbing that troublesome hand of hers, I quickly lift it up above her and roll on top of her, pinning her to the bed under me. I stare into her surprised eyes as I slowly interlace our fingers above her head, watching her every expression.

"Are you ever going to stop teasing me?" I whisper to her, my breath ragged.

"No, probably not," she breathes out.

And then my mouth is on hers.

I squeeze her hand in mine and she slides her other one up my bicep, which flexes at her touch.

Whatever shyness she was experiencing earlier, it sure as hell is gone now. But I realize, as I take her mouth again, so is mine.

She kisses me back fiercely as her free hand continues to explore. But this time, it isn't hesitant at all. Her touch slowly trails from my biceps to my chest, then she moves those fingers around to my upper back. She grips me, *hard* and I breathe her name against our frantic mouths as I slide a hand under the small of her back, pulling her even closer to me.

Somewhere in my mind I think about how I will never get tired of her touching me like this. Or kissing me like this.

Because this is everything.

She is everything.

I pull on my shirt as I walk into the kitchen. My head is still in a daze from whatever the fuck got into me back there. Even though we haven't even gone further than kissing, I still can't believe how bold I am around her. I never realized that just kissing could make me feel this way. That it could be so much.

I casually wonder what in the hell happened to the *old* Steven.

Oh yeah, that's right. I think. He fell through a portal into a land of magic and monsters, was saved by a beautiful girl, died nineteen times, saved the girl and after ultimately confessing his love to her, they went running off into the sunset...

Every. Ten. Minutes.

Jesus fucking Christ, no wonder my head's a wreck, I think as I grab the flint and steel off the hook behind the stove and crouch down to light it. Even experiencing this antiquated lifestyle was a shock when I first got here. And now, here I am. Lighting the stove with a goddamn knife and a rock without even a second thought.

But as archaic as it is, there's also something so simple about it. Life is different out here, slower somehow. I'm not even sure if I will want to go back to a world of modern amenities. I've never been one to be impressed by fancy things anyway, and I like the life I have here with Ali.

Maybe when, *or if*, Ali and I get back, we can have a little cabin somewhere. One away from town, with no electricity. We can have a garden and- I shake the thoughts away, well aware that I'm getting way ahead of myself.

I am just beginning to wonder where Ali ran off to when I feel her arms wrap around my waist from behind. She rests her cheek on my back and I place one hand over hers as I continue to stir the eggs in the make-shift pan. When she releases me, heading over to sit at the table, I glance over my shoulder at her.

I can't help but return her smile.

I have found myself smiling a lot these past few days, and I'm not mad about it.

"So, what would you like to do today?" she inquires.

"Do you remember what happened the last time you asked me that question?" I laugh, remembering how badly I wanted out of the house and then thinking of everything that happened because of it.

"You're right. You are certainly not allowed to pick anymore," she says as I dump the bacon and eggs onto our plates. She sits there thinking for a few moments, then starts a stream of consciousness that I'm barely able to keep up with.

"We could get to work on expanding the fence around the pastures, or start in on translating more of the books. We have to update the maps from this last trip, so we remember where the new hiding places are and where the boundaries stop and we have to reorganize the map room, it's such a mess. We also have to add to the daylight marks in the armory. How long was it? Three weeks? And we lost a lot of supplies out there, so we could start re-making them. Or we could train, or-"

"Ali," I say, hushing her up as I set a heaping pile of food in front of her. "We just got back, don't you want a little down time?" I ask, sitting across from her and digging in.

"We don't have time for that. If we ever want to find a way out of here, then we have to keep moving. You said it yourself, we can't just give up," she says.

"And we're not going to, but that doesn't mean that we have to spend every second trying to get out of here. Think about it Ali, we might never get back to the valley. I hope we do, but the reality of it is that we might not. If that's the case, then I don't want to look back and realize that I wasted my whole life trying to get out, when I could have... *lived.*"

Her anxious eyes meet mine, then soften, and I can tell she is seriously considering what I just said.

I'm not sure when I became such a romantic, but I've been thinking about this a lot lately, and I just wanted to get it out.

So there it is.

"Back home," I continue, "I took everything for granted. My house, my friends, my family. I wasn't living, I was just killing time, waiting around for the next day, or *year*, or the next time we moved. I was waiting around for my life to start, never knowing when or *if* it would. When I fell through that portal, I felt like my life was taken from me before it even started. But now, I feel like maybe I have a second chance to make it right. I can't wait around until we find a way out to start living, I want to start it now. And I want to start it.... *with you.*"

Ali puts her face in her hands and is quiet for a long moment. I pick at the food on my plate and wait patiently for her response.

"I thought that..." she says softly, trying to find the words. "I thought that by admitting to myself that I *liked* my life here, that I was somehow giving up on my old one. That I was letting my family down. But you're right. I've been so caught up in getting to The End of this, I've made myself miserable. I haven't let myself be happy, but ever since you got here... I am. I'm happy with you, Steven. I don't know what's going to happen to us, but I'm with you. No matter what."

Chapter 37

"So, what *do* you do for fun around here?" I ask Ali as I hop up to sit on the stone counter next to the sink.

"You're looking at it," she laughs, holding a soapy plate out of the water.

"No, seriously," I continue. "We've jumped off a waterfall, and I know how you love beating the shit out of me in the training room, but what else?"

"Umm... I don't really know..." she says, staring out the window. "But I think... I think we should do whatever the hell we want. After that last map run, I think we've earned it."

"I agree," I smile at her.

Whatever the hell I want... I add silently to our conversation and then give her a quick flash of a memory, one that involves my hands in her hair.

The sudden projection catches her off guard and she drops the dish back down into the sink with a *splash*. She raises her dripping wet hands up and stares at me, wide-eyed.

She is soaked.

It's hilarious.

Her red cheeks and shocked face make me burst out laughing. I hop down off the counter and try to run, but it's too late.

The back of my head and shirt are suddenly drenched. Now I'm the one in shock and she's the one laughing.

"Alright, alright. I deserved that," I say. And before she can escape me, I catch hold of her waist, pulling her up against me. She squeals and we both laugh as I hold her tighter.

"Okay, what about fishing?" Ali says with a chuckle, her face suddenly beaming. "You said you liked it back home and well, I have the gear?"

"Oh hell yes, let's do it!" I say excitedly.

I remember her telling me on that very first day that she likes fishing, but it isn't something that we've made the time for since I've been here. Well, unless you count the few minnows that I stabbed with a stick when we were out on the map run, but that definitely wasn't *fun*.

"But hang on, Ali. *Someone* got my shirt soaking wet..."

"Steven..."

"And now I have to take it off..." I say, slowly backing away from her.

"Don't. You. Dare..." she warns, but I don't listen.

I pull my damp shirt off, throw it straight into her face and take off running down the stairs to the first floor, with Ali close behind.

Ali and I stand in the supply room on the third floor looking over her impressive collection of fishing gear. She has nets, traps and a variety of fishing rods. Although the mechanics on the hand-made spools are a little rough, they are impressively clever.

We each grab a pole, net and tackle box to share. As we leave the room, I stare back longingly at the spearfishing gear.

I will definitely be back later to try that out.

I have no idea which way we are going, but I'm sure we will be using one of Ali's *ridiculous* tunnels. I say ridiculous, because they are *everywhere* and confusing as all hell. As many times as I've used them, I am still nowhere near figuring out where they are all hidden. Or where they all lead to. Every time I think I have it down, she will bring me to yet *another* hidden passageway.

Which is precisely what she is doing now.

Just outside of the living room at the base of the stairs, Ali leans over and pulls up one of the rugs on the floor, revealing a trap door.

Secret trap door in the floor. Of course she has one of those, I roll my eyes and consider how it's a miracle that I've never gotten myself lost in this funhouse.

Toting the gear, I drop about twelve feet down into the tunnel. I bend my knees and stick the landing, a trick I have been practicing after watching Ali drop the thirty feet off the front porch as easily as if it's a normal step. I'm just happy whenever I manage to not roll my ankle.

It's amazing how much your body can handle when you don't have the fear of permanent injuries holding you back. Even if I did break a bone, it would heal within a few hours. My ego on the other hand, now *that* would be bruised for at least a few weeks. If not the rest of time.

Ali would make sure of that.

Looking back, I watch as she lands gracefully behind me at the same exact time the trapdoor falls shut above her. She reminds me of a wild cat, graceful, strong and not a creature that you want to mess with.

Show-off, I say, but secretly, I'm impressed. No matter how hard I try, she is always just a little better than me at everything. I tell myself it's because she's been here longer, but that excuse will eventually run its course.

What? She shrugs, but I see that smug little half smile as she walks past me. I just shake my head.

The passageway is short. No more than a minute later, we step out of the tunnel and into the daylight. Looking around, I realize that we are on the other side of the mountain. I don't know how long it would have taken to walk the shoreline and around the cliffs to get over here, but I am suddenly grateful that this particular shortcut of hers exists.

I guess some of the tunnels aren't that ridiculous after all... I think, making a mental note to pay more attention to them.

There are stairs cut into the hillside, creating a trail of switchbacks that lead straight down to the shore. I shield my eyes with a hand and squint out toward the water, recognizing the half-moon shaped bay that you can see from Ali's bedroom. As I watch her making her way down the path, I realize that she is walking a little slower than she usually does, but not because of an injury this time. Normally, she would be miles ahead of me, but today, it seems as though she's taking her time. Like she's *actually* enjoying herself, which makes me smile.

At the bottom of the trail, we walk along the shore until we come to a dock. Tied to it, is a small wooden fishing boat gently bobbing in the water.

"You have a boat?" I gasp, thinking that we were just going to be fishing offshore.

This is even better.

"Yeah, I've got a boat," she says, tossing an oar in my direction. Somehow, I manage to catch it. "You know how to use that?" she asks, nodding to it.

"Better than Noor does, that's for damn sure," I joke and she lets out a hysterical laugh.

"Well that's not saying much, but *thank god* for that," she laughs again as she steps steadily into the boat.

"Where are we going?" I say, tossing in the gear and untying the line.

"I know a place," she smiles as I give the boat one good shove away from the dock and jump in, steadying myself as it rocks back and forth.

We make our way out of the bay and along the coastline, enjoying the sunlight as a cool breeze rolls off the ocean. A few minutes later, Ali signals to the mouth of a wide river and we make our way toward it. The river snakes inland and I watch as the choppy dark blue of the ocean quickly cuts off, creating a line of brackish water before fading to more of a soft green.

Along the shore grows a type of tree that I've never seen before. The roots are sticking up from the water in a tangled heap and it gives me the impression that the trees are trying to crawl away.

"It's a mangrove tree," Ali explains. "They make for good fishing, and I just like coming up here. It's peaceful," she smiles, looking around. And she's right. The water is still, the leaves gently flutter in the breeze and the only sound we can hear is the water being disrupted by our paddles. Looking around, I suddenly realize that it might even be peaceful here at *night*. The thick web of roots, all tangled together in the water and growing up onto the shore, will most likely keep any creatures a good distance back from the river once it gets dark.

As we travel upstream, the water becomes more and more crystalline until I can clearly see the rocks at the bottom. The mangrove trees shoot straight up into the sky, their reflections rippling on the surface of the water. The leaves overhead curve together, stretching out over the river and creating a natural tunnel for our boat to glide under. Vines hang down from the trees and it feels like we are in a different world. One that is peaceful and calm.

As the sun dips below the horizon and we paddle through the dark, I'm unable to hide my uneasiness. I can't see where we are heading, or even how close the shore is, but Ali continues on, unconcerned. As she guides the boat around the bend, the river widens, forming a large pool. I stare at the water, perplexed.

Because somehow, it's *glowing*.

I lean over the side of the boat and, looking down, realize that it's the rocks. Thousands of tiny stones seem to put off their own glow, causing the water to shine with a million different shades of greens and blues. I stare curiously. Then I notice that the canopy overhead is also glowing. I smile, recognizing the lanterns. There are dozens of them, illuminating the leaves.

It must have taken her hours to hang all of those, I think.

We let the boat drift as Ali drops the small anchor into the water. Looking around, I can already see several fish scurrying away from us.

The night is quiet, which means that I was right. If the creatures were able to traverse the swampy terrain, then we would have heard them by now.

Looking over, I see that Ali is already lying on the bench, gazing up at the domed canopy of leaves and lanterns. The lights above reflect in her eyes, making them sparkle even more than usual. The soft light makes her skin glow. I suddenly envision her all alone out here, spending hours hanging lanterns for no other reason than to create a magical place. A place just for her.

And she chose to share it with me.

Hell, she chose to share her whole *world* with me. When I first arrived, after she found out that I couldn't help her get home, she could have just left me behind, knowing that I would only be a hindrance. Or she could have given me some supplies and sent me on my way.

But she didn't.

She saved me and then she took me in. I don't know how I can ever thank her for that, but I plan on spending every day trying.

"Ali, this place..." I say.

"I know..." she says whimsically.

"Hey," I say, urging her to look at me.

Thank you. For everything, I add, but only in our minds.

Her eyes soften and her head tips to one side in sympathy. Words can't explain what I mean, but they don't have to. Because through our shared connection, she already knows.

Fishing rod in hand, I lay on the bench in the small boat and my legs are hanging over the side into the water. Ali has done the same and is lying on the bench opposite me so we are facing each other. She casts out the fishing line in front of her and reels it back in lazily as she stares up at the sunlight trickling in through the trees above. The wind rustles through the leaves and the frogs croak as the water slaps gently against the boat.

And I am enjoying every second of this.

"Okay, I've got one," I say to Ali, looking over at her. "What's your favorite ice cream topping?"

"Cookie dough, obviously," Ali replies quickly.

"You can't pick that!" I laugh.

"Why the hell not?" she chides.

"Because, cookie dough is a dessert in itself, or at least the makings of one. It's not a *topping*," I say.

"It is too a topping!"

"How?" I ask.

"By putting it *on top* of my ice cream," she glares at me playfully, raising her eyebrows. "So, wise guy, what's *your* favorite topping?"

"Chocolate sprinkles, obviously."

"*Oh my god,* you're so boring," she says, tipping her head back dramatically. "Okay, it's my turn," she thinks for a few moments. "What's your favorite thing to do back home that you can't do here?"

"*Hmm...*" I mindlessly cast the line back into the water, trying to think. "Well, there's a lot of things I don't mind living without, but my *favorite* thing... I'm gonna have to go with video games."

"*Video games?* Seriously?" she laughs.

"Oh come on, you just got mad at me for not liking *your* answer," I lecture.

"I know, I know. I guess I just didn't picture you as the *gamer* type..." she smirks.

"Oh yeah? How exactly did you picture me?" I sit up, suddenly curious.

"Well, I guess... oh never mind," she trails off. But there is no way I'm going to let her off the hook this time.

"Oh no you don't, now you have to tell me. How did you picture me?"

"Well..." she looks embarrassed. "I guess with the nice clothes, working out, knowing other languages and living in a mansion... I guess I pictured you as more... *studious*. But video games? It just seems so... *normal*. And also very nerdy," she says, holding back a smile.

"Hey, I'm also *studious*. And may I remind you which of the two of us built a library *and* an armory in their house?" I tease, but I know that Alexandra Cutter is as far away from *nerd* as you can get.

"Well, that's true," she smiles smugly.

"So what's *your* favorite thing back home that we don't have here?" I ask.

"Oh, me? Well that's easy," she says, reeling in her line again and taking her time with it.

"Yes?" I prompt, because I need to hear the answer to this.

"Video games." She doesn't even look at me when she says it, but I can see the smile playing at the corner of her lips as she casts her line back in again.

So I lean over my side of the boat, scoop up some water and splash her with it.

"Hey! What was that for?" she squeals.

"Because you just gave me shit about being a nerd two seconds ago and you play too? What the hell..." I ponder, because I'm honestly having a hard time picturing it.

"So how exactly did you imagine *me* in the real world?" She smiles and I can tell she's enjoying this.

"Um, I guess I pictured you as... *popular*?" I say hesitantly, but that doesn't stop the cascade of water that is immediately thrown in my face.

"No way in hell! *Popular*," she laughs. "I'm the furthest thing from popular, actually. It's a wonder that Makena still talks to me. I only ever hang out with Noor. Hence, the video games," she smiles and I just shake my head again. *How could I have gotten it so wrong?*

Once the shock of it has settled in, Ali and I end up launching into an hour-long conversation. We talk about what games we've played, which are our favorites and which ones we wish they would release a new one for. I can't believe that in all the time we've been here, this hasn't even come up. It seems like a lot of things haven't really come up, but now that we are... Well, whatever *we* are, they're starting to.

I suppose it also took a while for me to adjust to this new world. How to survive it. It's no wonder that all normal conversations were abandoned.

At this moment, I also realize how closed off Ali was when I first got here over two months ago. She had been kind, yes, but she also kept the conversations quick and to the point. Now that she is starting to open up, I find that I'm learning something new about her every day.

The sky turns to night and our secret little dome of light is glowing bright once again, shutting off the rest of the world. I'm not sure how long we've been out here, but it was nice to lose track of the daylight cycles. Sitting here in this little boat, with no worries in the world, was exactly what we both needed. Tomorrow, we will get back to training, chores and translating those damn books.

But for today, this is it.

And it is everything.

"Okay, my turn. How about your favorite thing *here*, that you didn't have back home?" Ali asks, switching up our earlier question.

I look over at her.

I see the lights sparkle in her eyes, the way her soft red curls are pulled over one shoulder, and I realize that it's an easy answer.

The easiest answer in the world.

"You," I say plainly, because it's true.

A shy smile flickers at the corner of her lips as she meets my eyes. I move over to her bench, straddling it to face her.

"Well, *I* was going to say magic, but I guess you're okay too," she says, still smiling.

We study each other for a long time. I grab behind her knees on either side of the bench and scoot her closer to me. And then I notice the hitch in her breath.

The hitch in mine.

I haven't kissed her since this morning, but fuck if I haven't been thinking about it all day. I lean in, allowing our lips to touch before slowly coaxing hers open. I keep my grip behind her knees and let my lips move over hers, breathing her in. My head spins and although I keep my movements slow, I deepen the kiss. Moving a hand into her hair, I realize that hers are already in mine. We pull each other close and I let the pleasure of it wash over me.

When our lips finally part, she closes her eyes, steadying herself. She blinks, slowly coming back to reality. I drop my hands back down to her legs, not wanting to fully let her go.

"Okay, that's it," she says, still in a daze. "Who was she?"

"What?" I say, genuinely confused.

"Who was she? The girl. The one who taught you to kiss like that?"

Well, fuck.

I knew this conversation would come up eventually, but does it have to be *now*? I move my hands off of her knees and back to mine as I consider my options.

I could simply kiss her again, causing her to forget the question in the first place. *No, that wouldn't delay it for long enough...* Or maybe I could just lie about it? *Yeah right, I'm shit at lying.*

Or maybe I could convince her that-

My thoughts break off, because she is staring at me, clearly concerned by my reaction. Which leaves me with one option.

The truth.

"*Um...*" I start lamely, scratching the back of my neck before trying again. "Well, I..." *god*, why is this so difficult?

I stare down at my fidgeting hands, take a deep breath and just blurt it out.

"Ali, you're the first girl I've ever kissed."

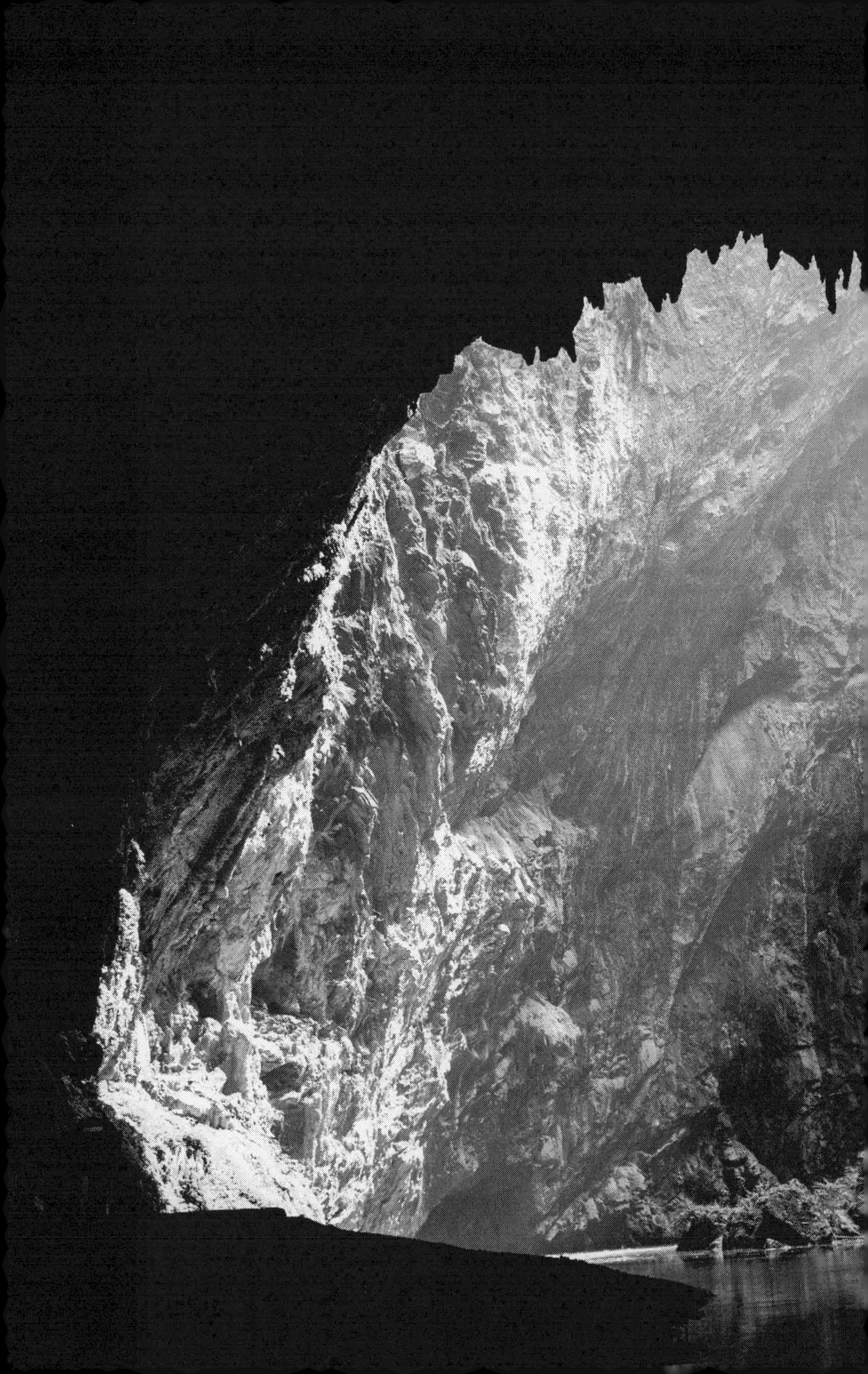

Alex

Chapter 38

I stare straight at Steven. His declaration has left me... *stunned*.

How could *I* have been his first kiss? So many emotions flood through me, I'm not sure which one of them to feel first.

And don't even get me started on the *thoughts*.

Steven clearly knows what he's doing, there's no doubt about that. My stomach does a little dance just thinking about it. He is kind, charming and has a body that would have anyone around my age blushing, so how is it that the girls in those big, fancy cities weren't all over him?

I can't wrap my brain around it.

I figured that at some point, someone back in Chicago or New York had rocked his world. Figured that they taught him everything he knows, but that their relationship eventually fizzled out when he moved away. And as much as I hate those thoughts, I already came to terms with them.

But *this*? This is something that I hadn't even considered. How is it possible that he's never kissed anyone? And how could I have been so wrong about him, *again?*

I look over at him. He's staring down at his fidgeting hands and it almost looks as though he's... *embarrassed?* He doesn't have a thing in the world to be embarrassed about, so his reaction confuses me.

But now that I think about it, it makes sense. I just assumed that all the times he was hesitant or shy was a lack of attraction. Then I thought that maybe he was simply doing it out of respect, that he was taking it slow for me.

And maybe he is, but now I have to consider that maybe his shyness is something else.

Maybe he's just as terrified about this as I am.

What if he's worried about making a mistake, or fucking the whole thing up, same as me? I thought I was alone in my inexperience and now, finding out that I'm not, has a sudden wave of relief washing over me.

He's sitting there, all distraught and I have to figure out what I am going to say to him. My first thought is to tease him, like I always do, but seeing how much this affects him, I decide against it.

I lean down, trying to see under his shaggy hair to those deep blue eyes. When they meet mine, I realize that not only does he look embarrassed, but also *guilty*.

Does he think he did something wrong? If so, that's a load of shit. He has done *everything* right.

More than right, in fact.

I don't know how it's possible in this short of a time, but he is everything to me. He has become my whole world. After everything I went through, I've found myself starting to open up. To feel like myself again. Another thing I didn't think was possible.

He brought me back.

"Steven," I say softly. "I don't have the faintest idea how any girl in their right mind passed you up. But... I'm glad they did. I'm glad I was your first. And you should know..." I take a deep breath, "that you were mine."

Well *that* gets his attention.

And now I'm the one who's blushing with embarrassment.

Those dark blue eyes with their now purple hue in the dark dart to mine, the shock spreading over his face.

"But... how?" he murmurs, a slow smile deepening those dimples in his cheeks.

"Well, I was just wondering that same thing about yo-"

And then his mouth is pressed firmly against mine again. But this time, it is anything but sweet like the last one. This kiss leaves me feeling breathless and frantic and I never want him to stop. I grab his shirt and pull him closer to me, my tongue finding his. I can't breathe, can't think and the whole world just melts away. I casually wonder if he knows the effect he has on me.

My heart is beating out of my chest and I feel the urge to be closer to him. *I need him closer.*

And then, he lets go.

"Shit, Ali, I'm sorry, I just-"

"You just what?" I stare at him, *daring* him to stop.

"I just... oh, fuck it," he says and then grabs my face and pulls my lips back to his.

We ride back to the house in the little fishing boat, but this time, we sit on the same bench. Our weight definitely offsets it, but I don't care.

I steal glances over at Steven, recalling the most recent memories of us, and I can't keep the stupid smile off my face. I also can't help but notice that he is doing the same.

The moon and the stars over the ocean are incredible tonight and I make a mental note to come out here more often.

As we glide through the dark water, I think back over the time since Steven got here. So much has happened over the last few months and yet, I feel like I'm just now starting to get to know him. But I realize that maybe that's because I haven't let my walls down, haven't given him the chance. Because I still find myself not believing what is happening between us. Here is this perfect, gorgeous guy and he is choosing to love *me.* I'm secretly afraid that one day I will wake up and it will all be over.

That this has all been just a dream.

But every day it isn't over. Every day, I love him more. *And, don't forget, he loves you too,* I have to keep reminding myself. *And you were his first kiss.* I almost giggle at the thought. I suddenly wonder what the hell is wrong with me? Because this isn't *me.*

Is it?

"Hey, Ali?" Steven says with that deep-in-thought look about him again.

"Yes?" I ask.

"I just... what I was trying to say back there, is that... Well, I've just never done *this* before," he gestures between the two of us. "I have no idea what I'm doing and I can't believe that I haven't completely fucked it up yet. But if I start to, please just yell at me or something..." he looks down at me and my heart melts at how sincere he is.

"Steven, you haven't fucked anything up, not even a little bit," I smile at him. "And don't forget, I don't know how to do... *this...* either." I gesture as well, a little terrified by that thought.

"Ali, there's nothing you could do that would ever change the way I feel about you."

My heart nearly stops at that.

"*Really*... but what if I started snoring or something?" I ask in an attempt to regain my composure as well as my train of thoughts.

He laughs, but then grows serious again.

"Even then. Although, in that case I might need you to make me some ear plugs. I need my beauty sleep," he smiles.

That one gets a laugh out of me, because Steven is always asking me to make him stupid things that he could very well make for himself. But I know that he would rather be clinking away in the armory than messing around with magic or anything practical, so I generally give in to his requests.

"So..." I say hesitantly, because I have to ask. "You said I was the first girl you kissed," I blush again. "But what about relationships? Is there someone back in the valley who's devastated you're gone?"

"Um, no. No one in the valley. Well, I guess no one *ever*, actually. We just moved around too much, I never really saw the point. Besides, no one was ever... *interested*. Nerd, remember?"

"Bullshit, they weren't! I've seen guys half as hot as you leave a trail of broken hearts in their wake, so I don't believe that for a second."

He is quiet for a long moment and then he gets that grin that always lets me know when he's about to say something moronic.

"What?" I say frustratedly.

"You think I'm *hot*?" he wiggles his eyebrows at me.

I slap his arm.

"You're insufferable," I say.

"*Hmm*, insufferable, intolerable, unbearable?" he offers.

Smart ass, I tell him, because it drives me crazy when he does that. And he does it, *all the goddamn time.*

"But hey, since *you* started it, how many boyfriends have you had? Or *girlfriends*?" he asks, and I roll my eyes at him. Because he sounded a little hopeful with that last part.

"Well, none actually. But I did have a fiancé," I say, looking out over the water as I try desperately to keep my face serious. Steven stops paddling and stares at me wide-eyed, the blood draining from his face.

"Yeah, it's kinda hard to talk about," I continue. "His name was Logan. He asked me if I would marry him and I said *yes*. And then in first grade, his family moved out of town and the heartbreak of it was- *Ow*!" I laugh, rubbing the arm that he just shoved.

"Don't do that! *Christ*, Ali," he says, putting his face in his hands and shaking his head.

He's adorable.

But I'm not sorry. He had *that one* coming.

As we pull up to the dock, I hop out to tie up the boat.

"But seriously, Ali," Steven says, stepping onto the wooden platform next to me. He puts his hands on my waist and quickly spins me around, pulling me against him. As he looks down at me, I notice that his hair has fallen over his eyes again, making my heart skip. "How. In the hell. Has no guy ever kissed you?" he speaks slowly, his voice deep. I lose myself in his eyes and suddenly feel weak in his arms, unsure of how to respond.

"I um..." *find it hard to speak when you stare at me like that.* He smiles at my internal comment, but I continue. "I guess that I just never really liked anyone, not like *that*. Until, well, there was this one guy. He washed up on my beach and he... he saved my life," I say, staring up at him.

"I think *you* saved *me*, remember?" he smiles down at me.

As we stand on the dock, I hold him tighter, thinking about how I'm going to explain what he did for me. That he did save me. That before him, I was done. I was a shell of a human, lost to a world of loneliness. A soul without life. A body with no more steps to take, a voice with no breath. And now that I'm thinking about it, maybe I was always that way.

Even before this place.

But I can't find the words or the courage to say all that. So I simply wrap my arms around his neck just as the sun settles below the horizon, beyond the half-moon bay, and watch the sky explode with stars once again.

Chapter 39

"Come on, you gonna take all day?" I say, twirling a wooden practice sword, as I stand in the training area in the armory. Steven is still standing in the doorway, his own wooden sword limp in his hand, his arms crossed stubbornly.

I try not to notice how his biceps bulge when he's standing like that, but I can't help it.

"Ali, come on, this doesn't feel right. I don't want to hit you," he says.

"You said that you wanted to take training more seriously," I remind him.

"Yeah, *on my own* and against that stump over there. Not against *you*."

"That didn't stop you before?" I argue.

"Yeah no shit, because *before* you kicked my ass every day. Now, I might actually hit you for once."

"You won't hit me. And if you do, I'll heal in no time," I say quickly, eager to see what he learned out there on his own. "And besides, I'm hoping that *I* will actually get to train this time too," I say with a smart grin.

"Oh yeah? And what's that supposed to mean?"

"It means that up until now, you've been as worthy of an opponent as the stump. Now get your ass over here and try to hit me!" I say.

He stands his ground.

Stubborn. That's what he is. Does he actually think that he can hurt me? "Okay fine, I admit it. Up until now, I've been going easy on you. But now I won't," I say, tossing the wooden sword aside. I pull the dagger from my boot and hand it to Steven. Because I have a point to prove.

"Ali, what the hell am I supposed to do with this?" he says, staring at it.

"You're going to throw it at me," I say, dead serious.

"No fucking way."

"Yes, fucking way," I say stubbornly, heading back to my side of the training area. "Now, throw!"

"Ali, I didn't want to accidentally hit you with a *wooden* sword, what makes you think I'm going to throw a knife at you on purpose?"

"Okay, fine. Throw it next to me then," I say.

Grumbling, he takes position, brings back his arm just like I taught him, and throws it.

Ten feet to my left.

"Seriously?" I say, walking over to retrieve it.

"Ali," he grumbles, reluctantly taking the dagger back. "I still don't know why we'r-"

"Just throw it."

He focuses and throws again. I can see from his release that the knife is going to be several feet away. *Close enough,* I smile and less than a second later, I am standing four feet to my left, casually twirling the dagger around in my hand.

He just stares at me, his jaw open.

God, I love messing with him.

"What the hell, Ali! What the *fuck* was that?" he says.

"*That* was me proving a point. "

"*A point?* Ali, you just moved faster than the knife. Holy fucking shit," he runs a hand through his hair and then is quiet for a long moment. "You really have been going easy on me, haven't you?" he says, looking back up at me.

"Yup."

Again, with the hair thing.

"Hold up, can *I* do that too?" he beams.

"I don't see why not. I didn't show it to you before because well, it never came up. But you also weren't ready for it. Using magic like that, before you're used to it, wears you out and probably would have gotten you killed. *Trust me...*" I mumble, because the first time I did it was a complete accident and it didn't end well.

"So what else can we do, or can *you* do, that I don't know about?" he asks.

"I think that covers it. And it's really not that exciting. You can just move a little *faster* when the occasion calls for it, kind of like when you focus in and hear the creatures outside. It's too difficult to keep it up for a long time and takes a lot of concentration, so I don't use it that often."

But for some reason, it has been getting easier lately. I briefly wonder why, before storing that thought away for later.

"Man, why do you get all the *superpowers*?" he complains and I let out a chuckle.

"Well I can't teach you how to read minds, but I can show you how to do that one. But not right now. Right now, we're training, not learning new tricks. But I promise, if you're about to hit me in a way that would cause more damage than a bruise, I will move out of the way."

"Have I ever almost hit you in a way that would cause more damage than a bruise?" he asks hopefully.

"No. No, you haven't," I smile.

I have to admit, Steven is definitely better at fighting now than he was before our little *outing* across the countryside. The few days of real-world experience taught him more than I could have in months of training. Now, he is more confident with his movements, more sure-footed. He grips the sword tighter and brings it down using all his weight.

And he is fearless. But that much I already knew.

The change in him is exciting and I can't help but smile whenever he isn't looking. Because I'm finally able to fight him, *actually* fight him. I don't have to hold back nearly as much as I did before. And I keep to my promise that I will use magic to move out of his way if it comes to it. But it hasn't come to it.

Not yet at least.

Still, I have worked up a sweat beating him, and I find the challenge thrilling. Once I teach him to move *faster* using magic, then our training sessions will start to get really interesting. My competitive nature is looking forward to it.

Steven lunges at me, sword first, breaking me out of my reverie. I dodge the jab and decide that it's time to bring this to an end. I'm bruised, tired and I want food.

He jumps forward again, this time bringing the sword down above my head. I raise my own sword to block it and then, ducking down, I knock him off his feet as I pass him. He falls to the floor with a *thud* and I quickly disarm him, throwing his sword, and mine, well out of the training area. Then I stand over him, crossing my arms.

"What's the matter, giving up so soon?" he coughs out.

"Says the guy on the floor. You lost, I won, *again.* Now get up so now we can eat," I smile.

I start to walk away, but Steven grabs my leg and I go down *hard*. And as glad as I am that he's getting over the whole *I don't want to hurt you* thing, this one hurts like hell.

Laying on my stomach, I moan, then roll to my back. Steven crawls up beside me and props his head up with one arm.

"Okay. *Now* we can eat," he smiles and I roll my head to the side to glare at him.

"You know this means I have to get you back at some point," I say.

"Oh I know. But for now," he leans in close, "it was worth it."

I look straight at him and he must see the flash of light behind my eyes, because suddenly, he's no longer smiling. Before he can do a thing about it, I have him face-down on the floor, his hands pinned behind his back.

"Fuck! Ali that's cheating," he complains into the stone floor.

"Well, so is knocking a girl on her ass when she's walking away," I retort.

"How else am I supposed to beat you?" he says. I know damn well that the compliment is an attempt to get out of the little predicament he is currently in, and unfortunately, it works. I let his hands go, then sit on the floor next to him as he rolls to his back.

"You're a sweaty mess," I say, looking down at him.

"Oh yeah?" he says, and he has that look in his eye.

"No, Steven, don't-" *too late.*

I'm on my back, *again*, but this time, Steven is on top of me. He lets his weight pin me to the floor and, before I can protest, his lips are moving against mine and I completely forget what I was supposed to be complaining about.

Chapter 40

It's strange how quickly our lives have changed since getting back from the map run a week ago. Not only are Steven and I *together*, but we both seem to have a new, brighter perspective on things.

Well, except when it comes to the books.

Those continue to grate at our sanity on a daily basis.

Steven and I are sitting on the couch in the living room, my legs draped over his lap and a fire blazing in the stone hearth. We each have a book that we're working on translating and there's piles more of them on the coffee table next to us. At least neither of us have to use the key to translate them anymore. We've spent so many hours staring at the damn things that we both have the language from Steven's tattoo memorized at this point. But every book we translate turns out to be more of the same. More about plants, about weapons, potions, etcetera, etcetera. Even the big book upstairs is a whole lot more of building things, creating things, but no *escape plans,* unfortunately.

At least, not that we've found.

I look over the top of my book at Steven, who is rubbing the back of his neck, brows furrowed as he stares at the page in front of him. Suddenly, he slams it shut, tosses it onto the coffee table and flicks his pencil across the room, finished with this project for the day, apparently. I smile.

"We have to be missing something," he says, tipping his head back to rest on the couch as he stares at the ceiling.

"Well, we could always go on another map run," I say jokingly, which earns me a glare, before going back to my book.

Steven is quiet for a long moment. Then he jumps up abruptly, tossing my legs off him.

"*God*, Steven, what?" I say.

"That's it! Ali, that's it! You figured it out!" he says, his eyes ecstatic from whatever epiphany he just had.

"And... what exactly did I figure out?" I say, confused.

"The *maps*. Ali, it's the maps!" he beams.

"What about the ma-"

And then it hits me.

"Ali, it's the inscription around the edges, it has to be!"

The realization of what he is saying slowly sinks in, but then I understand. I stare back up at him, hope in my eyes. "You're right, it's the only thing we haven't translated! Why wouldn't the way to get out... be written on a *map?*"

"How did I not think of this before?!" he says, running into the map room, frantically clearing the books from the table. I rush to help, moving piles over to the side tables, the bookshelves and even stacking some on the floor. Then we pull out every single map we can find, including the ones pinned to the walls and toss them into a large messy pile on the table. The ones rolled up clink against the wood, threatening to roll off.

Some of the maps are duplicates that cover the same area, only on a different scale. All the maps that are of the *same* scale fit together in order to show a larger area. But as much as I have tried to keep them organized, they're still a mess.

I don't even know where to start.

"Steven, look," I say several minutes later, a map in each hand. "This one has the inscription only on one side and this one has it on two," I stare at them curiously, wondering what it means. Steven is holding up his own maps and turns them so I can see.

"These two don't even have any of the symbols. I guess we start by finding the ones that do?" he offers.

We go through every single map systematically, which takes more than a minute. Once we have finished, I look at the scattered pile on the table, and what they have in common hits me straight away.

"Steven, they're all the same scale. Which means-"

"That they all fit together. It's *one* map," he stares at me wide-eyed.

A moment later, we are frantically throwing the pages around, trying to piece them together.

We quickly run out of room on the table and end up placing them on the floor like a giant picture frame around it. The chairs are now thrown haphazardly into the living room and Steven and I are standing on top of the table, maps in hand, as we try to match up the missing pieces.

I've always been a fan of puzzles, but *this*... this is the jigsaw puzzle from hell.

We have to use the topography to match up the edges, only problem is, some maps show nothing but ocean with no distinguishing landmarks.

Like I said, *hell*.

We stand on the table and walk around, hopping down to match up the pieces. Then *moving* piece after piece when we discover that we had it wrong.

The process is grueling. But finally, the frame is complete.

Steven and I each take a piece of parchment and get to work copying down the inscription. I step away from the table stiffly as I stare down at the translation of symbols that repeat themselves over and over along the edges of the map.

INTO THE FORTRESS YOU MUST GO

CATCH A LINE OF FIRE THAT IS AGLOW

COMBINE WITH EYES THAT CANNOT SEE

LET GO AND TO THE END IT WILL TAKE THEE

"A goddamn riddle?" Steven groans. "Whatever happened to a good 'ol fashion *X marks the spot?*" he says, muttering profanities under his breath as he walks away.

I ignore him, my eyes still fixed on the page. I re-read the words again and again, hoping that it isn't true.

Hoping that I've got this wrong.

"Into The Fortress you must go... catch a line of fire... eyes that cannot see... into The Fortress... line of fire... *fuck!*" I push away from the table, muttering my own choice words as I do. I am vaguely aware that I'm chewing on my cuticle, something I haven't done for a while. I pace back and forth, trying to think of anything *else* it could mean, anything at all.

But I come up short.

I know what it means.

"Goddammit!" I continue pacing, because this can't be happening.

"Ali, what? What is it?" Steven asks, all hopeful and optimistic, but I'm too in shock to respond.

His hands find my upper arms and he stops my frantic motions, forcing me to look at him. But I don't want to.

I want to get back, but not like *this*.

There has to be another way... my thoughts trail.

"Alexandra, talk to me! What do you know?" he says desperately, but I just cover my face and shake my head. After a long moment, Steven's big hands gently move mine away and I'm forced to face him.

"Do you remember," I begin slowly, "how I told you that I'd found another portal? But that it didn't take me home?"

"Yes, I remember. You said that the creatures..." he looks away, catching on to where I'm going with this.

I continue. "In *that place*, there's no sunlight. So the creatures are out *all* the time. Not only that, but do you remember your dream? The one with the explosion? The one where I fell..." I squeeze my eyes shut from the memory.

"Yeah, I remember. You were running through that creepy castle and-"

"Not castle, Steven. *Fortress*."

Chapter 41

"Ali, is all this really necessary?" Steven complains as I help him cinch tight the metal chest plate to his torso.

"Yes," I say plainly. Then I dig around one of the chests in the armory for something that will fit his legs.

"But if you're only *showing* me the portal, why do I need this whole... getup?" he asks.

"Because, I'm not just showing you the portal. We're going in," I say nonchalantly.

"What!" he shouts. "Ali, are you insane? We can't go in right now! We don't even know what it is we're supposed to do once we get there!"

"We're not *going in*, going in," I roll my eyes. "We're just stepping through so you can see it. The area near the portal is safe... *relatively*. So the armor is just a precaution."

"Relatively. *Great,*" he says sarcastically, then buckles the leather straps around his thigh to hold the armor in place as I start donning my own.

"I could just tell you about it, but it's hard to explain. And do you remember how tired you were when you came through the portal to get here?" I ask.

"So you think I'm going to get that tired again," he says.

It isn't a question.

"If we plan on actually going in there, you're going to have to get used to jumping through without wanting to take a nap within the first five minutes.

So, I figured, we might as well start now. If you're up to it, that is." I look up from what I'm doing, just now realizing that maybe I should have asked him first. *Shit.*

"I'm up for it," he says without even thinking about it. "Any idea how many times it will take?"

"Well, for me, it was probably ten or so before I didn't notice it anymore. But I was also here longer than you before I went in. I was already pretty used to the magic, so I don't really know what it will be like for you. Here," I say, handing Steven a leather hood.

"What's this?" he asks, eyeing the crudely stitched together fabric questioningly.

"It's a hood. Helmets block your vision and make it hard to turn your head, so I came up with this. It won't stop an explosion or a sword, but it does stop an arrow. Well, stops it enough that it won't kill you..." I trail off.

"And you know this because..." he says, staring at me.

"I only showed you my *deaths*, not my *close calls.* It still hurts, but trust me, it works. Now pipe down and put it on," I smile at him, pulling my own hood forward so it hangs around my face protectively.

I look up, noticing the small smile tugging at the corner of his mouth.

Then I realize that this is the first time he's seen me in full armor. I'm wearing a custom formed-fitting piece of protective metal for my torso, arms and legs and braided strips of leather to form the gauntlets that swoop down, covering the backs of my hands. Add to that the hood, weapons and tight brown leather that covers anywhere the armor doesn't, I'm sure I look ridiculous. It's much tighter than I'm used to, but the last thing you want when you are running or fighting for your life is for your outfit to get in the way.

"Hey, no teasing!" I lecture.

"I wasn't going to tease you..." he says slowly, his eyes trailing over me. Then he gives me that sexy as hell grin, letting me know *exactly* what he thinks about the outfit.

I blush, not sure what to say.

"But I do know one thing," he continues, giving me a crooked smile.

"And what's that?" I roll my eyes, playing along.

"I definitely don't look as cute as you do," he says teasingly, knowing damn well how much I hate the word *cute*. I give him one good shove on his chest plate and he stumbles a few steps back, laughing.

And then I get a good look at *him* for the first time.

"So?" he says, giving me a goofy Ironman stance. I laugh, shaking my head at him, but honestly... he looks like a warrior.

A very attractive warrior.

Clearly, he made that chest plate himself at some point when he was messing around in here, because it fits him *perfectly*. The form-fitting piece of metal showing off every muscle. Which I am absolutely *positive* was not an accident.

The hood makes him seem more like a character from one of our video games, which I find... *hot*. Under the hood, his wavy brown hair falls over his forehead and he looks out at me from those devastatingly deep blue eyes. He rests his hand on the hilt of his sword casually, looking like... well, like he was born for this. He is flat-out sexy as hell and I'm not sure how I am going to concentrate with him wearing... *that*.

He also looks intimidating. If I didn't know him, I wouldn't mess with him.

But because I do know him, I mess with him.

"You look... *cute*," I say, because no way in hell will I ever tell him what I actually think about him in that outfit. He pretends to be offended, but I can tell he doesn't believe me.

He knows he looks good.

Staring at him, I can't help but think... *knight in goddamn shining armor*.

I mentally roll my eyes at the irony of it. Because isn't that what the childhood version of me always wanted? A knight in shining armor to sweep me off my feet? That is, until I grew up and realized that in life, no one is coming to save you.

You have to save yourself.

That's what I learned out here, alone. Here, in this place, I don't need a man to save me. I can damn well save myself.

But ever since Steven got here, it's made me rethink everything. Maybe I don't need him, but I *want* him. Want him by my side.

Want him to be a part of my life.

And maybe, just maybe, we can save each other.

I buckle on my sword as we make our way out of the armory and down the hall toward the ladder. I step onto one of the rungs and, holding on with one hand, look back toward Steven.

"You ready for this?" I ask.

"Ready. What floor are we going to?" And I think for a moment that he's a little *too* chipper for where we're about to go.

"We're going down. *All the way* down, past the first floor," I say.

"But... the ladder stops at the map room?" he says, confused.

"It won't this time," I smile slyly at him and then slide down out of view, looking up to be sure that he is following. He hasn't done this with the armor yet, but nevertheless, he's right behind me. He seems to pick up everything faster than I thought he would. And he isn't just *good* at everything out here, he's *great* at it.

Which I find infuriating.

I approach the first floor and, without slowing down, I kick the upturned lever sticking out from the stone wall. The once solid floor beneath me falls open, allowing the ladder to extend further down beneath the mountain.

"Oh, what the fuck!" I hear Steven shout from above me and I chuckle.

As we continue down through the stone tunnel and I feel the pressure build in my ears from the sudden drop in elevation, I decide that it's probably time to give Steven a little bit of a warning.

"Hey Steven, don't freak out, but your view is about to get a little... larger. So just hold on, okay?"

"Ali..." he lectures from above, a hint of terror in his voice.

And then it happens.

The ladder is no longer attached to anything. It plunges down out of the ceiling and into a massive cavern. I look around with a broad smile, never getting tired of the sight. There are stalactites the size of buildings jutting down from the ceiling and everywhere you look there are equally as large tunnels branching off in all directions, expanding out so far that you can't see the end of them through the haze of stale air.

Between the stalagmites scattering the floor are large, dark pools of water that overflow and pour into each other, traveling down into the darkness further than you can see. The ceiling and walls are lit with the same glowing vines from the greenhouse. Only, these grow wildly, hanging down everywhere in a mess of glowing green against the jagged stone walls.

"Holy shit, Ali!" Steven barks out.

"I warned ya!" *Sorta.*

"Yeah, well you could have warned me a little sooner! And with a little more detail! *Fuck!*" he gasps and I have to assume his reaction is due to the unknown distance we would fall before hitting the bottom.

At least he didn't let go of the ladder, I shrug.

We fall through the center of the expansive space and, as we approach the platform at the bottom, I begin to moderate the speed of my descent.

"Alright, time to start slowing down!" I shout up toward Steven before landing easily on the stone platform.

The cavern is essentially a bottomless pit, with large stone ledges and platforms protruding out everywhere, creating a maze of pathways between the pools of water. I can hear droplets as they fall from the vines overhead and splash in the glossy pools, reminding me of a slow rain as they echo off the stone walls.

Steven slows to a stop and then climbs down the last couple of steps. He tosses his hood back and looks around, awe-struck. I smile again, realizing how much I enjoy showing him my world.

Our world.

"Ali, this is incredible! Ya know, now that I'm not on a ladder. Hang on," he says, looking back and forth between it and me. "How in the hell did you get that all the way down here?"

"Well, one section at a time and a lot of hanging upside down. Not gonna lie, that wasn't my favorite project, but I got sick of having to climb up and down a rope every time," I shrug.

"Ali, you're insane."

"I know," I smile, because it was insane. But when you're stuck somewhere, alone for six months, you tend to do crazy things to keep yourself occupied.

And even crazier things in the hopes of getting out.

"How far down does it go?" Steven says, warily making his way over to see what's below the ledge.

"I have no idea. I've dropped a few torches, but their light disappeared from view before they ever hit the bottom. So try not to fall in," I add.

He smiles, but instinctively steps away from the edge.

"Ali, is that the portal?" he says suddenly, looking toward the far side of the cavern beyond the pit.

In one of the dark pools, there's a pile of rocks jutting out from the center of the water. They level off, forming a large plateau, and the stones continue up in the center of the flattened space, creating a large, squared archway. It's filled with the same mysterious substance as the portal Steven and I fell through back in the valley.

It resembles water, clear and moving, but it's filled with more stars than the night sky. Unlike the portal back in the real world, the liquid doorway has a mysterious iridescent purple hue, which infects the rocks around it. Cracks of purple light splinter out over the structure and surrounding stone. The suspended liquid moves all on its own, shimmering like waves on the sea.

"This way," I say, breaking Steven from his trance-like state.

We make our way down the stone stairs that are cut into the wall.

Stairs that *I* did not make.

Stairs that were already here.

They wrap around the pit and lead us to the path surrounding one of the pools. The stillness of the water's surface reflects the glowing vines, hiding the darkness that lurks below. It looks... *unsettlingly* peaceful.

"Can we swim down here?" Steven asks, mystified by the pool's allure.

"Well..." I say, rolling a large rock into the water with my foot.

Almost immediately, several large tentacles shoot out from the darkness, engulfing it. Steven jumps back and I hear the unmistakable sound of crushing rock. Then I cover my face with my hands just before the creature sprays us both with water and tiny stones. The pungent smell of dead fish and sulfur assaults us immediately and I pull the edge of my hood over my nose in a failed attempt to obstruct it.

The creature's dark skin pulses with an iridescent glow as it slowly snakes its way back down into the abyss.

The water calms as if nothing had disturbed it.

"Okay," Steven says slowly, wiping the water from his face. "No swimming in the creepy pools. Got it," he smiles over at me, amused, surprising me again at how well he is able to adapt to this crazy world.

Not to mention how well he's able to put up with my bullshit.

We continue on and when we walk up the last set of stone stairs, Steven stops dead in his tracks at the edge of the water, staring at the portal.

"It looks a lot bigger than it did from up there," he says, looking up at the massive doorway pulsing with liquid stars.

Between us and the portal are rocky pillars, jutting up from the deep and surfacing just enough to create a stone path in the dark water, leading over to the portal. There's no way to see just how deep down the water goes, but every once in a while, you can see the shimmer of one of the squid-like creatures as it leisurely swims around the pillars far beneath the surface, using its tentacles to propel itself along through the murk.

Carefully, we step from stone to stone, making our way over to the jagged edges of the island then climb the rocks leading up to the portal. As we stand here on the platform, I can feel the pulse of the portal on my skin. Looking over at Steven, I can tell he feels it too. The power and magic emanating from it is intoxicating, drawing you in. As I watch Steven stare into it, wide-eyed and entranced, it reminds me of the moment when I saw the portal for the first time.

I found myself stuck outside at night and was in need of shelter, *fast*. And so I ran into a nearby cave. Lantern in hand, I decided to explore while I waited for daylight. Not long into my walk, the wall opened up into a massive cavern. I had nearly fallen from the ledge. Seeing the portal for the first time took my breath away. I remember sitting down in that opening, my legs weak, and cried for nearly an hour.

Because I *thought* I had found the way out.

The way home.

Now, standing next to Steven, I instinctively look up, immediately finding the narrow patch of darkness a few hundred feet up on one of the cave walls. I stare at the very same spot that I sat in that day, remembering the brimming joy I felt.

Little did I know that the portal would bring nothing but horror, heartbreak and disappointment.

Along with fourteen additional deaths.

"Ali, what is it?" Steven says, breaking the silence, but my eyes stay fixated on the small opening in the far wall.

"Nothing. I just... it took me so long to get down here and then..." my voice trails off.

He reaches out, grabbing a strap on my armor and tugging me close to him. He wraps his arms around me, understanding.

"*God*, I really thought it was the way out," I say into his chest. Then I lean back, shaking off the memories. "You ready?" I ask, looking up at him.

"Probably not," he says, letting me go and pulling his hood back up over his head. Taking a deep breath, he takes my hand and we give each other one last nod.

Then we step forward into the sea of stars, disappearing from the world we know.

Chapter 42

The heat hits like a wave, flowing over me until my entire body is surrounded by it. I struggle to breathe as the hot air fills my lungs. The shocking temperature difference between the cold, damp cavern and the dry heat of this place is staggering no matter how many times I've been here.

And speaking of staggering...

"Shit, Steven!" My hand is still in his as he starts to collapse, threatening to take me down with him.

Hearing my voice, he manages to come back to reality just enough to stabilize himself. I crouch down, pulling his arm over my shoulder and wrap a hand around his waist as I drag him away from the beating pulse of the portal. The stars try to follow us, but once we are far enough away, they let go of their hold and break off, settling back into their suspended state within the frame of the arch. As soon as the connection is broken, Steven stands a little straighter and is able to hold most of his own weight.

"How ya feeling, soldier?" I ask, because it looks like he's going to be sick.

"I'm... okay. I think... But *god damn* it's hot! Is there any air in here at all? Or maybe a nice breeze?"

I chuckle. "Yeah, sorry, no breeze. This is about as cool as it gets, but you get used to it... sorta. Can you walk?" I ask.

"Um, yeah, I think so," he says, taking a few hesitant steps forward.

Satisfied that he isn't going to topple over, I let go. As much as I like to be near him, I'm already sweating. But it's either wear the armor, or get shot by an arrow.

Or a ball of fire... I muse.

"This area isn't usually too bad," I say to him. "But look alive, nowhere is safe in here. We're going to walk out to the edge so you know what we're dealing with and then we're getting the hell out of here. Deal?" I say, pointing toward where the cliff walls on either side of us open up and the ground stops.

"Deal," Steven says slowly, but I'm not sure if he even hears me. Looking over, I can see by the upturn of his hood that he is taking in all of what is, yet another, sprawling world.

Only, this place is unlike anything that exists on the outside.

It's as if this whole world has been swallowed up by a cave of deep crimson stone walls. Even the air has a reddish tint to it, bathing everything in its hue.

There are endless tunnels that burrow deep into the cliff walls, and beyond them, wide open spaces. Unlike the cave beneath the mountain, which could fit several large buildings, this cave has hundreds of miles of its own landscape, hills and mountains that could easily fit several *cities*, all suffocated inside a stone prison of carmine.

The dark ceiling looms high above us. Its details are almost impossible to make out through the haze of heat that permeates this entire place. Particles of ash swirl through the air like snow, but it's anything but peaceful.

Uneasy, is the word I would use.

Because I know what that ash came from. And looking over at Steven, I can tell he does too.

There is something harrowing about this place, you can feel it in the air. The cavern is steeped in perpetual darkness, lit only by the lava below and the luminescent stones that are embedded within the cavern walls.

Steven looks over at me and gives me a quick nod, signaling that he understands the danger of this place and that he's ready to get this over with just as much as I am. I nod back and put my hand on the hilt of my sword as I start forward quickly, scanning the open area as I go.

It only takes a few minutes before we are nearing the edge. I slow my pace to a walk, waiting for Steven to catch up so we can walk forward together.

We step up to the ledge, which is somewhat reminiscent of standing on top of the tallest mountain above our little house in the cliffs, looking out over the world.

Only *this* world is desolate.

Below us is a large ocean. But it's an ocean of lava instead of water. It boils and swirls, its slow currents streaking it with shades of red, orange and yellow. Around the shores are cliffs of red stone and rocks shooting up into the air.

Atop the cliffs are miles of forests. But the trees here are not quite... *normal*. Their trunks are twisted, their leaves a perpetual shade of red and brown, unable to grow vibrant in the heat. Gnarled vines with large spikes shoot up from the ground, giving the area an even more unfriendly air to it.

And then there are the islands.

Scattered all around the cavern like clouds are platforms, suspended in mid-air. The tops of them scattered with the same crimson trees. There are rivers and streams of lava, flowing through the landscapes and over the edges of the cliffs to meet the ocean.

Fiery waterfalls flow straight out of the ceiling, landing on the floating islands until the molten streams wind their way along their surfaces, pouring out over the edge and continuing on their journey.

It's a world of fire and death.

"What's that?" Steven asks, pointing straight out across the ocean to the far side, to the dark looming shadows that lurk there.

"That, is what we're here for," I give him a look and he immediately understands.

Far across the lava, beyond the cliffs and hills of crimson stone, past the warped trees of red, is The Fortress. Hidden away in the shadows.

Rising straight out of the lava, the crimson brick pillars hold the structure high into the air, taller than any skyscraper.

Taller than any mountain.

The massive fortress with its endless towers and battlements stands out from the more natural surroundings. A sinking feeling forms in my stomach just from the sight of it.

"Who do you think built it?" Steven asks.

"I have no idea. But whoever they were, they're long gone now."

"Ali, how did you get all the way over there? It doesn't look possible," he says, studying the harsh landscape.

"The short answer? I didn't. Not the first time. Well, not even close to the first time, actually. But I made it eventually and, lucky for you, I drew a map," I smile at him. "But it still won't be easy. It's a long way, and the path isn't exactly a straight line."

"Yeah, I can see that," he says, looking a few feet to our left at the gaping hole in the stone. One wrong step and you would be falling straight down the crevice into the lava below.

"Now, let's get out of here. We'll do this again tomorrow," I smile at him, receiving a glare back. He's clearly exhausted and I'm my usual self. A fact that is undoubtedly annoying him.

We are nearly halfway back to the portal when I hear the unmistakable *woosh* of an arrow. Steven and I both drop to the ground as it whizzes over us, piercing through the space that our bodies previously occupied.

See, that's why we have the fancy getup, I say, smiling over at him. At least his instincts are still intact, even with the fatigue.

Well, I didn't really need it if I was just going to drop to the ground anyway, he argues.

Another *woosh*, a clang, and then I hear Steven moaning next to me. I look over frantically, seeing that an arrow has just hit him straight in the back, leaving a small dent in his armor. I know immediately that it won't cause any permanent damage, so I have to cover my mouth to hold back the laugh that is trying to escape me.

What was that, Steven? I couldn't really hear you complaining about your armor over the sound of you getting shot! I laugh.

Ugh, dammit Ali! Shut up and start running!

We both stand and head straight for the portal. As the arrows fly past us left and right, I focus, feeling the magic run through my body as I dodge them at an inhuman speed. I turn to look at Steven, making sure he's doing okay and then, I see it.

Under the shade of his hood, a purple flash of light flickers behind his eyes and a smug smile spreads across his lips as he dodges an arrow that *should* have hit him.

I stare at him in shock. *When did he figure that one out?* I wonder. He winks at me and then picks up the pace, running past quickly and jumping through the portal before me.

When I land on the other side, back in the cavern beneath the house, Steven is standing there, looking smug as all hell.

"Alright, tough guy," I roll my eyes at him, because I know what's coming next.

"I didn't think I could do it, but I did. And the look on your fa-" he cuts off suddenly, looking unstable.

Fantastic, I think sarcastically, then use my magic to rush over to him, making it just in time to help him collapse to the ground.

Chapter 43

"Ali?" I hear a groggy voice say. Looking over, I see that Steven is finally waking up.

"Well that's a weird place to fall asleep," I say before taking a huge bite out of my sandwich, masking my smile.

Steven looks around, confused. I left him exactly where he collapsed earlier, on the stone landing in front of the portal. But I brought him down a pillow.

He stares at it, then around the cave.

"I passed out, didn't I?" he groans.

"Yes. Yes you did," I mumble out through a mouthful of food.

"Are you eating a *sandwich* right now? I'm over here unconscious and you're eating a sandwich?" he says disbelievingly.

"What?" I say, my mouth still full. "I got hungry," I shrug. "Why, you want one?"

He lets out an exasperated breath, then slowly stands to his feet, walking over on shaky legs. He sits down next to me on one of the rocks as I pull out another sandwich from my pack then hand it over to him.

"How long was I out?" he asks.

"Um... a couple of hours."

"Shit, we've been down here a few hours?"

"Well, *you've* been down here. I ran upstairs, got out of my armor, made a few sandwiches, watched some cartoons..."

He leans over and gently bumps his shoulder against mine, smiling at me sideways.

"And I see you couldn't wait to get me out of mine too," he teases, looking down at his body, which is now armor-free. This earns him another eye roll from me.

But I did help him out of it, knowing damn well how uncomfortable it is to sleep in.

"What the hell happened?" he asks, rubbing his neck.

"It's the portal. When you first got here, you only went through once and you slept for most of the day. You just went through one *twice*. And your little magic trick back there didn't help either…" I eye him pointedly.

"But you have to admit, the magic trick was pretty badass," he says and I can't help but smile at his dimpled grin.

"I honestly thought you'd be out for longer," I say, relieved by how chipper he's being, considering the circumstances.

"Well, I'll probably be out again pretty soon, but this time I'll try laying down first," he smiles. "*Huh*," he says, stretching. "I thought I would hurt more from the fall."

"You probably would… if you actually fell. Good thing I was here to save your ass, *again*," I say dramatically.

"Dammit, I guess I owe you one," he says.

"And I will be happy to call in that favor anytime I see fit," I say, dusting the crumbs from my hands as I stand. "Now, think you can climb a really big ladder?"

Steven looks up toward the distant ceiling, then hangs his head back down with a *huff*.

"Maybe I'll just roll off this rock and let the giant glowing squid things eat me. It's probably easier to walk back from the island…" he mutters.

"Oh, don't be so melodramatic," I say, helping him to his feet.

"Maybe I'm being over-dramatic, or excessive, or-"

"Steven, don't you start with me."

"Or… *ostentatious,*" he smiles.

"I swear to god Steven, if you do that the whole way up the ladder, I'm pushing you off it."

Standing under the waterfall, I realize that nothing feels better than being clean after that place. I almost gave in and came up here while Steven was still passed out, but even with being sticky from sweat, dirty from head to toe and hair full of ash, I didn't want to leave him for that long. Not down there.

I dry off quickly and pull on my clothes, eager to get back to the house.

Steven, I'm back, I say to him as I walk inside.

Hey Ali, I'm in our room, he replies and his response has me blushing. *Our room*. I smile to myself as I make my way down the hallway. I hadn't really thought about it, but he's right.

It is our room.

He's been sleeping in my bed every night since the map run. He even dragged his mattress back to his old room days ago. And I'm certainly not about to ask him to leave. Not only do I want him close to me, but I always sleep better when he's around.

When I walk through the door, Steven is standing over by his side of the bed. His back is to me and my heart sinks when I see the dark red stain spreading across his shirt.

"Steven, you're bleeding!" I say, staring at it. The arrow must have broken the skin after all.

I stand perfectly still, finding my own panic strange. Bumps and cuts don't usually phase me, but there's something entirely different when it comes to *him*...

"I am?" he says, trying to look back at it. He winces from the movement.

"Go sit down, I'll get a rag," I say, heading over to the basin in the far corner to soak a piece of cloth. When I come back, Steven is sitting on the edge of the bed struggling to get his shirt off.

"Here, let me," I say, climbing over to sit behind him. Reluctantly, he lets me help.

Stubborn, I admonish. He mentally grumbles through our connection and I can feel how much he hates feeling weak.

Another thing we have in common.

I hold his shirt away from the wound and slowly pull it up and over his head. After a few more winces, it's finally off and I look down to examine the wound on his back. The laceration is just below his left shoulder blade and I'm pleased to find that it isn't too bad.

I've definitely healed from worse. And even though the bruising is still dark and the cut angry, there's already a little bit of yellow healing around the edges.

"Well, will I live?" he asks smartly, glancing back at me.

"You'll live. But the bedsheets won't unless I get this bandaged up."

"Well, we'd better save the sheets then," he says, trying to be clever, but I can hear the weariness in his voice.

I clean the wound as gently as I can, but still feel him wince under my hand. Even though I have personally given him greater injuries than this more times than I can count while we were training, it still strikes me how much I care for him.

How much I hate to see him hurt.

When I'm finished, I fold a piece of fabric several times and press it to the wound delicately. Now, the only thing left to do is get the bandage to stay there.

As I reach over, picking up the long strip of fabric that I tore earlier, I catch my eyes wandering freely over his back. His sun darkened skin, the tattoo down his spine and the strong muscles that ripple every time he breathes sends these feelings straight through my entire body. I can't suppress my sudden breathlessness or how much I want to run my hands all over him.

Then I smile, deciding to take my time with the last part of this chore. I hold the fabric in place with one hand and begin slowly, very slowly, wrapping the bandage around him, making sure that the back of my fingers trail along his skin as I go.

"Ali," he whispers in a deep cautionary voice, clearly knowing damn well what I'm doing.

When I've gone as far as I can reach with one hand, with my fingers hovering right around his ribcage, one of Steven's hands covers mine for a moment, holding it there briefly before taking the bandage from me. With my hand now free, I slide it over him slowly, touching his skin freely, feeling the muscles beneath my fingertips as I make my way around the other side. I take the gauze from his helping hand and when I am finished with the first time around, I have to do the whole thing over again.

Sometime during the second pass, I notice that Steven is breathing a little heavier than when we started. Which makes me smile, because I am too.

When I finally tie off the fabric, securing it in place, I wrap my arms around his waist and rest my cheek on his bare back, being careful to avoid the wound. When he reaches up, holding my arms against him, I shut my eyes.

I love being this close to him.

He rubs his thumb over my arm and then slowly releases my grip. I want to complain, but when he stands up and turns around, he gives me a look that says he is anything but finished with me.

I bite at my bottom lip to hold back a smile as I raise myself up on my knees and wrap my arms around his neck. Our bodies press together, his hands resting on the small of my back as he stands beside the bed.

After a moment, he takes my face in his hands and looks down at me, studying my face with a smile that makes my heart leap.

"You know, someone took me through a portal, *twice,* and now I have to sleep. And that particular someone, is making it *really* difficult to want to do that right now," he says deeply, a dimple playing at the corner of his mouth.

"Well, then you should probably sleep..." I say, staring up at him with big hopeful eyes that convey how much I disagree with that statement.

"Dammit, Ali," he says, his lips suddenly on mine as I fall back onto the bed with him on top of me.

Chapter 44

I jump through the portal and land in a crouch on the other side. I whip around, drawing my sword and raising it in a defensive position.

A second later, Steven leaps through, sword already raised. The metal blade glints red in the crimson light as it comes down quickly, clattering with mine as I block his blow. The weight of him sends my feet sliding backward across the stone ground, but I hold my position. I hear an arrow as it whistles through the air and give one hard shove against Steven's blade so I can jump back and evade it. The metal armor I wear clinks with the motion and despite the heat, I pull my hood back into place over my forehead.

Then I let Steven see the flash of green behind my eyes and give him a roguish grin. He meets my gaze, showing me the purple flicker of his own as I lunge for him, moving at inhuman speed. He jumps back just as quickly, then tries to return the favor. I evade the jab and attempt to slash at his right shoulder. He blocks, and we continue to circle each other in the open space.

The sound of another arrow perks our ears and without taking his eyes off me, Steven turns sideways, letting it pass before he strikes out again.

At first, we started training in here for the sole purpose of getting accustomed to the heat. But we enjoyed the thrill of evading arrows while we sparred so much, that we opted to train down here all the time. Because we are wearing armor, and since we both can move *faster* now, the wooden swords were left behind and we have been training with the real ones.

I sort of miss training in the armory. The ease of it and the *temperature*, but for where we are planning to go, this type of training is necessary.

And I can't deny that I find it exhilarating.

I wouldn't say Steven is *better* than me at fighting, and even if he was I would never admit it, but his skills have increased rapidly over the last several weeks. And finally, we're a fair match in a fight. His fatigue from going through the portal has long since worn off, but we continue coming through daily, just in case. Because when we actually set off on our next journey, we want the best chance at surviving it.

I dodge another blow and strike out with my own. I spin around, crouching low and swing my sword with both hands, right toward the metal armor on Steven's thigh. He blocks it and then twirls our swords free of each other, making another move against my opposite side. I block, swinging at him again and again, pushing him toward the cliffs against the far wall.

I almost have him cornered and he knows it.

Just before we reach the fallen rocks at its base, he smiles at me and then turns, running toward the rubble. I relax my stance and stare after him, wondering what he's up to. He leaps up onto one of the rocks and then stares back at me with a look, daring me to join him.

And because I'm not one to back down from a challenge, I do.

We stand on the unstable pieces of stone, lashing out at each other with swords and fists and kicks. My eyes flicker again, helping me keep my balance on the crumbling stone as I block every blow. The sweat drips down my face, but I ignore it. I haven't actually beat him in a while, seeing as most of our matches end in a draw, so I'm determined to emerge victorious.

And clearly, so is he.

We continue across the jagged rocks as we fight, sword against sword, the muscles in my legs and core burning with the effort to stay balanced. I slash down toward Steven's head and he blocks. Arms raised, he holds our position and stares at me, a dimple appearing when the corner of his mouth lifts in a smile.

What are you up to... I say, narrowing my eyes at him. We don't dare speak out loud in here, otherwise the creatures high above on the cliffs would most likely crawl down to join us. A few arrows here and there are fine, but the last thing we need is an all-out battle.

His smile widens and I cock my head.

He feigns a blow to my right and I move to block. After realizing his sword is not against mine, I watch as he does a backflip off the rock and lands perfectly on the stone ground twenty feet below. I roll my eyes and shake my head at how pleased he is with himself.

Show off, I say, jumping down to run after him.

What's the matter? Can't get a hit in? he teases.

The ego on this man... it's... well, I suppose it matches mine.

Hey Ali, he says as I continue to throw blows at him, *you remember that one time I beat you? Maybe you should just give up now?*

Hey Steven, you remember that time you fainted? I retort.

I didn't faint, I passed out. It's different!

It's not! I laugh as the battle continues.

I don't know how long we've been sparring for this time, but it seems like we can push ourselves a little further each day. We're accustomed to the heat at this point, as miserable as it is. I barely even notice the armor anymore. Steven and I have both incorporated magic into our motions as naturally as if we were born with the ability.

And who knows, maybe we were.

I think back to when I first got here and how using magic, even just a tiny bit, drained me like I had just ran a marathon. Now, using it is easy. Like it's a part of me, a part of *us*. And ever since Steven got here, I can feel that part of me growing stronger. The connection we have to each other, to this *world* and everything in it, is undeniable. It's as if we can reach out and touch parts of it, because we are a part of it.

A soul belonging to two worlds, I think, realizing just how much our tattoos ring true. Our souls belong here, just as they belong to the world we left behind.

Eventually, our determination gives way to exhaustion and we lower our swords, calling today's match a draw.

Panting and fatigued, I make my way over to Steven so we can head back toward the portal. I didn't realize how far our fight had taken us from it today. Goes to show how comfortable we've become in this place.

I wonder how long we've been at it this time and glance down at my watch, force of habit. I immediately roll my eyes, seeing the dial rotate rapidly. The damn thing never works down here.

Or maybe time doesn't exist down here...

I hear another *woosh* and quickly raise my sword, hearing the loud *clang* as the arrow bounces off my blade, inches from Steven's head.

Thanks for that, he says, winking at me.

Does this mean I win? I smile sweetly back at him.

Absolutely not, he replies, draping his armored arm over my shoulders as we walk back toward the portal together.

I sit on the edge of the bed wrapped in a towel and stretch my sore neck as I attempt to brush through my wet curls with my fingers. It seems that I come away more and more sore each time we train.

Because every time, we train harder.

But I ease into the pain, knowing that I will heal quickly. That I will be stronger for it. Back in the real world, I was always relatively active, but it wasn't until I got here that I started actually working out. At first, it was just something to do. Something to help with the loneliness. But I quickly realized that the stronger I was, the better chance I had of surviving out here. And now, training with Steven, I've never felt as strong as I am now.

I've also never felt so much like myself.

Even though my six months alone were a living nightmare, it gave me the time to find out who I really am. Without the noise, without other people, spending that much time alone forces you to know yourself. Forces you to survive against all odds, even when you feel like you can't go on. I just didn't realize that until Steven dropped into my life.

I thought that my time out here alone had broken me. Thought that because I hadn't found a way home, that I was weak. But I'm not. Because scared, little five-foot-five *me* was able to save him. *I* was capable of showing him how to survive in this world. I didn't realize how much I grew, how much I learned or how brave I had become until he washed up on my beach. Until I was confronted with my old self in his terrified eyes.

And then he told me that I was the strongest person he knew.

Over and over, he *trusted* me, relied on me, with no questions asked. He never doubted me, not even for a minute. And slowly, I started to consider that maybe I am strong. Maybe I can do this. That surviving out here didn't break me.

It only made me stronger.

Steven showed me that I could be proud of what I've accomplished, proud of how I survived, of who I am as a person. And for the first time in my life, I started to believe in myself. All the broken pieces of me started to fall into place and I found that my world was starting to make sense again.

It makes sense, because *he* is in it.

According to the marks in the armory, it's been over a month since that first map run. Since I shared my memories with him.

Since he found out what it's like to die.

After we finally made it back home, Steven confessed to me how he never really lived prior to being here, but that he wanted to now.

That he wanted to live this life *with me.*

And he's right. Because what is the point of getting to The End, if you don't enjoy the journey? What is the point in fighting, if there is nothing to fight for?

Steven had been waiting around for his life to start, but me? I was actively *running* from mine. Back home, all I wanted to do was leave that small town. To get out. Steven made me realize that I've been doing the exact same thing here. I've been running from my fears instead of standing my ground. Searching for a way out instead of appreciating what I have.

But it's time to stop running. It's time to fight, not just for a way out, but fight to *live.*

To have a *home*.

Because if all our efforts fall short, then this is it. This is our home. This is our life. And we damn well better not waste it.

So every day, we train harder. We fight. But we also take time for ourselves. And in doing so, we've created a life here.

A life together.

I smile at the thought, looking around our bedroom with its ocean view and fluffy pillows. I reach out, touching Steven's baby blue T-shirt that he abandoned on the bed earlier, blushing at the memory of how it got there...

Ali! Holy shit, Ali! Get in here! Get in here right now!

I jump up, panicked by his urgency. It barely registers that I'm still in my towel as I run out the door to find him.

What could have happened? Did something get into the house? Is he hurt? My thoughts race.

"Steven? Steven, what is it?" I shout as I run down the hall.

"In here!" he shouts back.

I turn the corner, run through the living room and into the map room. I see Steven standing there, leaning on his hands over the table, looking down at a book.

A book.

A book that better say "exit here," or he is going to have a long walk back from a certain island for giving me a heart-attack...

"Ali, you won't believe what I found. This book, it's-" his words cut off as he finally looks up at me. My hair is dripping onto the wooden floor, puddling at my feet, I'm holding the towel together at my collarbone and there's a look of annoyance plastered on my face.

"Oh... um... sorry, I thought that you were... um, well, I thought..." he stutters, trailing off.

"Steven, what did you find?" I say, trying to draw his attention back to whatever it was that had me racing out here. He shakes his head to clear it and stares back at the book.

"This book, it's about the creatures. All of them. At least, I think it's all of them. It says what they look like, what they can do, and it says their weaknesses," he looks up at me with bright eyes.

"So what? We know most of that already." *And I know it from experience...* I think darkly.

"No, Ali. I mean *all* of them. Even the ones in that hell hole on the other side of the portal," he says.

I stare at him, trying to figure out where he's going with this, until he continues.

"Like the ones who shoot *a line of fire*," he says and suddenly, I understand. "Ali, I know what we have to get from The Fortress. And I know how to kill them."

Chapter 45

I rush over to the table and stand next to Steven, looking down at the open book in disbelief.

"What does it say?" I ask urgently, completely forgetting my previous annoyance, because *this* was worth the heart attack. Steven stands still for another moment. He's acting strange, like he isn't used to me standing so close...*weird.* A second later, he pulls himself together enough to explain.

"Okay, so you know those creatures you told me about? The ones that live around The Fortress, the ones made of fire? Well it talks about them here," he says, pointing to a passage, one with his handwriting scattered all around the margins. "It says that when they die, they don't turn to dust, they melt... *back into the lines of fire from which they came.*"

"Holy shit," I smile.

"I know. But wait, it gets better. It says they shoot fire," he says.

"Yup, I know that part," I say, *remembering*.

"Well, the fire can only last for so long and then they have to sort of... *re-charge.*"

"So... if they have to re-charge, then..." I say slowly, piecing it together.

"Then we have a window. A time that we can kill them without getting fried. It's not long, only about five seconds, but it's something," he says, studying the page again.

"Something? Steven, this is huge! I've never been able to get close enough to kill one, and we didn't know what we needed to get. But now we know.

Now we won't be going in there blind," I say, looking back down at the book, already formulating a plan in my mind. "Steven, I think this could work," I say after a few moments, then stare up at him with bright eyes.

"I think it could too. I was thinking-" his sentence breaks off as his eyes meet mine for the first time since I've been standing here.

Then he lets his eyes wander down and I suddenly realize why he's acting so strangely.

I'm still standing here in only my towel, and even though Steven and I have lived together for months, it's a little different now.

Because he isn't *just* my roommate anymore.

"I think... we need to finish translating the rest of that book," I say quietly. "See if there's anything else in there we can use. But I think I'll go put some clothes on first..."

"I think that's probably a good idea..." Steven says slowly, trying unsuccessfully to hide his smile as I make my way toward the hall. As I do, I can feel his eyes on me. They feel like fire on my skin.

"Oh, and Ali?" he says before I can turn the corner. "I'm sorry... that I interrupted you..." he says slowly, letting his eyes trail over me once again, not even trying to hide it this time.

"No, you're not," I quip back. His eyes shoot to mine and I hold them.

"You're right, I'm not," he smiles and shrugs. I blush, before disappearing quickly down the hall.

It took us the rest of the day and most of the night, but we have nearly finished translating the entire book.

The Book of Monsters.

I was right, in that I did already know most of it just from experience, but there were still some surprising details that will certainly come in handy.

And then there are the creatures that I *haven't* seen before.

A shiver runs up my spine as I realize how much of this world we have yet to explore. All the creatures we have yet to encounter.

But even more terrifying than the thought of what else lurks in the dark, is that the book doesn't have any pictures. No matter how well it describes the creatures, we won't really know what we're up against until it is staring us right in the face.

Then there's the small, unsettling fact that we won't be able to translate what creature is on the very last page at all.

Because the page is missing.

It was torn from the binding in haste. By who and why, are questions that I try not to think about too much.

"The eyes, Steven! I found the eyes!" I say, beaming. He leans over, reading what I translated in the margins.

"You're right, *the eyes that cannot see...* that has to be it. So what is that thing? And how do we kill it?"

"Well, I've seen them before, so I know what it looks like..." *and what it feels like when they hunt you,* I think, not letting him hear it. "But I've never killed one. It says here that only something quicker than light can. I know we can be *fast*, but not *that* fast. And I've tried arrows before, that *definitely* doesn't work..." *Yeah, because the damn things can teleport,* I leave out again, because I'm not really ready to talk about it. Not yet. There aren't a lot of things out here that scare me anymore.

Those do.

"Quicker than light, *great.* So I guess we'll just take this one creature at a time then?" he asks.

"Sounds like a plan to me," I say, realizing that the creatures that shoot a line of fire somehow seem less... *horrifying*.

"Now, we just have to figure out how to bring back the fire they leave behind without burning ourselves. Got any ideas?" Steven asks.

"Not a clue," I say, staring off. "Unless... Steven, I've got it! The big book upstairs!"

"What about it?" he asks, confused.

"The *glass*. I finished translating the page with the glass bottles. Some to hold magic, some to hold potions and one glass vial to hold... *fire*."

We both shoot up from the table.

Steven shoves me back down into my seat, making a run for it, but I'm still faster. I trip him, but he only stumbles for a moment before he's grabbing at the back of my shirt, yanking me backward and laughing hysterically as we race each other to the ladder.

Chapter 46

I'm standing in the armory, staring at the marks carved into the stone wall. We've already put off our journey through the portal several times, and so we decided to put a date on it. Now that we know what we need to do, there's no reason to delay any more. *As much as I want to...*

I pull the dagger from my boot and make another mark. *Tomorrow*, I think.

My stomach drops.

We only have one more day in our home, one more day safe in the shelter of the cliffs, and then tomorrow...

Steven steps up behind me and puts a comforting hand on my shoulder. I lean back into him and he circles his arms around me as we stare at the marks on the wall together. It feels as though the weight of both worlds is suddenly on our shoulders. I think about my mom, my friends, about how worried they must be.

I think about what they *think* happened to me, to Steven.

I shudder.

I have to do this for them, but I also have to do this for myself. It's like Steven said, we need to know that we've done everything we can to get back to them.

"So..." Steven says, looking down at me and then pointedly eyeing the wooden practice swords leaning in the corner. I roll my eyes.

"I thought we agreed we wouldn't train on our last day. *Save our energy* and all that," I turn in his arms, looking up at him.

"Well, then don't consider this training," he says with a sly smile.

"Oh yeah?" I say as he backs away from me toward them. "Then what would I consider this?" I say, playing along.

"*Fun*," he says, tossing me a sword.

He gives me a giant grin and then takes off running.

I laugh. But if he wants to play, then I have no problem indulging him. After all the time we've spent taking training seriously, it feels nice to be a little carefree for a change.

Nearly an hour later, I'm surprised to find that I haven't even broken a sweat. After training on the other side of the portal, in the heat, with full armor, this feels like nothing.

And I have to admit, this is *fun*.

We leap from one wooden table to the next, knocking tools to the floor and laughing as we chase each other around the entire room, not just in the area designated for training. My cheeks hurt from how much I've been laughing and I'm secretly a little angry that his attempt to brighten my mood worked so well.

I fight off blow after blow as Steven swings at me again and again.

I raise my sword above my head, quickly noticing that Steven is in no position to block, and almost feel sorry for the bump I'm about to leave in his skull. But only a little. He would do the same to me.

My sword comes down and just before it makes contact, Steven *catches* it.

With. His. Bare. Hand.

I stare, confused, because I never considered that he would use his *hand* to stop it. I'm even more surprised that I didn't break it. But when I look down from his hand, clutching my sword above our heads, down to his eyes, I find them already fixed on mine.

And I instantly know that training is over.

Somewhere in the distance I hear the clatter of wood as his sword hits the stone ground. I slowly release my own grip as Steven flings it across the room without taking his gaze off me. I hear it hit hard, but my eyes stay locked on his. A purple spark lites behind those dark blue eyes and less than a second later, he's pressing my body against the far wall.

His hands are suddenly in my hair, pulling my lips to his. And although his lips are soft, his kiss is rough and relentless. And I can't get enough of him. I wrap my arms around his neck as he presses me into the wall even harder.

Feeling brave, I lift myself up and wrap my legs around his waist. His lips leave mine for a moment as he works to catch his breath. I wonder for a brief moment if what I did was too much, but then he slides his hands down my body, pulling my legs tighter around him and gives me a smile that makes my heart stop before covering my lips with his once again.

He kisses me frantically, eagerly, and our closeness makes my head spin. Knowing that he's as desperate for me as I am for him causes chills to run over my whole body.

I feel like nothing else in the world exists. No monsters, no magic, no desperate suicide missions through *hell* in a futile attempt to get us out of here...nothing. In this moment, there's only us, only our bodies as they intertwine.

Nothing else matters.

His body presses against mine, in tune with the rhythm of our kiss. I could die. *Actually* die from the way he's holding me, pressing me into this stone wall. I bite his lip playfully and he groans, releasing me. I reluctantly slide to the floor as he staggers backward, running a hand through his hair and taking a deep breath as he turns away from me.

"I'm sorry, I-"

"No," he says firmly, looking straight back at me. "Don't ever be sorry. Not about *that*," he says. I study the smile on his face and it makes me realize that he's just being a gentleman, *again*. I give him a coy smile and he returns it, those dimples deepening in his cheeks just as I can feel the heat rising in mine.

"So... how about we get some fresh air? I know a place," I offer, because as much as I would love to spend the day inside with him, I'm also fully aware of where we're about to go and I want one last day in the open air. One last day of sunlight before we're stuck in the bowels of hell for god knows how long.

"I could use some air," Steven agrees wholeheartedly. He walks over to me and places a tender kiss on my lips before taking my hand and leading me out of the armory.

The midday sun shines bright overhead as we run through the green grass of the meadow outside the house. I look around with a newfound longing and appreciation.

We don't know how long we'll be stuck on the other side of the portal and I want to take it all in while I still can. The trees, the birds, the glistening water of the stream as it gently flows over rocks and laps at the shoreline.

And then there's Steven. With his bright smile and shaggy hair as he runs beside me, clearly enjoying the beautiful day as we follow the river downstream.

We get to the top of the waterfall just as the sun begins to duck below the trees. We aren't safe up here after dark and I make a mental note to expand the light barricade once we get back.

I usually swim in all my clothes, but looking down at them now, I decide that I'm sick of running back home with them sopping wet. Any self-consciousness that I once had around Steven has long since been nullified. Living with someone for as long as we have will do that. He has seen me with bedhead, bruises, broken bones and when I'm a sweaty mess after training. So I figure there isn't anything left to feel embarrassed about at this point. But as I take off my boots, followed by my pants, I'm suddenly grateful that everything I have out here is relatively modest. The boy shorts and sports bra are practically a swimsuit anyway. I pull my shirt off, tossing it to the ground and I'm about to make the jump down to the water when I notice that Steven is *staring*.

"What?" I say, exasperated, hoping that he isn't about to tease me and make this awkward. *This is practical, right?* I think, suddenly feeling a little embarrassed. Even though we sleep in the same bed every night, this is the most exposed I've ever been around him.

"Nothing... it's just... if you brought me here to cool down, then you're off to a hell of a start," he says. His voice deep as he gives me that crooked grin of his.

"Calm down, *Romeo*, we're going swimming. *Just* swimming," I roll my eyes, but inwardly, I feel relieved. My awkwardness immediately dissolves, because he's attracted to *me*. That fact gives me more confidence than I've ever had and I can't help but smile.

"*Just* swimming, got it," he says, taking his shirt off in a way that makes my heart stop.

Shit. I gape at him, feeling the blush immediately flood my cheeks.

And then the sun goes down. *Thank god.*

"Last one down might get shot!" I shout playfully as I run past him, flying off the edge backward and landing several seconds later in the cool water below.

As I resurface, Steven is already splashing down next to me. I wince as the water drenches my face then splash him in return.

"Oh, *now* you've done it!" he says, chasing me through the water.

He eventually catches me and I scream as he pulls me to him, then laugh as he tickles my sides. I scream out again, then shove him under.

When he comes back up, he tries to glare at me, but he fails miserably.

He shakes his head, grinning, before his large hands find the bare skin of my waist and he pulls me closer, wrapping his muscled arms around me, pressing our bodies together. He pulls us over toward the rock in the center, leaning against it so we're no longer treading water.

Then he kisses me.

The water on our skin makes him feel impossibly soft. I can't help but relish every touch, every motion of our mouths. The kiss has me feeling... weightless. Like I'm floating in his arms.

I never want it to stop.

We swim and float around the swimming hole, laughing and talking, for several daylight cycles before making our way back over to the little rocky island in the center. We spend a long time sitting back-to-back, saying nothing as we look out at the world. The flowers in the grass, the wind through the trees, and the sounds of birds are so peaceful. So *alive.*

And then there's the stars at night. *So many* stars.

Even the sounds of creatures in the dark are a welcome comfort when you know you're safe. I tip my head back, resting it against Steven's back and close my eyes, breathing in the cool, crisp air.

"Steven, how long's it been?" I ask.

"Since..." he prompts.

"Since you got here. I haven't counted up the marks for a while," I wonder, having been too pre-occupied with the marks ahead. That, and Steven is usually the one who carves them into the wall whenever he's in there.

He's quiet for a moment, contemplating my question.

"I think it's been around four months," he says easily.

"Four months? Really?" I ask, turning to sit beside him.

"Yeah, can't you tell?" he asks with a mischievous smile before playfully rubbing his stubbled face against my cheek and then down to the crook of my neck.

"Okay, okay! I get it! Stop! Steven, stop it!" I laugh as he trails kisses down my neck.

Several minutes later, I grow somber, considering what he said. "Four months. Which means..." I trail off.

"Ten months," he says, looking at me. "You've been here for ten months."

That shouldn't hit me in the gut like a ton of bricks, but it does. Realizing it, Steven wraps an arm around me and I lean into him, feeling the comfort in his embrace. As heartbroken as I am to have been out here for this long, I still can't help but smile.

Because I'm not alone anymore.

I don't just have company, I have *him*. Even through the sorrow, my heart warms at the thought.

"Hey, Ali? There's something I've been wanting to say to you. And, well, since I don't know what will happen...how long we'll be in there..."

I tilt my head to look up at him, but he continues to stare off toward the shore, lost in his own thoughts. Ones he's not letting me hear.

"I'm sorry, Ali," he says, surprising me.

"Sorry for what?" I pull back so I can see his face fully, because I can't think of anything he should be sorry about.

Is he sorry for how long I've been out here? Because I could say the same for him. Four months is a long time to be away from your home, your family.

Your *world.*

I know that better than anyone.

"I'm sorry I gave you my heart in that cave and that I haven't been able to say this since... I think I've been afraid to. But what we're about to do, well, I'm just sorry I waited until now," he says and I can't get a read on where he's going with this.

"Say what?" I ask hesitantly.

Does he regret what he said in that cave? Is he nervous now, because he's about to take it back? If that's the case, I don't think my heart can bear it. I suddenly feel dizzy. I can't look at him. *No, no, no...*

"Ali, look at me," he says, clearly picking up on my panic. When I don't, he uses his thumb and forefinger to tilt my chin up to face him.

The second my eyes meet his, I realize that I'm terribly mistaken. A wave of relief washes over me. Because he's looking at me like I am his whole world.

How could I have doubted him? *Because he's your world, Ali. And that won't ever change. Even if it does for him...* The thought terrifies me.

"Ali, I love you. You are everything to me. I'm sorry I haven't had the courage to say it since we were in that cave, but I've wanted to. I've wanted to every day," he says sweetly, his eyes staying steadfast on mine.

And I don't know what I've ever done to deserve him.

"You have nothing to say sorry for, because... well, I haven't said it either. The cave just felt... surreal. I wasn't sure if, when we got out of there and after everything, you would feel the same. But you do, I know you do. I guess I was just afraid to bring it up, because if I did, maybe it wouldn't be real anymore," I blink.

"It's real," he whispers.

"I love you too, Steven," I say, my voice hitching with emotions. He smiles down at me as his thumb brushes my chin. Then he kisses me softly.

So softly.

When he pulls back, he gazes into my eyes and our fingers intertwine as we enjoy our last moments in the sunlight.

Chapter 47

Steven and I walk out of the portal and into the heat, just like we've done countless times before. Except this time is different. This time, we aren't going back.

The goal is simple: get to The Fortress, get the fire, and get the fuck back home.

Easy.

Yeah right, my brain says, already mocking me. This is going to be *hell* and I know it.

Steven and I are dressed in our full armor and hoods, swords at our side. I have a dagger in my boot, like always, and noticed earlier that Steven strapped one to his bicep as well. We carry our packs, full of the same supplies we took on the map run. Only this time, we brought more food. My stomach turns just at the thought of how long we went without. We are not about to make that mistake again.

Especially in here.

We also brought along with us several of the glass vials that will *supposedly* hold the fire once we kill the creatures. The fact that we have no way of testing whether or not that will work is doing nothing to calm my uneasiness. We know that the creatures can be killed and we know how to do it. But actually succeeding, without getting ourselves killed in the process, is going to be a whole other matter. Because five seconds is all we have. Only five seconds before the creatures can recharge and light us up like a torch.

But first things first, we have to get to The Fortress.

Although I've made the journey before, I know firsthand that it won't be easy, even with the map that's tucked inside my pocket.

Over the last several weeks, Steven and I also came up with a plan for if, or more likely *when*, one of us is killed. When you appear back on the island, you have yourself and your clothes, but that's it. All weapons and supplies will be left at the place where you died. Which, if you ask me, is horribly inconvenient.

So we devised a plan.

Whoever survives will gather the dropped supplies, find a safe place to hide, and then wait until the other can find their way back. That way, we can guarantee nothing is lost and we can move forward *together*. Having been here before, I know damn well that if this is going to work, then we will need to rely on each other. Need to have each other's backs.

So we will hide, and we will wait.

It's a good plan, but one I hope we won't have to carry out.

At least, not too often.

I have no illusions about this being a walk in the park. I don't even mind that I will probably die for the eighty-seventh time. Because by now, *hell*, I'm used to it. *Well, as much as anyone can get used to it.*

But watching *him* die? Watching *Steven* die?

My heart sinks at the thought.

A sudden flash of a memory, of watching him falling down into that ravine, of losing him, assaults my mind. I didn't know if he could survive the fall. Didn't know if he would come back. What I felt in that moment… I quickly push back the thought, replacing it with determination.

Because I am *not* going to let that happen again.

This time, I will be there for him.

Steven and I run across the familiar flat area where we've been training and continue on until we are standing at the edge. As we look out over the ocean of lava to The Fortress, with its dark haunting towers looming in the shadows, I suddenly remember how far it is.

Our last map run's gonna feel like a stroll through the meadow after this one, Ali. I mentally prepare myself.

We make our way along the edge until we are standing above a smaller ledge far below. There's already a large rope tied to a rock from my last little *adventure* down here, snaking across the ground in front of us before disappearing over the ledge. I glance over at Steven and he gives me a quick nod of acknowledgement.

I grip the rope, walking backward over the edge and down the cliff. Steven follows and after a short hundred-foot climb down, we're standing on the narrow stone ledge at the bottom.

Now that we're closer to the lava, the temperature has increased substantially. I'm suddenly grateful that we spent so much time training down here. This type of heat isn't exactly something you can ever really get used to, but at least we're not immediately incapacitated by it.

We run along the rocky path, staying close to the cliff wall and keep our guard up, searching for anything in front of, or *above*, that might try to kill us.

I glance over the ledge, realizing that the lava can't be any more than a few hundred feet below us. I can easily hear the crackling of it, and the smell of sulfur burns my nose and throat.

Ali, to your right, Steven warns in what I've started to think of as his "military" voice. Short and to the point. I look up slowly and see the skeleton high above us crawling along the cliffs like a spider, its bow draped across its back. I look around, finding three more in the vicinity, but none of them seem to notice our presence. The natural noises of this place mask our footfall, but it would only take one misstep, one loose rock, to have the creatures immediately lock on to our position. Moving quickly and quietly, we keep our eyes glued on the creatures until they are far out of sight.

Several minutes later, we reach an area that opens up. It's similar to the training area in front of the portal, only much larger. There are several patches of the ground that are on fire, most likely caused by some creature that passed through before us.

Steven looks over warily, but we continue on, walking side-by-side around the flames and across the open space, making our way toward the trail that leads up the inclining rocky slope ahead.

Hours later, we finally reach the top. I have to stop for a moment to catch my breath. Steven stands next to me, putting his hands on his knees and giving me a look that says he's grateful for the respite as well.

I gaze around curiously, surprised we haven't been ambushed yet. *Well, there's still time,* I remind myself.

You see over there? I say to Steven, pointing toward where the crimson stone ground gradually fades to patches of dark brown. *We'll have to go around.*

That's right, creepy quick sand. I'll try not to fall in, he grins. I smile, because even in his mind, the inflections in his voice hold that same touch of humor. I never thought anything could make me smile down here, but here he is, standing there making jokes. Proving me wrong.

I continue to stare at him, realizing that he doesn't even have to *say* anything to make me smile. Tan skin, dark brown wavy hair touching the tops of his dark blue eyes that look one-hundred percent purple in this light, and that damn baby blue T-shirt. It's poking out from the edges of his armor, the soft pastel contrasting against the heavy leather and metal armor that covers it. I shake my head, amused. Because here's this *warrior* standing in front of me and he's wearing a goddamn designer T-shirt.

What? he asks, staring at me warily.

Nothing, I say, shaking my head before taking off at a steady jog, looking for a way around the sand.

Well, here we are.

Running.

Again.

I take a giant leap off the ledge, giving me the boost I need to clear the large crevice in front of us. As I fly through the air, I try not to think about what's below. Steven is right behind me and the second we touch down on the other side, we take off running.

And why are we running this time? Because an *army* of skeletons is after us.

I grit my teeth, hating the sounds of their bones scraping together as they give chase, the grating noise amplified by the echoes bouncing off the surrounding rock.

Arrows fly at our backs and we use magic to evade as many as we can, but we can't dodge them all. I know I've been hit several times, but the armor seems to be holding up, because the strikes haven't slowed me down. Not yet at least. I hear arrows clanking off Steven's armor as well and silently hope that one doesn't slip past the protective covering.

After the first little *incident* with the arrow a few weeks ago, Steven took the time to reinforce all of our armor.

And right now, I'm glad he did.

We slow our pace, suddenly realizing that the arrows have stopped. I turn, looking to see if we finally lost them.

Just out of bow-range, the creatures are standing in a line, right at the edge of the fissure we jumped over.

Why are they stopping? I've seen them jump further than that before, Steven asks.

The creatures here are extremely territorial. So if they've stopped, that means we're no longer in their territory... I explain, because I've seen this before.

So... if we're out of their territory... then whose territory did we just step into? he asks warily. I stare back, staying silent. Because he isn't going to like the answer to that question.

Just keep your eyes peeled, maybe we can slip through unnoticed, I say. But I already know that there isn't a chance in hell of that happening.

Unnoticed. Sure... he says sarcastically, clearly not believing me as he scans the forest we're walking into.

The stone ground fades to dirt and our footfall is silenced by the crimson grass that blends in with everything else in this place. The trees are taller than any I've seen in *either* of the outside worlds. They loom over us, their branches clawing at the air like they are their own type of creature, ready to pounce. Their twisted roots spread out along the ground, tangled with thorns that snake out across our path. Bright red vines hang down around us. I move them aside with my sword as Steven follows close behind.

I don't always walk around with my sword drawn, but in the forest? *Hell* if I'm putting it down.

Because I know whose territory this is.

As we walk among trees, I suddenly miss the wide-open spaces we traversed to get here. Although there were no places to hide, at least you could see what was after you. Here, the branches sway in the heat and the leaves fall, the constant movements hiding the creatures that lurk in the shadows.

I continue on, until another huge tree juts up in front of me. Holding onto its twisted trunk, I clamber over its thick roots and drop the short distance to the ground.

Then, I stop dead in my tracks.

Steven steps down next to me and I quickly whirl around, clasping my free hand over his mouth. He stares at me questioningly, then looks over my head. His eyes widen, his face pales and he takes a stumbling step back, replacing my hand with his own. He starts to heave and, ducking behind a tree, he throws up as quietly as possible.

Yeah... that's about the reaction I was expecting, I think, looking back toward the carnage, cringing. There's a massive hog, larger than a buffalo, suspended by its back legs several feet above the ground. One long jagged cut splits its body in half and it's been disemboweled. *Gross.*

Thick coagulated blood seeps down its body and slowly drips off of its large tusks. The internal organs were pulled halfway out of the creature, spilling out and across the ground in front of it.

The sight of a *fresh* kill would make anyone's stomach turn. But this looks and *smells* like it's been here for a while. The meat is clearly spoiled, which makes watching the creatures who are currently *eating* it, even worse.

The stench of rotting flesh makes my eyes water and I'm just about ready to join Steven behind that tree, when I notice that there are only two creatures standing around for their evening meal.

That's odd, they usually travel in larger groups-

Suddenly, my eyes go wide. I run back to Steven, who's still hunched over, his hands on his knees.

Alright, it's time to go, you can throw up more later, I say urgently.

Ali, what's- he starts, but the rustling trees beside us answer his question.

We take off running through the brush. My stomach sinks, knowing that the way we're heading is taking us off course. But after a quick look behind us I realize... we don't have a choice.

Because they've seen us.

Chapter 48

The sounds behind us grow louder as more creatures join the brigade that's after us, but we keep on running. I watch as Steven leaps over a thorn bush ahead of me. He's at least six inches taller than me, can jump higher than me, and yet even he barely cleared it.

Which means there's no way that I'm making it over, I realize. *Unless...*

Suddenly, my instincts kick in and I concentrate, feeling the magic that's all around me. I pull it from the air, from the trees, from... *Steven*?

I can *feel* him. Feel his magic.

Glancing up, I watch him turn back toward me, the light flickering in his eyes. I let his magic join mine, and then, I jump.

I clear the thorns by well over a foot, hearing Steven give a loud *whoop!*

I start laughing, figuring we don't need to be as quiet when they're already after us.

"How did you know you could help me?" I shout up toward him as we run.

"I didn't, I just felt that you needed it," he calls back to me.

I wonder for a moment what else about this world we have yet to discover.

"*Woah,* Ali, stop!" Steven says suddenly, putting an arm out. One that I immediately run into. I grasp his armor, holding on to steady myself. I breathe heavily.

In front of us, the ground gives way and another forest spreads out far below us. But *this* forest isn't colored in the usual crimson variety, it's a fusion of striking shades of aqua blue. The bright colors stand out in stark contrast from the red walls surrounding it. I find it… *unsettling*.

"What the hell kind of tree is that?" Steven asks me.

"I have no idea, I've never been this way before," I say, looking around warily.

"Shit," Steven says and it only takes me a second to figure out why.

Because we're trapped.

The creatures funneled us through a valley of cliffs, too high up on either side to attempt a free climb. Looking around, I realize there's no other way out.

Except for *down*.

It's then I hear the sounds of the horde, making their way noisily through the crimson forest behind us. The ground shakes and the trees sway from the force of their heavy footfall.

I look over at Steven, the mutual understanding in our gaze.

"Well, let's hope the branches break our fall," I say, looking down to the forest of blue. "You ready to jump off a cliff?"

"Do I have a choice?" he asks.

"Hey, I've jumped from higher," I say, taking a running leap off the edge.

"Yeah, but you *died*!" Steven shouts after me. I burst out laughing even as I fall. As fed up with my humor as he probably is, I'm beginning to really appreciate his.

I hit the first branch so hard it knocks the wind out of me. But after that first one, the next thirty or so don't seem as bad.

The final twenty-foot drop to the ground however, that one gets me.

I try landing in a crouch, but between the weight of my backpack, and the numbness in my limbs from the fall thus far, it throws me off balance, sending me forward.

I hear the bone crack in my wrist, not even feeling the pain.

But I know it's coming.

Ope, there it is, I groan a moment later, but immediately get to my feet. I hold on to my wrist, looking for Steven.

I hear the sound of breaking branches overhead and look up. My brows furrow as I watch him fall. *He's definitely not going to land on his feet.*

I rush toward him before he even hits the ground. When he lands straight on his back, I hope that maybe his backpack will break his fall.

It doesn't.

He lies perfectly still. My eyes find his leg, which is now bent at an impossible angle.

"Fuck, Steven! *Steven!*" I shout, throwing myself down beside him. But when I see the pained look on his face, I quickly let out a breath. Because he's still alive.

"Hey, I'm here, I'm right here," I whisper, before looking around in a panic. I have no idea what creatures are down here. Whose territory we just fell into. But whatever they are, no doubt they heard our fall.

I look up, finding the creatures that were previously chasing us lining the ledge above. They watch us for several long moments before, one at a time, they slowly turn around, disappearing from view.

Satisfied that nothing is *immediately* trying to eat us, I turn back to Steven. He's groaning softly, his eyes pinched shut in pain.

"God, Steven," I say quietly, looking him over. "I know your leg is hurt, but where else? Do you hurt anywhere else?" I say, having already started feeling around his neck, to the back of his head, and down his spine. He groans again and my heart hurts from the sound. Seeing him like this is *unbearable*.

I bite my lip in an attempt to keep it together.

"Steven, I have to put your leg back into place so it will heal properly, okay?" I warn.

He doesn't say a word, but he manages to open his eyes, giving me a weak nod. I touch his face gently with my good hand and he leans into it.

"I'm so sorry, this is really going to hurt," I say gently, making sure he's prepared for what I'm about to do.

"You know this from experience?" He attempts to smirk, but I can tell the motion pains him.

"Yes. But I had to wedge my leg between two rocks to set it, so be thankful that you have my delicate fingers," I try to joke, but it comes out weak.

"I like your fingers," he says, wincing as he reaches up to hold them to his face, then gently pressing them to his lips. "Don't worry about me, I can handle it, okay?"

I nod, but secretly, I'm trying not to cry.

"That's my girl. My little warrior," he says weakly before pinching his eyes shut again in pain. He's clearly delirious, but the sentiment still catches me off guard. And it's so sweet that I suddenly find and take hold of my missing courage.

I am going to fix that damn leg, then I'm getting him the fuck out of here.

It takes me a moment to survey the damage and another to get myself into position, but if anyone knows about broken bones, it sure as hell is me. I've lost count of how many I've broken, bruised, fractured or dislocated since I got here. But it *well* exceeds my death count, which is saying something.

"Okay, you ready?" I say, sliding my broken wrist under his leg so I can use my arm as leverage, then place my good hand in position.

"Yeah, I'm rea-" his voice cuts off at the sharp *snap* as I quickly pop the bone back into place. He lets out a pained shout followed by an intake of breath through clenched teeth.

"Goddammit, Ali. *Fuck!*" he says, his body lurching from the pain. I secure a few broken sticks around his leg for support, and he moans again as I cinch them tight with the twine I pulled from my pack. He curses as I tie it off and then settles his head back down, an arm draped over his face as he breathes heavily. I watch his actions, relieved that he seems to have a full range of motion, which means any other injuries he has aren't as serious and will heal quickly enough.

I look around again, finding nothing but the twisted roots and the warped trees for as far as I can see. But whatever hadn't heard us fall, most certainly heard Steven scream.

Which means that it's time to get out of here.

I sling my backpack on with a wince. My wrist is throbbing now, but I don't have time to deal with it.

Steven struggles to sit up and if not for our situation, I wouldn't have let him move at all this soon after a fall like that. But we don't have the luxury of sitting around.

Crouching beside him, I wrap one of his arms over my shoulder, my good arm around his waist and help lift him to a standing position.

I glance up toward where we fell, quickly getting my bearings. I know the direction we need to go, I only hope that there's a way to get back up from down here. This journey will be hard even on familiar ground, so the sooner we get back on course the better. But right direction or not, I don't like that we're heading into a warped version of the forest above. And I definitely don't like the fact that we are traveling *under* it.

"Think you can walk?" I ask because we have to start moving.

"Yeah. Yeah I can," he breathes out through clenched teeth and I give him a skeptical look. "Yes, it hurts like hell, but I know I just made a whole lot of noise, so I'd like to get the fuck out of here."

"Alright, hold on to me," I say, gripping him tighter and holding most of his weight as we head off into the forest.

It's eerie how similar it is to the forest above. The tree trunks are knotted, winding together along with the thorny vines. They crawl across the ground and shoot straight up in some places, creating walls of spikes and sticks. There are even the same softer vines that hang down from the trees all around us. The only real difference is how the leaves and grass are a piercing shade of blue, with that same color snaking through the browned tree bark like bolts of lightning.

As we continue on, I suddenly get this strange feeling crossing over the back of my neck, making the hairs there stand on end. A shiver runs up my spine and it feels like someone, or *something*, is watching us.

Stalking us.

I feel it again, but brush it off. *I'm probably just being paranoid.*

We stumble along together, exhausted and in pain, but we just keep going, searching for a safe place to hide. To heal.

What the fuck was that? Steven says a few minutes later, stopping in his tracks. His head darts to one side and he stares curiously toward one of the trees. Its blue leaves gently rustle, but there's no breeze down here. It's as if something just brushed past it.

Maybe I wasn't imagining it, I think as uneasiness spreads through me.

And then I realize what's happening.

Fuck! I say, sliding my arm out from Steven's waist to stand in front of him. I quickly move a hand to the side of his face, urging him down until our foreheads are touching.

Look at me, Steven. Look straight at me and don't look away, I say frantically.

Ali, this is great and all, but do you really think it's the best time for that? he teases as his eyes move to look around.

Shut up! Don't. Look. Anywhere. Else. My tone snaps him back into defense mode and he looks straight into my eyes, understanding my warning.

Ali, what's happening.

The eyes. The ones that cannot see. It all makes sense now, I say, piecing it together for the first time. *As long as our eyes can't see them, then they can't see us...*

Shit. Ali, are you sure? he asks.

I'm sure. But there's not just one out here...

How many? I can feel them, but I can't seem to focus... he says uneasily.

That's because they never stop moving. They only appear for a second and then they disappear, it's how they hunt. They circle you, make you want to look for them, make you feel like you're going insane. But once you actually see one... my eyes go dark and I feel a warm tear run down my hot skin.

It's okay Ali, don't think about it. Just look at me, I'm right here. I'm with you, he says, moving his hands to gently cup my face.

I want to get lost in those eyes, in his words, in the comfort of his touch. But I can't stop thinking, *this is it.*

This is where the journey ends.

We're going to die here. And when we do, we will have to start all over. *Will we even want to start over? Want to try again?*

I feel a prickling feeling run up my left arm and I can see in Steven's eyes that he feels it too. It doesn't take us long to realize why.

Because it's standing right next to us.

Chapter 49

I have to bite my lip to not scream. I hold my breath and feel my body start to tremble with fear. The figure is standing right beside us, no more than a foot away.

Out of the corner of my eye, I can barely make out the shape of it. Its skin is a dark black, like a void threatening to suck us in. Its legs are almost as tall as me and sickly thin. Its arms jut down, with large hands that hang past its knees. I can see long, spindly fingers that twitch and curl, as if they are waiting to grab something.

And I know from past experience that these creatures are nearly ten feet tall.

My stomach turns.

I'm frozen in place, holding my breath as another tear slips out. But I don't blink. I stare straight into those dark purple eyes. They are my rock. My safe place.

And they are just as scared shitless as mine are.

Then the creature moves and I almost jump. Steven and I are both trembling now, but we hold on, keeping our eyes focused on each other and away from the creature that hunts us. It moves slowly, deliberately. I've never seen one stand in the same place for so long. But maybe that's because I've never seen one for more than a few seconds... another shudder runs through me.

Because a few seconds is all it takes.

After a moment, I finally realize what the creature is doing. It's crouching down. *Why?* I wonder.

Steven, don't look, stay with me, I urge, but even in my mind my voice sounds shaky.

Ali, I'm with you, I'm here, he says, but his voice trembles too.

I suddenly feel a wave of anger, because we came all this way, and for nothing.

We're going to die.

I see the bottom of its jaw first. And then its teeth take form. They're black, same as its skin, but sharp as spikes, each tooth larger than my dagger. They're dripping wet with something and I'm glad the only view I have is blurred through my peripheral. It continues down and the pit in my stomach grows as I realize how *wide* its mouth has opened. The bottom of its jaw is almost down to my elbow and I'm just now starting to get a view of its upper teeth. It must have unhinged its jaw, widening it to attack. But it hasn't.

Can't attack yet... I realize.

Not until we look at it.

It continues to lower itself down and I understand what the creature is doing just as Steven does.

The eyes, we say at the same time. It's lowering itself down so we will see its *eyes*. I give Steven one last look, before we each squeeze ours shut.

I quickly find that the darkness is more terrifying. Because *now*, I don't know what's happening. I can still feel the creature beside me, *feel* several more circling us.

But I can also feel Steven.

His large hands have moved, and he's holding the back of my neck, gentle, but firm. My hand is still on his face and his forehead is pressed against mine. I can feel the motion of his breaths.

His rhythm is steady.

It anchors me.

Then, I feel the hair on my skin settle and the electricity running down my arm dissipate just as quickly as it came.

After a few moments, I slowly open my eyes and find Steven's staring back. A wave of relief washes over me as I realize that the shadow standing beside us, is gone.

I think I might collapse with joy, but we aren't out of this yet. We have to find a safe place to hide. To heal. I wince as I once again become aware of my broken wrist tucked into my side, but I'm reluctant to move, so I keep my forehead pressed against his.

Steven's hands move from my neck to pull my hood back up, his eyes never leaving mine.

If we just look at the ground, we should be okay, right? he asks.

I think you're right. I don't think they can see us, or at least, they can't attack, if we don't look at their eyes.

He smiles at me and, taking advantage of our proximity, he leans in, giving me a deep but brief kiss that leaves me breathless, before stepping away and pulling his own hood into place over forehead.

He nearly stumbles, forgetting that he can't walk on his own. I quickly wrap my good arm back around him as we continue on, trying to navigate our way through the rough terrain with our view limited to the ground beneath us.

After several minutes, we reach a stone wall and follow along it until we come to an opening, leading us into a large cave. Once inside, I dare to look up. There are narrower tunnels that branch off and I don't even want to think about what could be hiding in the dark.

There is a shallow alcove in the wall, close to the entrance. It's high enough up from the ground to be easily defendable and because this cave has several entrances, it offers us more than one way out if necessary.

Nowhere is safe in this place, so for now, it's enough.

Steven tosses our bags up onto the high ledge and I look over at him, suddenly unsure how he's going to get up there with his leg. But apparently, his upper body strength seems to be working just fine. He jumps up, grabs the ledge and pulls himself over with only a few winces.

Great, I think, wondering how in the hell *I'm* going to get up there with a broken wrist. As I stand there, trying to figure out which footholds I can use that will accommodate climbing with just one hand, I notice Steven looking down at me, confused. He knows that *normally* I could scale this in my sleep, so his confusion quickly turns to concern.

I'm fine, I just need a little help, I say, reaching my good hand up toward him. He leans over, lending a hand, and I grasp his forearm just as he holds mine. He pulls me up and over like I weigh nothing, then immediately starts looking me over, trying to pinpoint my injury.

Stop that. Really, I'm fine. It's just my wrist, I say, trying to assuage him. In reality, it hurts like hell. Steven must have guessed as much, because he gives me a look of concern mixed with annoyance as he pulls the first aid kit from his pack. He gestures for me to come closer to him, giving me a "don't mess with me" sort of look. And because my wrist hurts too much to argue, I move closer, holding it out for him with a wince. He wraps it carefully, but firmly, and the relief is almost immediate.

But so is the exhaustion.

I don't know how long we've been awake, but definitely longer than we're used to.

After checking on Steven's injured leg, I help him find a position comfortable enough to lie down, then curl up next to him. We stare up at the stone ceiling for a long time, silently watching the twinkling of the tiny glowing stones embedded in the dark crimson. Like little pricks of sunlight trying to break through the veil of darkness.

Hell of a day, huh? I say, chuckling.

He rolls his head over to look at me and smiles brightly.

Hell of a goddamn day.

When I wake up, I move my wrist around instinctually and am pleased to find that it's completely healed. I sit up quickly, suddenly panicked, because I know how long we must have slept for that to happen.

I half expected to be woken up by an arrow or some other creature trying to kill us during the night, but I'm pleasantly surprised to be in one piece.

Looking over, I see Steven beginning to stir as well. As he wakes, he gives me that dimpled smile, then looks down at his leg, attempting to move it.

How is it? I ask, concerned that it hadn't set right after what we put it through yesterday.

It's... it's fine, he says, surprised. *I think it's healed. But no more jumping off cliffs today, deal?*

Deal. We'll wait until tomorrow, I say and can't help but smile as I take a deep, relieved breath. Not only because he's feeling better, but because now we can continue on sooner than later. I know from experience that it's never a good idea to stay in one place for too long.

Not down here.

As we walk, hoods up and heads down, I realize that this part of the forest is somehow cooler than the rest of the world. *Yeah Ali, if you can consider the temperature of the sun as "cooler,"* I lecture myself. But as the patches of turquoise blue grass slowly start to fade back to red, I can feel the temperature starting to rise with every step.

Steven and I walk close to each other, not wanting to risk being separated and only dare to look up once the warped turquoise landscape is far behind us.

When we finally do level our gaze, we don't look back.

Our number one goal now is to get back to the path above. Because getting lost in here would be the end of it. And going back through that last forest... Well, that isn't a great option either.

After what seems like ages, I finally see a hint of those familiar crimson red vines, winding down from the stone ceiling. Steven sees it too and with a quick glance at each other, we run toward it.

Above us, there's a vertical cave, leading straight up through the stone ceiling, allowing the vines to make their way all the way down from the area above. Grabbing hold of the scraggly, trailing plant, I yank as hard as I can, testing my weight. Steven grasps a bunch as well and lifts himself up by it, smiling over at me when it holds.

Well, what do you think? he asks, looking up through the cave covered in vines. *It's a long way.*

Not up for it? I tease.

What do you think? he says, giving me that crooked smile and a wink before pulling himself up, hand-over-hand, using only his arms to climb.

Show-off, I say, but quickly follow after him.

Once up in the cave, the climb becomes easier as we use the stone walls for a foothold. We quickly scale it, side by side.

When we climb out, we're back in the crimson forest. Thankfully, there are no signs of the creatures that we ran from before, so I pull out the map, studying it. Once I have our heading, we continue on over rocks, roots and thorns, until the trees begin to clear.

We did it. We made it out, I say excitedly. Steven smiles at me. I run forward, my eyes on the trail up ahead.

Until suddenly, my feet are yanked out from under me and I land on my face in the red grass. My vision starts to blur and I try desperately to blink back the fog. I think I see Steven running after me, but he's upside down, which doesn't make any sense.

I must have hit my head *hard*, because the world is spinning.

It just keeps spinning.

"Ali!" I hear his thick voice shouting my name, over and over. But then his voice and the world begins fading to black.

Chapter 50

"Steven?" I mumble. My head begins to clear and blinking, the world slowly comes into focus. Only, it's upside down.

No, not the *world.*

I'm hanging upside down.

I look up, and my eyes follow the rope tied around my ankles to the pulley system hanging in the tree, to the counterweight. I shudder at the realization.

This trap was set on purpose.

A memory of the disemboweled hog suddenly floods my vision, causing my stomach to turn. I look around, searching for Steven. I'm horrified to find him also hanging by his feet, several feet away. My heart sinks and my pulse starts to beat faster.

Because he isn't moving.

Steven! Steven, wake up! I shout, but there's no answer. I want to shake him awake, but I can't reach him. We're hanging at least fifteen-feet up and my backpack is lying on the ground below me.

Along with my sword and my dagger.

Shit! They must have fallen out of their sheaths.

Turning my attention back to Steven, I move back and forth, using the momentum to swing myself from one side to the other, until I'm able to reach out and grab one of the leather straps on his armor. We sway for a moment and as we slowly start to still, I reach over, grabbing onto him with both hands.

Then I start shaking him.

Steven, wake up! I shake him again. *Oh god, please don't be dead!*

Well, I'm not God, and I'm also not dead, his voice says in my mind even before his body starts to stir.

I want to hit him.

I decide against it, but only because I can't tell if he has any injuries or not.

Are you okay? I ask in a rush. He rubs his head and looks around.

Shit! And yeah, I'm fine, but shit! he says, suddenly realizing our predicament. He immediately reaches for his sword and groans when he finds the sheath empty. Then his hand moves to his bicep and he unties the dagger from its sheath, turning back to me with a satisfied grin.

Well, look at you, I say, smiling back.

Holding the knife in one hand, he grabs hold of my forearm with the other and I grip tight, giving him a quick nod. With little effort, he uses his strength to reach up and slice through the rope above my feet with one quick slash. My body immediately falls and I feel the quick jerk in my arm when our grip holds and we swing through the air.

Dangling below him, I look up, meeting his eyes for a long moment. Once again, lost to them.

Steven gives me a mischievous smile and then, he drops me.

I land easily, but look back up at him with a glare.

Hey, a little warning? I chide.

You have to admit, you had that coming. You always have that coming, he says with a quick raise of his eyebrows. Then he puts the blade between his teeth, reaching up to climb his own rope to cut himself free. But before he has the chance, we hear the barrage of grunts and heavy breathing from the nearby forest.

The creatures are heading straight for us and *fast*.

Ali, run! Steven shouts in my mind.

I quickly grab my sword and duck behind a tree, pressing my back to it.

Maybe they won't see him? I hope, but as I listen, I hear the creatures slow to a halt.

Right under him.

It's then I know for certain that they were the one who set the trap. I just have to wait for them to let their guard down so I can get him out of here.

Suddenly, I hear the sound Steven makes when his body hits the ground. I wince, squeezing my eyes shut.

After taking a deep breath, I slowly peer around the tree, finding that Steven is completely surrounded. Two of the creatures have him by the arms and he's struggling against their grip, unable to escape.

The creatures stand tall, resembling men, only brawnier. Their thick stocky legs jut down from their torn leather pants like chunky tree trunks and ripple with an impossible amount of muscles. Their arms and chests are just as muscular under their leather tunics and every inch of their skin is covered with long, brutal scars.

And if the scars weren't threatening enough, their faces certainly are. It looks as though their noses have been smashed in and the two large breathing holes in the center of their faces remind me more of a pig's snout rather than an actual nose. Their thick teeth are yellowed, protruding straight out and coming to sharp points. A longer tooth sticks out further than the rest on either side of their toothy mouths, curving upwards like small tusks.

And their *eyes.* With no pupils, the off-white of them seem to glow against their ragged, leathered skin.

They don't speak, but the way they grunt to each other makes me think that they're intelligent enough to communicate. That, and their clothing and weapons are clearly by design.

I've taken on these creatures before, but never more than one at a time. They're ruthless in a fight, as if they were built for it.

Even though I'm stronger now and faster, the hoard around Steven is more than he and I could handle *together*, let alone on my own. I know that running into the thick of it now would be suicide. But the images of those same creatures devouring the rotten flesh off that hog makes me realize that I don't have a choice. I would rather risk dying to save him, than let these odious creatures do the same to him.

If I can just free him, then maybe we would have a chance. I raise my sword and, gripping it tightly, look around the tree again, deciding on my plan of attack.

Steven struggles against his captors and I watch as one of the creatures steps up behind him. This one is larger than the rest and has a scar that runs down its face, intersecting its left eye. The way the others act around it lets me know immediately, *this one's in charge.*

A sick smile of yellowed teeth spreads across its face in a satisfied grin and I watch as it strikes the side of Steven's head with the stock of its crossbow, knocking him out cold.

Anger flares up inside of me as I watch the creatures make some sort of noise that can only be described as laughter. The shock of that act delays my plan, but it hasn't changed it. Not until one of them throws Steven over their shoulder like a rag doll and the entire drove takes off running.

I watch until they're out of sight, then step out from my hiding place, standing alone in the clearing.

Fuck! Why did they take him? Why didn't they kill him? I wonder, grabbing my pack, and tossing Steven's into a nearby shrub until we can come back for it later.

And we will come back for it.

I pick up my dagger and slide my sword back into its sheath as I stare at where they disappeared through the trees.

Then, I narrow my eyes, pull up my hood, and take off after them.

The creatures destroy everything in their path, so it isn't difficult to follow their trail. The *distance* they have run so far, however, is beating me down.

Don't they ever sleep? I wonder.

We've been traveling non-stop for about two days. Two *real*, twenty-four hour long, days if I had to guess.

My exhaustion makes it feel longer.

I've been watching from a distance, so I know they're still carrying Steven. Know that he's still alive. Which, at this point, is the only thing that's keeping me going.

If the creatures would have just stopped *moving* for ten goddamn minutes, then I could have snuck into their camp and gotten him out of there. But they haven't.

They just. Keep. Running.

And so do I.

I'm sitting on a branch at the top of a crimson tree and peering out from its branches, studying the structure in front of me. The giant stone building was built half on land and the other half straight out into the lava. It isn't as tall, or as expansive, as The Fortress, but it's sure as hell a lot larger than any buildings I've ever seen.

The stone bricks that make up the building are completely black, causing it to loom over the landscape like a shadow. Unlike the castle, with its million entrances and windows, this is *fortified*. It reminds me of a medieval bastion and even looks like it's seen a war or two. Some of the stones have crumbled down and are now sticking out from the lava below. Entire sections were clearly blown to pieces, the gaping holes revealing the endless stone staircases that spiral up through it.

All-in-all, it looks *ominous.*

From the safety of my perch, I search for a way in. There's a bridge leading from the hillside to what is clearly the only entrance, about halfway up the building. It's heavily guarded by more of the same pig-looking creatures. Only, they're dressed in golden armor, and are clearly well armed. With no visible way to get past them, and no way to fight them off on my own, I have to find another way in.

And then, I see it.

Climbing down from the tree, I start the long hike down the rocky hillside, keeping clear of the creatures standing guard around the perimeter, and staying out of sight.

I make my way down the sloping stone hill until I'm walking along the shore of lava. I tug at my armor in a failed attempt to cool myself down.

I stand at the base of the structure and look up, suddenly feeling dizzy. The sheer size of it is unsettling. But no more than twenty feet above me, is a large hole blown into the corner, revealing a blackstone staircase. From where I'm standing, the creatures guarding the bridge won't be able to see me. Which makes it a perfect place to sneak in undetected.

I find a narrow space between two rocks and quickly stash my pack before looking back up and taking a deep breath.

"Hold on Steven, I'm coming," I whisper aloud and in my mind. I've reached out to him hundreds of times over the last two days and the fact that he hasn't replied, means that he's either still passed out, or that he's dead and our mental connection doesn't work on opposite sides of the portal. *We should have thought of that. Should have tested it.* I shake my head, frustrated.

He was alive when they carried him in there an hour ago, I remind myself again, hoping that it's still true. The fact that the creatures made the effort to bring him all the way back here, gives me hope that there's still time to save him.

I reach out, finding a handhold in the cracks of the blackstone, but I immediately draw back.

"Shit!" I say, shaking my hand and looking down at the red burns that are already spreading across my fingertips.

And then I watch them disappear.

What in the hell? I think, because I've never seen a wound heal that fast before. *Must be this place...* I shake my head, then quickly pull out my dagger and cut some of the leather from the tunic under my armor.

It's torn in several places anyway.

Wrapping the fabric around both my hands, I start to climb. It's still hot and I will probably have some burns even through the material, but it's tolerable. I quickly scale the stone and pull myself over the ledge. Standing, I begin to draw my sword, but quickly realize that the stairwell is too narrow to wield it.

I don't like this... I grumble, drawing the dagger from my boot instead. Then, taking the stairs two at a time, I make my way up into The Bastion.

This place isn't nearly as large as the Fortress, but it's sure as hell just as confusing. I've been wandering around for at least ten hours and I haven't seen any sign of Steven. Exhaustion and frustration is wearing me down and I'm getting desperate for any sign that he's okay. I need his help, need some clue as to where to find him.

Steven, please, where are you? I reach out again, cursing when there's, yet again, no reply.

Normally in these types of situations, I would be talking to *myself.* But instead, I've spent my time in these incessant stairwells yelling at *him.*

I swear, if you're still alive when I find you, I'm going to kill you myself. This place is shit.

God, I fucking hate stairs just as much as you hate ladders.

I don't want a damn cake when I get out of here. You sir, are going to have to figure out how to make me some goddamn ice cream.

And cookie dough.

At this point, I must have this entire place memorized. Because I've been going in circles. Some of the staircases lead to small chambers, others to larger rooms, but most of them lead to *nothing.*

Like a goddamn funhouse.

The stairwells either open up to the side of the structure, revealing the sheer drop to the lava below, or they dead-end into a wall of blackstone.

And it's really starting to piss me off.

Steven... where the fuck are you?

I watched the creatures carry him over the bridge, so I know he has to be here somewhere. I also know that I have to be missing a huge part of this structure. Because I haven't seen any of the creatures yet.

Not one.

Which is unsettling.

Goddammit, Steven...

I stand at the end of yet another staircase, looking out of the crumbling stone wall over the world of lava. The particles of ash swirl through the air with my every movement.

There's a lot of it around here.

Holding on to the edge, I lean out, trying to get my bearings. Several feet to my left, I see another opening. Only, this one isn't made from a blast. And it hasn't eroded from time. It looks like it was made on purpose.

Like a window.

My relief is short-lived once I realize what I have to do to get over to it. Looking down at the lava far below, I tighten the leather around my hands and shake my head at the stupidity of what I'm about to do.

Steven, I swear to god... I say before pulling myself out of the safety of the stairwell.

Finding my first foothold, I hold myself close to the stone wall on the outside of the edifice. Although I don't have far to go, that doesn't change the fact that there's hardly anything to hold on to. My fingers, already burning from the heat, shake with the effort it takes to hold my weight. My boot barely has an inch of ledge to step on and I just hope that the stones won't crumble away beneath my feet. I shimmy my way along the wall, breathing heavily and trying desperately not to look down.

Once I'm finally close enough to reach the ledge, I swing a leg over the windowsill and pull myself through with a grunt. I hop down into the room and quickly pull out my dagger, but there's no one here.

I sigh with relief before moving deeper into the building.

I find myself in a long hallway. As I slowly make my way down it, I stay close to the wall as I search room after room. This part of The Bastion looks more lived-in and less like an endless maze of deserted tunnels and staircases.

Which means I'm getting close.

There are rooms with tables and chairs and some that look like bedrooms. As I walk through the threshold into another chamber, I find myself in some sort of loft that looks over another area down below. I head toward the railing, but when I hear the grunts, I quickly back away from it just as one of the ugly creatures ambles past on the floor below.

I lay on my stomach, the metal armor shielding me from the heat radiating off the stone floor, and quietly crawl toward the banister. There are three of them in the room below and the sounds they make are a mix between having a party and arguing.

I stare at them curiously.

One is sitting on a chair in the corner and it holds a large container of liquid that sloshes around, making a mess. Its grunts sound almost like a laugh and by the way its body convulses, I figure that's exactly what it's doing.

And then I notice what the creature is wearing.

Steven's armor.

The chest plate is nowhere near large enough to cover it's brawny chest, but it's draped over the creature all the same, the leather straps that dangle at its sides bouncing as it laughs.

The other two are clearly arguing. Looking over at them, I see they are fighting over Steven's hood. Like children with a toy, pulling it from each other's hands and causing the other to grunt loudly in protest.

The sounds of these creatures arguing over Steven's things as if they are *entitled* to them, and the thoughts of what they did to him in order to get them, cause a flood of anger to boil up inside of me. I hear the one in the corner laugh again, and well, that sends me over the edge.

They tore him away from me and they are *laughing*.

It's possible that they have already killed him and they are *laughing*.

I suddenly feel overcome with a familiar type of rage, one that I haven't felt for a while. It's the kind of instinctual anger that kept me alive out here, back when I was alone. It's *visceral* and I slide right back into it, letting it overtake me.

If Steven is alive, then he's going to need that armor back. If they killed him already, well, then this is *revenge.*

Either way, I'm going to kill them.

I roll to my back and slowly draw my sword. I didn't plan on making a scene, not unless I had to, but this is personal.

I *want* to kill them.

All of them.

I grip the handle of my sword tightly with both hands, then quickly stand, leaping over the banister. I land the blade in the top of one's head to break my fall. It explodes into a cloud of ash as the others just stare at me, stunned. The creature directly in front of me grips the leather hood in its oversized hands, looking horrified as it holds the fabric closer. As if that could protect it. I quickly snatch it away.

Then I sink my sword into its stomach.

The one in the corner has stopped laughing and is staring at me wide-eyed, clearly unprepared for any sort of attack. Before the creature can even blink, my dagger is sticking straight out of its face. The cup drops, landing on the ground with a clatter, the dark liquid spilling out onto the floor. As it slowly seeps toward my foot, I realize that it looks a lot like blood.

I re-sheath my sword and dagger, then pick up the chest plate from the chair and look around the room. There are doorways that lead off in various directions and one whole wall opens up to a balcony with no railings. As I walk out onto it, my heart stops.

Because there is Steven.

Five stories below, on an island of blackstone rock surrounded by lava, he is chained between two pillars. His lifeless body hangs there, arms outstretched, suspended by shackles that are digging into his wrists. He's on his knees, his ankles also chained down to the stone. His favorite light blue shirt is now in shreds and it's covered in blood.

His blood, I realize.

Even from here, I can see the dozens of angry cuts slashed across his bare skin beneath the torn shirt.

God, Steven, what did they do to you? I nearly sob.

But the feelings of heart-wrenching sorrow that clutch at my chest are going to have to wait. Because he's still breathing.

And I'm going to get him out of here.

Chapter 51

I drop the armor to the stone ground with a clatter and step off the balcony. Turning mid-air, I grab the edge of the stone as I fall and swing myself onto the platform below. I look around, scanning for any sign of the creatures, but this place is deserted.

The area reminds me of a courtyard, with two structures facing each other, their balconies jutting out as high up as I can see. Although, unlike a normal courtyard with flowers and a sitting area between the two buildings, this one has a floor of lava and a garden of crumbled stone.

Whatever was here before, has since collapsed, scattering the lava below with stone debris. There are broken archways, pieces of what were once rooms and turned-over stairways, all sticking up from the molten liquid to create walkways and platforms leading to the other side.

There's another balcony two floors down to my left, a sprawling gap between us. I take a running leap, clearing the span and landing easily. And then I jump again. And again. In less than a minute, I make it to the ground floor.

Then I see the stairs. *Dammit.*

At least the way back up will be easier.

The heat rising from the lava, which is now only a foot away, is excruciating. I have to get Steven out of here and *fast*. I don't know how long he's been chained up down here, but I don't think anyone could withstand this sort of temperature for any extended amount of time.

I look around again, still not seeing any sign of the creatures.

That's when I notice that the entire first floor of both buildings is a series of open-faced rooms and alcoves. Unlike the nearly empty rooms on the floors above, these all contain *weapons*.

Lots of them.

They're hanging on hooks, piled in barrels and chests, laying on tables and even propped against walls.

Well, that's handy, I muse.

I run into one of the alcoves, desperately searching for something I can use to break the metal shackles. I pick up a small hatchet, testing its weight, but then immediately trade it for a giant axe that is leaning up against a table. It's extremely heavy.

Perfect, I smile.

I run along the ground floor until I'm standing across from Steven, the lava spreading between us. My heart aches again at seeing him like this.

Not wasting any time, I jump from stone to stone until I land on the large platform that he's chained to. Eager to get to him, I drop the axe and run.

I fall to my knees in front of him and look up into his blood-smeared and soot-covered face. I push his wet hair back from his forehead and study him, thankful that he seems to be in one piece. Touching his face, I realize that he's burning up. I feel like I could die from this heat and I've only been down here a few minutes.

Has he been down here this whole time?

I urge myself not to think about it.

Steven! Steven, I'm here, wake up! Wake up! I say, my face close to his. I see movement behind his eyelids and nearly gasp with relief as he slowly starts coming to.

"Ali?" he says slowly, his voice groggy. Once his eyes are able to focus, they go wide and I hear the chains rattle as he pulls against them.

No! Ali, you can't be here! Get out of here, now! Hurry, before they come back! His voice is low, exhausted, but the urgency and the anger is unmistakable.

I'm not leaving without you. Now hold still so I can get these chains off you, I say, running back for the axe.

"*Agh!*" He snarls through clenched teeth. *Dammit, Ali! You shouldn't have come down here! You have to go. Now!*

He struggles to get his feet beneath him so he can stand, but stays hunched over, breathing heavily from the effort.

God, what did they do to you? I stare.

I reach for the axe, but just before I can grab it, a bolt whizzes right past my hand and I snap it back.

"Shit!" I mumble, looking up to see where the shot came from. A few floors up, one of the yellow-toothed creatures stands on a balcony, reloading its crossbow. Another one steps out next to it and then another. Suddenly, the angry grunting noises are coming from everywhere, all at once.

Soon, they will *all* know I'm here.

Another creature steps out from a nearby doorway, crossbow loaded and pointed straight at me. I hear the *click* as the weapon discharges and I duck. It barely misses me.

Then, I don't think, I just *move.*

Grabbing the axe, I run across the platform toward the creature, then leap over the lava and bury it deep in its chest before it has the chance to reload. Four more creatures step out from another room, flooding into the small armory I'm standing in. I take one more down with the axe before switching to my sword to finish off the other three.

I stop for a moment. Realizing what I just did.

Five. I killed five already.

I didn't come in here expecting to win any battles. I just hoped I could find Steven alive and sneak him out. I've never taken on this many before *and survived it.*

Maybe Steven was right. Maybe I'm stronger than I've allowed myself to be.

At this moment, I realize that I would do anything for him.

For us.

The sound of bolts rain down outside the room, clinking on the stone and breaking me from my thoughts.

Because Steven is still out there.

I look around and see several crossbows hanging on the walls of the armory, but I have no idea how to shoot one. And then my eyes land on the bow and quiver of arrows sitting on one of the tables. I head over to it quickly, because I sure as hell know how to use one of these. As I grab the weapon, I can hear Steven shouting, but looking over, I see that it's most likely out of frustration rather than pain, because it doesn't look like he's been shot yet.

He's gripping the chains in his large hands, trying to *yank* them right out of the stone pillars on either side of him. The muscles in his chest and arms bulge from the effort. His hair and shirt, what's left of it anyway, are damp with sweat, clinging to his nearly bare skin. His abs clench with every rattle of the chains.

I stare at him.

Am I still staring? I should stop staring.

I bite at my lower lip.

"Ali! Are you going to stand around enjoying the view or are you going to get me the fuck out of here?!" he shouts, frustrated.

"Alright, alright!" I pick up the axe and haul it over my shoulder as I quickly make my way back over to him.

"Get down!" I shout as the bow clatters to the stone, the axe already swinging through the air. Steven ducks as I crush the chain between the heavy blade and the blackstone pillar, releasing his right hand. Just then, a few more of the creatures make their way down to the ground floor, using their sturdy legs to hop from rock to rock, heading toward us and moving *fast*.

I look at Steven, still chained down by his ankles and other hand.

There just isn't time.

"Leave the axe!" he says, realizing it too. I hand it to him before I pick up the bow and leap off the platform.

I head toward the oncoming group, dodging the volley of bolts coming from above. I'm finally beginning to hone in on the sounds of the crossbows. Knowing what to listen for, what to feel for, gives me a heads-up as to where they are coming from and how many of them there are.

Still, I'm getting really sick of being shot at.

I hear the faint click of another weapon and feel the familiar wave of magic run through me as I step out of the line of fire.

Rushing up one of the fallen staircases, I stand at the top, above the five heading toward me. I pull an arrow from the quiver on my back, take aim and release. I hit one of the pig-looking creatures in the center of its forehead, knocking it backward into the lava. It sinks down slowly, the ash spreading across the surface of the molten liquid.

"Okay... okay," I say slowly in approval, looking at the weapon.

I pull the magic through me again and concentrate. Within exactly four seconds, the others are sinking down to join their ugly friend.

I look up, counting twelve more on the balconies above. With twelve more arrows released, their heavy bodies fall, fading to pieces before they have a chance to reach ground level.

Finally, I think, relieved to *not* be dodging bolts for a minute.

As the ash floats down around me, I turn to see two of the creatures heading toward Steven, their crossbows raised. He's released his other hand along with his left leg and is now hacking at the last of his chains. Two more quick motions have arrows whizzing past him, bursting the creatures behind him into flurries of dust.

Steven whips his head up and looks at me, surprised. In his efforts to escape, he hadn't heard them coming. He gives me a quick nod of gratitude before going back to what he's doing.

I jump down from my perch onto a lower platform, then make my way over to him just as he breaks through the last chain and looks up at me.

"You ready to get the hell out of here?" I ask.

Before he can answer, I hear the click of a weapon and watch as a bolt heads straight toward him. His eyes flicker, but it's weak. He moves to the side, but isn't quite fast enough and the arrow grazes his right shoulder.

But he doesn't make a sound. He doesn't even *flinch.*

I stare at him.

Even as the blood trickles down his arm, he ignores it. He just looks around, taking in the location of his enemies before deciding on his plan of attack.

I know that *this* is what we've been training for, but actually seeing him like this...

My stomach sinks.

I whip my bow around, aiming toward where the shot came from and watch as the creature steps out of the shadows. I take aim and release. But the arrow that was aimed for the creature's snouted face suddenly bounces aside like it's nothing more than a toy ball, the creature's gold-plated arm deflecting it.

I lower my weapon, because I recognize this one.

It's almost twice as large as the rest of the creatures and has a scar running through its left eye. I also realize that it is standing directly between us and the stairs to get out of here.

"He's their leader," Steven says from behind me. "We should go a different way."

"There's not another way," I say to him, because getting lost in there again isn't an option. Not when we're trying to escape. Not when these creatures know the halls.

Leader or not, I remember the pleasure that this particular creature found in knocking Steven unconscious and feel the anger rising up inside of me once again.

This creature took Steven from me once, I'm not going to let it happen again.

We're getting out of here, but not before I turn this vile beast to ash.

A wide toothy smile spreads across its face, as if it's already won this battle. The gesture does nothing to dissuade my determination.

In fact, it may have just fueled it.

Glancing over, I watch several more creatures jump down from a balcony, joining the ones that already flooded in from the halls.

And then I watch Steven.

He's already managed to find a sword, a crossbow, and is busy leaving a trail of ash in his wake. I smile, surprised at how efficient he is. He switches back and forth between the two weapons as if he's done this a million times before.

The bolts start flying again as reinforcements appear above us. Crossbow in arm, Steven starts shooting the creatures off their balconies without even a glance in their direction at the same time he wields his sword, easily taking down the ones swarming him.

Clearly, he has a handle on it.

And so I turn back to the creature who is their leader, hold my bow at the ready and wait for it to make its move.

We stand on the ground floor under the protection of the floor above. And now, it's just the two of us.

And I'm going to enjoy this.

But then the ugly creature drops the crossbow. Without taking its eyes off me, it reaches over to grab a golden sword, one larger than any I've seen before. Its yellow teeth spread into a sickening grin.

"So that's how we're going to play this," I say, tossing my bow aside and drawing my own weapon. It looks pathetic in comparison.

Without warning, the creature runs at me, making a grunting war cry that's probably meant to terrify me.

It's loud, sure, but I'm not backing down.

A bulky arm raises the heavy weapon over the creature's head, ready to strike. I concentrate, waiting for just the right moment. As it swings the blade down, the metal glints in the light, reflecting and looking almost molten itself. I jump to the side, faster than the creature's eyes can see.

Faster than I've ever moved before.

It looks at me, confused, while it slowly works out what's happened. Because not only did I jump out of the way, but I already severed the arm holding the sword.

The beast howls and staggers backward, anger flaring as it watches its lifeless arm and weapon fall to the stone ground in front of it.

Steadying itself, it fixes its soulless white eyes on me then charges forward with an open hand, the one it still has, heading straight for my throat. I pull out my dagger and stab it through the creature's outstretched palm, causing the stumpy fingers with long yellowed nails to curl as it cries out in pain.

I plunge my sword into its stomach, glaring into its soulless eyes, watching as the scarred skin on its face slowly flakes off until its whole body crumbles, disintegrating into ash at my feet.

The creature's armor clatters as it hits the ground and I watch a tiny ring of keys thump to the cracked stone floor.

I stare at my bloody sword and dagger for a long moment, paralyzed by the realization of what I became in these last few moments. The person this place made me into.

The person I don't want to be anymore.

I quickly push those thoughts aside.

When I turn around, I find Steven standing several yards behind me. He's breathing heavily, still gripping a sword in one hand, a crossbow in the other.

I quickly notice that it's *his* sword. I stare at him questioningly.

Where did he find that?

"I watched them throw it over there in the pile," he says, tilting his head toward one of the alcoves with a shrug.

I take a moment to look around the courtyard. The volley of bolts has completely stopped, replaced by a snowfall of ash, gently floating down from the balconies above. Then I hear a grunting noise to my left and before I can even glance toward it, Steven has shot the creature between the eyes without even taking his off mine.

The chain links that still hang from his wrists clink as he lowers the crossbow to his side.

"You came for me," he says, his tone deep as he walks toward me. "That was an *incredibly stupid* thing to do."

"Well, I guess we're both inclined to do incredibly stupid things," I whisper, meeting his eyes and never wanting to let them go.

He sheaths his sword in one smooth motion, then tosses the crossbow aside, taking one long step toward me. He throws my hood back then runs his hands into my hair, pulling my mouth to his for one quick, hard kiss. The relief of having found him alive, of having his strong hands holding me again, of his body pressed against mine, washes over me.

"Now, let's get the fuck out of here," he says, stepping back.

I feel a little dizzy.

"First things first," I say, dangling the ring of keys between us. He tips his head sideways, eyeing them curiously. Then he smiles, shaking his head in disbelief when he figures out what they're for.

Or recognizes what they are for.

I drop down to unlock the shackles on his ankles and then stare up at him as I slowly rise to release the ones from his wrists. They fall, clattering to the floor.

Suddenly, my concern and anger flare up all over again as I take in the sight of Steven's wrists. I gently turn them over in my hands, and an aching pain shoots through my entire being.

Now that the shackles are gone, I can see the angry burn marks and the deep cuts where their edges dug into his skin over and over. The image of him chained up, passed out and hanging helplessly from them, flash through my mind. My heart hurts as I stare at the angry wounds encircling his wrists. I clench my jaw, fighting back tears.

Steven softly tilts my head up and gives me a sweet smile, reminding me that it's okay.

That it's over.

I swallow back the heartbreak and my anger, knowing that we need to get moving.

"This way," I say, pulling my hood up and heading toward the blackstone staircase.

I notice Steven rifling through the weapons in a nearby chest, then watch as he pulls out a crossbow. He looks at it curiously, then throws the strap around his shoulder and grabs a few bolts before following me out of the room.

As we climb the stone stairs, heading toward the floor that leads to the window and our escape route, something registers in my mind. I stop, whirling around toward Steven.

He runs straight into me.

"What do you mean you *saw* them throw your sword in the pile? You were awake? I was calling for you, going crazy looking for you and you were *awake!?*"

I suddenly realize that I've never actually been angry at him before, but *this* certainly qualifies.

"Ali, come on, we can talk about this later," he says, trying to move past me.

"No, we can talk about it n-" The loud grunt that comes from the stairwell behind us has me saving that thought for later.

I pick up the pace as I continue up the dark passageway, barely lit by a few dim lanterns.

How could he not say anything? I fume, but know he's right. I have to let this go. *For now.*

When we finally reach the fifth floor, I head out onto the balcony and pick up Steven's armor, tossing it over to him. He stares at it questioningly. Then a slow smile spreads across his face. He looks up at me out from under his too-long damp hair.

Then, raising one eyebrow, he gives me a knowing smile as he brushes the ash off it.

Chapter 52

Steven and I are standing at the top of the crimson cliffs, looking back down at The Bastion. The creatures haven't come after us yet, because they're still frantically searching *inside.* We know, because we can hear them from here.

None of them could have guessed that we would be leaving from anywhere other than the front door, let alone escape so quickly. The fact that I had memorized the way out gave us a head start. By the time they realize we aren't there, we will already be miles away. And, as exhausted as we are, we want to put as much distance between us and this place as possible. So we run through the forest until the war cries and angry grunts slowly fade into the distance, replaced by the quiet crackling of lava and the eerie echoes that constantly reverberate in the distance through the caverns.

It's going to be at least a two-day journey back to the clearing where the creatures set the snare and captured Steven. But I know that neither of us will make it that far without sleep. So we run as far as our legs can take us, until we both slow our pace to a staggering walk, crippled by fatigue.

So far, the red forest has been quiet. I have to assume that's because all the creatures that usually reside here are all back at The Bastion. *Looking for us.*

After a while, Steven and I manage to find an area of dense trees surrounded by thick foliage backed up against a large outcropping of crimson rocks. Using the vines to climb over the thorny bushes then jumping down into the clearing hidden behind it, we find ourselves tucked away, where nothing that walks by could see us.

It seems as safe a place as any in this godforsaken part of the woods.

I drop my pack to the ground, then remove my armor, immediately reveling in the freedom. I lie flat on my back in the red grass, breathing heavily. Steven slowly settles down beside me.

We lay here in silence until our rapid heartbeats begin to slow and I can breathe normally again. Steven smiles over at me, but I can't seem to make myself smile back.

Because I can't stop thinking about what happened back at The Bastion.

"How long were you awake? Did you hear me calling for you?" I say, trying desperately to keep my composure.

"Ali, I don't want to talk about this. Can't we just forget it?"

I sit up and stare at him.

"No, we can't *just forget it.* I followed those creatures for two days straight without stopping, without *sleeping*. Then spent another lost in those stairwells. I didn't know if you were alive or dead and I couldn't find you. Why didn't you say anything? You could have at least let me know that you were-" I cut off my rant mid-sentence as I look him over for the first time.

Really look him over.

He's clutching his side, clearly still in pain from one of his injuries. It's been *hours* since we left The Bastion. The fact that it hasn't healed yet, means that it was worse than it looked. I look away, setting my concern for him aside for a moment, because this is important.

"Why didn't you say anything?" I say, softer this time, but he doesn't say a word. He just looks at me with sad eyes. I stare back at him.

And suddenly, I understand.

"You... You didn't *want* me to find you," I say quietly. But it isn't a question.

He takes a deep breath before answering.

"No. I didn't," he says, looking away.

"Dammit, Steven, we talked about this. We're a team. *I'm with you,* remember?" I say, the anger creeping back into my voice. I spent *days* looking for him, wondering if he was even alive, wondering if there was a chance that I could save him. I risked my life and he hadn't said a word.

"Ali, I just... couldn't tell you," he says softly.

"You *couldn't* tell me? Tell me that you were alive? Tell me where you were, tell me that-"

"I didn't want to, okay!" he shouts, standing to his feet. It catches me off-guard.

I've never heard him shout before, at least, never at me.

I look around, worried that the volume will attract the attention of some creature, but he doesn't stop.

In fact, he gets louder.

"I didn't want to tell you where I was, because I didn't want you to find me. I didn't want you anywhere near that place. In case you haven't noticed, we heal a whole hell of a lot faster in here, which means that when they were using me as *target practice*, they didn't have to wait very long before they could do it again. They almost killed me, over and over and over and I wish they would have. I *wanted* them to. Because if I died, the pain would be gone and I could find my way back to you. If you came to get me... if you went to that place... *fuck!"* his voice breaks off and he rubs a hand over his face, his jaw tight, his fist clenched at his side as he paces back and forth.

Then he levels his voice to barely a whisper. "Ali, I would have stayed in there for an *eternity* before I watched them do the same to you," he stares straight at me, breathing heavily, and I can see his eyes are filled with unspilled tears.

"Steven, I-" my voice cuts off and I can't breathe.

I look over the almost-healed scars that cover every inch of his strong arms. Then I look down at the ones on his stomach and chest, realizing that they don't match up with the tears in his shirt.

His shirt has *so many* more.

My world turns upside down as I take in the reality of what happened to him. The reality that I *didn't* get to him in time.

They tortured him.

I should have gotten there sooner. This shouldn't have happened. He didn't tell me, because he was trying to protect me. And I was angry with him. Why didn't I get to him sooner?

I feel helpless, useless. They broke him and I wasn't there.

I didn't save him.

And now? There's nothing I can do to take back what they did to him, no way for me to save him from the memories.

So I do the only thing I can do.

I stand up and throw myself into his arms, letting the tears stream down my face. It takes him a hesitant few seconds before he accepts my embrace. Then he wraps himself around me, burying his face into my neck.

I hold on to him.

And he *clutches* at me.

Then, he starts sobbing in my arms.

Steven is leaning against the stone wall and I'm laying back into him. He holds me in his arms, not wanting to let me go. We are *exhausted*, but neither of us can sleep.

"Steven, I'm so sorry," I say quietly.

"You don't have anything to be sorry about," he says into my hair.

"No, I do. I'm sorry that I was stupid and got us stuck in that trap... I'm sorry that I didn't get to you in time-"

"Ali-"

"No, Steven, I have to say this. I'm sorry for what you went through. I would have done anything to stop it. And I think, if I were in your place... I think I would have done the same thing. I wouldn't have wanted you there either," I finally say, turning to look up into those purple eyes. They are so weary, so full of torment. "I can bear my own pain, but I can't stand seeing yours. I'm sorry I was angry at you. But I need you to know that you don't have to worry about me, I can take care of myself."

He looks down at me, a smile playing on his lips.

"Alexandra Cutter, I knew you were tough, but *holy fuck*. By the end there, I was starting to feel bad for those hog-faced creatures," he gives a small laugh and then grows serious. "I understand why you were angry. And you're right. We're supposed to be a team and I shut you out, so I'm sorry too. But don't think for one second that I doubt you," he says and I can see in his eyes that he means it. "Oh and Ali?"

"What?" I look up at him again, curious.

"Remind me never to piss you off," he smiles widely and I lean into him, listening to the sound of his heartbeat until we both drift off to sleep.

"Well, this is it. Do you want to head back home? We can give this some time and try again later?" I ask Steven as we stand in the clearing, the ropes from the snares still hanging from the trees overhead.

I'm not sure how he's holding up after everything he went through. Now that we're back on the trail, we could easily head back home.

"No," he says quickly. "I don't want all of this to have been for nothing.

And besides, I have my badass partner back," he says, bumping my shoulder with his.

"Well, I think my partner is becoming pretty badass himself," I smile back, remembering the sight of him. Sweaty, his shirt torn, the chains hanging at his wrists, wielding a sword *and* a crossbow. I'm not sure how many he killed back there at The Bastion, but even with his injuries, he certainly did some damage.

"Well, you ready to do this, my little warrior?" Steven says, giving me that adorable sideways smile.

He stands at the trailhead that leads to The Fortress, holding out his hand to me. I take one lingering look at the path leading back home. Then, I place my hand in his as we head down the long road.

The one I've been down before.

But this time, I'm not alone.

Chapter 53

Steven and I stand side-by-side, staring up at The Fortress in front of us. It's *daunting*. The towers, battlements and curtain walls seem to go on for miles. And I know from experience, that they probably do.

"How do we get inside?" Steven asks, looking up at the towering structure.

"That way," I say, pointing to our right where the rocky cliffs lend a hand. The fallen debris has piled up, creating an easy climb up the jagged rocks to one of the lower windows leading inside.

Not wanting to be hindered by our packs, we decide to only bring along what we need. As we take inventory of our supplies, we find that all of the glass vials in Steven's pack are crushed, most likely from his fall down into that warped biome of eerie blue. I broke one of mine at some point, but still have four of them intact.

But we only need one to catch the line of fire.

I hand two of the vials to Steven and tuck the others into my pocket.

We wedge our packs between two rocks at the base of the tower, then spend the next few minutes covering them with dirt and rubble until they are effectively hidden among the debris before we start the climb. With every step, the pit in my stomach digs itself deeper. I don't know what lies ahead of us, but if it's anything like the last time I was here, I'm not particularly looking forward to it.

Standing just below the tall, narrow window that leads inside, I look back at Steven.

Okay, here we go. Keep your head up, keep moving and-

Stay strong, he smiles, finishing my sentence.

I smile widely back at him, then grab hold of the windowsill, pulling myself up just far enough to see inside. The stone is hot on my hands, but it doesn't burn me, not like at The Bastion. Deeming it safe, I draw myself through the opening and into The Fortress.

The five-foot drop into the corridor plunges me deep into a nightmare.

One I thought I escaped long ago.

The hallway is endless and seems to elongate the more time I spend staring down it. The torches flicker from their sconces on the walls and the sound of my footsteps echo, making their way down the hall without me. The stench of the stale, hot air makes it hard to breathe and the familiar sinking feeling that always accompanies this place washes over me.

Steven hops down beside me, reminding me again that I'm not alone this time. I look over at him and with one last nod, we take off running down the long hallway.

As we near another corner, I crouch down to peer around it. Seeing that the passageway ahead is empty, I signal to Steven and we move forward again. I'm not sure how many hours we've been running around the endless maze of hallways, but finally, we find our way to another staircase. Bringing us one floor closer to our destination: the top.

We draw our swords, slowly making our way up, but discover *another* series of intersecting hallways.

As we run past window after window, I consider crawling out one and *climbing* the rest of the way. But between the memories of being shot at with arrows and fire, the explosions, and the skeletons crawling up the walls faster than should be possible, I decide that maybe being on the outside of The Fortress isn't actually the best idea.

Halfway down another hallway, I suddenly stop dead in my tracks, causing Steven to almost run into me.

Ali, what is it? he asks.

Listen...

We're both quiet for a moment and then his eyes go wide with the realization. It's the sound of a crackling fire.

Only, it's *much* louder. Much *closer.*

The noise is quickly replaced by what sounds like a flame thrower and we watch as the intersecting hallway ahead of us lights up like a missile silo.

We stand perfectly still as dozens of skeletons pour out of the now burning hallway, crawling along the ceiling, the walls, before dropping to the floor in front of us with a clatter, heads clicking and twitching from side to side as they listen to their surroundings. Steven and I slowly look at each other, not knowing what to do. If we move an inch, they could pinpoint our location in less than a second. If we stay here, then we risk the chance of them running straight into us.

We don't have the chance to decide. Because behind the skeletons, the flames move, rising up from the floor and slowly taking shape to form a figure. It glows with hot, molten liquid swirling around its frame, and I can feel my skin burning, even from here. Silently counting, I look over at Steven.

He's counting too.

It's been five seconds since the last blast of flames, which means... *time's up.*

Run! I shout and we both sprint down the hallway. The skeletons draw their bows, taking aim, but quickly realize that *we* aren't the biggest threat.

Steven runs ahead of me down the hall and darts around a corner to his left. We have to get out of this hallway, *right now.*

I round the corner after him, but stop dead in my tracks.

I don't even notice the heat that sears at my back.

My body goes cold.

Because standing in front of Steven, is another breed of skeleton. Unlike the others, this one's bones are as black as night. There's no trace of skin left anywhere on its frame. I immediately notice that its head doesn't twitch around to listen.

Because its dark eyes can *see* us.

Standing at nearly eight feet tall, it looks straight over Steven's head. Looking right at me.

But I don't return its icy gaze.

The only thing my eyes can see is the dark blade of its large stone sword protruding out of Steven's back, dripping with his blood.

"No!" I scream.

But it's too late.

Steven slumps over the sword, his arms and legs going slack. His blood pours to the floor and I feel like the world has stopped moving.

My world has stopped moving.

I watch with horror as the life slowly leaves his body. Then he disappears, taking part of my soul with him. There's a split second of searing pain that tugs at my chest the moment he's torn away from me. For a moment, I feel like I'm dying too.

Then I'm alone.

It only takes a moment to realize that the creature has a new target. *Me.*

As the flames behind me dissipate, I step back out into the hallway, the ground noticeably hotter beneath my feet. As tears fill my eyes, I stare at the creature and start counting.

One. I take another step back, standing in the middle of the hall.

Two. My tears begin to fall.

Three. The skeleton steps forward, raising its blade slowly to my chest.

Four. It draws back the sword, ready to strike.

"Five." I jump backward, into the safety of the next hall, and watch as the creature is engulfed by flames. Raising my sword, I take one hard slash, severing its head from its bony body.

Emotionless, I barely notice the burning tears running down my face, can hardly hear the ear piercing screams. Its body bursts into black ash, floating down the hall with the conflagration as if the pieces were being swept down a river.

When the fire dies out, its lifeless skull clatters to the ground at my feet.

I wipe away the tears and force myself to focus.

I step over what's left of the wretched creature, pick up the weapons and armor that Steven's death left behind, and take off running down the corridor. Desperately seeking a safe place to hide.

Chapter 54

Ali! Are you okay? Please be okay... fuck! Steven's voice pleads in my mind.

I found a small room in one of the towers and I'm now hidden beneath a crumbling staircase. It isn't a great hiding spot, but I managed to shake off the creatures that were following me, so it will have to do for now.

Yes, yes I'm fine. I got away. God, Steven, it's so good to hear your voice. My heart aches at the sound of it. I knew in my mind that he would be alright, but watching him die like that...

Are you okay? I ask urgently.

You mean, other than running into a sword? he tries to joke.

Oh Steven, I'm so sorry, I say, the horror of it still clouding my mind.

It's okay, Ali. Really, I'm fine. It was pretty quick. I'm almost home. I'm just grabbing a new sword and then I'm coming back.

It's okay, I'll just-

Don't even start with me, Ali. We're sticking to the plan. You hide and I'll be there as soon as I can. After seeing those flame-throwers in action, it's going to take the both of us to take one down, he says.

Okay, I'll wait for you. But please, be careful, I say. It takes him a moment to respond. When he does, his voice is softer, calmer.

I will. And you too.

I smile, relieved to be able to talk to him, to feel him as if he were right here next to me. I want to talk more, but he's going to have to concentrate to get back here safely and I need to focus on staying alive. My hiding spot will only work so long as nothing comes this way. I need to be ready to move, and *fast*.

I sit down on the hot stone ground for just a moment, realizing that it's the first time I've stopped moving since we got to this place.

My legs ache with relief.

I lean back against the wall and hear a strange *click*. A second later, the wall behind me draws back. I jump away from it, startled and staring in confusion. After a few strange noises, the wall recesses even further, then slides to the side, stone scraping stone, until it reveals a hidden staircase. I stare, wide-eyed as I step slowly toward it, peering inside.

The narrow passageway is dark and the air smells musty, like a tomb that hasn't been opened for centuries. The winding stone stairs curve down, so there's no way to see from here where they lead to.

But I'm about to find out.

After setting down Steven's armor, his sword and that stupid crossbow I've been hauling around, I take one last look around the room. I know I won't be able to stay in one place until Steven gets back anyway, so I might as well explore.

I grab a torch off the wall and, against my better judgment, I head down into the darkness.

The stairs seem endless. And I'm starting to get a little dizzy from the constant downward spiral, but at least it's cooler here than in the halls of The Fortress.

When I step down from the last step, I find myself walking forward into a large room.

Not room, I realize. *A great hall.* One that you would expect to find in a castle like this. Only, I've never seen anything like it here before.

All the ceilings in The Fortress are tall, but here, they're *massive*. Large round columns are spread throughout the room, towering a seemingly impossible height. I marvel, noticing how every single piece of stone is intricately carved. The walls, floors, columns and archways are all decorated with twirling designs. The patterned stones look ancient and almost... *regal*.

At the far end of the large room, there are several wide steps, wrapping around a large platform.

On the platform, lined side by side, stand ten massive thrones.

What the hell? I wonder, making my way slowly down the center aisle toward them. I walk up the steps, standing next to the throne at the end of the row. They are carved from the same dark crimson stone as The Fortress. But unlike the rest of the castle, which is crumbling to pieces, this room seems untouched by time.

I walk down the row, studying each throne carefully. They are all a little different, not in size or shape, but how they have their own uniquely carved design, each one just as intricate as the next. Walking along them, I notice the inscriptions carved into the stone backrests. Each one in a different language, and none of which I can read.

Until I get to the two thrones in the center.

I recognize the symbols immediately. One is the same language as Steven's tattoo, and the other language is from mine.

I know by heart every intricate line of Steven's tattoo, so I recognize some of the words straight away. Then I grin at *how* I memorized that tattoo. I blush as I picture him shirtless in our bed, my fingers trailing over the dark ink flowing down his muscled back.

My stomach and heart ache at the fond memory, because he's not with me right now.

He should be here with me.

Suddenly, the entire room shakes beneath my feet and dust falls from the ceiling.

I know that sound... I think, looking around the windowless room as if I can see what caused it. Clearly, one of the creatures outside is blowing holes in the castle again.

Which means that it's time for me to go. If this room is going to collapse, I sure as hell don't want to be inside it when it does.

I look back at the inscriptions longingly, frustrated that I don't have time to translate them.

Wait a second... I think, setting my torch down and pulling out the map I have tucked in my pocket. Scattered throughout the room are large fire pits. Ones that must have once roared to life, filling the room with their light. Grabbing a piece of charcoal, I flip the map upside down and place it over the inscription. The one carved in the same language as Steven's tattoo.

The same language from the books.

Rubbing the charcoal over the parchment, I watch as a perfect copy of the letters transfer clearly onto the page. I smile, then carefully fold up the map, sliding it back into my pocket.

The room shakes again, causing my torch to roll off the throne and fall to the floor with a clatter. I pick it up, then take one last look around before heading toward the stairs. I climb them two at a time, but that isn't fast enough. The tremors shake the stairwell and more than once, the quakes knock me off-balance, slamming my shoulder into the stone wall in the narrow passageway.

When I finally reach the top, I duck out of the hidden doorway, then nearly jump out of my skin when the heavy stone opening slams shut behind me.

Chapter 55

The ground shakes again and I'm not sure how much longer this part of The Fortress will remain standing.

I have to get to another tower.

Ali? Ali, are you okay? Steven asks frantically.

Steven? Are you here? Are you back at The Fortress? I ask, a little out of breath after running up god knows how many flights of stairs.

No, I'm not. I'm making good time, but it's still going to be another few hours before I get to you. What happened? Are you in danger?

How does he know? I think curiously. *Um, not in danger... yet. But I'll keep you posted on that...* I say slowly, watching as another explosion sends pieces of stone flying past one of the windows beside me.

Fuck! I hear him curse, feeling his magic urge him to pick up the pace. But no matter how fast he runs, he won't get here in time.

I'm on my own.

I quickly run up another set of stairs and my heart sinks. Because outside the tower I'm standing in, is the outer walkway.

I'm at the top.

Staring out over the parapet, I decide that this is *not* where I want to be when things are currently exploding. I turn quickly to go back down the stairs, but five large, dark skeletons block my path. Swords drawn, they start after me.

Shit! Backing away, I draw my own sword.

There's nothing on these creatures to *stab*, other than bone, so according to the book, the only way to kill these things is to decapitate it. Only, I don't have a flaming hallway to use as a distraction this time.

And this time, there are five of them.

With all my strength, I take a swing, aiming for the first one's neck. The creature raises its own blade quickly and our swords clatter, metal against stone. I see a quick glimmer of light run up the creature's blade, then watch in horror as my sword breaks. In. Half.

"Dammit!" I shout.

Now it's time to run. I turn on my heels and take off across the top of the wall. Suddenly, a loud screeching noise causes me to buckle over. The deafening sound has me throwing my hands over my ears just as another explosion knocks me fully to the ground. Clamoring to get up, I stare wide-eyed at the gaping hole in the path behind me. The ground shakes again and I can tell that The Fortress was hit somewhere else, only further away.

Which means there's more than one...

I run headlong toward the next tower, fear and adrenaline urging me forward. I just have to get inside.

Steven, I think. In my terror, I can almost *feel* him here with me.

Then I catch sight of something. I turn, the blur of white unrecognizable as the creature shoots past the wall I'm standing on, rising up quickly through the air next to me. My eyes grow wide as I watch the creature's ascent.

As I lay eyes on it for the first time.

It's unlike anything I've ever seen. Hovering high above me, it's easily the size of a house. The giant malformed creature is a burnt shade of white, making it stand out from the dark world around it. Its large, black eyes droop as if haunted by a million souls. It drifts high above the castle, long sickly tentacles hanging beneath it, curling and waving through the hot air.

Then it fixes its eyes on me. They turn to red, glowing with anger and fire. I watch with horror as its face *splits in half,* revealing row after row of mangled teeth. A glowing ball of light forms in the back of its throat as smoke billows and falls from its open mouth.

It screeches again and the piercing sound paralyzes me. Looking up, I see it release something from the bowels of its throat. It only takes a moment to register that the ball of fire is coming at me, and *fast.*

Finding my feet again, I run.

The explosion lands hard behind me and the force of it sends me flying through the air. I look down, watching as the ground beneath me disappears. My stomach drops when I realize there's nothing between me and the lava far below. I close my eyes and the memories of what it feels like to fall, to burn to death in that molten ocean of pain, floods my mind.

I can't die like this, not again.

My body strikes the stone wall of the tower and I know immediately that something is broken. More than one something, probably. But a few broken bones are *nothing* compared to how I'm about to die.

I slide down the hot stone, then land hard on the edge of the parapet. The force of the impact causes me to lose my breath and I'm suddenly sliding over the edge. My hands slap at the bricks, scrambling for anything to hold on to, until my fingers manage to latch onto a small crack between the stones.

My fingers burn from the sudden strain.

The shooting pain from whatever is broken races through my body in waves and I know I won't be able to hold my weight for long.

I look around, but there's nothing else to grab onto. No way to pull myself back up. My feet kick uselessly over air and lava and I can feel my trembling fingers already beginning to slip.

Alexandra! I hear Steven shout in my mind.

The pain in his voice is heart wrenching.

I wish it could have been different, wish that I could be here for him. But I won't be. His desperation won't save me.

In my delirium, I can almost feel him here with me, just for a moment. One comforting moment. But I know the feeling is unfounded. That he's hours away and I'm going to die.

A single tear falls down my cheek as reality takes hold.

I love you, Steven, I whisper just as my hand slips from the hot stone.

Suddenly, there's a sharp pull in my arm and that feeling of falling abruptly stops.

I blink. Because I don't understand. It doesn't make any sense.

It's not possible.

I find myself looking up into dark purple eyes flickering with a bright, vibrant light.

I am lost to them.

Brown curls hang away from his forehead as he leans over the edge looking down at me, his strong hands gripping my arm.

He caught me.

"You're here," I whisper as another tear escapes. "*Don't let me go.*"

"I'm here. I've got you. And I'm not letting go."

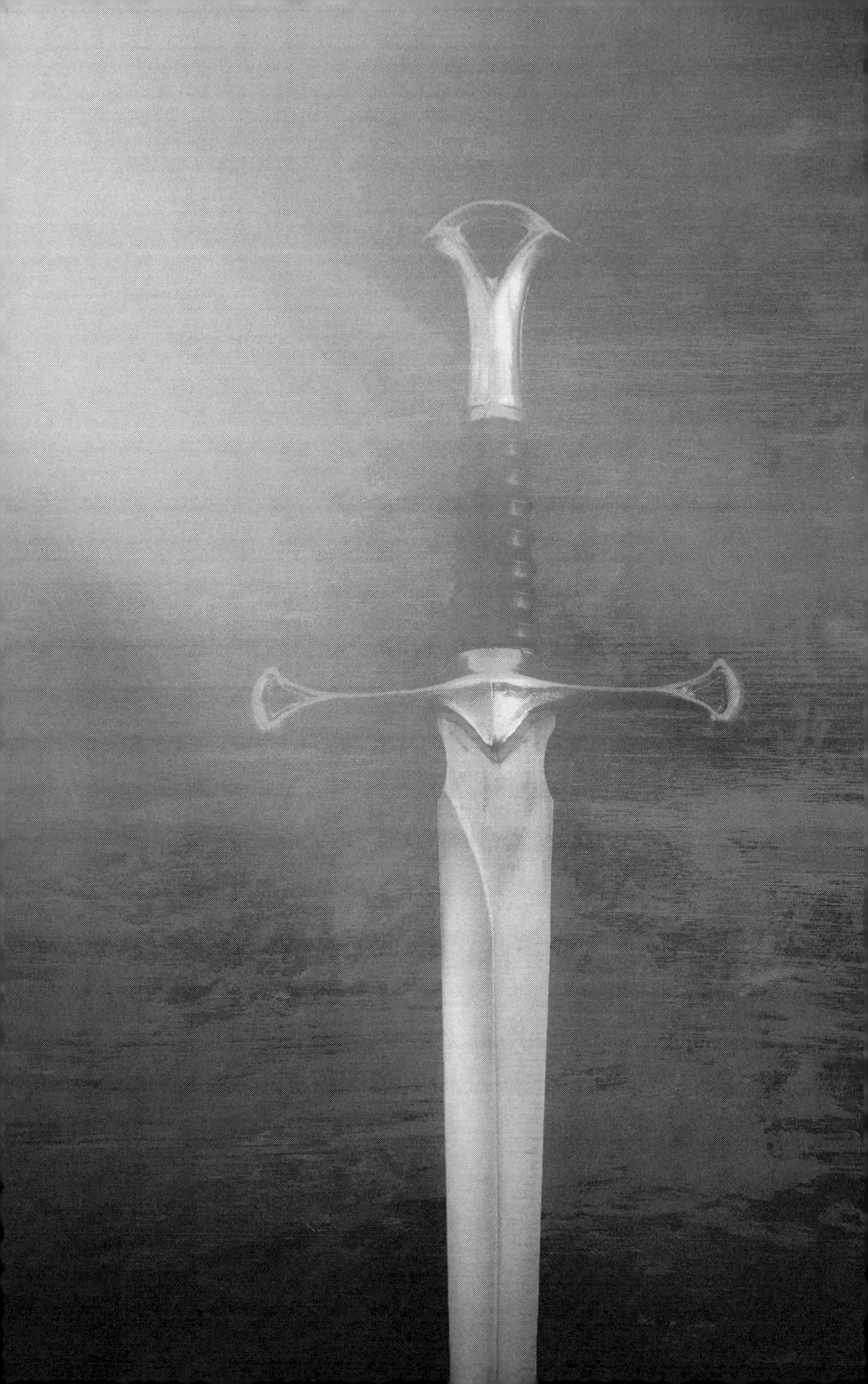

Steve

Chapter 56

"*Agh!* Fuck!" I shout, pounding my fists into the sand of our *favorite* island, as Ali likes to call it. It's dark, and the cool breeze rolls over my skin. It feels incredible after spending the last few weeks in absolute *hell*.

It feels even better after being stabbed through the chest with a giant sword.

I take a deep breath of the fresh ocean air, but I can't breathe yet. Because Ali is still in there, still in danger.

I have to get back to her.

As I head for the trapdoor, something comes up from the deep, charging straight at me.

"I don't have time for this shit," I mumble.

The creature's arms are outstretched, its large hands heading for my throat. Taking a deep irritated breath, I watch with disdain, waiting for it to come closer. When it does, I reach out and grab both of its wrists, breaking them instantly and sending the creature to its knees, howling. I step behind it and crank its neck. After a loud *snap*, it explodes into ash.

And that's when the arrows start.

I quickly evade several dozen before kicking the lever and jumping down through the trapdoors just as they fall open. I grab hold of one of the panels and swing myself away from the annoying-as-fuck pile of hay, landing in a crouch next to it before making my way down the tunnel.

As I run through the woods, I hardly even notice the arrows being shot at me. I feel the familiar sensation of magic as I concentrate on the air around me, using it to urge my body forward faster, outrunning the onslaught until I'm in the clear, nearing the footbridge. I duck under several tree branches that are sticking out into the path, but as I run past, they snag at the already ruined baby blue T-shirt that I, for some reason, am still wearing.

I look down at it, the fabric torn to pieces. My jaw clenches at the memories of what caused the damage. Anger boils up inside of me and I tear it the rest of the way off. I look down, staring at the pieces of it in my hands. I suddenly realize with a strange sense of nostalgia that it's the same shirt I was wearing when I got here. I hold the once soft fabric between my fingers, now completely stained with blood, and think about the boy who wore it when he fell through that portal. It's then that I understand something Ali once said to me. *I don't even know who that person is anymore.*

And she was right. That person, that *boy,* he's dead.

I am someone else.

The fabric slips through my fingers and I watch as it slowly falls to the ground. Then I step over it, leaving it behind on the path.

I don't look back.

Ali! Are you okay? Please be okay... fuck! I call out to her, needing to know if she escaped the creature that killed me.

Yes, yes I'm fine. I got away. God, Steven, it's so good to hear your voice, she responds.

I audibly sigh in relief. It's good to hear her voice too, but that doesn't stop my frantic pace to get back to her. I'm already nearing the house, suddenly realizing that I must have been moving *fast,* because it's only been a couple of minutes.

Are you okay? she asks and I almost laugh. Because isn't *that* the question of the goddamn year.

You mean, other than running into a sword? I tease, hoping my humor will assuage her concerns.

Oh Steven, I'm so sorry... she says, sounding devastated.

It's all fun and games and sarcastic comments when she talks about *her* dying, but she just can't take a joke when it comes to me getting hurt. And somehow, I find that endearing.

It's okay, Ali. Really, I'm fine. It was pretty quick, I say, but that's a lie. Because it wasn't quick. And it hurt like fucking hell. *I'm almost home, I'm just grabbing a new sword and then I'm coming back.*

It's okay, I'll just- she tries to argue.

Don't even start with me, Ali, I say, knowing exactly what she's trying to pull. And I'm not going to have it. Not for a second. *We're sticking to the plan. You hide and I'll be there as soon as I can. After seeing those flame-throwers in action, it's going to take the both of us to take one down.*

Okay, I'll wait for you, but please, be careful.

The sweetness in her voice makes me stop and I take a breath. I stand there in the meadow, running my fingers through my hair. I look up at the night sky with its now familiar array of stars. *So many stars.*

I don't know how, but she always manages to calm me down.

I will. And you too.

Running into our bedroom, I head straight for the closet. Some of my clothes are still in my old room down the hall, but most of them have *somehow* found their way in here.

Which makes me smile.

Looking around, I suddenly miss the quiet moments Ali and I used to have back here at the house. But I know that *those* moments are what we're fighting for. Neither of us can have a life, a *real* life, if we stop trying to get back to the one we left. We owe it to our families, to ourselves, to do everything we can to find a way back to them.

So we will keep on fighting.

I smile, touching one of Ali's shirts that's hanging right next to mine. But then I halt my hand, my fingertips feeling the rough fabric. Staring at it curiously, I realize that I've never seen her wear it. When I pull it out, holding it up, I immediately see why.

It's a dingy shade of green and even though it's clearly been cleaned, that doesn't hide the large bloodstains covering it. It has been torn, repaired and torn again. Reminding me of the one I just left behind.

And then I remember a time I saw her wearing it.

A faint flash of a memory appears in the back of my mind. The memory of a shy, sweet girl in a missing person poster. I suddenly realize that *this* is the shirt she was wearing when she disappeared. The one she was wearing when I watched her die.

Fifty-two times.

The memories of her first few days are something straight out of a nightmare. *So why does she keep it?* I wonder vaguely, but quickly shrug off the thought. Because there isn't time.

I pull on a clean white T-shirt, run down the hall and skid through the living room, almost tripping on one of Ali's goddamn rugs on the way to the ladder. I climb up it quickly, making my way into the armory in no time at all.

I strap on a spare sword as I head back to the ladder and practically jump onto it, sliding quickly down to the first floor. I slow my descent in order to find the lever that's discreetly tucked away beside the ladder. *Ali and her secrets,* I think, shaking my head and wondering how many more she has hidden away.

The trapdoor disappears beneath me and I plummet down until I'm in the open air, dropping through the center of the large cavern. As I fall, my vision blurs and I see flashes of something that isn't there.

Can't be there.

Images of a large, medieval throne room fill my head, but just as quickly dissipate.

What the hell was that? I wonder, shaking my head as my vision returns to normal.

When I near the bottom of the ladder, I slow, then jump the rest of the way. I take the stone stairs three at a time, then run along the path and across the stepping stones to the island.

I don't stop, not even for a second, before leaping through the portal.

Chapter 57

The air is stiflingly hot down here and I already miss the outside world. I have been using magic to push myself forward through the crimson landscape, knowing damn well that it could wear me out.

But I keep going.

I've already run into several creatures, but none of them stood in my way. Not when I'm trying to get back to her.

Killing them was as easy as breathing.

As I calculate my progress, I realize that the path to The Fortress seems a whole lot shorter when you actually keep to the trail. Mine and Ali's little *detours* on the way there caused our trip to take *weeks*, rather than the couple of days that it should have. But at the pace I'm currently setting, and how far I've already come, I plan to cut that time in half. Which means I should reach her in only a couple more hours.

But a lot can happen in a few hours. Especially down here.

As I run, I think back to the first time we went off track. How jumping from that cliff, breaking my leg, was such a considerable hindrance. It somehow seems laughable now. If I only knew back then how much worse it could get...

My mind clouds with the memories. Waking up in The Bastion, my wrists burning from the hot metal, the blood dripping down my hands as the shackles slice through my skin again and again. The sounds of chanting grunts above me and then the searing pain, over and over, as arrow tips pierced my skin. The creatures are playing with me, like a new toy, and everyone wants a turn.

I watch them, scattered around the courtyard of stone and magma, cheering each other on as they line up. One after another, they tear through my skin with arrows and blades. They break my bones with mallets and fists. My head spins with the pain, unable to pass out.

Unable to die.

And then I hear her voice calling out to me.

And she's fucking pissed.

But I hold on to that voice. I can't respond, because I can't let her find me. Can't let them do *this* to her.

Every time she speaks, I focus only on her voice, on *her*. I listen to the way she articulates every word, the way she says my name. I cling to every nuance of her voice like it's my lifeline, even as my own body convulses against the chains. In those dark hours, she is my strength.

Suddenly, a feeling that's somehow stronger than those horrible memories pulls me from the hopeless spiral I'm sinking into.

Something's wrong.

I can't tell what, or how I know. But somehow, I know that Ali is in danger. And I haven't reached her yet.

Panic builds in my chest.

Ali? Ali, are you okay? I ask frantically, hoping that this feeling I have is wrong.

Steven? Are you here? Are you back at The Fortress? she asks, and I don't like how she feels in my mind when she says it.

Something is definitely wrong.

No, I'm not. I'm making good time, but it's still going to be another few hours before I get to you. What happened? Are you in danger?

Um, not in danger...yet. But I'll keep you posted on that... she says slowly and through our shared connection, I can feel her heart quicken. Which answers my question.

She's in danger. And I'm. Not. There.

"Fuck!" I shout, quickening my pace and feeling that familiar *pull* inside of me. The pull that urges me to get to her.

I have to get to her.

Even though I know there's no chance of reaching her in time, I have to try.

I throw myself across a large creeping crevice that cuts through the crumbing stone ground, jumping farther and higher than I knew I could, then continue running.

I don't know how long I've run for, but it feels like eternity.

Suddenly, I drop to the ground, clutching at my head as I press my palms against my ears, trying to block out the deafening, screeching sound that seems to originate from inside my mind. My ears ring and the noise blots out all others.

What the hell is that? I look around frantically, but I don't see anything aside from the familiar, empty landscape.

And then, the world surrounding me transforms.

Chapter 58

I know when I'm dreaming, I always do. Because it feels *real,* more like a memory. This one is pretty much the same as all the others.

Only, it's not.

Because this doesn't just *feel* real.

It isn't a memory. And it isn't a dream.

"This is real," I whisper. I'm standing on the top of the battlement, staring at Ali. She's hunched over, her hands pressed against her ears. An explosion knocks her to the ground and I nearly go over myself.

"Ali! Ali, answer me! Can you see me?" I shout for her, but she doesn't show any signs she's aware of my presence. She runs away from the explosion, heading in my direction.

Then, she runs *through* me.

I quickly look down at my body, confused, then behind me, seeing her retreating figure.

What the hell is happening? How am I here, why can't she see me? I wonder.

I turn to follow her, but suddenly, she stops. Her head tilts upward, like she's looking at something. I follow her line of sight, but don't see anything other than the dark red stone of the cavern in the distance, the ash swirling in the air around her.

Her hands shoot to her ears again, but I can't hear anything other than the eerie noises that always permeate this place, the hissing of lava far below. The sounds are muffled, and I wonder for a moment if maybe I'm asleep after all.

Then Ali is running again. I can see the light flash behind her eyes, the look of horror and determination as she runs faster.

But she isn't fast enough.

No. Not again. I can't watch this again. I have to get to her.

The ground explodes right behind her and stone shrapnel flies in every direction as the floor collapses. The force of the blast sends her flying through air, over the lava and into one of the towers high above.

"Ali!" I shout, running toward her. I watch with horror as she falls, barely landing on the path below. She scrambles, trying to hold on to something, anything. But she's still sliding, closer and closer to the edge.

She's going to fall. My heart pounds in my chest. *I have to catch her.*

But I can't. Because I'm. Not. There.

Then the image of her, the one I'm clinging to, slowly fades away, disappearing like a dream. I find myself back in my body, kneeling useless on the ground, *hours* away from The Fortress.

Away from her.

"No, no, no!" I shout, clenching my fists tightly at my side. *"Alexandra!"* I shout, my whole body shaking with the urgency to get to her. I won't accept that I can't save her this time.

I won't.

I *have* to get to her.

I love you, Steven, her soft voice whispers the words in my mind and I can feel the sorrow behind them. I can feel her fear, her hopelessness.

It breaks my fucking heart.

I squeeze my eyes shut and feel that pull like I never have before.

When I open them, I feel the hot stones beneath my knees, see Ali's small fingers as they lose their grip. Watch as she slides backward off the ledge.

I lunge for her.

Just as her hand slips from the stone, I grab her arm, holding her weight as she sways helplessly beneath me.

Ali's eyes shoot open and the shock in them is reflected in mine.

I think of all those times I couldn't save her, couldn't get to her in time. All the times I watched her die. The times I stood by, helpless and heartbroken.

How? I wonder. But whatever is happening, however I got here, it doesn't matter. Because *finally*, I. Saved. Her.

"You're here," she says almost inaudibly as a tear slides down her face. *"Don't let me go."*

I barely hear the words, but they flood my mind with so much force, so much longing, that it brings a newfound confidence into my own.

"I'm here. I've got you. And I'm not letting go."

I am *never* letting her go.

Ali manages to reach up with her other hand, wincing as she grasps my forearm. She isn't all that heavy, but I can feel the exhaustion starting to seep through my entire body, all the way to my bones. Pushing back the fatigue, I pull her up and over the ledge and we fall backward onto the hot stone.

I lay beside her, suddenly out of breath. When she turns toward me, she reaches out a hand to touch my face. I watch, curious if she even *can*. Wondering if I'm really here.

Or maybe I'm still back on that trail.

But when her fingers brush my cheek, I lean into her. My breath hitches and I close my eyes. Because I can feel her.

"You're really here," she whispers.

I reach a hand up to hold hers closer, then turn into it, kissing her palm.

"I couldn't let you fall," I say, because it's the truth. I stare into those scared, green eyes and want to stay in them forever.

But forever can't happen if we *explode* right now.

Keeping her hand in mine, I help her to her feet.

"*Agh*!" she exclaims, grabbing at her side. I wince, remembering the force at which her body hit the tower above. How she fell back down onto the hard, stone walkway.

"Here, come here," I say, pulling her toward me, then carefully lifting her into my arms. "I think it's time to get off the roof," I say, smiling down at her as she nods tiredly in agreement.

Holding her close, I run inside the nearest tower, then quickly make my way down the stairs. Finding the room empty, I decide it's as good a place as any to rest. To figure out a plan.

Then I notice the objects hidden under the crumbling staircase. My armor, my sword and dagger, along with the crossbow I stole from The Bastion. That's when I realize that *however* I managed to get here, it hadn't allowed me to bring the sword I was carrying from the house. I'm suddenly grateful that Ali took the risk to retrieve them for me. Because we are going to need all the help we can get.

"Alexandra Cutter, did you kill some poor creature to get my armor back again?" I say with a sideways smile to the girl still in my arms.

"Well, it did stab you, so I figured it had it coming. And it wasn't *just* for your armor," she smiles wryly. "I know how much you like your sword. I do, however, regret hauling around that goddamn crossbow. It's heavy as hell," she grins again, but it's strained. I can tell the pain is getting to her. I shake my head, because even injured, she's still my feisty little warrior.

I set her down carefully onto the floor, then grab my armor, pulling it on over my white shirt.

"Um, Steven?" she asks, staring up at me. "What the hell happened back there?"

I cinch tight the leather straps, then pause what I'm doing to glance back at her.

"I have no fucking idea," I say.

"How did you get to me in time? I thought you were still hours away?"

"I *was* hours away," I let out a breath. "I honestly don't know. I just knew that I *needed* to get to you and so... I did. It felt-"

"Natural? Like it's a part of you?" she adds, saying the words before I know them myself.

But she's right.

"Yeah, just like that," I say curiously.

"I feel the same way, when we talk. I guess you have your own superpower after all," she grins up at me. I return her smile, then frown, noticing her empty sheath. "Yeah," she says, observing my line of sight. "You know those big, ugly skeleton creatures that are running around here?"

"We've met," I say dryly, then smile. Because that's something Ali would say. She smiles too before continuing.

"Well, don't try and hit them with a sword..." she trails off.

"Shit, really? I thought you just had to chop its head off?" I say, strapping my dagger back to my arm above the elbow.

"Yeah... that works if you can manage it. But apparently, their weapons are *reinforced* or something. When it used its sword to block my blow, mine broke in half."

"I told you we should have brought the *big* sword," I say with a crooked smile, teasing her. She rolls her eyes at me.

"Here," I say, handing her my sword. I know she can wield it, and I'm already comfortable with the crossbow. As she takes it, she struggles to stand up. I offer out my hand to her, but she refuses it, like I knew she would. But I had to try. I will always try.

Stubborn, I admonish. She ignores the comment.

"I think I'm okay now, it must have just been a bruise," she shrugs. Then winces.

Liar, I say. Because after watching the way she got to her feet, how she's struggling to take a full breath, she *definitely* broke something. I study her, trying to determine *how* stubborn she plans on being. I consider for a moment if there's any chance in hell of talking her into going straight home.

"Steven, we can't leave yet," she says seriously, already knowing what I'm about to suggest.

I stare at her for a moment, then take one long, deep, exasperated breath. Knowing there's nothing I can do when she decides to be stubbornly unyielding.

"Okay. So what's the plan?"

Chapter 59

The plan is stupid. But we don't really have a choice. After everything we went through, after making our way here, we can't leave empty handed.

Our first step is to block off all the entry points to the rooftop. The last thing we need is to be dealing with all the other creatures that lurk in this hell-hole when we're trying to kill the most dangerous one.

Well, *one* of the most dangerous.

I'm still not entirely sure what caused the gaping *holes* in the pathway, but I hope to hell they won't be coming back anytime soon.

Ali is currently sitting outside one of the towers, a scowl on her face as she watches me move stone after crumbling crimson stone, stacking them up in the doorways to the other towers.

We had a very long discussion about whether or not she could help with this part of the plan. Clearly, I won that argument.

I managed to convince her that she needed to rest, and to heal, for as long as possible if she wanted to help with the more dangerous part of the plan. So finally, she conceded. But she isn't happy about it.

Hence, the adorable glower.

I slide one last large piece of broken stone over a gap leading to the stairway and look around, satisfied. The only problem with keeping the creatures *off* the rooftop, is that we are now trapped *on* it.

Like I said, the plan is stupid.

I head back toward the tower where Ali has been sulking, brushing the dust and ash from my hands as I do. The glass vials she carried were shattered when she slammed into the tower, which only leaves us with the two that I previously tucked into the straps of my armor. It's a miracle they're still intact. I slide one into my pocket and hand Ali the other, because we can't risk losing the last of them. And I'm not exactly sure how this will all play out.

Looking down over the parapet, I realize how accurate the Book of Monsters had been. *The creatures certainly do come out of the fire*, I notice.

Before deciding on this harebrained plan, Ali and I spent some time watching them fading in and out of the molten liquid around the large supports of the battlement as if they were a part of it.

Now, all we have to do is get one up here, kill it, get the fire and get the hell back home without dying.

Fantastic, I think. Once again amused that Ali's sarcasm is starting to rub off on me.

The trickiest part of this plan will be getting only *one* of them up here. And so we watch, waiting for the opportunity.

Ali and I are each standing in front of one of the towers opposite each other. The path separating us is further than I would like, but this is our best chance.

Ali leans over the edge, a large piece of stone in her hand.

Watching, waiting.

When the time comes, she looks over at me and I give her a quick nod, loading a bolt into my crossbow. I'm not sure what it is about this particular weapon that had me interested enough to grab it as we fled The Bastian, but right now, I'm glad we have it.

Ali quickly jumps up onto the ledge, showing no sign of the pain I know she's still feeling and peers down to the lava below. Holding out the rock, she takes aim, then drops it. The second it leaves her fingers, she jumps back onto the stone path and runs into the tower, hiding behind the wall next to the open doorway. I do the same, my back against the stone in my own tower as we wait.

I hear the sounds of a rushing forest fire shooting up high above the wall, then settling back down onto the walkway between us. The ardent light coming from the creature casts shadows onto the crimson bricks in front of me, letting me know that it's right where we want it to be. I jump out, standing in the threshold to face the blazing creature.

"Hey, asshole! Over here!" I shout, waving my arms, then duck back behind the wall, pressing my back against it.

I'm hidden away less than a second before the creature attacks. *Whoa!* I look away, shielding my eyes as I feel the air and heat flying past me in a rush.

The temperature rises, quickly becoming unbearable. The oxygen is sucked from the room, fueling its rage. I hold my breath, and I'm not sure how much longer I can stand it. But then the fire stops.

The second it does, I gasp for air. I raise my crossbow, quickly turning the corner and making my way out of the tower. I head straight toward the creature with long, deliberate steps. It fixes its attention on me, billowing smoke and shooting out no more than sparks. Then it begins to shake and I can feel it growing hotter by the second, even from here.

My five seconds are almost up.

Right on cue, I hear Ali's voice coming from the other side of the large structure.

"Hey! Come and get me!" she shouts, her voice firm. The creature turns quickly, immediately sending a line of fire in her direction. I hope to god she got behind the wall in time, but I push the thought aside and force myself to focus. I take aim, stepping even closer to the creature until I'm only a few yards away. We only have one shot at this. If I miss, I won't have time to re-load.

The fire dies out and I stand my ground as the flickering form turns to face me. It tries to glow hot again, the flames spinning around it like a violent whirlwind, but it's too late.

Because I'm already in position.

"Gotcha," I say quietly, pulling the trigger.

The bolt shoots out at an impossible speed, the stock digging into my shoulder with its release. It shimmers with light for just a second and I watch with wide eyes as it splits into three pieces. The center bolt stays fixed on course, but the other two veer off to either side, looping around, until all three find their mark in the creature's blazing body. I shield my face with my arms just as a pulse of heat and light knocks me off my feet.

Just as quickly as the heat comes, it disappears, leaving nothing but the mild throbbing pulse from the burning skin on my arms.

I look up warily and watch as what remains of the creature melts down into the pathway in front of me. The thick glowing liquid flows between the bricks, *turning back into the lines of fire from which it came.*

"Ali! Are you okay?" I shout in her direction, because I haven't seen her since the blast.

My panic begins to rise.

When she steps out from behind the crimson brick wall unharmed, I let out a breath I didn't know I was holding.

"I'm good. You?" she asks, eyeing me over. I look down at my arms and find that the third-degree burn marks are already disappearing.

"I'm good," I say, standing to my feet and pulling out one of the small glass vials. Ali makes her way toward me. She's still favoring one leg when she walks, but she's no longer holding her ribcage. Which means that, thankfully, they must be nearly healed.

We stand on either side of the melted pooling of fire, each holding a glass vial. Each secretly hoping that this will work.

"Okay, here goes nothing," she says, crouching down. I match her movements, leaning over the glowing liquid, getting as close as we dare. I pull out the plug with my teeth, then hold out the cylinder of glass, trying to figure out how the hell I'm going to get the liquid inside without burning myself. The fire flows slowly, lines of burning hot lava, and I'm suddenly unsure if this little glass container is capable of containing it.

Suddenly, I watch, awestruck, as a few glowing droplets slowly rise up, hovering above the stone. It vaguely reminds me of the magic surrounding The Big Book back at home. I stare curiously as the liquid slowly pulls into the glass I'm holding, filling it.

I seal the container, then slowly rise to my feet. The hovering liquid that still remains suspended in the air falls back down to the stone with a splash.

I study the vial. It's hot to the touch, but so is everything in this place. At least the glass seems to be holding. Looking over, I watch as Ali's big eyes examine her own, the glow of it illuminating the soft features of her face.

It's then that she looks up at me. We stare at each other and there's this strange emotion building up inside of me.

It almost feels like *hope*.

And then the ground shakes, reminding us that we aren't out of this yet.

"Okay, time to go," Ali shouts, but I'm already following her to the far tower.

With a grunt of effort, I quickly slide the stones away from the opening in the floor, revealing the staircase leading down.

Back into The Fortress.

Into the darkness.

Into the endless maze of hallways.

Because Ali is still healing, I insist on going first. Reluctantly, she agrees. Most likely because I have the crossbow and we both know she isn't healed enough to be wielding a sword. Especially my sword.

And she knows me well enough to know that I really, *really* want to use the crossbow again. It's clearly enchanted with some sort of magic, and I'm eager to get back home and figure out how I can do this with all our weapons.

As we make our way down the corridors, I raise my crossbow to check every corner, like a soldier clearing a building. Every time we spot a creature down one of the long halls, we head in the opposite direction as silently as possible. The last thing we want is to draw attention.

We have what we need.

Now we just have to get out.

These fucking halls are endless. Even though we're moving quickly, it's still taking Ali and I way too much time to find our way back to the window that leads out of The Fortress.

But finally, we see it.

I climb out first and then reach a hand back down to help Ali through.

"All that running around gave me time to heal, but I'll take your hand anyway," she says and I can't help but smile at her. Because she is stubbornly indestructible.

She takes my hand and I easily pull her up and out onto the crumbling rocks beside me. With every step, every rock we climb down, I feel a heavy weight beginning to lift. Because we are finally out of that place. Finally free of the endless hallways, free of the labyrinth from hell. I find that I'm already looking forward to getting back home.

Back to the open air.

I'm relieved to see that our packs are still right where we stashed them, hidden among the rocks at the base of The Fortress. Not wanting to hang around any longer than we need to, Ali and I quickly sling them on. I smile over at her. Then, taking her hand in mine, we head toward the trail.

Toward *home*.

But we only make it a few steps before stopping dead in our tracks.

Because across the large open space spread before us, standing among the trees, is a line of figures. It takes my eyes a moment to focus, but when I do, I realize that the brawny creatures, with the smashed-in snouts and ugly teeth, are the same creatures from The Bastion.

Only, there are *hundreds* of them.

And they look pissed.

Chapter 60

The front line of creatures start toward us, their snarls and grunts echoing off the surrounding cliffs on our left. To our right is the ocean of lava. And our backs are up against the curtain wall between the towers at the base of The Fortress.

Which means we're trapped.

The only way out is through the creatures, which isn't even an option, or *up*, back into The Fortress. It's not a great alternative, because if we can get inside so easily, then *so can they.*

But we don't have a choice.

Still holding Ali's hand, we back up slowly toward the place we just escaped. For a moment, I tell myself that we just need to find a place to hide until they give up the search.

But I know these creatures better than that.

They will never give up.

Just then, an ear-piercing shriek perforates the air, and then another, followed by several explosions that shake the ground violently, sending Ali and I to our knees. We cover our heads as rocks rain down around us.

When the dust clears, I look up.

"No," I whisper. The rocky path leading up to The Fortress is *gone*. The explosions hit the castle, destroying the window we crawled out of and causing the rocks leading to it to crumble the rest of the way down, spreading out at the base of the wall.

Now, there's no way back up.

My stomach sinks as reality sets in. The only way out is forward. And *forward*, means getting past those creatures. The creatures who want us dead.

Or worse.

They move toward us slowly, weapons raised. Next to me, Ali holds my sword defensively in front of her just as I cock my crossbow.

We glance warily at each other.

Steven, what the hell is happening? If they wanted to kill us, they would have done it already, she says, staring quizzically at the creatures.

I know... I say, wondering the same thing. I study them for a long time.

It's then I know what I have to do.

I straighten and, handing my crossbow over to Ali, I raise my hands up in a ceasefire gesture, taking two slow steps toward them.

Steven, what are you doing? Ali urges, panicked. But I ignore her.

"What do you want?" I shout toward the creatures. They stop moving and their grunting grows silent.

I don't need to count to know how many they outnumber us by. Sure, Ali took down dozens of these creatures back at The Bastion single handedly and I can certainly hold my own, but not against this many.

Not against an army of hundreds.

If there's something I can give them in exchange for Ali's life, then I am going to do it. Even if I have to sacrifice myself, I'm going to make sure that she makes it out of here. If one of us can get back home with the fire, then all of this will have been worth it.

I look out over the throng, waiting for an answer to my question. A question I'm afraid I already know the answer to.

They stay quiet, but I spent enough *quality* time with these creatures to know for a fact they can damn well understand me.

Suddenly, one of them lowers its crossbow. It takes two strides forward, matching mine, as it steps out of the crowd to face me. Without saying a word, the creature slowly raises a hand, uncurling a thick finger. Pointing it behind me.

Pointing straight at Ali.

A shiver runs up my spine as my fears are confirmed. I turn slowly to look at her and see the horror in her eyes, because she knows it too.

She killed their leader.

Now they want revenge.

They don't want to kill us, they want to take us back there. To take *her* back to The Bastion. And even though Ali doesn't know the full extent of what they did to me when I was imprisoned there, she knows enough to be terrified.

I watch as a tear slowly slides down her face. And the hopelessness in her eyes brings out a new type of rage from deep inside of me. An anger I didn't know I could possess.

Ali is *strong* and they are taking that away from her. Making her think that she isn't. It's clear in her eyes that she has lost all hope. And seeing them do that to her?

I fume at the thought.

Isn't what they did to *me* enough?

There is no fucking way in hell I'm going to let them take her. Not while there is still a breath left in my body.

She. Is. Mine.

And they can't have her. They will never have her.

"Ali, give me my sword," I growl as I stalk back toward her with determined strides.

"Steven, what are you doing? There's no way we can kill them all, we've lost," she says quietly, devoid of all feeling. "Here," she says, not meeting my eyes as she hands me her dagger.

The implications shoot straight through to my heart. I want to kill them.

All of them.

"Don't you *dare* give up on me," I say, taking her firmly by the shoulders. I lean down, pressing my forehead against hers. I close my eyes, feeling close to her for one last moment. When I lean back, I tip her chin up, forcing her to look at me.

"Ali, I need you with me. Are you with me?" I whisper urgently, our breaths an inch apart.

"But how-"

"Are you with me?" I say again, my tone serious, my eyes locked on hers. I'm asking her to trust me and if this is going to work, then she will have to. She takes a long moment to answer, those sad, green eyes staring into mine. Then I see the flicker of light emerge behind them and I feel her strength, her magic, as it joins mine for a brief, confirming moment.

"I'm with you," she says, her voice suddenly steady. I straighten and she hands me my sword.

I pull up my hood as I turn to face the creatures. With deliberate steps, I walk straight for them. Their grunting tones turn to more of a mockery at the sight of one man heading toward the legion of armed creatures.

I look behind me one last time and watch as Ali slides her hood into place as well, a smile playing at her lips.

That's my girl, I say, turning back toward the creatures. Smiling, I slowly raise my sword.

And then I disappear.

Chapter 61

I materialize directly in front of the creature who stepped out of the crowd. Its shocked, white eyes meet mine, but only for a moment.

Because my sword is already through its chest.

It turns to ash, its body floating away in the hot breeze, joining the endless particles that will forever drift in this godforsaken place.

I stand staring at the front line and watch as a mix of confusion and terror spreads across their toothy faces. I cock my head and, with a sly smile, I disappear again, re-appearing at the far end. I slit another one's throat and the creature next to it grunts, jumping back in surprise. It raises its crossbow frantically, then lets out a shot.

But I'm already gone.

The doubts and fears of not being able to save Ali, not being able to get to her, have completely vanished. Because I've already done this. On the top of that battlement, I got to her in time.

I saved her.

And moments ago, at the base of The Fortress, surrounded by these creatures with no way out, in that moment when she had given up, I knew I had to save her again. Because I'm fighting for more than our lives.

I'm fighting for *hope*.

I'm not sure what took me so long to realize this part of me, to realize what I can do. The feeling is instinctual, that *pull* inside of me, the *need* to be somewhere else. I suddenly realize that it was never a weakness. My entire soul has been pulling me to where I need to be all along.

I was just never brave enough to listen.

I realize that I'm not helpless. I don't have to stand by while the world falls apart. I have the power to do something about it. And now I know, it's a power that's been here all along.

My soul knows where it wants to go and it appears before my body, giving me the opportunity to see the world before I become a part of it. It's just like in all my dreams, when my soul needed to be here, needed to save her. But back then, I wasn't strong enough. Not until I found Ali. She is strong and fierce and she showed me that I can be strong too.

She is my strength, I think, and not for the first time.

I pull myself again to another area on the battlefield, realizing that with every jump, I become stronger, faster. Whatever *this* is, it's a vital part of me. I suddenly feel like I've spent my entire life sleeping.

But now, I'm awake.

I move through the crowd of creatures, killing one after another. The organized line of brawny warriors spread out, their confusion causing them to break their defensive lines. As they start to scatter, it becomes easier to pick them off.

I turn back to check on Ali, knowing damn well that she won't be able to sit this one out for long. Sure enough, I quickly find her among the crowd of chaos. She's already right in it with me.

Just like I knew she would.

And *apparently*, she's figured out how to use the crossbow.

Bolts are flying, splitting through the air, taking down creature after creature, the ash exploding around her. I have to admit, she's a good shot. It's an added bonus that this particular crossbow assists her efforts by turning every one shot into three. I watch for a moment as she walks toward the onslaught, bow raised. She is sure-footed, deadly, and the creatures suddenly look just as terrified and confused by her as they are of me.

But deadly or not, the sheer number of creatures heading her way is daunting. I want to make sure that she is strong enough, that she has a fighting chance. So I pull the magic to me and open it up to her, just like I did in the crimson forest when I helped her escape these very same creatures the first time. Having noticed, she looks up and smiles at me. Then I see the flicker behind her eyes and I can *feel* her. Her power pulses through me and suddenly I feel stronger too.

Because we're stronger together.

Our magic flows freely between us and I give her a broad smile before I disappear again, heading toward my next target.

I pull myself behind a group of five and shake my head as they fumble with their crossbows, caught off guard by my appearance. As quick and strong as they are, I know they're not up to the mark with hand-to-hand combat.

But I am.

Giving up on their crossbows, they start closing in on me, fists at the ready. They pull out a variety of small golden knives and swords from their belts, but I can tell just by the way they are holding them, hesitant and unsure, that I don't have anything to worry about. All at once, the large creatures run at me, snarling from behind their large, yellowed tusks. After stabbing one in the chest, I duck to avoid a blow from a large fist. I spin around, swiping its feet out from under it and feel the ground shake when it connects with the stone.

Another comes at me with the stock of its crossbow, but I step to the side, grabbing it out of its hands, then jamming the weapon under its chin and pulling the trigger. It crumbles into ash and I use my sword to quickly finish off the rest of them.

I'm used to moving *fast*, Ali and I have plenty of practice with that, but now, I'm beginning to combine our training with my newfound *ability*, if that's what we're calling it. I'm not just moving fast, I'm also disappearing for split seconds at a time, only to reappear in a better position to strike. The creatures quickly become frustrated, unable to keep track of my movements, which gives me the advantage.

I reappear again, this time directly between two of the creatures. They quickly turn to face me and I wait for them to take aim. When I hear the *click* of their weapons, I disappear, watching from afar as the bolts release from their crossbows and they wind up shooting each other right in their snouts.

I suddenly feel a different, yet familiar, kind of pull inside me. The one telling me that Ali is in danger. Looking over, searching through the throng of ash and angry creatures, I see them closing in on her on all sides. Clearly frustrated, I watch as she tosses the crossbow aside.

It's empty.

She pulls out her dagger and, after flipping it around her hand with a flourish, takes a defensive position, gesturing with her hand for the creatures to come at her.

What the fuck does she thinks she's going to do with that tiny dagger? I wonder. Sure, she's good with it, but she isn't *that* good. There are way too many of them, and she is surrounded.

I'm just about to disappear and go help, but I pause for a moment when I see the flash in her eyes and the sly smile on her lips. I watch closely with narrowed eyes, wondering what she's up to.

All of a sudden, every single creature in her radius drops to the ground, clawing at their ears and the sides of their heads until they are bleeding.

I appear behind her, arms crossed in confusion as I look around at the creatures surrounding her, crippled with agony.

"What the fuck was that?" I stare at her curiously, more than a little impressed. And more than a little in love.

"Apparently," she says, striding casually over, stealing the dagger from the scabbard on my bicep. "They don't appreciate the sound of my voice. At least, not when it's screaming in their heads," she smiles up at me.

I look down at her and give her a crooked smile. Then she raises both daggers, twirling one in each hand. I shake my head as she slowly backs away, a smug little smile on her ash and dirt covered face.

This girl, I think with pride and amusement as I watch her use nothing but two small daggers to take on the hoard. The creatures are easily double her size and her frame seems impossibly small standing beside them. And that's when I realize this isn't a fair fight.

Those creatures don't have a chance in hell against her.

Hand-to-hand is her specialty, I should know, she's kicked my ass more times than I will ever admit. Pairing that with whatever hell she's wreaking in their minds gives her enough of an advantage that she can take on several at a time without even breaking a sweat.

I watch as the ash swirls around her with her every motion.

Clearly, she doesn't need my help.

So I disappear, heading back to take out the rest of them.

I step over another large body, looking around as it disintegrates into ash. This wasn't a fight.

It was a *slaughter.*

The crimson stone in front of The Fortress is now stained an even darker shade of red and the air is so dense with the floating particles of our victory that I can barely see through it.

I wipe my sword on my pants to clean it, because well, they're covered in blood anyway. As I'm sure the rest of me is as well.

I look over at Ali, and can't help but smile as I make my way over to her. Seeing her like this reminds me of how fierce she can be.

As if I could ever forget.

Her stance is defensive, her deliberate and calculated eyes scan the area around her. She fists the two daggers backward, keeping them level with her chin, as they slowly drip with thick blood. Her long, red hair flows out from her hood, the ends of it stained a deeper shade of crimson.

Her eyes catch sight of me walking toward her, and she takes one last look around before she slowly relaxes, lowering her weapons. When her gaze finds mine again, it softens, then fills with a mixture of surprise and triumph.

Because we won.

Chapter 62

After the battle outside The Fortress, the walk back to the portal isn't so bad. Ali and I know the way and know what areas to avoid. We continue to stay alert, stay out of sight, but we walk easily, knowing that nothing we come up against will be able to stop us.

Not now that we know what we can do.

There have been a few run-ins with skeletons, but we hardly even stopped our conversation as we swiftly dealt with them.

Which makes me realize something.

Maybe the reason we aren't afraid of this world is because now, we're a part of it. *A soul belonging to two worlds,* I think, glancing toward where the words are hidden just below Ali's armor. She walks ahead of me in the open space, and as we near the portal, she turns back to smile at me.

We made it.

Together, we step out of the infernal world and into the cold of the cavern beneath the cliffs. The sound of dripping water echoing off the walls has never sounded so good and I take a deep breath, letting the cool, damp air fill my lungs.

Ali heads for the ladder without saying a word and I follow close behind. It's surreal, going home after so long.

How long has it been? I wonder. It was probably only a few weeks, but who the fuck knows. It feels like *ages.*

When I step off the ladder into the map room, I walk over and stand next to Ali. She's looking around as if she's never seen it before. So am I.

We stand there for a long moment, just staring.

I feel numb. Like what I'm looking at is too good to be *real*, that at any moment, it will all disappear, replaced by flames and monsters and death.

But it doesn't disappear.

We're home.

It's as if everything was frozen in time during our absence.

I look at the large wooden table in the center of the map room, the chairs scattered around it. I look at the books, neatly lining the shelves and the parchment maps tied neatly in their scrolls. I look past it to the living room, with its soft hand-made feather couches and fluffy pillows. The wall of dark glass gives us a view of the meadow down below, of the trees outside. The waterfall.

It all seems so... *normal.*

It feels safe, comfortable, and I want nothing more than to curl up on that couch with Ali in my arms. But after I take a quick glance down at my blood-stained armor, finding the ash and dirt covering every inch of my body, I realize *that* dream isn't exactly an option at the moment.

"Um, I guess we'd better get cleaned up," Ali says, clearly in the same state of mind as she pulls at the ends of her blood-stained hair. "This is going to take me forever to get out, why don't you go first?" she smiles sweetly and I can see the exhaustion already starting to take hold.

"I have a better idea," I say with a sly smile.

We leave our packs in the entryway and walk out onto the front porch. I squint, holding up a hand to block out the unfamiliar light of day.

The fresh air happily invades my burning lungs.

I look over at Ali and then grab her hand, intertwining our fingers as we drop down to the grass, not bothering with the ladder.

The thirty-foot drop doesn't seem that high up anymore.

As we near the falls, I can already feel the soft mist cooling my hot skin. I walk with Ali on the little dirt path until it turns to stone, leading into the vine-covered grotto behind the waterfall, sheltering us from the outside world.

The rumble of crashing water makes it next to impossible to talk to each other, but these days, we hardly ever speak out loud anyway. Sometimes, we don't even bother with complete sentences. Through Ali's power, she can simply open her thoughts to me, allowing what we are feeling to flow freely back and forth. I've never been so close to anyone and I realize that maybe it's because I never wanted to be.

Because I never had her.

Behind the falls, I watch as the sun streams through the mist, creating rainbows that reflect all around us. I feel the cool air and gentle mist of water hitting my face. Then I look over to Ali. Her hood is still raised as her head tips up, transfixed on the falling water. The daylight makes her eyes shine in a way they didn't when we were down in the below, in The Nether. I stare at her for a long moment.

Even covered in sweat, ash and blood, I can't help but think, *she's so fucking beautiful.*

Suddenly, I need to be close to her. Need to get her out of that armor and feel her body against mine, need to know that she is safe. That *we're* safe.

That this is real.

I push back her hood and stare into those eyes. Then I frantically start to unbuckle the leather straps on her armor. She looks up at me and her urgent fingers start doing the same to mine.

Damn this fucking armor, I complain and my heart fills with the sound of her laughter as it echoes off the stone walls.

It's so good to see her *smiling* again.

As I pull the final leather strap through the hoop, Ali raises her arms. I lift the armor up and over her head, tossing it aside before she helps me remove my own.

I pull the last piece of leather holding my sword in place and look up at her, letting it slowly fall to the ground. *Finally* free of all restraints.

She rushes into my arms and her mouth immediately finds mine. My lips move greedily against hers and I pull her closer, my head spinning as I melt into the softness of her.

It's been too long since I was able to hold her in my arms like this.

It feels like coming home.

The cool mist of the falls clings to my skin, causing ash and dirt to start running down my face, reminding me of what we *actually* came down here to do. I lean back to look at Ali, smiling lightheartedly. I touch her hair and she laughs, looking me over as well.

We're a goddamn mess, but I'm not about to let her go so soon.

I kiss her again, easily lifting her off her feet as she wraps her legs tightly around my waist. I step back onto the wooden platform, into one of the smaller streams coming from the falls. Ali's warm hands hold my face as she moves her lips against mine. The water drenches our mouths, our skin, our clothes, washing away every last trace of that place.

Her lips are soft and wet and I hold her close to me, deepening the kiss as the sun slowly falls beneath the horizon. Ali has, of course, filled the entire grotto with lanterns, sealing us in to our own little world, safe from the creatures outside.

After a moment, she leans back, brushing the wet hair away from my eyes as she studies me. I watch her as well, taking in every inch of her. Her eyes, her full lips and all the freckles that scatter her cheeks. I study how her wet hair falls perfectly around the soft features of her face. Features that are no longer hardened by the harsh lines of sweat and sorrow. She's still my little warrior, but there's also something else about her now.

Something new, something bright.

Even after everything, she's *smiling*.

We both are.

And then her eyes slowly wander down to my shirt. Following her gaze, I feel the need to respond. *Um, yeah. My blue one got a little... torn to shreds,* I say.

I know... That's not why I'm staring... she says, looking up at me out from under long lashes. I stare at her curiously and then back down at my shirt.

It's white, and... it's soaking wet.

Oh, I smile, understanding. I can almost feel my dimples appear as I look back up at her, finding a blush blooming across her cheeks, how she's biting her bottom lip. *God*, she drives me insane.

If you wanted me to take my shirt off, you could have just asked, I say, pretending that my heart isn't currently beating out of my chest from the way she's looking at me.

No, you can leave it, she says and through our shared connection, I can feel *exactly* what she is feeling.

I make a mental note to wear this shirt more often.

She runs her hands from my chest down to my stomach, tracing every line that's now clearly visible through the sheer fabric clinging to me. I look up and close my eyes, letting the water cool my warm face, trying desperately to regulate my heartbeat as I feel her hands explore.

I run my hands along her thighs, pulling her tighter to me. Then her soft fingers trail up my body and over my neck. She grabs my chin, tipping my face back down to look at her. Her eyes flicker to my lips, and she leans in, letting hers linger only inches from mine. She keeps us like that for a long moment, her shuddering breath intertwining with mine. I know she's teasing me again, but I'm done playing games.

Because this girl, this incredible soul, *she's mine.*

I quickly run my hands up her body, into her hair and pull those smirking lips against mine. I take everything I want from this kiss, give her everything I have, everything I am. And in this moment, I know that for the first time, she gives her everything to me as well.

Because I am hers.

Chapter 63

I wake up suddenly, my heart beating fast. Until I realize where I am.

My body relaxes as I focus on the light flooding in through the glass wall in our bedroom. I watch the clouds float past outside, see the bay sparkling far down below.

Ali is curled up next to me, still sound asleep. She's all soft features, messy red waves of hair and completely at peace.

Which for her, is rare.

I don't know how long we slept for, but *god*, we needed it. I wrap an arm around her and she subconsciously snuggles into me, burying her face in the crook of my neck. I casually play with her silken hair, and rest my cheek on the top of her head, relaxing back into the pillow.

I take a deep breath, and close my eyes, taking comfort in feeling her this close to me.

It's then I realize, there's nowhere else in *either* world that I would rather be.

After breakfast, Ali and I walk back downstairs to the first floor. She's wearing one of my T-shirts, which looks huge on her, a pair of shorts, thick socks and her hair is pulled up into a messy sort of bun on top of her head. After living with her for so long, I'm used to seeing her *around the house* wear, but after watching her slaughter hundreds of creatures as we fought side-by-side in battle just a few days ago, it suddenly feels strange to see her like this. We just got back last night, and she already looks so comfortable, so *relaxed*. Whereas I'm a little on edge.

She's still a mystery to me, still stronger than me, and I love that about her.

"Hey Ali, can I ask you something?" I say, because now is as good a time as any.

"What is it?" she says curiously.

"Your green shirt, the one in the closet," her eyes fall and she closes them for a moment, as if talking about it brings everything back. "Why do you keep it?"

After taking a deep breath, she looks back up at me.

"Because it's important. As much as I *want* to forget, I feel like I need to remember," she says softly.

I grab her by the hand, drawing her into me. I place a kiss on the top of her head and just hold her. Because she is so much stronger than she knows.

It inspires me.

I run a finger over The Big Book on the fifth floor, letting its magic surround me. Somehow, the feeling is stronger now, more... familiar.

Or maybe I'm stronger now.

I look over and watch as Ali carefully places the two vials of fire into a small chest, then slides it back onto the shelf before backing away.

"Well, we *caught the line of fire,*" she says, lost in thought. She shakes her head and I already know what she's thinking.

So much work for such a little thing...

"Maybe we can wait until tomorrow to *combine with eyes that cannot see,*" I joke and she lets out a strained laugh. Because we aren't doing anything for a while.

The greenhouse and the animals down in the fields desperately need attention and the house is an absolute mess. Not to mention, we need some time off. Because *hell*, we deserve it.

We agreed that finding a way home shouldn't stop us from living our lives, so we are going to do just that.

We are going to *live*.

But taking the time to live doesn't mean we're giving up. We will never give up. We will continue to train, continue learning about this crazy world and once we have put some time between us and our last journey, then we will come up with a plan.

And whatever road lies ahead, we sure as hell will be ready for it.

"Steven?" Ali asks from nearby in the armory, where she's watching me attempt to fix up our armor. Everything we managed to come back out with had certainly taken a beating and I've come up with some ideas of how to reinforce them.

"Yeah?" I stop hammering for a moment and wipe the sweat from my forehead with the back of my arm as I straighten, looking over at her perched cross-legged on top of one of the wooden tables.

"Why don't you ever talk about your parents?" she asks.

I rub a hand down my hot face, frustrated by the question. But I figured this conversation would come up eventually. Especially since I've been *actively* avoiding it.

"Because I'm still pissed at them," I say quickly, then continue hammering away at the metal, probably a little harder than I need to.

"Why?" she asks curiously.

I step back, tossing the hammer back onto the anvil.

"Because," I say coldly, hoping she will get the picture that I don't want to talk about it and just let it go.

"Because..." she prods.

I sigh, unsure why I thought I could get away with a short answer in the first place.

"Because they're the reason I'm here," I say angrily. "When we got to Garda Valley, I thought for a moment that I finally found a place I wanted to be. A place that could be *home.* And they were going to take that away from me. *Again.* So I ran. I ran, fell down that hill and I ended up here. It's their fault for always making me move around, never letting me feel like I had a home and now... *I'm gone.* They're probably going insane looking for me and there's nothing I can do about it," I say, sitting on the bench beside Ali, burying my face in my hands.

"I lived in that town my whole life. I couldn't wait to get out of it. I *planned* to get out of it. You got to see the country, hell, the whole *world* and you got to see it with your family. What's so bad about that?" she says, her tone soft. And I know she's not arguing, not lecturing, she's just trying to understand.

"Because I never had a *home*. There was no point in having friends, or planning for the future, when we would just move away from it. I wanted to think about the future, *my* future, but how was I supposed to do that when there was nothing I could count on?"

She sits quietly for a moment, contemplating.

"Did you ever tell your parents?" she asks.

"Tell them what?"

"What you just told me. Did you ever tell them that it wasn't just about *moving*? That you didn't feel like you could have a home, friends, or even a future, when you moved around all the time?" she asks.

"No, of course I didn't. They wouldn't understand and they wouldn't care," I say, getting up to go back to my project. Because this conversation is ridiculous.

"They would care, you know that. And how do you know they wouldn't understand if you never told them?" she says plainly, causing me to look up at her. "Maybe your parents know you better than you think. Maybe, when you get back, you should give them the chance. They might not be able to give you what you want, but they love you, so they will at least listen."

Goddammit. Why does she always have to say things that make sense? I bring the hammer down again as I think about what she said.

After a few minutes, I shake my head, because Ali is always doing this. Always calming me down, or giving me the space I need to work out whatever shit is going through my head.

Then being there for me whenever I'm ready to talk about it.

I grumble, then look over, my expression softening when my eyes meet hers.

"Thanks, Ali," I say, my voice barely audible. She gives me a small, warm smile, and I return it before going back to my project.

I hit the hot metal again and again, but I can't help but think that maybe she's right. I didn't give my parents a *chance* to make it right. Because I never told them the truth about how I felt, not really. I lashed out with snide comments and constant complaints, but I never told them how much it meant to me to feel like I had a home. A future.

I set the hammer down again, running a hand through my damp hair and look back over at Ali. She's sitting on that table, perfectly content watching me work for hours on end. Because she just wants to be with me.

And then it all makes sense.

What I feel for Ali puts everything into perspective and I realize something. My parents didn't care where we moved to. Because their home is with each other. *With me.*

I am their home.

And now, *Ali is mine.*

Chapter 64

It's only been a few weeks since Ali and I made it back through the portal, and I'm surprised at how quickly we've fallen back into our normal routine. Now, it feels like our time in that hell-hole didn't even exist, like it was just a bad dream.

But it wasn't.

What happened in there changed us. And I know there's no going back.

After almost losing her, what happened to me in The Bastion, the battle, I half expected to return with a lifetime's worth of nightmares to keep me awake, but I didn't. Every night, I sleep soundly right next to the girl of my dreams, knowing that whatever happens, I can protect her.

Hell, *she* can protect *me.*

And on the nights when the dreams do find their way back to us, we take them on together. We're a team, and there's nothing in the worlds that will ever change that. Even if we find our way back, I know beyond a doubt that this girl is *my* whole world.

Ali and I spent the entire day hidden away in our secret cove, tucked within the safety of the mangrove trees.

On our way home, we sit side by side on the little bench of the fishing boat, slowly rowing through crystalline water. As I listen to the water gently lap against the boat, feel the cool breeze on my face, I find myself thinking about the dreams again. About how they consumed nearly every night's sleep up until sometime after I got here.

When did they stop? I wonder curiously. It's one of the many things I haven't quite pieced together.

"What are you thinking about?" Ali asks, looking over at me out from under long lashes. I think again how nice it is to see her this relaxed.

"I was thinking about the dreams. The ones about you. I haven't had one for a while..." I trail off.

"Isn't it obvious?" she smirks, and I glare back.

"What have you figured out," I say, trying to hold back a smile, a little frustrated that she's been keeping me in the dark.

"Well, it took me a while to piece it together, if that makes you feel any better. But I don't think they were dreams," she says.

"What do you mean?" I ask curiously.

"Before you got here, you had nightmares of me dying, of you trying to save me, but you couldn't get to me. I think that was when your powers started. Only, you didn't know how to control it, or weren't strong enough. Or maybe you had to be *here*, in this world, before you could..." she muses.

I row slowly, thinking about that. It makes sense. In the dreams, I felt that *pull*, that *need* to get to her. That same pull I feel when I disappear.

"You think that my soul appeared, I just couldn't pull myself to you yet... so all those times, I was *actually* here," I say, slowly piecing it together.

"Exactly," she says with a smile. "And I think I felt you, some of those times at least. I felt you here with me. I just didn't understand it, not until you got here. Even on that first day, you felt... *familiar*. When you saved me on the battlement, I could feel you again in that way. I recognized your *soul*, because I felt it before."

I stare off, not sure what to think about that. It feels like a lifetime ago, being back in the valley, but even then, my soul was trying to be *here*.

To get to *her*.

"But I didn't always feel that pull," I add. "Sometimes I had the same dreams over and over. They felt so real. I was *terrified*, like *I* was the one who was dying-" my voice cuts off and I look straight at her. "Holy fuck. Those were *you*."

"Yeah, sorry about that... I guess you weren't the only one who couldn't control your power. Whenever I was asleep, when everything came flooding back, I must have opened my mind up to you, sharing the memories without even realizing it."

We stare at each other for a long moment, both thinking the same thing. Knowing that even before I got here, somehow, we were already connected.

I smile. Because deep down, I've always known that.

"Hey, let's stay out here a while," Ali says softly, nodding toward the setting sun as it dips below the horizon, disappearing into the sea. And so we let the little boat drift out into the open water.

A few minutes later, I'm lying on the bench, staring up at the night sky. It's a clear night and I feel a kind of peace wash over me. Because I've never seen so many stars.

"Hey, Steven?" A hesitant voice says beside me. I use the hands that are behind my head to lift myself up, turning to look at her. I notice she's holding a small package.

Curious, I sit up to face her.

"What's this?" I say as she hands it to me. It feels like a wooden box, wrapped in parchment, a tiny bow of twine tied perfectly on top. I smile at that.

"Well, according to our marks, you've been here about six months. Which means I've been here about a year, right?" she says.

"Yeah, that's probably about right," I say, having no idea where she's going with this.

"I went missing in May and well, you said your birthday is in May, so..." she says with a shy smile.

"Ali, is this a birthday present?" I stare at her, *shocked*. After all we've been through, after everything that's happened, this girl remembered my birthday.

"It's not much and it's not a cake, but I thought... well, I thought that maybe you would like it," she smiles up at me. "Seventeen, right?"

"Yeah, seventeen," I manage to say with a chuckle, because I can't believe it. Can't believe that I'm seventeen, that I've been out here with Ali for six months. Can't believe that she got me a *present*.

I quickly unwrap it.

Pulling the top from the box, I pause, staring at what's inside.

"Do you like it?" she asks, worried.

"Ali," I breathe out. I quickly look up at her, a broad smile spreading across my face. "It's... *perfect.*"

I look down again. Nestled inside the box is a watch. Its golden face matches the one on Ali's wrist, only slightly larger.

And it's calibrated to the twenty-minute daylight cycle.

The thick leather band definitely makes it more my style, as opposed to the delicate golden chain on hers. I remember how fragile it felt when I wore it after rescuing her and how I asked if she would make me one. That was *months* ago.

And she remembered.

It must have taken her hours to make it, even with magic. My heart fills at the sentiment. Because it's the nicest thing anyone has ever done for me.

As I gently pull it from the box, I rub my thumb over the face of it. Flipping it over, I notice that there's an inscription carved into the back of the smooth metal. The letters are small, but perfectly clear.

And they are written in the same language as my tattoo.

At this point, I have no trouble reading it. I quickly find that the inscription is similar to our tattoos, and yet so different. Because this is just for us. This is *ours*.

MY SOUL BELONGS TO YOU

YOU ARE MY WORLD

I smile, then look back up into those sad, green eyes.

No, not sad. Not anymore.

Emotions flood my own eyes as I reach for her. I gently grab her wrist, unclasping the golden chain that she always wears. I meet her eyes, gripping the delicate watch between my fingers as I feel the magic running through me.

I hand it back to her, and she looks down at it curiously. Then her eyes snap back up to mine, a smile spreading across her lips as her own tears threaten to fall.

There's no question that our souls belong to two worlds. The one we left behind, and the one we are undoubtedly a part of now. But my soul belongs somewhere else now too.

My soul belongs to her. She is my world, and no words could have conveyed it better. So I inscribed the same ones on the underside of her watch, but in the same language as her tattoo. Because those words are not just for me, they are for us. And they're not just words, they are a *promise*.

It wasn't until I was lost that I found my home, I say to her through this connection we share, because I want her to feel every word. Know the truth behind them. *Ali, you are my home.*

And then I hear her voice, soft and sweet in my mind.

And you were right, she says, looking down at our fingers as they intertwine.

About what? I ask, watching her curiously.

I feel like I'm lost to a dream too... she says. Then her eyes snap to mine. *Don't wake me up.*

Epilogue

Alex

I'm standing in the greenhouse, a small smile tugging at the corner of my lips. I brush the dirt from my hands and turn around, casually leaning against the raised flower bed and wait.

Steven appears in front of me and I find his hands are already on my hips, his lips already on mine. I chuckle.

You're getting good at that, I whisper in his mind.

What, the kissing? he says, teasing me. He knows what I'm talking about.

Well, that too, I suppose.

I always know when Steven is about to appear, because I can feel his soul before I can see it. But lately he's been appearing a little *faster*, trying and failing, to catch me off guard. After the battle, we integrated it into our training. Since then, I have to admit, he's getting better at it.

He kisses me again, long and sweet before stepping back, studying what I'm working on.

"I'm trying to decide if I should plant these or-" my voice cuts off.

Something happened.

I can't tell what, but I can *feel* it.

"Hey, do you want to go up top? Watch the sunset?" Steven asks me suddenly.

"Um, yeah... I do," I say, confused, because that's exactly where I feel like I need to be. Which is strange. I haven't felt the urge to be up there since...

"Race you up!" Steven says with a smirk. Then he winks at me, and disappears.

"Great," I mumble, then begrudgingly head toward the ladder.

"Goddamn ladder," I mutter to myself as I near the top rung where Steven has the *courtesy* to hold the trapdoor open for me.

"Took you long enough," he says, a smug smile on his face.

"Leave it to you to develop a superpower just to avoid a damn ladder," I say, grumbling. I'm starting to get really tired of his bullshit, but I guess I had it coming.

"Why did you want to come up here anyway?" I ask. There's a sunset every ten minutes, so we've already seen *thousands* of them.

"Um… I'm not sure. I just felt like I needed to," he says nonchalantly. But I felt it too.

It was that same *pull*, that *need* to be up here.

And then it hits me.

"No fucking way…" I say, staring at Steven with wide eyes. I open my mind to him, letting him hear my thoughts, because it's easier than finding the words to explain it.

And we don't have much time.

His eyes go wide, matching mine, as we run out the door.

Standing on the edge of the cliff at the top of the highest mountain above our house, we look down at the island.

Far below on the tiny island across the sea where we first arrived, is a person.

A person lying in the sand.

Steven and I look at each other for a long moment, not believing if this is actually real.

And then it gets dark.

"I guess… I'll meet you down there?" I say, smiling over at him.

"Not a chance. I'm with you, remember?" His eyes find mine and I hold our gaze for a long moment, knowing he means it. Without breaking the contact, I feel his fingers take my hand in his.

And together, we step off the cliff.

End of Book 1

Acknowledgments

I don't even know where to start, except by saying thank you. Thank you for taking a chance on a new author and the very first book she ever wrote. When I sat down and typed up the prologue "just for fun" back in 2022, I had no idea where this journey would take me. So thank you for coming along on this ride.

I have to thank Hannah, because this book is your fault. When I read your manuscript for the first time, I cried. I was so proud of you. Of your determination, your indefatigability, and your excessive use of sticky notes. Because you didn't just write a book, you fought for it every day. You inspired me, and I set out to find something I wanted to pour that much love and heart into. Funny that it turned out to also be books, but I guess we shouldn't be surprised.

Mom, thank you for being the very first person to read my manuscript, and my very first fan. You've always been my biggest supporter in every crazy thing I decide to do, and I could never thank you enough. Love you!

To the rest of my family, thank you for your encouragement and endless support. Every single one of you has helped me get to this point in some way and I will forever be grateful.

To my editor, Jasmine, thank you so much for jumping in on this project. Your support has meant the world to me, and my book wouldn't be where it is today without you.

To my Bookstagram family, because that is what you are to me, my found family. I could not have done this without you. Thank you Meghan, Kelly, Erin, Allie and Joyce for all you've done to help me through the publishing process and for all your support. Thank you to my entire street team, who took the time out of your busy lives to support me and my book. Your constant positivity brings a smile to my face everyday.

And thank you, Grayson, for telling me to trust myself at a time when I didn't.

About the Author

I grew up in a small town in Northern California where I now live with my husband. I always loved books, but it wasn't until I finished writing my debut novel, Lost to a Dream, that I decided I wanted to turn my passion for telling stories into a career. It's a goal I strive for everyday, over late nights and lots of coffee. Whether through writing or audiobook narration, books are my passion. I hope you enjoy my stories as much as I love creating them.

linktr.ee/courtneyrosaleen
www.courtneyrosaleen.com

instagram.com/courtneyrosaleen
goodreads.com/courtneyrosaleen

Made in the USA
Columbia, SC
11 August 2024

841acde5-3ae8-4834-bee9-b1c2abbece8bR01